BUSHMASTER FALL

BUSHMASTER FALL

by Carl A. Posey

DIF

DONALD I. FINE, INC.

New York

Library of Congress Cataloging-in-Publication Data

Posey, Carl A., 1933–
    Bushmaster fall / by Carl Posey.
        p.   cm.
    ISBN 1-55611-245-9
    I. Title.
    PS3566.O67B87   1991
    813'.54—dc20   90-56067
                                             CIP

Manufactured in the United States of America

10 9 8 7 6 5 4 3 2 1

Designed by Irving Perkins Associates

*To F.E.E. with gratitude
and great affection*

AUTHOR'S NOTE

Although I spent much of my youth in and around what we used to call jungle, credit for my discovering the true miracle of the tropical rainforest goes mainly to a handful of wonderfully articulate experts, in particular: Adrian Forsyth, whose *Portraits of the Rainforest* and (with Ken Miyata) *Tropical Nature: Life and Death in the Rain Forests of Central and South America* are incomparable expeditions into that strange and beautiful world; Andrew W. Mitchell, who, in *The Enchanted Canopy,* uniquely reveals the arboreal laboratory of the canopy naturalist; and *Exploration Fawcett,* the timeless Bolivian bush tales of Colonel Percy Harrison Fawcett, edited by his son. One hopes that *Bushmaster Fall* conveys some sense of the riches to be found therein.

I am also grateful for the considerable technical assistance generously given by a Vienna friend, Edward Kerr, to help get nuclear facts right. Such errors as may remain I claim as my own. And, as always: hurrah for P!

The players and institutions in *Bushmaster Fall* are imaginary and do not represent reality, past or present. Any perceived resemblance is purely coincidental.

ALEXANDRIA, VIRGINIA
1991

Part I

THE FALL

1

For the rest of his life, Krylov marveled at the fact that he had first heard of the Beni Fall from the only man, as far as the world was concerned then, who'd seen it. He had come to Santiago for a conference on radiological safety, held, as they always seemed to be, in a country without much radiology. His Safeguards bosses in Vienna had thought it would be good for him to attend, as he and Oldenburg, an intolerable Dane, were already doing the inspection for Brazil's Angra-1, just an enormous continent away. Krylov had felt a bit brave, coming to Santiago. Chile had not had diplomatic relations with the Soviet Union since the Allende days, when Mother Russia had verified that she could be precious little help at the end of the day. They were still airing out the embassy over on calle Colon. Any Soviet stood out in a place like Santiago, where the faces were British, Italian, German, and ancient Indian, and not a Slav in sight. But Krylov would have stood out anywhere he went, one of those big, fit men you see all over Europe, light as boxers on their feet, big Mongolian wolves in the well-tailored sheepskin that KGB officers wear when they travel in the west. He quickly sensed a vacuum of personal danger. The Chileans were so numbed by referenda, strikes, poised elections, and hard-faced old men in uniform waiting restlessly in the political wings, that he could have been a green Martian and nobody would have blinked. No one even looked at him, except Mason, the man who had seen the Beni Fall.

Mason had intercepted him at the mezzanine bar of the Hotel Carrera, once a very dangerous place for Russians, plainclothes-men everywhere, now also rendered impotent by the prospect of uncertain change. Krylov and Mason had stood at the bar, more or less shoulder to shoulder, with their *pisco* sours, the great hall of the lobby buzzing and murmuring around them, the security people gathering in small pods here and there among the pink marble pillars. "My name's Mason," the man had said in American English, extending a hand to shake. Krylov, not wishing to confound anyone with his true origins, had introduced himself as Calvin Hobbs, an astrophysicist just going home to Victoria from a week at the observatory in La Silla. Canadians, he had discovered, were hated nowhere in the world, and everybody liked astronomers.

Mason had been delighted, of course. Not often he got to talk to an expert. His strong, drink-reddened face had become happy, the pouched blue eyes smiled. He was, he said, a decent amateur; as a pilot, you had to know something about the stars. They talked about his being a pilot, flying one of those old DC-8s full of fruit up to Miami after midnight two nights a week, and about the atom, the trouble in the Gulf, the pros and cons of *pisco* sours. Not wanting to spend the evening with his fellow conferees, a few of whom he saw emerge from the cop-per-doored elevators across the room, Krylov had decided to hang on to this American, who seemed to have a story to tell, and offered excellent cover besides.

They wound up at the Siratorio, up Providencia way, for din-ner, "on the Dominion Astrophysical," as Krylov put it, playing Hobbs. And there, over tumblers of a terrible Chilean vodka named Mirnoff, Mason told him that it had been he who'd seen the Beni Fall. Like nearly everyone else in the world, Krylov had never heard of it. He supposed it must be like the Fall of Tehuántepec, obscurely Latin and historical, but he gave Mason a show of interest. "You did?" he encouraged, with a smile.

It had happened not quite a week ago, Mason said. He'd caught that flicker of welding-white light in the dark glass of the DC-8's windscreen, and could not take his eyes away. Even though something in him yelled that the sudden flash must be an electrical fire, and his reflexes yearned to scan the four tiers

of engine gauges glowing on the chipped metal . . . he stared
at the Fall. Mason had been the only one aboard to see it. The
pilot and engineer had crawled aft half an hour out of Santiago,
wanting naps while Mason drove the old tramp along the
rough terrain. He flew on autopilot, nothing much on his mind.
. . . Mason went silent, then, and watched his reflection drift
like a ghost past the silhouetted cordillera as the restaurant
turned slowly on its pedestal. Krylov imagined how it must be,
alone on the flight deck. He thought Mason must have been in
the midst of those imaginary conversations people have with
former spouses, bosses, loved ones, and children.

They'd got out of Santiago a good six hours behind schedule,
Mason resumed after a while, their flight plan, their Miami
clearance, everything totally fucked up, and everyone a bit raw
at being stranded by some thirty-year-old gremlin. The DC-8
had come off the Douglas line in Long Beach in 1959, the year
Mason reckoned his adult life had really started—the fuse of
marriage and children had been set, the military career faded
neatly into an airline job. An airplane as old and rickety as he
was, he explained, sometimes needed a lot of help. They were
not airborne until 2:00 A.M. "You're very much alone at that
hour," he told Krylov. "There's nothing on the radio, no running lights, nothing at your altitude. The only other traffic's
Cessnas coming out of the Beni with a load of paste. You see
them against the snow, their exhaust way down in the rocks."
He grinned quickly, modestly, letting Krylov know he was better than the expressionless young aviators you saw around
Miami International and Medellin. On the night of the Fall, if
they were flying at all it was under a stratus deck that had
blown in off the cold Pacific to fill the western valleys. Like
islands in a cloudy sea, the mountains glowed, vast negatives of
rock and snow, their hard edges softened by the touch of night.
Off to the east lay the jungle, impenetrably dark except where
early rainy-season lightning flashed quickly, like distant artillery. The sky . . . well, it was that southern sky, crossed by the
dense, luminous wash of the central Milky Way, stars like fields
of diamonds, dimensional, fat and glistening as raindrops.

It had flown suddenly out of that field of light, like something crashing through a transparent sphere on which the stars

were borne, very high and a bit to the west of Mason's northerly heading. Because the bright object seemed to climb, he knew it approached him, following a northwest-to-southeast course. Thin, sure, and beautiful, the line curved across the sky, so steady that it might go on forever. Then, as quickly as it had appeared, it vanished.

A fractional second later, there it came again, this time many more lines fanning out from where the first had been, like a hand opening into fingers of light. There were about five of them, Mason thought; in fact there had been a dozen. As Mason watched, the fingers stopped climbing dead ahead and began a long descent. Halfway to the almost imperceptible line of the eastern horizon, they again winked out. Mason thought that would be it, the chunks of whatever the object had been—a meteor, a re-entering satellite—raining on the forest, utterly swallowed up by it. Abruptly, the eastern sky lit with what must have been a hundred points of light as though each finger had exploded into a score of smaller sparks, which faded like coals from a cigarette before the jungle took them in.

"A perfectly thrown rock," said Mason. "That was what the Fall was like, a white-hot stone skipping across heaven." Mason laughed then. As a matter of fact, it had looked like something thrown—perfectly thrown by the hand of God. Had it reminded him of anything else? "An aircraft?" Mason laughed again. "You don't mean an aircraft, you mean a UFO." Actually, there was never a moment when he thought it was anything but an object from space. He'd been an amateur astronomer, back when he'd had a place to put a telescope, and he knew a meteorite when he saw one. Otherwise he wouldn't have called in the sighting. But people did, you see, that was how the world learned about supernovae and meteors and comets, people called them in.

"In the old days," Mason said, "I might've given a talk on the Fall to the Rotary Club or Jaycees, they'd always been after me for something. Of course, if I was still in touch with *them* I wouldn't have been there to see it. Thing is, Cal, I was the only witness. In all the world, I was the only one to see it. Without me, it would have fallen like the proverbial tree in a forest . . . it wouldn't really have happened without me there to witness it." Mason nodded toward the turning night. His voice went soft with loss. "It made me feel special for the first time in . . . Christ, in centuries, it felt like. My name was on the IAUgram that went out on the meteorite. For a while I thought they were going to call it the Mason Fall. Course, they finally went with geography . . . as is proper." Mason peered at the darkness, as though another swarm of objects were about to incandesce above the cordillera. "At first I took it as an omen. I really believed it was a sign my life was going to change. I don't know what I expected. Maybe just a letter from a grownup kid." He shrugged like next week's suicide. "Naturally, it wasn't anything. The goddamned stars don't know we're here."

The El Beni Fall did alter Mason's life, though. Three days after their talk, when Krylov was back at Angra-1, Mason, Captain Henry, and a Panamanian flight engineer named Vallerino took off from Arturo Merino in a twenty-year-old stretched DC-8, carrying fresh fruit to the northern winter. Santiago radar lost them at 7:37 A.M., without a peep on the radio. Searchers took three days to find the airplane, which was strewn like a big candy wrapper across the empty brown foothills northeast of La Serena. Of course, the suddenness of it and the silent radio caused some bomb talk back in Santiago, but that faded. Bomb or no bomb, the loss of three foreign airmen with marginal safety records and a few tons of grapes was no Lockerbie. Nobody tried to reassemble the aluminum puzzle that had rained down upon the Equis Valley, just as, for a long time, nobody tried to reconstruct the Fall. The scattered shards of airplane stayed where they had fallen, except for movable chunks that made their way into local home and lawn decor. Experts on the flight line at Merino reached their own conclusions: the crew had done something, God knew what, that pushed an old airplane beyond her endurance.

Reading the dozen lines the *Herald* carried about the incident, Krylov thought it merely sad, for he had liked the pilot; a terrible business. It was very late in the game before he realized Mason had been murdered for telling a secret Russian that the meteorite had looked like something thrown. Someone had been watching in Santiago after all.

2

The night of the Fall, Joly Goodpasture decided to spend the hours until sunrise in what he called Arachne's Palace, a wood and metal platform nearly fifty meters off the ground in the main branchings of a great brute of a jacarandá tree from which cable walkways radiated out for hundreds of meters into the surrounding canopy of the rainforest. As they always had, the early rumblings of the rainy season made him restless, loosening deep memories and longings. There was all that secret life up there, the screech of bugs and click of bats, the palpable stealth of tree boas and anteaters, all those hidden bargains struck between animals and plants. At these times, Goodpasture began to hope that the creatures he had spent his life studying might let him into their richly intertwined lives for a few hours. He was like God, he thought, a bit old, a bit worn out, wanting a weekend among friends.

On any other night, Rosa, the Guarani woman of fifteen who cooked, kept the laboratory picked up, and now and then slipped like a dirty child into the empty hammock of Dr. Goodpasture, might have tried to stop him. Going into the forest canopy on the system of ropes and *jumars* was always dangerous, but it seemed especially so to her on that one night of the month when he drank a liter of nearly frozen Russian vodka up on the platform. Large and pale in khaki, he made a ghostly figure in the dusky half-light, a spectre hovering in the growing darkness of the understorey. Watching him, she felt numbly

that her heart must break, but not her fear of his falling. No, this *carayba,* this white man, cracked her heart by leaving her thus easily, ascending out of her world into an inaccessible, coldly *ingles, boracho* one of his own. . . . Feeling the warm touch of anger, she averted her eyes and suppressed such thoughts. They were like darts to the devils who swarmed through the forest, and she would not lay an inadvertent curse upon her doctor. But, year by year, as he became more and more the center of her existence, she wanted more from him—a touch, a loving touch, perhaps. If something happened to him . . . she would search out a *surucucu,* a bushmaster, to bite her. . . . She shivered at the thought of the big viper, who could not help striking until all his venom was spent. Still, she would do it. Better the *surucucu* than life without the doctor, which would be a litany of famines: no home, no work, no money, no food, no family. . . . It played like a sad cascade of song. In that life a Guarani man would give her a litter of small children they would not be able to feed unless she became a whore or a political or planted coca for the *narcotraficante* in a sunlit patch of the high forest.

Looking toward him, she saw him begin to fly just off the ground, swinging on the twin ropes. She shuddered. Tomorrow was the Day of the Dead, when one could think of nothing but the lost souls. They roamed the forest in the form of animals and evil spirits; for all she knew, the doctor's science put him in touch with them and they all sat around the high, fragile platform in the treetops, sharing vodka the way he had done when the North Americans were here. In any case, it was not a time for her to interfere. She watched as he pushed one *jumar* clamp up its rope, secured it, then pulled up the other, fastened that one, and repeated the process, like a large, clumsy spider slowly moving up a web. A few tens of meters off the ground he vanished into the jungle evening.

Much later she saw a match in the black night around the platform, and the red breathing of his cigar. Finally, when the rain blew in and the trees thrashed in the wind and lightning winked at her with the evil eye of the ambient crowd of invisible deceased, she thought she heard the slurred, incomprehensible language of his singing. Chilled with superstition and fa-

tigue, she lay in Goodpasture's hammock and listened to the storm race through their corner of the Beni. She was sleeping when Goodpasture became the other witness to the Fall.

Until he read about the meteorite in the international edition of the *Miami Herald* two weeks later, Goodpasture suspected the lights had been the cold hundred-proof Stolichnaya percolating through his cortex, the alcohol molecules queued up like sinners waiting to cross into the liver. Vodka had drawn stranger pictures for him; it had even set him like a Russian on a windowsill above dark cobblestones . . . but of course the window had overlooked the steep, snowless alleys of La Paz, not St. Petersburg. He would have let the Fall go as a vision, then . . . except that the lines across the darkness possessed an element of draftmanship that forced him to consider that they could be real. But real what?

Even without the Fall, it would have been a remarkable night. The thunderstorm's great exhalation of wind and rain caused even his jacarandá to genuflect and dance; the forest echoed with the shot-like cries of failed branches, no longer able to carry their burden of lianas and bromeliads in the tempest. The rain swept at a flat angle over Goodpasture's platform, the swollen drops big as pale grapes, smashing against the wooden slats. His long, rusty hair flying madly in the wind, his red face gleaming with excitement, Goodpasture rode out the storm in a partly sheltered corner of the platform, watching the world disintegrate around him, feeling the crazy rise and fall of his *Dalbergia nigra* beneath his feet. As he always did, he waited for the awful crack to come like an explosion from the rose-scented branches suspending him, and then the plummet through darkness. . . .

In the canopy, Goodpasture had liked to tell the graduate students who had trickled through the El Beni Research Centre back when the project was still alive and funded—he hurried past the thought, not wanting to be bitter on a rare night aloft— you waited to hear that rupture under you, to hear it at the same instant you began to fall. He would tell them this when they'd gathered on the platform with him to experience the jungle night, before they had used the jerry-rigged cables and suspended walkways to creep out into what always felt to him

like thin air, no more substantial than a child's improvised tree house. Their eyes would widen and they would peer into the darkness, conscious of every acceleration of the huge rosewood tree in the light winds, feeling through their young, tanned skins the frailty of everything that supported them.

God, how he missed those days now, he thought, sadness like a chill against him. Those had been the days of Amecos, as they called it, for Amazon Ecosystem Study, pronounced of course very much like *amigos*. Typical American touch. They'd come in with scientists from Bolivia, Brazil, Peru, Venezuela, all eating and living on what the Americans put into the experiment and the few scraps the British sent to keep Goodpasture going, to explore the way water and chemicals moved around in a sample parcel of rainforest. Mere luck they'd chosen El Beni. Juan Levy had directed the project, had brought in the engineers to stick up steel meteorological towers in the forest, to add the diesel generator and the IBM computer workstation to the facility. They'd built three bungalows with screens and porches, kerosene refrigerators, running water. They'd left behind a Land Rover and a Zodiac inflatable boat with a big outboard on it; if he'd known how to use it, they would have left the little airplane as well. Bloody fantastic, it had been, like the excitement that visits a quiet village with the discovery of gold, and leaves deep silence behind it when the lode plays out.

But Goodpasture had lived too much of his life nearly alone, nearly in silence, to miss the young faces or the action or the money very much. He missed old Juan Levy. Some nights, he and Levy, two big men with an unspoken desire to go a little mad, would ascend to the platform and drink vodka and smoke cigars. Sometimes they talked all night, sometimes they sat in comradely silence, quiet as Indians. The slight warmth of their camaraderie blazed like a bonfire in the cold worlds each inhabited—it was as much heat as either man could stand. Goodpasture had marveled at the daily transformation of Levy. Directing Amecos, bringing together the dynamic strands of research planes and river boats and ground stations into a kind of data-gathering symphony, Levy must have resembled his father, whom he had described as a State Department Jew. His voice rang like an opera baritone's across El Beni, getting the work done. But at the end of the day, Goodpasture saw the other side of Levy impose calm silence, a stoic willingness to be content with little, and that odd invisibility of the Indian. His mother had been a maid from up by Antigua when she met his father in Guatemala, and Juan had grown up in Guatemala City. Yes, he missed old Juan, he truly did. It surprised him, for Goodpasture could not remember ever missing anyone before.

He chuckled mournfully at all the memory and pulled on the frosty bottle, now streaked with dark fingers of condensation. He supposed he still climbed the ropes to drink and have a cigar and perhaps sing a bit of opera to recover those nights and the odd chemistry of their friendship. Where was Juan now? Doing science, is what Levy would say, probably with a sneering laugh. Doing science. And I, thought Goodpasture, what am I doing? He closed his eyes. The platform rose and fell like the deck of a doomed ship, but he was conscious of no trace of fear. The storm had a kind of warmth of its own.

Anyway, you had to ignore the possibilities. If you loved, you didn't think about loss. If you married, you ignored the prospect of divorce. If you conceived, you tried to forget infant mortality. If you used the ropes and *jumars* to ascend into the canopy, you didn't think about the lines parting, or the deadly fall, or how quickly the ants would do a job on you. . . . Thinking about possibilities made life too frightening. The beast in the jungle business, where you waited eternally for something awful that never came. Goodpasture had ignored the possibilities steadfastly, and so had avoided almost all of them beyond the decay of a young man's brilliant field work into the stable, rather plodding work one did in middle age. And hope, he wondered now. What of hope? Or was his life at El Beni merely functional despair? Instead of doing science, he was doing time. He would have to tell Juan about that one, some day, in a venue still to be determined. Meanwhile, at fifty, the only fatal possibility that interested him was the ropes and the supporting branches; they must finally realize their potential for mischief and cast him down. Sometimes the prospect scared him shitless. But on this night, nothing was more trivial than a deadly plunge. "Why," he whispered to the buzzing that had risen in the rain, insects celebrating the grounding of the bats, "break a bone at my age and think how long it'll take to heal." Thousands of years, probably. He pulled at the bottle. Epochs. Depends what kind of curse you're sailing under. He grinned and lifted his leathery boy's face to the night, to the flashes of lightning, the slap of rain.

> *Du kennst mich nicht, du ahn'st nicht, wer ich bin*
> *Befrag' die Meere aller Zonen, befrag'*
> *den Seemann, der den Ozean durchstrich,*
> *er kennt dies Schiff, das Schrecken aller Frommen:*
> *den fliegenden Holländer nennt man mich!*

As though he sang the storm away, the rain ceased, the clouds galloped off toward the sierra, leaving the sky so clear that the Milky Way made a glowing smoke of stars above him, broken only by the silhouetted branches of the crown trees, which yearned toward the cloud of light. The insects went quiet as the night became dangerous with the click of bats returning to the hunt, and here and there the crack of some poor bastard tree limb, belatedly surrendering to the weather. But nothing seemed to have failed in Arachne's Palace, which meant he didn't have to worry about getting up in the morning with all the other spiders to repair torn nets. He filled his mouth with cold vodka, let the dense fluid tug at his neurons. You could study this and study this, he used to tell Levy and the young faces. You could study it forever, and never get it right. The comment always made the Americans look away (but not Juan; he understood), embarrassed by the willingness of a British cousin to give in, to lack scientific hubris. But it was true, you never even scratched the endlessly camouflaged surface of the forest, or if you did, you arrived at another untouched layer that would not be explained by the first one. It gave nothing back. The goddamned ants, those tadpoles looking up from their bromeliad tanks, the endlessly foraging capuchins, nobody noticed you at all, except perhaps to get out of your way, to yield. Oh, you could watch, and you could work out the scenarios of cooperation and conflict, but the why of it was always hidden. How did a tree know to offer food to ants, how did it know they were there, how did it know when they weren't? Where and in what language was all this stuff written down, anyway? And yet, the central mystery of this world had sometimes cracked a portal for a moment, an hour, once for an entire day . . . it had let him see it as God might.

He cocked his head, listening. The fading noise of insects seemed almost to whir out of him and he felt as though his very mind flew with the huge water drops that gathered at the pointed leaftips to fall like parachutists, flattened in the air until they smashed against the broad leaves of the lower storeys. His tree, his platform, the web, his own breathing, all moved on the heaving breast of the forest. "God," Goodpasture whispered passionately, his throat constricting. "What a place this is!"

Like a cosmic reply, the bright sky was laced suddenly with a dozen moving lights, seeming to rise toward him from the north, then poise, as though hovering; then, beautifully surreal, they spread apart and he could see they were not standing still, but falling toward El Beni, toward the very *Dalbergia nigra* in which he lay. Nervously now, he sipped from the bottle, wanting the vodka to hurry on its circuit through the brain, wanting the vision erased if it was false, explained if it was not. The lights winked out. Good, he thought, good. He stood with some difficulty, the wiry body of the naturalist suddenly the unsteady shell of an old boy full of vodka. It was unfair, he thought, to ask a man to work a puzzle through a blurred pane of drink. Unfair.

Again, the sky responded to his thoughts. The lights reappeared, multiplied twenty-fold, falling gently as flares into his remote and unconnected part of the world. They were the color of electricity, but still only points of light . . . no, small *disks* of light; he could just discern a geometric form within the dazzle. The objects fell and fell, so close he thought he must be able to catch them as they approached the platform, but then, perhaps a hundred meters (perhaps ten miles; the sky offered no sense of scale) above the dainty clustered leaves and pale flowers of the jacarandá, the nearest one vanished, or, rather, the geometry disappeared, leaving nothing but a glowing cloud, as vague as the smear of stars beyond it. In a second, it was gone, and Goodpasture decided it must have been the vodka doing strange things with the Milky Way. Had there been a muted pyrotechnic sound? Had he really seen a kind of luminous dust descend into the wet treetops? He could not remember. Looking back at the sky, he found no trace of anything. A dream, then. He settled back upon the platform and took a long pull from the nearly empty bottle. A fine old dream.

But, reflexively, beyond the veil of alcohol, his mind had got out Occam's Razor and had begun reckoning the simplest explanation for what he had seen. You did that, working all your life trying to understand creatures that would not communicate with you, but seemed to chatter endlessly to one another in a language of sound, color, and chemistry. You went for what could be proved, what made sense. Without such discipline, you could explain anything. After all, nothing accounts for strange airborne lights better than visitors from other worlds. The trick was never to presume full comprehension of anything, for that was not what the cosmos had intended—although it would take most Americans, perhaps all but Juan Levy, a bit longer to know that.

When his *Herald* finally reached him and he read that there had been a meteorite in El Beni on the night of the apparition, he thought that was an explanation of convincing simplicity. The article said the meteorite apparently cracked apart when it first hit the atmosphere, then shattered further against the denser air closer to the surface. Quoting a pilot, the story reported a kind of symmetry among the descending points of light, which Goodpasture himself could verify. Taking the Razor to the incident, he found that a meteorite, possibly a rather special sort of meteorite, was about as much explanation as was wanted. Except, the underground skeptic could not help but wonder, why would a meteorite appear as points of light that winked out, winked on, and vanished? "Goddamn it," Goodpasture growled, "You can never understand it all. I tell you and tell you." He took a mouthful of iced vodka and let the dizzying load of alcohol slide down his gullet drop by drop until he felt its paralytic touch within the stomach. Yes, except that something in him *did* understand and just wasn't talking. "Jesus, Juan," he told his vanished friend, "I'd sure like to talk to that pilot."

It was not until about three weeks after the Fall that Goodpasture realized he had been unconsciously searching for some physical evidence of a meteorite. Going out to check his insect traps, wandering through the dense, dusky land beneath the canopy, he'd been keeping one eye open, trailing his sensors so to speak, and had come up with nothing, as though the thing had just vaporized a few hundred meters above the research station. He didn't believe it. You'd always get a fragment, some small shard of chondritic rock; and it would leap out as an unfamiliar object in this closely known domain. Still, for all those days there was nothing, and Goodpasture forced the Fall into the corner of his mind reserved for puzzles and mysteries. He had other, more immediate problems than the fate of rocks from space. Something was happening in the Beni, something like a plague.

3

He saw the first sign on his way up the Chipirirri for his customary Thanksgiving dinner with the Petersons, a missionary couple from North Dakota, their mission school poised on the river's rim well upstream, where the water came shooting out of the gorges and abysses of the foothills like something crazily uncontrolled. Of course, the jungle torpor quickly tamed the flood, spread it into a branching Chaparé and Chipirirri, slowing the water until, brown and utterly composed, it meandered through the forest toward the distant sea, creating muddy oxbows and lagoons.

Down by the research station, the currents were slow enough that the Amecos Zodiac fairly flew along, skipping like a well-thrown rock across the dark water, Goodpasture resolutely at the helm. It had been better for the soul to be ferried upstream in a cayuca by a pair of Guarani boys, but that had been the journey of a full day. The Zodiac could make the run in a morning and needed no rowers, although by the time the Mission was just a bend or two away, the Zodiac's noisy outboard could just hold its own against the current. In the old days, he would have taken the station's surplus Rover and driven the fifteen miles or so on the Todos Santos road, which was not too bad if the rains hadn't turned it to muck. Roaring along in the car, one had felt utterly alone. The great trees rose like a colossal natural wall on either side, and there was no one to be seen except the Earth's various children, some in the trees, some in shacks and huts along the way, everyone sustained to about the same degree in a universe that seemed somehow fair and egalitarian. The animals foraged where food took them. The humans did the same, cutting and burning enough ground to grow casava and yams and maize for the year or two of life left in the infertile land. Through good times and bad, that was how it had been, everything steady-state, as though time suspended in the hot humidity of the rainforest. Back then an *indio* would ask you which side of the river you lived on. That had been the size of the old world.

Goodpasture shook his head sadly. "No more," he whispered into the great racket of the outboard that seemed to him to poison the marvelous silence of the place. "No more."

More than vast amounts of water had come down from the highlands since then. Every mestizo in Bolivia, he thought, had decided to move to the frontier, what he rather sneeringly called the wild east, searching for fortune in the form of reduced misery. The government was after people to grow cash crops for export, and you saw a lot of cattle now and great diesel trucks dragging cut mahogany and rosewood carcasses down the nasty, scarlike trails their masters sawed in the very flesh of the forest. And there was coca.

The Todos Santos road going toward the mountains became a nearly continuous strip of miserable houses made of found wood and tin and thatching, plain as driftwood, set upon concrete blocks in weeds along the road. A bacterium's paradise, and a rat's as well. It was like a film of Bolivian poverty, each frame a similar tableau of silent men, women, and children with faces as inscrutable as monkeys'. They wore polyester pants and shirts or dresses from the factories of the mysterious Orient, and the ubiquitous sloganed T-shirt. What could Caltech or Oxford mean in a world bounded by Todos Santos, El Crucero, and the Rio Chaparé? To Goodpasture the mystery was as impenetrable as the forest wall. Behind each shack, a modest garden was planted with potatoes and corn and, farther off the road, like a tiny nursery orchard of blackthorn, a plot of rowed *Erythroxylum coca* rising to the hot sunlight that clearing forest trees let in upon them. These pretty bushes with their finely tapered leaves, white flowers, and red berries had truly buggered up the world. For now, instead of the wood-paneled, worn-out trucks of before, there were the new Nissans and Toyotas, full of comfortably furtive men wearing opaque sunglasses and bearing some godawful automatic weapon capable of felling trees. Another impenetrable mystery. How could men bring such arms into the forest, where people still hunted with bows and arrows and ancient shotguns? And how is that different from bringing in *This Bud's for You* T-shirts and the idea of farming for money instead of one's survival? Goodpasture thought it would be hard to choose between the *narcotraficantes* and the cattlemen, who'd turned the forest farther east into verdant islands in an ocean of savannah.

But one had to move cautiously here, for the arguments began to narrow toward what he thought of as the naturalist's puzzle. Were the old days more important than the present? Were monkeys more important than people, were people more important than trees? Each question cascaded down and down, unanswerable at every level. No one knew. You have to remember, he reminded anyone who'd listen, that no one knows. Maybe it is wrong to put the people first; maybe it's wrong to winnow through one species and tag some as friends and others as enemies. For all one knew, the rainforests were *supposed* to be used up, hacked away and burned and given over to the growing of drugs for one animal species—maybe it all connected in some inevitable ecological necessity that was still impossible to discern. Maybe, Goodpasture thought, we are heating up the Earth by burning the rainforest because great Nature whispered to us about a coming ice age. The naturalist's puzzle. It could turn you inside-out faster than the black holes and cosmic strings of astronomy. And the great wariness such possibilities induced might also account for the odd, stilted tone of journal papers, that reduced non-human life to kneejerks, quirks, and appetites, with the rich vitality drained off into Science.

In fact, Science marched through the forest with him. At intervals along the banks Goodpasture could just make out the ghostly skeletons of metal observation towers remaining from Amecos. They dotted the jungle all the way from the Ichillo and Chaparé northwestward to the Rio Beni. Now the raised shacks were deserted, empty and derelict as the watchtowers along the Czech border, rusted, covered with ant highways and epiphytes. Now and then, tramping the forest, he'd come upon the rusting metal legs incorporated within roots groping earthward and lianas rising toward the light. Sometimes there would be an instrumented drifter washed up along the river bank, or the silver hide of one of the Amecos tethered balloons, which had been used to hoist sensor packages fifty meters above the canopy. The skins lay upon the vaulted roots and sub-storey scrubs like desiccated elephants, the shining bags collapsed around their pod of rusted-solid electronics.

A lot of waste came out of a project like Amecos; the environment under study became littered with the means of studying it. Amecos had begun with the towers and balloons, the river boats and airplanes, two years ago in September, the last third of the dry season, when the farmers liked to begin burning off their patch of forest for cattle or yams or coca or whatever. The sky darkened steadily and the setting sun looked like a bag of blood until the first rains rinsed the air. The study had run through the rainy season into the following May, when, as though a celestial switch had been thrown, the sky went dry again. The scientists issued a press release to the effect that the data stored on ten thousand rolls of computer tape was a detailed snapshot of the rainforest as it had been during the nine months of the study—that, plugged into a numerical simulation on a supercomputer, the data would let them predict how the forest moved chemicals and water, day to day, season to season. One of the colorful expressions coined by a NASA publicist was that the study would show how the Earth's lungs worked. But a lot of people had not been so sure Amecos was a good thing. Most *indios* took it to be the harbinger of some further but as yet undefined form of white mischief, and waited stoically for the scientific mask to be whipped away, revealing the familiar face of exploitation.

Well, it had quieted down pretty quickly after that press conference, he thought now. They coined a few more phrases that made Man sound terribly powerful and Nature terribly weak and stupid. They'd shown one computer rainy-season model run that Goodpasture thought impressive. It showed the plume of Krypton 85 tracer percolate up out of the high trees of the forest canopy and drift on winds into the foothills, moving just opposite to what he would have expected. Then the scientists had gone back to where they'd come from, leaving the derelict structures to rot in the forest. "What will archaeologists make of these things, anyway?" he grumbled now. "What kind of culture builds useless shit that lasts forever?"

The thing was, Juan Levy had known the program was a load of cock. You always sensed he wasn't into the science of it, although he'd known how to chat it up, how to turn the clever, headline-shaping phrase, how to persuade the *indios* that Krypton 85, while mildly radioactive, wouldn't hurt. Maybe it was having a fraud of a project to run that had put Juan up in the canopy with Goodpasture and the vodka. But, no, it had been something more, something Goodpasture had never quite been able to see, a kind of melancholy resistance to Amecos, faint as the scent of flowers upon the jungle air.

The river narrowed, nozzling the current so that it tugged at the tiller wrapped in Goodpasture's big, freckled hand, and he felt, as he had so often before, the touch of dry mountain air mixed into the dense, hot atmosphere of the lowland forest. The sierra made a white smoke of snow across the sky in front of him. Rising in a series of progressively more barren foothills, the land marched up and up, shading from green to the lavender of haze and rock, which blurred into the flank of the massif. Up there, in the vast wasteland of the Altiplano, human life proceeded as miserably as it was possible for it to do, or perhaps, thought Goodpasture, as God had intended life to be. Bad as it was, the Aymara preferred it to the eastern forest, where, it was said, they would die from heat or drown in the humidity. Christ, the Altiplano could make even an unbelieving biologist feel the cruel touch of Heaven.

Perhaps, as in the rainforest, life up there had once been fair, although he rather doubted it: the place shimmered with inequity, fixed, inscrutable. He could not bear to visit the high plains, the misery sucked at him too hungrily; now, when he traveled, he shut his spiritual eyes when the plane took off from Santa Cruz and didn't open them until he was outbound from La Paz. Well, he could not stand the unfairness that had eaten away the egalitarian ways of the rainforest, either, and so on trips to the Mission he kept to the river, untouched by what happened beyond the screen of trees. The occasional beat of an army helicopter or drone of a small *narcotraficante* plane kept him in the present, as did the faint distillery odor downwind of a concealed laboratory, or when what had seemed to be a basking cayman along the banks turned out to be a human corpse with neither head nor hands. But one could still travel the Chipirirri and the Chaparé with one's spiritual eyes shut nearly tight.

Nor, thought Goodpasture, snorting now at his deep seriousness, was a visit to the Mission an occasion to open them very wide. He had endured all but one or two of the Easters, Thanksgivings, and Christmases of the past decade with the Reverend Elmer Peterson and his family, and would have quickly abandoned the tradition except for Patricia Peterson, the minister's extraordinarily plain wife, whom Goodpasture had once loved. The thought of her, familiar as she had become with time, produced a small but pleasing excitement. Goodpasture laughed aloud, his spirits soaring. He turned his full attention to navigation and began to scout the steepening banks for a suitable landing that was not too far from the Mission, but out of sight of it.

It was then that he saw the monkeys.

They were brownfaced capuchins, *Cebus apella*, stern little chaps with cowls and eternal frowns, so essentially bright that Goodpasture always thought them somehow underdressed. Beyond a doubt, they were the smartest primates, present company excepted, in the forest. He thought he might have met these fellows before, on one of their foraging campaigns through Arachne's Palace. There were ten or twelve of them, about evenly split between males and females, always with a couple of juveniles and always a baby clinging to its mother. Their leader was a tough-looking ten-pounder, big for Cebus, who traveled like a colonel of infantry behind a protective screen of favored males and females. Out on the perimeter, the out-of-favor males did their work as sentinels, and sullenly—of course, capuchins always looked sullen—brought up the rear.

They were usually the first to see a predator, and the first to be taken.

The odd thing today was that you almost never saw Cebus on the ground. It was too damned dangerous. Most of their lives they spent in the canopy, up where the big cats were too heavy to go. But for some reason these had abandoned the safety of the treetops for the river bank, where they stood like a crowd of little hairy, unhappy people on a bare patch of ground jutting out of saw grass and lianas. The leader, whom Goodpasture recognized from an odd trapezoid of nearly orange fur near the neck, sat some small distance away from the others, restlessly plucking at his fur, rubbing his hands, but also keeping an eye on his followers. They looked for all the world, thought Goodpasture, like people at charades. But what was their leader trying to tell them? When the monkey tugged at his fur, it came off in great tufts. He cried out in an odd, aimless way, and rubbed his torso, then crept to the water, where he splashed himself, keening all the while. When he returned he still sat apart from them, and when some of the infants one normally saw playing with the dominant male ventured too close, he snarled and bared his long canines, frightening them back to their mothers.

Goodpasture pushed the Zodiac past the troop, who had heard him but were not quite ready to flee while he was still on the water. Then he cut the motor, letting the boat swing back toward them on the current so that he could beach it some twenty meters upstream. The inflated hull bumped aground and he secured it with slow, deliberate motions, not wanting to frighten the little gathering away. The leader ignored the intruder, and continued to rip away at his hair, and went back to the water. At this range, Goodpasture could see he moved like a very old man, with a clumsy, knuckle-dragging lurch, his tail hauled limply along behind him.

As one of the dangers of being a naturalist was to reduce everything to mechanical behavior, another was the impulse to see animals in human terms. Goodpasture knew the rules better than most, and yet, what could this tableau be if not a kind of charade? You didn't need a doctorate to see the old boy was trying to warn the others away, doing the heroic, leaderly thing right up to the bitter end. Here is what I've got, he was telling them, and you mustn't get it. Leave me with it. These male capuchins were as brave as Richard III at such times, monkeys of truly regal stature—stalked by a harpy eagle, the most frightening creature in their forest, the little capuchins would all vanish, terrified, leaving their leader to shake his fist and yell at the intruder. It was like yelling into the face of Death herself.

The big male began to cough uncontrollably. His face retained its earnest, apprehensive frown, but his eyes swam with what could only be fear. Yes, thought Goodpasture, and it's more than just a flow of juices or a raised voltage to the brain. It's being *afraid*. After a moment, the monkey lay on the cleared space, breathing hard, a pink string of thick mucus and blood dripping from his jaw. He no longer addressed his troop. He had turned his face to the wall, the way an Apache would, knowing the end was near. The others fluttered quickly into the green tangle. Goodpasture could hear them break their silence as they hurried back to a safer altitude; they would have a new leader by the time they regained the canopy, no doubt one of those poor boys who'd spent his life riding the perimeter. Animals were lucky, though. They had memory but no grief. Except . . . why wouldn't they? It would not be that surprising to discover a capuchin female tearfully mourning the loss of her grand old monkey lad. The man laughed at this. "You used to be a scientist, old son."

He stepped gingerly ashore, not wanting to soil or wrinkle the khaki shirt and trousers Rosa had ironed for him. The dying capuchin heard his footstep and arched his neck around to see what came. He tried to rise but could not get his limbs properly arranged to do it. "Just me, old boy," Goodpasture crooned in a soothing voice. "Just your old compatriot from up canopy way, come to see you right. Don't get excited, don't move. . . ." The capuchin struggled once more to rise, and Goodpasture stopped. The monkey wasn't seeing very well, and, only a few meters away, one could tell how sick he was. Large patches of fur were gone and Goodpasture could make out swollen, red-rimmed lesions dotting the exposed pinkish-grey skin. Watching the man, the capuchin attempted a brave snarl, but only gurgled and began to cough once more. "There, Sunny Jim, there, there, there," murmured Goodpasture, advancing a few more steps. "We'll have you good as new."

But the monkey had lost interest in the man. It sighed, its body relaxed, and, as death generally came in the jungle, was suddenly no longer alive. Goodpasture knelt beside the corpse, pitifully smaller than a human fetus, thin-limbed and frail, the face, now emptied of all vitality, frozen in a defensive grimace. Carefully, Goodpasture touched the fur with his fingers, ready to leap away from the teeth if he'd misread the signs. But the figure on the bare earth did not move. In a minute or two, the ants, beetles, and birds would move in and undertake the fallen leader. Goodpasture lifted the thin, wiry arms and probed the fur. "Well, now, you scoundrel," he said at last, "and where have you been? Some whorehouse up Santa Cruz way?" Near the lesions were tiny crystals not much larger than grains of salt, but bright as sequins. Glass, maybe. Sometimes you heard a troop getting into a house and trashing it with their curiosity. Maybe this old boy got into somebody's party trimmings— some of the Beni's ranchers might have such stuff around. Goodpasture put a broad hand under the dead monkey and picked him up. In the Zodiac he found one of the large freezer bags he used to hold samples, and put the monkey into it, along with stones for added weight, sealing the bag with a twist of coated wire. "We'll just take a look at you, old son." He tied the bag to a thin nylon line and lowered it into the stream. That way, it would keep and wouldn't frighten Patricia.

4

The Mission crouched in a clearing that looked as if it had been kicked in the side of the forest by a great, angry foot; the debris of its creation lay in a timeless compost along the edges, blending into the high grasses and tangled curtain of lianas and fern and beadlike mosses. This narrow perimeter of fertile earth had been planted with potatoes and cassava and yams, and even a small stand of coca bushes, back where they could grow unobtrusively without the jungle drinking all their light. But in the clearing itself, a multitude of bare or booted feet had tramped away all possibility of further vegetation. Gaunt chickens strutted the barren, rust-colored ground, pecking mindlessly at the planet, and every volume of hot shade held its cloud of gnats and stinging flies, which crawled drowsily upon the beige, ribby mongrels napping as though dead in any shadow they could find. A handful of mean cinderblock buildings had been arranged around the open area, their flanks once stuccoed white, but steadily discolored where they sucked up the color of the clay and mildewed. They were roofed in galvanized metal painted blue, as the Reverend Peterson had once explained at some length, to signify Heaven. The minister, Goodpasture had decided early in their relationship, liked his symbols simple, but richly enfolded in explanation. As they did everywhere, a squad of boys wearing the black shorts and white shirts of all schools, kicked lazily at a matching, clay-reddened soccer ball, which the minister, always mindful that example may turn even an Indian practical, kept always taut with air.

The main building was a low cruciform whose three blunt wings housed a chapel, classroom, and meeting room, where, on high holidays like this one, Patricia Peterson and her little entourage of Guarani women prepared dinner for the children of El Crucero and the bush settlements thereabouts, along with a few distinguished adults. Another blue-roofed structure on the downstream side of the clearing was surrounded by a rough corral fence, and held the Mission's scant livestock—a cow, a bull, a family of pigs that roamed the place like naked Caucasian dwarfs. On the upriver side was what the Petersons called the Vicarage, a stained concrete box with the same blue roof, a screened porch, a radio aerial, and a few courageous bougainvillaeas brought over from Santa Cruz. Their vined branches were almost bare of leaves; the few magenta petals they retained trembled precariously in the still air of the forest, like dead leaves always just about to fall. The Vicarage indeed. To Goodpasture's English ear, the term clanged brassily. Only an American, he thought, could use the term here without irony.

Clinking with duty-free-store plastic bags full of Chilean Riesling and two liters of Tanqueray from Her Majesty's glorious locker at Embassy La Paz (as Juan Levy had called it, laughingly), Goodpasture hesitated on the rim of Peterson's clearing and lifted his face to the air, like a wolf. One always seemed to be stepping aboard the other man's ship, a feeling Goodpasture quickly suppressed, as it seemed to give the minister power over him. Fact is, he told himself, it's just a guilty twinge that comes from returning to the scene of a petty crime. As between the two of them, him and Peterson, the clearing was the public domain. Still, he could not help testing the atmosphere for signs.

Beyond the pungent barnyard scent of cattle and pigs, he discovered guinea fowls roasting, stuffed with rice and spices one's nose had forgotten how to read, potatoes baking, yams, and pies—oh, yes, there were pies, banana ones, he thought. Across the clearing, like a caged beast, the generator droned mournfully. Voices rose and fell on the still air, American voices, male ones, female ones, the sounds of humans speaking English and Spanish and Aymara, as unintelligible as the whir of insects floating in the shade. Yes, and there, he caught the thin, reedy sound of Patricia, where she led her little Indians toward the Great Meal. Goodpasture chuckled. Nowhere in the rainforest were women so skilled at preparing the holiday cuisine of North Dakota. Her voice rose once more among the murmuring others, and he smiled, pleased to hear her in this haze of evocative sensations, which seemed like a spell cast deliberately to charm him. He uttered almost a bark of ferocious delight.

Just at the instant of giddy high-spiritedness, the dying Cebus leapt into his consciousness. Only God knew why one had such short circuits, but there it suddenly was, the poor sod of a capuchin dying of nobody knew what; his plague monkey. The dead animal had followed him the half mile from where he'd moored and covered the Zodiac, and he realized that, in fact, he had kept the beast in mind ever since putting it in the water, trying to work the puzzle of its death, a puzzle that seemed to be missing half its pieces. As he pushed along a track toward the Mission, his brain had been sorting primate diseases and found nothing that explained the odd behavior or the death. But now, he told himself, it was time to put the blasted creature away. This was to be a trip brimming with rare pleasures, and not ruined by some preoccupying mystery.

He was still engaged in such imaginary conversation when he pushed past the screen door into the meeting room. Long tables flanked by benches had been set and the children had decorated the walls with primitive drawings of Pilgrims and American Indians, pumpkins and turkeys, which, Goodpasture thought, they must have found bloody bewildering. The aroma was enough to bring a strong man to his knees. He saw Patricia the whole length of the room away, and called, "Happy Thanksgiving, Pat," and carried his bag over to her. She gave him her unaffected grin, which he quite liked to see—she had another that was so manifestly contrived he could not look at it.

"Hello, Joly." Her voice was almost completely lacking in resonance—there was, as Goodpasture put it to himself, no scream in it. They shook hands, both trembling with the contact after long abstinence. The rare touch of a lover brought an astonishing change in her. She flushed, and where one moment there had been a skinny, doughfaced woman of forty-five, her long nose always a bit runny and red, her small brown eyes watery and almost without lashes, and thin brown hair that gave real meaning to the term mousey—here was someone rather pretty. Christ, he thought, with roses in her cheeks she could still almost make his heart leap. Not the way it once had, of course. Back at the beginning, he'd thought she must be the love of his life, a creature drawn to him through time by the shaking out of bones between two jungle mothers, his in Bristol, hers in Bismark . . . something cosmic and fine. Now he viewed it more as a bargain of the type struck between every living thing in the rainforest, not so much destiny as ecological necessity. Still, he had to make himself release the familiar warmth of her hand.

Goodpasture had never quite understood what it was that had drawn him so powerfully. His first glimpse of her thin, slope-shouldered silhouette against the river years ago—Christ, ten years it must have been—had brought a covetous chuckle from his heart that surprised him. Who was this plain woman, that she pierced him so readily? For years, he had treated his feelings as a boyish crush, a secret he would keep forever; but when, on Thanksgiving five years ago, he had found himself sitting alone with her in the darkness and full of malt, and confessed the emotions of that first glimpse, she had immediately reciprocated. When he had next seen her, at Christmas, they had embraced, whispering warm secrets, trembling in one another's arms. On the following Easter they had lain down together in the forest, the naturalist hoping he had found a spot where they could have half an hour without snakes or ants, and made love like glowing savages. He had never seen her naked in daylight, and knew her body only from touch and what could be discerned in celestial light. Watching her, he thought how unremarkable she was beneath the long bottlegreen skirt and white cotton blouse—mere teabags of breasts, genitals with a tired air about them, pale and bluish in moonlight, hairs spare as trees in the Altiplano. . . . Goodpasture grinned for her. Reality didn't seem to matter, for he had never got enough of her.

But what he liked best, he thought now, was seeing her work. Perhaps it all came down to that, her seeming willingness to do any amount of hard, hard work. The idea had come not from watching her at the Mission, or listening to her talk about the missionary life they'd led on an island in Lake Superior where she had nearly lost all her teeth, and where, she said, she decided there must be a Joly Goodpasture somewhere with her name on him. Instead, it came from a night when she had left a cloud of menstrual blood on his lowered trousers. Pantless, he had watched her bend like a Guarani woman over the shallow water of the dark river, rubbing endlessly, endlessly, rubbing as she cooked, as she sewed, as she cultivated her small garden, until every last molecule of blood was gone. She may have been driven by a fear of discovery; but it had been hard work. He liked to see her at her work, then, and thought that labor must be what she was really all about. It was real, and when she was genuine his heart crept irresistibly toward her. Often she was not, and now, as he looked at her, he saw that other, disingenuous creature rise behind her little eyes; the rose withered in her cheeks, she went suddenly, appallingly, plain and stupid. Behind him, Goodpasture heard the screen door bang and knew that Elmer Peterson had entered, for there seemed to be less light in the room.

Goodpasture turned to find Peterson almost within reach. "Elmer," he told the man, "thanks for having me in." It was what he always said. It spun like a winged seed into the vast opacity that seemed always to surround his host, who smiled miserably.

"Hello, Joly. Glad you could make it." His greeting was as standard as Goodpasture's, the second half of an incantation with which they began, uttered in a voice as flat and empty of large forms of life as the North Dakota prairie. Goodpasture thought it was the voice one would use to beg a wife not to leave or whine about not being able to stick this life much longer, both of which, according to Patricia, he did regularly. The two men shook hands, the minister taking the other's in a mock-meek, perfunctory way, releasing it quickly. One would have known the man wasn't much for touching even if his wife had not exposed the trait.

Although, Goodpasture thought, you didn't need a disillusioned spouse's disclosures to know all you needed to about Peterson. Her confidences had only confirmed the impressions given so strongly by the man himself. He was ascetically slender, a bit under six feet tall, although he looked both taller and shorter than that; a long torso had been incongruously joined to legs a size short. His face was narrow and pale, its cheekbones sharp as a starving Indian's, and almost perfectly rectangular beneath a spray of dark blonde hair. Sad blue eyes peered out of this gaunt mask, whose broad, thin-lipped mouth seemed always about to wrinkle in a sob of despair. It was, Goodpasture had decided when he first beheld it, the face of a Scandinavian suicide. The odd thing about it was that, despite all those fine, high, febrile emotions written on him, Peterson was somehow coarse and unfinished. His long arms ended in knobby wristbones and the thick, curled claws of a dirt farmer, and his clothing for some reason always looked fresh from the rack of a dry goods store, as though he were a robot who had been built and clothed in a day. And yet, a kind of humor radiated from him too, as though Peterson had discovered an amusing irony in all that was sensed and seen and said about him. How much of this was merely a defensive illusion—a quiet man always seemed to know every damned thing—and how much real awareness of what went on around him was, Goodpasture thought, about the only thing he didn't know about Elmer Peterson. As, he added to himself with harsh irony, when the end of the affair finally came, there would be nothing Patricia would not tell her cuckolded husband about *him*. For an instant, as in the strobing light of a thunderbolt, he saw clearly the awful stupidity of going on with her.

"We're eating up at the Vicarage this time," Patricia put in nervously. The *Vicarage*, as though it were a fine house on a hill! He flashed what he intended to be daggers at her, but then, discovering that color had risen once more to her cheeks, that she was pretty again, his bad temper flew off into affection. He felt the familiar odd excitement of being near her, no doubt as easily detectable to others as a cloud of musk, and something else. . . . He glanced at Peterson. God, it *did* feel like war about to begin! But, of course, that was out of the question.

There could never be that much warmth between them. Do you know about us, Elmer? he silently asked the man. Do you find us funny in that hidden, bitter way of yours? Ah, God, just look at him. The man's flaunted despair was too much; Goodpasture turned aside.

"Some people here you should meet," said Peterson, implying that his gravitation had drawn guests of quality. Like his salutation, it was an invariable opening, a promise endlessly renewed as he and Patricia organized now this holiday salon, now another. They made no intellectual pretensions, but took whom they could. At Easter last there had been two Mormon boys, clean-limbed and mechanical, rapt with their mission to Bolivia, and a plump young man of about thirty dressed in the denims of the American west, a gold chain about his neck, his tender pink feet clutched in expensive leather sandals hung with turquoise beads. He had patiently explained to Goodpasture that he held the equivalent rank of a Roman Catholic bishop in a sect that seemed close to Peterson's, somewhere along the baggage-strewn path from Lutherans to Unitarians. The Christmas before there had been a former independent candidate for president of the United States, and his quiet, disheveled wife, both of them half mad from the heat, mud, and insects. People were always coming to the Peterson dinners on their way to save the rainforest, but often left soon afterwards, sick and swollen with bug venom and not caring whether the place was turned into mahogany furniture and fast hamburgers or not.

One Christmas, he couldn't think which one, they had even had the area's ruling *narcotraficante*, Congreve, which everyone pronounced cone-*gravy*. He had come, and his nasty pit bull that ate enough meat to keep a Guarani family alive for another rotten month, and a squad of Uzi-bearing bodyguards in jeans, T-shirts, mirrored sunglasses, and what Juan Levy had called gimme caps, one size fits all; bigger dogs, who ate very little. As he had no other name, Congreve had no history, beyond the hint of Chile in his surname and the fine bones of his face. You saw those cleanly drawn gentleman's faces all over South America, but nowhere was it more striking than in the mines of Chile, where, in the sudden illuminations of moving shafts of light, a begrimed peer of the realm would leap out of darkness, or a prince, or a king, all laboring like mules within the shell of a mountain. Congreve had that face, but also something junglish under the skin, an inner Indian that might explain the absence of biography. No doubt the man had come over from the northern desert of Chile, to La Paz, then down to the frontier, Bolivia's wild, wild east, working in the boomtowns that spread through the forest from Santa Cruz. He had discovered that a little coca could put him into a great house on a fifty-thousand-hectare ranch, give him the wealth of the Church and the power of Hitler. You could almost smell a tendency in him to break out in cruelty, that it lay beneath the surface as acne underlies the skin of adolescence. Ascetically slender, Congreve nevertheless radiated terrible appetites. The jungle around his plantation was said to be a cemetery of ruined women, abused unto death by him or his minions. Thus, despite the gawdy rings and Rolex, the overlain gold necklaces visible within the fine cotton collar of his shirt, Congreve was more than merely cheap and shallow: he was bloody dangerous.

In fact, it had been pretty awful sitting down to eat with him, he brought so much death to the table. Dining in his presence was like eating popcorn during a pornographic film in which every human aspiration reduced to organs and orifices. Something in the man had evoked the cruelty, the absence of restraint, you saw sometimes in children, the blank spots of childhood preserved in a forty-year-old.

The *traficante* had looked up at him in that instant, held his eyes with his own pale English ones. Something? he had seemed to ask. *Something?* Goodpasture had wanted to say, Yes, you make me wish I was almost anything else. But it would have brought trouble to the Petersons. Yes, he thought now, and to me. Admit your fear. Christ, you could barely do Patricia after.

"A good table, today," Peterson said.

"Anyone I know?" As soon as the words were in the air, Goodpasture saw what the Petersons had done. Patricia went pale, the color drained from her face. Watching her feet, whose long toes slid like short fingers just over the ends of dark leather sandals, he knew even before Peterson jumped in with his reply.

"Congreve came. We didn't think he would, but he did."

"I didn't see his car or his boys."

"Flew over," Peterson said proudly. "Helicopter's out behind the Vicarage."

Sure enough, Goodpasture could just make out the drooping tip of a rotor blade behind the buildings; it swayed in the meager breezes of the clearing. You heard talk that the *campesinos cocaleros* were being driven out of business by the fall in coca leaf prices, that they had given up coca growing to get the government bounties for switching to macadamia nuts or citrus or flowers, that they had finally found the hard slog of hauling and selling coca leaves too hard, now the price had dropped to nothing a kilogram. You heard that the farmers were fleeing a dying industry. Maybe so, but, really, Goodpasture thought, it was just a lull; the government, the Americans, lacked the staying power of their national addiction. Once Bolivia had its own Shining Path riding shotgun for the *narcotraficantes*, life would resume. The Bolivian economy ran off the flywheels of its conegravies, billionaires with so much gold in their kits they would be rich forever. Private army rich, Croesus rich—helicopter rich. And if one day a few billion weren't enough, they'd find somebody to grow more leaves. The bright green groves would run across the mountains like verdant wildfire, far from roads and government patrols. "Congreve," Goodpasture muttered. "Wish I'd known."

"Would it have kept you away?" Patricia asked.

He heard the complaint on the thin voice, and wondered at her challenging him in front of her husband, flinging her lover's rights at him, her face glowing with a bright patch of aroused color in each cheek where even the blind could see it. But not the complacent—Elmer Peterson saw nothing that would jar his assumptions. "Not likely," Goodpasture said, deciding to surrender. She became pretty again, but he could not quite forgive her. She knew what he thought of Congreve and his boys; he had told her at some length as they'd lain in the breathing bottom of his inflated boat after that horrible dinner. So why, he silently asked her now, knowing my dislike in such detail, do you have this devil in for Thanksgiving dinner with me? A bitter suspicion revived within: they used Congreve to service their fantasy of being gentlefolk, having the baron down from the manse on holidays. Still, thought Goodpasture, forcing himself to cool down, one understood that the years upon years of living without comfort up in the Dakotas could make gentility urgently important to her. The vicars of his own childhood had done much the same thing, drawing aristocrats, often highly dubious ones, around their mean condition like a fine cloak. In any case, he thought, you didn't tell your lover what you thought of her pretensions: she might reply with what she thought of yours.

"He brought some house guests," she said.

"Charmers all, no doubt."

"Actually, very nice people." Her voice had gone quite cold, as she lost patience with him.

"A woman from Greenpeace," Peterson put in.

"And others," Patricia said, closing the thought. "Go meet them. I'll be up in a little while."

Feeling himself somehow jettisoned from the hall, Goodpasture numbly followed the minister out into the sunlight. As they started across the hard, beaten ground toward the Vicarage, he became conscious that Peterson watched him pensively, and wondered if Patricia's little outburst had caused something to snap into place after all. Goodpasture smelled anxiety and tension in the man, and felt a moment's pity. But, no, it had nothing to do with him. He looked into Peterson's flat blue eyes. "Something wrong, Elmer?"

"Naw," the man replied, slipping into the coarse accent of the prairie farmer. "Not really." But Goodpasture could feel a kind of magma of words building up inside the minister, as if he were about to erupt into speech and tell his version of All.

The prospect of such a decantation repelled Goodpasture, who wished now to hurry into the shelter of others, even if they were Congreve and his boys. But all he said was, "Good."

Peterson halted, still studying Goodpasture. "But it did surprise me, your not liking Congreve." He called him *cone*-gravy; his Spanish had always been resolutely American, spoken with a determined John Wayne accent. "I thought everybody around here liked him."

"I wouldn't have liked Robin Hood either."

Peterson ignored the sarcasm. "Everybody here just about lives in his shadow, and we're no different. He's the only protection Pat and I've got out here, aside from God I mean. I think the Lord must have put him here partly to look after our Mission."

"He moves in mysterious ways indeed."

"Course He does," Peterson continued, unperturbed. "I mean, everything, *everything*, is locked up in mystery, that's why everything rests on faith. You never see God's intentions whole, or even very clearly. . . ." He waved his farmer's hands in frustration as his surplus of words became a shortage.

But Goodpasture was touched, in a way, to hear this man he despised expressing almost what he himself had pondered so many times—touched, and a bit contaminated, as if Peterson's brushing that central truth brought him uncomfortably close, and jarred one's assumptions about being wiser than a missionary. "You're becoming a regular seminarian, Elmer."

"I don't know about that," the man modestly replied. "But I know that our protection isn't the only reason Congreve's here. God wants something else. He wants us to get to know this man, to know him through and through."

"But why?" A rising note in the minister's voice chilled Goodpasture; he heard the keening of some hidden madness and, for the first time, felt a ripple of fear, suddenly not knowing what this utterly predictable man would do.

"To look into him."

"Suppose Congreve's just a murderous little thief who's got lucky?"

"If that was true, God wouldn't have arranged all this."

"My point exactly."

"Know thine enemy, Joly. Know thine enemy," he repeated, his voice trembling with its burden of certitude. "God wants us to . . . contribute. I wouldn't say this to anyone but you, Joly. The thing is, Pat and I have been terribly selfish. We've been together, and close, you know, closer than I can explain, for so many years. We're just a kind of single entity. Often all we see is the other person. Sometimes we've even excluded our children, even God . . . although we've tried to make amends. But now we see that He wants us to put something more back, to make up for our having this great happiness together. God brought us into a country that will always be strange to us, and we've spent these years waiting for Him to show us why. I figured for the longest time that He'd intended to teach us to turn more toward people outside our marriage. But now I understand He had something else in mind. A couple of years ago, it must be now, He began to reveal his intentions. He brought us Congreve."

"Ah." Goodpasture could barely speak. The man's complacency, his pretending to knowledge of divine tactics turned Goodpasture cold, tight-lipped, and furiously angry. It was just this kind of mad, egocentric exposition that had led Juan Levy to call the Petersons the king and queen of bullshit. But, good Lord, one needn't be buried in the stuff this way.

"Course," the man went infuriatingly on, "we have no idea where it goes from there. We wait for the next sign . . . for God to show us His hand."

"I see." I see, Goodpasture thought, a small, mendacious world of horrible affectations. There's the bloody Vicarage, which is just this miserable block structure ahead of us, and there's this great love of yours who sees the world only as it frames you, who, incidentally, have been made to wear a set of antlers that would dazzle an elk. I see a husband and wife with a good deal of stupidity shared between them, like those grey women with the single eye. For a moment he tried to imagine Patricia and could conjure nothing but her ugliness—that, and his own rash of jealousy where the man's complacent confidence had rubbed him raw. Perhaps, he thought, that was just what Peterson had in mind. For a moment, he thought that he might give the minister the miracle he wanted and tell him about the meteorite fall. But, seeing the terrible, destructive belief that there would be a sign shine like madness in the minister's eyes, Goodpasture could not bring himself to feed it. He felt immediately relieved, of anger, of jealousy, of all his burdens, and when he remembered this moment afterward, he would feel that same quick flooding of relief, that it had not been he who had lighted Peterson's fuse.

"Do you?"

"Do I what?" Goodpasture had no idea what the man could be talking about.

"See."

"Oh. Well, I see you've given all this a good deal of thought." I see you're as crazy as you are full of shit. He stepped toward the Vicarage, eager for Peterson's awful friendliness to end. "All this theology has given me a thirst."

Peterson laughed softly, with just a note of an ascetic's contempt for appetites.

"And I want to see what this Greenpeace woman looks like. Things've been quiet down at the station."

Again Peterson laughed, like, thought Goodpasture, a deaf man deriding music. Well, one supposed that took a kind of confidence, after all.

"Here we are," the minister announced, all trace of that shrill voice gone now, along with the bogus intimations of close friendship. Only the flat prairie of the man's speech remained. For a moment, Peterson studied his companion, peered into his eyes with his own lightless, unhappy ones; then, with a flinching gesture that contained a visibly pained decision to endure the day, he yanked on the screen door that had sealed the Vicarage. The wood, swollen by the returning moisture of the rainy season, stuck, and Peterson had to work it furiously before he could wrench it free of the frame; finally it opened with a great clatter and his grunt of annoyed effort.

The door sprang open like a curtain, revealing surroundings that Goodpasture thought of as profoundly familiar, although nothing here was his. The single large room was sparsely furnished, mostly pieces of wood and canvas that the minister had made himself. The walls were bare except for a few wedding photographs and what must have been a church congregation of red Indians up in the Dakotas somewhere, and another that showed Patricia, young, slender, and surprisingly radiant in a setting she had once explained was an island in Lake Superior. They had experiences that her husband called their towering moment in that place. Whatever it may have done for him, it had cracked her ability to hope and put her in bed (well, inflatable boat) with Goodpasture. The concrete floor had been partially covered with mat rugs in bright colors, and there were pillows of a bright appliqué everywhere, the fruit of the sewing station she had near one window. It had always been extremely moving, to Goodpasture, to come upon her at her appliqué, like seeing a beloved woman at the piano, except, he was careful to note, now everything was so goddamned clear, no music came forth; just the bright cloth she made into pillows and bedspreads and tablecloths. They had been years trying to figure out how she might construct him a wonderful macaw-like shirt without seeming to make him anything really personal. Thus far, the project remained stalled. She had moved their dinner table into the center of the room and set it with colored napkins and her grandmother's china and silver. It sparkled incongruously in the place, which no amount of appliqué could save from bleakness.

At the opposite corner of the room, Peterson had what he liked to call his study, a narrow Scandinavian student's desk in moisture-wrinkled teak veneer, a bookshelf with perhaps a dozen volumes in it—the Mission's account books, Bibles, and sermons from here and there. Neither husband nor wife seemed ever to have read a work of fiction. Beyond the wall lay their bedroom with its old double bed of dark maple and a small bathroom in which Peterson, ever practical, had installed a urinal; it might as well have been a porcelain phallus, so overtly did it mark out the territory of his part. Her pretty cloth was everywhere, beating back with color the grey concrete of the straitened missionary life.

The handful of people sitting beyond the door looked up, startled into distraction by the commotion of Peterson's entrance—looked up, Goodpasture thought, like animals looking into a sudden beam of light at night. They seemed never to have seen the minister before or to have realized that, beyond the screened door, a bare patch of earth and a forest and river and other creatures had continued their lives without them.

On one side of the tableau was a blonde woman Goodpasture knew immediately was an American from California, sturdy, her yellow hair cropped short. He thought she must be the

Greenpeace person and took her to be a late baby-boomer, near-ing forty, but a pretty girl. She would take sailboat-style show-ers, using little water and discharging little waste, opt for re-cycled paper shopping bags, eschew the use of aluminum foil, and steer around all the jagged reefs that dotted the channels of American life: electrical radiation; substances that, taken by the ton, caused cancer in rats; obesity; ionization of the wrong sort. And, he thought, she would not be averse to a bit of grass or the odd line of Congreve's profitably uncontrollable substance. All of this he saw immediately; what was concealed to him was her reason for being Congreve's house guest. Perhaps, given the man's reputation, it suggested that she had peculiar cravings of her own. He decided not to like her overmuch, in case she wound up in a shallow forest grave near Congreve's *finca*.

The man sitting next to her had the soft face and the worn black suit of a town Indian, Peruvian, perhaps, or Chileno, and exuded such gentleness as to seem priestly. He watched Good-pasture with eyes as dark and deep as a deer's, in which you could just discern the mad light of large ideas. Ideologues were all the same, you could spot them a mile away. Goodpasture wondered at his age: something between twelve and fifty, he reckoned, give or take.

A big hairy man sat not quite in the background. He was probably in his early forties, looked to be from up north some-where, Guatemala, perhaps, or Salvador. It took Goodpasture some moments to recognize him as Arias, one of the helicopter pilots from the Amecos project. A Salvadoran. The familiar face had partly vanished behind a black brush of mustache and a thick fall of curly hair over the collar of his soft blue, epauleted pilot's shirt. The eyes were still the opaque, hopelessly neutral eyes of the pilot for hire; windows to nowhere. With the ma-chine and the act of flight between them and whatever occurred outside their narrow domain, pilots were as friendly and neu-tral as stray dogs, and had somewhat the same manner. They were brave in their way, however, and took grand risks for money and because danger is often good for the head and heart. But courage had not served Arias well. He had flown cropdusters in coastal Guatemala for almost ten years, a long time to be soaking up pesticides through an airplane's seat cushion. Arias had told him during Amecos that back then he had gone every year, when the dusting season ended, to have his blood replaced in Panama. But even with that, put him in a wide hall and he would almost fall over on his back, disoriented as a sprayed weevil.

Peterson was making introductions. "Doctor Joly Goodpasture . . . he runs the Beni research station down the Chipirirri a few kilometers from here. Señor Congreve . . . I think you know one another . . . Señor Arias . . .

"We met," Goodpasture said, nodding to the pilot, but Peterson hurried along.

"And Miss . . . Jones?" he asked the blonde dubiously.

"Call me Teejay," she said. Goodpasture loved her accent, which was that clearest of American ones, the voice of southern California. Everybody in California sounded like Jane Fonda; they all sounded smart.

"From Greenpeace?" asked Goodpasture.

She laughed, natural as mother Earth herself. "Greengo. Everybody mixes us up."

"Ah." Greengo was the artful *nom de guerre* of an environmental group—a cult, as he thought of it—determined to save every bloody thing in Latin America, especially the rainforest. They were one of the many infantries of the environmental movement, ready to go anywhere and do anything . . . like the ideologue there. Except her constituency had no people in it —it was one of ozone molecules, rivers, shorelines, trees, pandas, dolphins, whales, birds: the constituency, Goodpasture thought, of a fantasizing child. She and the other Greengo soldiers weren't in it to govern or reform, anymore than the guerrillas were—all of them just wanted to be part of the action, whether out in a Zodiac under a whaler's harpoon gun, or up in the Peruvian mountains with the *Sendero Luminoso*.

"And Señor Palma," Peterson hurried along. "Mr. Palma is a healer, Joly. You might want to talk plants together."

"A healer." Goodpasture shook the man's small, tan hand, and saw that Palma's gentle face shared his contempt for this thin disguise. Herbal doctors still roamed the Altiplano, following their fathers and grandfathers as faithfully as any man on Harley Street—but this Palma was not one of them. His hands were girl-smooth, not stained by a lifetime of milking jungle plants and touching the sick poor. A pity he wasn't, they were wonderful for a biologist to talk to. No, this Palma thing was just about the opposite, Goodpasture reckoned. He should just come out and say that he tortured and killed his fellow men for a living, working in the name of some discredited belief. "What do you heal?"

"Everything I can."

"Everything. That's a good deal of healing." You heal the life right out of them, I hear.

"We keep busy."

"I can see that." Goodpasture looked around the group and thought that theirs was not really the gaze of dazzled animals, but of prisoners turning up their eyes to footfalls on the mesh above. But why would he think that? These people had to be the freest of the free.

Congreve was calling him, all false-hearty. "Hey, Doc-tor," he said, offering a heavily ringed hand for shaking, but without getting up. In this drab setting he seemed almost to glow. He wore a raw silk suit the color of cocaine and a fine black shirt within, open between the great wings of its collar to reveal pale, almost hairless skin covered by a filigree of gold chains. Suspended half in apprehension, half in pleased surprise, the man presented his fine British face as a boy might, except that this boy's eyes were empty of everything but dark instincts centered on cruelty and power.

People liked the roads and clinics he had added here and there in the Beni, liked having all that wealth between them and an unsmiling government they did not like and rarely saw: La Paz was light years from the forest. But Congreve had also brought something cold and alien as well. Most of the so-called drug lords in Bolivia were merely businessmen, and ran their traffic like any other commodities trade, surrounded by family members, and not much given to leaving headless, handless torsos in the Chaparé. Not being a Bolivian himself, however, Congreve had no inhibiting gentleness at his center, and began to fill what he must have sensed was a vacuum of cruelty in the region, carried out with the help of the tough, stupid brutes he imported from Colombia and Peru. Of course, *Sendero Luminoso* likewise abhorred a vacuum. People like Palma were beginning to drift across the Altiplano frontier, thinking that perhaps they could help people like Congreve.

Looking at him now, Goodpasture wondered whether any of the stories one heard were true. He thought that the man, as rumored, had succumbed to the same addiction he served in others; he had the subcutaneous restlessness, the mood always poised to swing, the guard-dog attentiveness of the addict. But Goodpasture could not square the rumors of a neurotic, health-obsessed recluse, the Howard Hughes of El Beni, with the hip aristocrat he saw today. Congreve wore his shoulder-length black hair in a small braid, Willy Nelson style, and his thin hands glittered and jumped in the light, little forests of heavy rings flashing green and red and diamond-white. His feet, the smallest Goodpasture had ever seen on a man, even one as small as Congreve, were shod in beige kangaroo-skin cowboy boots. He occupied the chair that Patricia and Peterson called His Chair, meaning the minister's. No doubt if they had not made some possessive reference to it, Congreve would not have chosen it now; but he could no more help taking what was not his than a *surucucu* could resist that second or third strike. Once provoked, the man had no more brakes than a viper, even if the prey were only a ragged old chair desiccated by a lifetime on the American prairie. If Patricia were beautiful . . . Goodpasture dropped the troublesome thought. Thank God she was not.

"Doctor," said Congreve, leaning forward without getting up, and sticking out his hand. "How you doing, brother?" His voice was a buzz; in Spanish it told you how completely the Indian ruled inside that small, finely made exterior. You also heard the hatred of all educated men. They said Congreve could not read or write, but Goodpasture thought that must be apocryphal; although, he thought now, the man might need to push the words along with guiding forefinger and silently moving lips.

"Happy Thanksgiving." Goodpasture gave the proffered fingers a hard shake, grinding the rings together as though accidentally. When he retrieved his own hand he was careful not to follow the impulse to wipe its palm on his trouser leg. "I don't see your pooch today," he said, wondering what the rotten little brute could be killing out in the clearing.

"Pooch?" Congreve frowned.

"*Perro.*"

He laughed. "I was just telling them, Doctor. Do you believe the fucker bit me?" Behind him, two bully boys with Uzis rolled their eyes and grinned at one another about such canine stupidity. "It musta gone loco." Congreve liked the sniggers that began to drop, coinlike, from the two bodyguards. "Loco," he repeated. "So, know what I do?" He looked around with his thin eyebrows raised interrogatively, teacher fashion. "Eh?"

I, thought Goodpasture, will die before asking. He looked at his companions, all transfixed by the question of whether Congreve's query was merely rhetorical or intended to summon some response from them. The blonde who wanted to be called Teejay looked around, mystified, signalling, Who, me? like a kid. But she didn't rise to the question; she kept her distance.

So did Palma. That left it up to Arias to answer, following his highly tuned sensitivity to his employer's needs. Goodpasture remembered the pilot's slavish tailwagging around Juan Levy back in the Amecos days. "What?" asked Arias. The voice had a dull, doped sound imparted not by drugs, but by years of absorbing pesticides. "What happened to the dog?" he persisted, grinning like one himself.

"After he bit me?" Congreve laughed, cold as a tolling bell. "We make him swim." Pause for effect. "Damn tough *perrito,* he go in the water from the chopper, maybe a hundred meters. He swim for the *finca,* you see. I think, Shit, this damn dog come back, okay, and then he go loco again and bite me twice . . . hell, he can give rabies . . . or AIDS." He laughed at the improbability of his ever contracting a disease of homosexuals. "You don't want AIDS from no dog, right?" No one contradicted him. "Before my boys can shoot him, this cayman come along behind. Them cayman, they can't help it when they see a dog swimming. Those four legs like wiggling fingers that say, Come eat me, come eat me. So they do. That is what happen to my *perrito.* It makes me . . . very sad." He lowered his eyes and let his mean little mouth crumple. Then he raised his finely cut face to his auditors, gave a great, hardhearted laugh, and pulled at the rum and Coke Peterson had made him. "That damn dog, though," he said at last, "he bite that cayman right to the end. Right to the end."

Christ, thought Goodpasture, moving over to the shelf where Peterson had set up his meager bar. Christ. "Gin?"

"Please help yourself."

He poured himself a tumbler of warm gin, added a single ice cube and squeezed a lime wedge into the drink. The dog stories would be better if one were drunk, he decided.

But, after giving Congreve their forced laughter, the group sank into an uncomfortable silence. Peterson, already fully decanted of words, did nothing to relieve it. Goodpasture sensed Congreve's restlessness and saw that the woman had also sensed it, the subaudible signals of dangerous bad behavior. Arias looked good-naturedly around himself, content as a farm animal, drinking only Coke. Of course his liver wouldn't want anything stronger. Goodpasture imagined that organ as a ruined palace, the pillars and corridors and chambers of it crumbled into rubble swept by dunes of yellow fat, with everywhere a trove of those big molecules from which lethal substances are fashioned. His brain chemistry would send one's equipment off-scale. For a moment, he saw Arias lying open, a shell of skin on an autopsy table. He imagined a crowd of doctors looking at the ruined liver, others shaking their heads over what they had discovered in the brain.

Thinking of autopsies recalled the monkey that waited for him in the river. He hoped a passing cayman hadn't taken a fancy to that plastic storage bag and stolen the Cebus and its cargo of plague. "Saw something peculiar on the way up," he told the silence. He felt the tension subside. The blonde smiled her relief at him as though they were kindred souls. Well, perhaps they were. She was young and fit, long legs with peasant calves and no panty line beneath the khaki slacks, always a good sign. Perhaps they were both looking for somebody. He thought he might be, given this ordeal by cone-gravy. Everyone watched him expectantly. "There was a troop of capuchins on the bank . . . with a very sick leader." Remembering the tableau, he found he could not share more than he had with Congreve; he did not want the many-ringed hand even figuratively touching his monkey.

"So?" Congreve wondered, puzzled anger building behind the voice.

"Only that it was unusual, seeing them out of the canopy. Puzzling behavior, we call it." He uttered a deprecating laugh intended to suggest that science could be silly.

Congreve flashed a look that said he didn't like pointless monkey stories.

"The monkey died while I was watching," offered Goodpasture. The Congreve wanted more. "I plan to autopsy the poor beast, see what killed him."

Palma, generously filling an ominous vacuum, asked, "You think it was a sign?" He had the velvety voice of a forest Indian, and his English had only a trace of Spanish in it. Goodpasture could imagine his using it to ask questions of a captured man, the soft voice like a cushion against the pain of interrogation. Palma chuckled, a warm shell of laughter enfolding a frozen core. "Perhaps 'sign' is too strong a term to use around a priest."

Goodpasture had to grin. The soft voice burrowed through the tense absence of conversation in the room, turning it over, fertilizing it with Peterson's sudden, head-wagging protestation, "But, I'm not a priest, Mr. Palma," holding up a thick hand against the notion. "I'm a missionary."

"But, to the monkey, you think it was . . . significant?" Palma peered unblinkingly at the Englishman, his eyes projecting that same gently persuasive note one heard in his voice.

Goodpasture shrugged, unable to look away. Why was Palma here, in the Beni? "But how would I know?"

"You are a scientist."

"All the more reason to be puzzled."

"You do not like omens, you scientists?" It was not really a question.

"There are ever so many things we don't like." Goodpasture had finished his gin and moved gingerly past Palma to pour himself another.

"Things are changing in Bolivia, though," Palma went on. "Omens perhaps show the way. Your dead monkey, now perhaps that is one. And there has been another, very unequivocal sign."

Everyone could feel Peterson's sudden tension across the room. "What was that?" he asked, his voice dull to hide some expectation. But Goodpasture knew before Palma spoke; it was inevitable that, somehow, the minister be brought to the Fall.

"On All Saints Eve," Palma murmured in that earnest, mildly exhorting tone, "there was a big fall of meteorites here, over the Beni. They even named it the El Beni Fall. I saw it in the newspapers. A pilot witnessed the actual thing. Like a cascade of light, he said. *Salto de luz*. Perhaps."

For a moment, all were transfixed by his words, and Goodpasture might have spoken of his own witness of the Fall. But Patricia swept into the room just then, bringing with her a flash of sunlight from the outside, and an odd radiance that excited Goodpasture, already primed by the vital presence of the blonde.

"Ready for that drink," she caroled happily, crossing to Peterson with a kind of flourish of her long, white skirt. Goodpasture's heart gave its little throb, wanting her at his own side, for she was pretty again, and, for whatever reason, he had let himself slide back into what passed in the forest for love. "Don't let me disturb you, Señor Palma. Please go on."

"He was talking about a big meteor in the Beni, Pat," said Peterson. She turned quickly toward him, frowned, trying to read his face, trying to discover the source of a worrying note she had detected in his voice. He's about to go bonkers on you, Patricia, thought Goodpasture. He's found a bloody sign. Abruptly he realized that she might be too, that the two of them might have a crazy alliance of divine intervention going on between them, one he could not penetrate—one he would not wish to touch with a three-meter pole. "Please go on, Mr. Palma," the minister said.

"There is nothing more to tell. But this cascade of light, this *salto*, must have been of a highly unusual character . . . a unique sight."

"Did you see it?" asked Peterson.

"That is also remarkable. Apparently no one did, only the pilot." Palma shrugged. "Of course, that is not the point. The point is that we begin to see signs. The Beni Fall. The dead monkey. There will be more, perhaps. I have noticed that when they begin to appear, you see them everywhere."

"Is there a monkey?" Patricia wondered.

"I found a dead monkey on the way up." Goodpasture grinned. "If you like, I'll show it to you later."

"*Ugh,* no thanks."

"But are these things not connected?" asked Palma, pursuing something. "Is that not what nature is all about?"

"Nature has not revealed to me what she is all about," Goodpasture replied stuffily, angry to have nature explained to him by some fucking little anarchist dynamiter from Peru.

"I am just an amateur observer, of course, but we healers learn a lot, travelling here and there. You see a strange thing here, and another strange thing there not long afterward, and soon you have a number of strange things. Then you ask yourself if they are not connected."

"And what do you reply?"

"I say one should never rule out anything."

"Divine or otherwise."

"Divine, political, biological. Everything is possible." Palma said it with the easy, shallow seriousness of the true believer, as comfortably immersed in dogma as a missionary.

Congreve interjected, "Hey, maybe it's some kind of judgment on *you,* Doc-tor. A plague star, eh." He laughed like a parrot.

"I haven't believed for a long time that meteors were thrown at us by God. Centuries, actually." Poor Peterson watched him balefully, the unhappy mouth working around words he would not utter. The man invited small cruelties. "What do you think, Elmer? Is this meteor business the sign you've been waiting for?"

"I wouldn't make fun of it if I were you, Joly," said Peterson. "We don't know what He will use to show us His Will." At that instant, a swirling gust of wind swept the clearing, raised a spinning column of dust, scattering the children who had begun to gather near the dining hall. The minister watched the dust-devil, then grinned at Goodpasture as if to say: See my power.

Congreve laughed, a trifle nervously Goodpasture thought. "I think He coming after me on account of that damn *perro.*" He spat out a harsh laugh then. God was not someone he worried much about; he had seen how well God protected the faithful all his life, and had given up on help from on high—Christ, God couldn't even protect people from *him.* "But, you know, I sure want a piece of that meteor," he said then. "What a chain it would make, eh? You find a piece of that meteor, Dr. Peterson, you save it for me, okay?" He fondled the gold links circling his neck. "I put it *here.*" For a moment he frowned over some abstraction, his empty eyes clouded with what Goodpasture thought, incredibly, must be belief. Congreve didn't think much of God, but a piece of a star, a meteor, that was different. Christ, you could see him working over the implications in his stupid, brainless way, like a dog solving the parable of a food dish that was now full, now empty. "People pay a lotta money for meteors. The *indios,* man, they go ape shit over stuff like that, they believe they come from the stars anyway. Maybe they trade me something better than coca, I don't know, magic or something. Maybe I become a famous *meteorero.*"

"A *meteoragroindustrialista,*" murmured Goodpasture.

"You got it, Doc-tor," said Congreve, his face letting Goodpasture know he'd heard the joke. "You watch. I confess the dog, your monkey come back to life."

"I shall alert the media." The warm gin percolated through his brain, rendering Congreve less dangerous. Goodpasture decided he needed a touch more and went to get it.

"Or maybe Palma here can fix it," Congreve ran on. "Maybe he comes with a miracle for El Beni." An odd, ominous turn, Goodpasture thought, for Congreve to slap a guest this way.

But Palma was unruffled. The darkness behind his eyes may have deepened, Goodpasture couldn't tell; something predatory swam around in there all the time, and then, now and then, you saw a dark ripple, maybe a fin. "I heal nothing but men," he said almost inaudibly. He looked into Congreve's dull black eyes. In Spanish he added, "I am not a pipe to be played, you know."

"Did I provoke you, Palma?" Congreve responded, also in Spanish.

"I was provoked at birth." Palma watched the older man steadily, his face clear of everything, showing not the slightest emotional weather. Goodpasture could see Congreve's inclination to provoke go out like an expiring flame, and thought that Palma must have powers of his own. For all we know he is President Guzmán himself. "But, as you would say," Palma went on, turning back to the Englishman, "we lose our thread."

Goodpasture felt a tickle of apprehension, now he had seen Palma make Congreve quiet; and yet he could not help wanting to play. "Probably the result of a cold front over Lake Maracaibo. Everything linked, you see."

Palma watched him with that same heavily neutral expression and Goodpasture turned away, feeling Patricia nearby, almost touching his flank with hers, although she faced the blonde. "It must be very exciting," she was saying, no doubt in response to some claim the woman had made for Greengo.

"What must?" he asked, putting himself firmly out of the line of further conversation with Palma.

"Teejay's with Greengo, Joly."

"Yes, Elmer told me." He looked at the blonde. Whatever she had said about her work, it had brought high color to her cheeks and, in her eyes, the light of unshakeable conviction. She was just like Palma or old Elmer there, cocooned in beliefs that were so strongly held as to operate free of reason. Palma would blow up the world to have his way, although he had no wish to govern, or make a broken economy spring back to life. Teejay and her chaps weren't problem solvers either; they ignored the conundrums of their cause: how to feed the people whose factories closed in the interest of clean air or reduced risks of injury. "Here to save our rainforest, then?"

"Not this trip," she replied. By God, he did love that clear-syllabled California voice. "We were up in Peru. They wanted to spray coca farms with Spike . . . put that stuff into a virgin ecosystem." She grinned with vast, but he thought bogus, candor. "But you'd know more about that than anyone."

"Well, I know the ecosystem's no virgin."

She laughed for him. He sensed Patricia, spiritually abandoned, falling off to one side, a bit piqued perhaps, but also drawn by the gravitations of her work: the task of finishing the table tugged at her like a moon. "Anyway," Teejay went on, "we heard they were planning a pilot defoliation project in the Chaparé, so here I am." She held out her palms, singer fashion, and added, "Ta-*da*."

"I hadn't heard about a pilot project."

"Maybe it's just a rumor, but we wanted to follow it up. I mean, are governments devious, or what?"

"Not very long ago," he said, hearing himself beginning to lecture, "yours was providing the lion's share of a rather big ecosystem study down here. Nothing very sinister, as far as I could tell. Measuring micro and mesometeorology, you know, uptake, chemical flows, that sort of thing."

"Amecos?"

"Yes."

"I always thought an acronym that sweet must hide something pretty awful." Her eyes were grey with jewel flecks of green and amber floating in the irises. Tiny laugh lines radiated out from their corners. Her nose had been broken, perhaps when she was a child, he thought, and now gave her a kind of severe, stony look in repose; but the mouth was broad and humorous, the short, thick hair darkening to a shadowy golden grey within. She had the permanent tan of someone who spent a lot of time in the water—the sun had dyed her right down to her skeleton—and she had an animated quality that, like the accent, he associated with California.

"You could say the same thing about Greengo."

"Touché . . . except, the government isn't in it."

"How on earth can you tell?"

"Because they try to use us. Because the DEA puts people in, sabotages our stuff. . . ."

Goodpasture smiled. "Enough, let's talk about something pleasant. Let's talk about your California childhood."

Again she laughed, rolling her eyes with great good humor. "Oh, boy, that obvious, huh?"

He thought it wonderful that she should be able to relax so utterly with him, in a room full of drug money, terror, and Christianity. "Actually, I'm very fond of California. Spent some time there, years back, guest lecturing and such stuff. Even choked with motorcars, it looked perfectly lovely to me."

"I've never met a Brit who didn't like it."

"Well, we have this residual thing about the American west. Red Indians, cowboys, gunslingers, the Grand Canyon, and those poor bloody people in the covered wagons. Imagine their seeing, when they'd just about got across Kansas, the Rockies rising ahead of them." He gave a great, admiring shake of his head. "We find it wonderful, in the old sense of the term, I mean. It fills us with wonder."

"And we adore the British. What a relationship."

"Yes, what a relationship. Requires considerable mythology on both sides." Through the gin slopping around within, he detected a muted signal for greater caution. Remember whose guest she is, he reminded himself. He looked into her clear, uncautious face. Pretty, golden girl, he thought, what are you doing with Congreve? "How does Congreve fit into your, *um*, movement?"

"You mean, what's a nice girl like me doing with a drug lord like him?"

"Something like that."

"It's a coincidence. We've wound up on the same side. He doesn't want his crops Spiked. We don't either, although our reasons are not . . . entrepreneurial."

"How long are you here for?"

She shrugged her broad, swimmer's shoulders. "Long as it takes."

"Perhaps you'd like to visit Beni station. Great eco-things going on there. A smashing observation platform up in the canopy." The invitation, he realized with some surprise, was overtly sexual.

"I'd like that," she said. But he felt his hold upon her suddenly weaken. They had come close together, like two hurrying ships upon the sea, linked for a moment across the turbulent gulf between them, which had seemed to narrow, bit by bit . . . but now he saw it widen. Too quick with that excited invitation, he decided. Hell, you could've achieved the same negative result by squeezing her breasts. "I'd better pitch in," she said. Then she gave an odd, diffident grin and leapt free, or so it felt to Goodpasture, to join Patricia at the table across the room. He watched them, two women chatting over the arrangements of flatware and candles and serving implements spread upon a woven tablecloth of reds and golds, another of Patricia's little ponds of color. It was a mistake to look at them together. Teejay's large, flawless face made Patricia's seem small and bloodless; beside the other's cropped golden mane, she looked nearly bald.

Goodpasture stalked over to the counter and poured himself another glass of gin. With a mouthful of the stuff, he went back to his watching, as detached now as a balloon skidding along the ceiling. Outside, the day's rain was beginning, the first large drops pounding like stones into the bare earth. Dogs flinched and trotted to shelter. Chickens ran for home. Across the way, the assembled forest folk, dressed for church in black trousers, white shirts, and white dresses, had regrouped after the dust-devil, and now filed into the hall for dinner. Peterson was talking earnestly with Palma, Congreve sat in his regal aura, speaking to no one. Arias sat tentatively nearby, cocked for fawning. Goodpasture turned his back to the women. One really could not get past the belief that a houseguest at Congreve's *finca* was inevitably co-opted sooner or later, by the legendary chemical and sexual games there. This meant the girl was either in grave danger or had some craving for what Congreve offered. Maybe she belonged to Palma. Either way, he told himself, it was an obstacle not to be cleared easily by an old jungle horse like you.

He thought with affection of his plain old minister's girl, pulled at his gin, and smiled. He wondered where she would put him at the table, and decided that his placement would be a talisman for everything. The sign. Usually she sat him next to her and they spent the meal with their adjacent thighs pressed together, making the hidden world beneath the table as hot as a cauldron. One year she had seated him in a more neutral spot, an exile that had filled him with melancholy. She had never explained why. Only much later on that day had she relented, yielding to him in the breathing bottom of the Zodiac. He hoped there would be no exiles for him tonight, for he had become rather fond of her again. At that instant, Patricia looked up, and saw how he watched her. Color suffused her sallow cheeks, the smile she gave him was shy, private, and enough to make his heart rap out a quick little jig. "Well, everybody," she called gaily, having to shout above the roar of rain on the metal roof, "It's time to sit down." Then, as they all moved toward her, she glanced from one to the other, and at the table, as though improvising an arrangement that had congealed long before. "Joly," she said, "you sit here, next to me." He poured down the last of his gin, a happy man at last.

5

The meal passed as in a dream, and almost in silence beneath rain that seemed to press the low structure into the bare ground, which soon ran with a tiny riverine network of tributaries and canals. Lightning flared in the windows, so close that its thunder cracked not a second later, and wild winds swept the place with shining bullets of water. It was not the crazy, waving ride of the canopy platform in a storm, but it suited Goodpasture, pleasantly glowing from the afternoon's ration of gin and altogether preoccupied with deciphering the messages flowing from Patricia through the warm patch where her right thigh pressed intermittently against his left one. The intermittence was troubling, for he took it as a kind of Morse code of impatience with him, possibly because he'd taken too much gin, or eaten too quickly or not enough. Mainly, he thought, he ate like a man paying tribute to the hard work his woman had done, work that reddened her hands and made her hair hang lank and thin—and, perversely, gladdened his heart.

The table was nearly quiet, for Teejay, the only truly animated person there, had been seated next to Peterson, whose silence drank in every sound she made, causing her finally to go quiet. Congreve fed the eternally hungry Indian within, focused entirely on the food and on replenishing it when it was gone, as though this meal would be his last for a long time. Palma nibbled, showing that even when confronted with one of Patricia's fine holiday meals, his appetites remained entirely political.

Goodpasture felt the man's soft, persuading eyes upon him a good deal of the time, but did not look up, nor did he venture glances at the unhappily stilled presence of Teejay. Now and then he heard a murmur of conversation about Palma's healing, the herbs, the traditions, the travels of the healer, seeing this and that. Christ, Goodpasture had seen some of the man's patients. How would a healer get the heads and hands back on? Arias had run out through the storm to tie down his helicopter and now sat like a clown, soaked through, quietly eating his portion as he waited for the order to fly.

The heavy beat of rain marched slowly off toward the mountains, and the room filled with slanting rays of sunlight for a moment before the sun touched and dropped behind the serrated peaks of the cordillera, blanketing the room in blue shadow. Hours before proper sundown, the diners sat in twilight, the steamy gloom relieved by flickering candles on the table. The sky above the sierra went peach-colored during their dessert, and was bronze when they leaned back with their brandy. Darkness fell as they gathered themselves to leave.

Goodpasture loitered in the Vicarage door as the Petersons walked their guests toward the helicopter, but returned Teejay's salute, and Palma's, before they boarded. Congreve had made no such gesture, which was normal for him; his little body, full of food, had run out of cocaine, damping his metabolic furnace and leaving him bloated and depressed. Arias had the rotor turning by the time they reached the helicopter, a Brazilian *Esquilo*. Strobe lights and beacons flashing, it spun a great dust cloud around itself and, nose down like a heavy, winged bug, ascended into the bright darkness of the early night.

The Petersons watched the aircraft circle for altitude before turning for Congreve's *finca*, some thirty kilometers farther out into the Beni. It seemed to Goodpasture that, at this moment, in the failed light, he could discern the webbing of umbilici connecting the husband and wife. He sensed an almost visible aura of intactness emanating from them, and realized, not for the first or last time, that they were, after all, reality, and his affair with Patricia merely a preserving fiction. Goodpasture would service her and take pleasure from her touch, demonstrating in terms that could be read by even the lowest primate that she was attractive to a competing male. It enhanced her value to her mate, added starch to Peterson's affections; his complacency flourished only when it was lightly cracked by his chronic fear of losing her. Thus, Patricia, whom Goodpasture saw as the engineer of all this, conserved her willingness to stay in the marriage, and her value as a female. With as little discussion or planning as a tribe of ants and a cercropia tree, the three of them had worked out one of the better ecological bargains to be found in the forest. She gave him blow jobs, he rendered her desirable. Goodpasture laughed into the night, struck by the transparency of their cosmic joke. The two figures across the clearing looked up as one, like animals in a herd, suddenly noticing a human observer nearby. Later they would puzzle together over the crackle of laughter that had floated to them on the humid night. Peterson would wonder whether Goodpasture had laughed at him. Patricia would wonder how he could be happy when she was at her husband's side. Well, he thought, the ants and the trees don't understand their bargains either.

"Don't be long, Pat," he heard the minister say, his flat voice slightly rounded with a begging note.

"I'm just seeing Joly down to the river. You can come too if you like." She always gambled with an invitation, but Peterson had never accompanied them.

"Hurry back." My God, thought Goodpasture. Was that a promise of lovemaking?

Her laughter reverberated with the excitement of deception. "Don't worry."

The man shook his head miserably. "Goodnight, Joly," he called.

"Goodnight, Elmer." Goodpasture stepped off the cement porch onto the spongy yellow ground, his cleaned boots searching for hard spots. Patricia fell in beside him and they marched off into the darkness, he thought, like lovers. At the far edge of the clearing, he stopped and looked back at the place. The minister stood outside one of the Vicarage windows, his body hidden in darkness, so that his unhappy face seemed to float in the lamplight. Goodpasture gave a final, insincere wave of his hand, and said to Patricia, "He doesn't seem very happy. Does he know?"

"About us?" She gave the watching figure a concerned glance, and then waved to him, a gesture like a trainer's signal to a beast. Peterson waved back and went inside. "Of course not."

"Just as well."

"We depend on his not knowing, Joly. As long as it doesn't hurt anyone, we can go on and on, forever." Forever. She said it breathlessly, urgently; but he knew that this notion of an infinite future arose from the same affectation as The Vicarage. Just for that instant, he wanted to walk away from her, renege on his side of their ecological bargain. But her excitement, rising hot and eager just there, within his reach, kept him within her circle. Her voice, when she spoke, contained the keening note of a randy, duplicitous woman ready to leap into space with her lover. "I love what we have together, Joly. I need you. I want you all the time."

"Yes, and so do I," although he thought he lacked conviction. Perhaps that was it, one loved the affair rather than the people in it.

They stepped out of the last of the light from the Mission. The forest, opaquely black beneath a new moon and full of the click of bats and sawing of insects, every living thing a trifle bonkers from the recent rain, took them in and rendered them invisible. She swung into his arms, they kissed, then continued walking gingerly along the path that took them toward the bend in the river where Goodpasture's Zodiac was moored. He kept them at an even, slowed pace, and walked with the high, deliberate steps of the Indians, so as not to surprise anything in the darkness; most things, if you didn't come thundering up to them aggressively, left you alone. They were utterly blind among the towering roots and lianas. The canopy shut out the wash of stars, all light. He wrapped one long arm around her, the hand cupping the ribcage, the very nice, firm ribcage, where the celiac artery drummed below the breast, and they walked in step, like people tied together. Seeing us, he thought, you'd think there was all that material apparatus between us, too. He chuckled softly with pleasure.

"What?" she asked.

"I was thinking of us out here."

"It's so dark."

"The better to carry out my nefarious plans, dearie." He put some heavy East End into the threat.

She laughed. "Nefarious, eh?"

"*Ahr.*"

"I have a surprise for you."

"Christ, I hope so."

"I'm wearing nothing underneath."

"Nothing?" He imagined her fatigued genitalia, the sparsely haired mound and softer parts beyond, waiting for him, unobstructed, all through the day, the meal, the brandy. His mind recalled the ocean scent of these, their sharp flavor. "All through dinner, sitting there taking everybody's picture?"

"Only yours, my dear. She only has eyes for you." She passed a flattened hand along his fly. "Well, and for my little cyclops there."

He brought her against him and, leaning down, raised the full white skirt, touched her buttocks, waist, belly, private parts with trembling fingers. Always, as they came together, tremors passed through them both, so urgent did their loving suddenly become. He picked her up by her underthighs and, releasing his member, pulled her upon him—it was as though they made love while drowning in a black sea. Always, he forgot until this moment the imperatives that had brought him to her in the first place, the deep but nameless chord she somehow touched in him. He wanted to spread her out on the ground beneath him, but was afraid of ants and snakes, and so he carried her, as she oscillated gently, farther toward the bank, out of the black wall of trees to the river's edge. He could hear a distant beat of helicopter rotors, the army or DEA out on a night patrol perhaps; and the whistle of a *traficante* plane descending without lights somewhere to the northwest, the scrape of a cayman launching itself into the stream, whose voice ran below all other forest sounds. Starlight silvered the Zodiac, the river, Patricia's pale legs and upraised face, the gleaming linkage between them. . . . "Ah, Pat, my God, Pat," he cried softly into the suddenly brighter night.

"With you I come and come," she whispered, panting, the

smell of her rising around them as from some fleshy jungle flower, "come and come."

He staggered the last few meters to the boat and laid her carefully down across its inflated hull, soft as a third body, and she took him in again, there upon the thin membrane that separated them from the current running below. Now they heard only the rush of water, the slop of the boat. At last, he lay back, his heart banging like an outboard motor, and she still at him. "You'll be the death of me," he murmured happily.

"No, the life, the life." She pushed him supine against the gunwale of the boat, spread him out. In the old days, before they had got much beyond a first embrace, she had announced, "I don't do blow jobs. It makes me gag." He had merely nodded, supposing there were things that he also would not do, although he had no idea what they were. But, in fact, she had been unable not to take him in her mouth. "I should get a bronze statue at the Mission," he had told her once, "for restoring oral sex to the Peterson household." He had been a little drunk. Patricia had not been pleased, and for a time had cut him off. But a relationship built on several hours' pleasure taken over a course of years had to be a forgiving one and such things were quickly forgotten. Tonight she brought him back to life, and drew him to her lips. . . .

The burst of light and racket and hurricane wind was sudden and terrifying. They had both drifted so far from the moment that the night's sounds, the rush of water, their own hard breathing, the beat of patrolling helicopters, the jungle noises, all blended in an ambient roar, like the endless sound in a city. The apparition caught him disoriented, unable even to imagine what it could be. A cayman, he thought, a mad dolphin, a jaguar leaping at them from the bush, for it was airborne. . . . His mind spun like a broken toy. Patricia stared into the descending light, and his member, poised like a gaping mushroom, seemed to look with her. And even as he saw her face, her horrified grimace, Goodpasture realized that this frightening confusion of sound and light was a helicopter, stealing up on them behind the sound-muffling wall of trees, to spring out overhead, and descend upon them, monstrous, blazing with light. He felt Patricia tense to flee, and pulled her into his arms, let her hide against him, shaking like a deer, while he spread her skirt to cover both of them. The flaming DEA, he thought then, the goddamned war on drugs dropping toward them, ponderous and lethal. He squinted toward the helicopter, expecting to see *Drugbusters* painted on the nose of a Huey. Instead, he made out *Agroindustriales Congreves, S.A.,* in streamlined letters along the fuselage of the *Esquilo,* and, behind the lights, he could just discern Congreve and Palma and the blonde woman, all gawping out the open side door of the craft. The *traficante* was grinning crazily, his inner supply of mad energy no doubt freshly restored, and held a microphone in the hand he was not using to hang on. "Hey, Doc-tor," he yelled into the mike, producing a metallic loudspeaker voice that filled the world, "you showin' her your dead mon-key?" Goodpasture decided not to move or try to reply into the gale of noise from the machine. "Is *that* your dead mon-key?" The night reverberated with the man's harsh laughter. Then, as Goodpasture made no response, the prank lost its appeal. The helicopter put its nose down and pushed out across the river. Not a kilometer away, Arias turned out all its lights and the machine vanished in darkness. Goodpasture listened until the slap of the rotor had drowned in the sound of the river and they were once more in starlight, alone. "I hope he gets what killed that monkey," he told Patricia. She said nothing, but hid against his chest. He touched her face and found it wet with tears. "I'm sorry," he whispered. "I'm so sorry."

He held her for a time. Finally, she stirred, sat up, and brushed away the tears, using some river water to rinse away the streaks. Then she lay against him, calm now. "Everything is changing," she said.

"Still, here we are."

"Yes, and here we go." She put her fingertips upon his face. "We can't do this again, Joly."

"Christmas is weeks away. Perhaps you . . . we . . . will be over this prank by then."

"It wasn't a prank. It was a deadly threat . . . to Elmer."

Christ, bloody Elmer. "It happened to *us*, Patricia, to *us*."

"I can't let them hurt him."

"Congreve only leaves the *finca* when you invite him. No bad thing if you didn't."

"And that Teejay woman . . ."

"It can't have been her first look at a dead monkey." He chuckled and gave her a squeeze. But her body had become stiff, she lay cold in his arms. "Look," he said, "it was embarrassing, but that's all it was. Lovers are always getting caught with their pants down, so to speak. Not the end of the world or anything."

"I have to go back."

"You're saying that, all of a sudden, because that little prick spied on us, we're quits? I don't believe it."

"But we are. We always knew it would end someday." And what was that he heard now in her voice? Relief? Was it *relief?* "I never said I'd give up my family for you."

"I never bloody asked."

"I have to go."

"Not yet."

"No, I have to go."

He heard the awful ring of good intentions in her voice. There would be a confession to Elmer, to spare him from hearing it all from Congreve, and this would set the stage for her rehabilitation. It would be as work to her, and she would do the necessary. She would betray every confidence Goodpasture had slipped to her, confess every phrase she had whispered about Peterson's frailty, penis, private habits, secret thoughts: after tonight, no surprises would be possible, she would see to it. She would tear it all up by the roots, and at the end they would have their marriage, and he . . . Goodpasture, the loyal preserving ant in their marital tree . . . he would have to think about what he salvaged, but it looked now very much like nothing. She would betray him. He must keep that act of treachery centered in his mental frame; it could transform the love that had flowed naturally from some cracked stone in him, into hatred. Already he felt an unfamiliar glare building within, stimulated by all her talk, all her thought, of saving bloody Elmer.

"When you have to go," he said quietly, "you have to go."

"I'm sorry," she said.

"Me too."

"I love you. I always have," she went on, dealing out the myth that her feelings had deep roots. "I always will."

"I shall take comfort from it." Comfort, O Queen of Bullshit.

"It's not us, Joly. It's . . . maybe it's the Fall."

"Eve could not have said it better."

"Really. Maybe the meteor really was a sign. Elmer thinks so."

"Elmer thinks he has a faithful, loving wife. I *saw* the fucking Fall. It was just a pretty bunch of rocks striking the earth after falling across the whole bloody universe. An accident. It didn't mean a bloody thing."

"I think it was a sign that everything would change. You, me, Congreve. The Beni. The world. Maybe it signalled the end of us all."

"The end of good sense, more like." The beginning of the age of bullshit.

"I have to go." She kept her head down and even in the pale light he could tell that all beauty had fled. Good. *Be* ugly.

"Think Elmer will put roses in those cheeks, Patricia?"

"I think he may try." She gave a self-deprecating smile at this. "Good-bye, Joly."

"Good-bye."

Then, quickly, in a rush, like someone fleeing for her life, Patricia pulled away from him, leapt ashore, and vanished into the forest. Did he want a bushmaster to nail her? He guessed not. A bad fall would suffice. A bit of fear, perhaps, some ant bites, to make up for the great emptiness that had begun to shape itself within him.

What would he do without her? He had no idea, simply no idea in the world. Their affair had been the only structure in his life since Amecos had run its course, the armature of his existence; one had been able to depend upon the holiday pilgrimages, the secret pressure of a beloved woman's thigh, the clandestine fornications in their inflated, floating bed.

What would he do?

Wearily, he stood, stretched his long body crossways and lengthwise, taking the cramps out of it, hoping to fill in around the expanding cave that seemed to be his center. He stepped out of the boat and went toward the wall of trees, thinking that

perhaps she waited for him there. But of course she was gone.
He might never see her again. Goodpasture bit his lip against
the sadness that rose like bile, knotting his throat. He wondered
when he had been so sad before this, and decided only in childhood had he experienced such swiftly settling melancholy. Hell,
until this moment, he had believed the apparatus of such misery had been ripped out long ago. He shook his head like a man
defeated. For a moment, Congreve's mad surprise, his *You
showin' her your dead mon-key?*, replayed; he felt the words drum
Patricia into him, into the earth. "My poor dead monkey," he
whispered after her.

The monkey. Glad to have something else to think about, he
stepped to the stern of the boat. The plastic bag was still attached and intact. He hauled it from the water and held it up in
the darkness. The little corpse sprawled stiffly, like a dead baby
in its sac, although . . . it had illuminations of its own. Like a
figure drawn around a constellation of stars, the monkey
glowed with points of light, scores of grains glowing the arc-
blue of the Fall.

6

A white-hot bolt of sunlight jolted Goodpasture awake. He opened his eyes to the unspeakable flickering brightness of the newly risen star seen through cracks in the forest wall, then turned away in pain. It took him a moment to remember where he was, why he lay in the bilge of the Zodiac drifting down the Rio Chipirirri. He floated on the run-off from last night's rains shed by the foothills, part of a dispersed squadron of tree limbs and other flotsam, but no bodies he could see. He remembered pushing off in the boat and paddling to mid-river; then, as the river broadened and slowed, he had fallen into a nervous, agitated sleep filled with light, noise, and unremembered threats. Through the night the boat had crisscrossed the meandering river, bumping along the shore, caroming back into the current, which swept it toward the far shore of the next bend. He shut his eyes, resolving not to scratch a patch of insect bites the night had brought him, and which began to cry out. At the other end of the boat, the dead monkey watched him steadily, no longer a constellation of blue stars, although Goodpasture could still make out the metallic dust in the brown fur, which glowed golden in the early, slanting light. The river moved like dense, brown molten metal, its dull surface blazing with splinters of reflected sunlight. Now and then a fish, fleeing predators or perhaps merely aspiring to something better, leapt into the air, poised for an instant's startled reconnaissance, and fell back into the turgid stream, leaving thick ripples going out and out across the slowly moving water.

The forest had begun to murmur before the sun cleared the horizon, and now its voice rose to greet the dawn. The treetops awakened like a vast, green city. Across the forest, platoons of red howler monkeys began their rough foraging through the treetops, pausing to greet the day with a great competition of ferocious booming voices, audible for miles, but no more threatening than the singing of frogs—the barks were intended to keep potential enemies well separated. Cicadas had begun their eternal thrumming, birds chattered and clanged in the canopy, macaws fluttering like yacht-club flags among the narrow shafts of light and shadow. Fragments of morning mist rose from the river banks and boundary trees into the hot sunlight pouring toward them from the east; the blue dawn quickly began to pale to the warm, hazy colorations of a tropical day. Far away in the east, a few small cumulus clouds floated in the light, infant storms waiting to be energized by heat and moisture.

Goodpasture groaned and shut his eyes against the light. Too much gin at Patricia's, he thought. And . . . too much something else. Only then did he remember why he felt so empty at the core. At first he could not recall much beyond the sudden light and sound, the sad lurch of the discovered lover's heart. . . . The memory clarified: the bloody helicopter and that sodded bastard cone-gravy, yelling through a loudspeaker You showin' her your dead mon-key? Christ. It had been only a minor insult from a man whose worst was terrible indeed. Who knows, from the helicopter it might have been rather funny, the two middle-aged anglos caught in the bilge with their pants off. But Congreve's insult had been the end of them. The end of everything, she'd said, the end of us all. In the hard light of morning, Goodpasture had to agree. The end of everyone. She had gone back to farm her husband's pain with penance, betrayal, and the admission of sin. And yet, for a moment, Goodpasture felt almost giddy from loss.

Then he cursed the morning, the memory, the woman who had walked away from him forever with such palpable ease. Forever, that word she liked to use about their love. "Sod you lot," he growled between clenched teeth. With an angry series of pulls on the starter lanyard, he got the outboard going. Then, needing risk, he gave the boat full throttle. The Zodiac leapt forward, its irritated buzz mingling with the day's chorus of birds, monkeys, and bugs. The wind in his face, Goodpasture raised his own peculiar tenor to the day, singing, or perhaps yelling,

> Wie oft in Meeres tiefsten Schlund
> stürzt' ich voll Sehnsucht mich hinab:
> doch ach' den Tod, ich fand ihn nicht!
> Da, wo der Schiffe furchtbar Grab,
> trieb mein Schiff ich zum Klippengrund,
> doch ach! mein Grab, es schloss sich nicht!

The Zodiac flew along, skipping like a flat rock on the slightest wave, ready to flip end over end, skittering dangerously around the twists of the stream.

> Ach, ohne Weib, ohne Kind bin ich,
> nichts fesselt mich an die Erde!
> Rastlos verfolgt das Schicksal mich,
> die Qual nur war mire Gefährte . . .

he sang, turning so wide that the far bank threw itself toward him. He hauled the boat around in a great, skidding turn that brushed the reeds along the shore and caused the motor to shriek as the screw bounced out of the water for a moment. He pushed the Zodiac through another wild turn, again nearly careening into the trees, but rescued its trajectory at the last moment. Behind him, he noted with some satisfaction, the calm surface of the muddy river lay ravaged by his furious progress: he wished that it would carry his scars all the way to the Amazon, all the way to the sea. But of course a river healed quickly, as everything did in the forest. Well, he amended, perhaps not everything. A sick monkey is a dead monkey. An empty man is an empty man. His hollow center dragged his spirits down. He throttled back on the final turn that brought him within sight of the sagging wooden pier Amecos had installed at the station. "Here we are, Sunny Jim," he told the corpse. "Home are the sailors." He switched off the motor and let the Zodiac coast to the dock, where he kept it off the ruined grey pilings with an outstretched hand, and pulled the boat along to its line, where he moored it.

The station had an awful quietness when the motor was still and the power generator had not switched on. Behind the trio of run-down wooden bungalows remaining from the experiment, the morning forest still hooted and howled; but the grove of trees and cutgrass in which the buildings stood was utterly silent. Ordinarily he welcomed the silence, taking it for tranquility. But this morning it had the same vacant quality he felt in his chest and around the heart. He picked up the bag containing the dead capuchin and headed for the building nearest the wall of trees. The structure was the kind governments raised to do a job, then left to rot in the wilderness when the job was done. The tropics had once been full of such buildings, wooden frames the forest could consume. He pushed his way past the screen door, which clattered shut behind him, into a small, plain room painted a light government green with sea-colored linoleum tiles covering the floor. The room was his laboratory, which meant it had shelves of dead things in bottles, including a regular parade of bottled poison frogs—a strawberry *Dendrobates pumilio,* in his flashy crimson leotard and purple tights; *D. auratus,* canon black on steel blue; *D. leucomelas, auratus'* black and yellow twin. Suspended in stances that made them seem alive, they looked like little figures from a comic book, the tiny superheroes of the forest. A maroon-topped card table and two folding metal chairs were set up under the window that faced north. The rest was government issue: a grey metal desk, credenza, bookshelf, assorted swivel chairs that leaked grey stuffing; an old Royal manual typewriter on a wheeled table, and, incongruously sleek, the Amecos workstation and small short-wave transmitter-receiver. A stainless-steel morgue table with a built-in drain stood along one wall, and a white refrigerator used for storing film, samples, food, and alcohol leaned against another, along with a narrow, rusted two-burner kerosene stove that had a sink and water tap on one side. The walls were bare except for a SPOT satellite infrared image of the Beni and a mosaic of tactical aeronautical charts covered with yellowing acetate that still bore phantom grease-

pencil designs from the days when Amecos was flying daily
sorties out of Santa Cruz. The plastic had begun to sag and
crack. Someone had left a 1988 calendar on which a pretty red-
head with a splendid body and grease smudges on her cheeks
was halfway out of a pink flight suit.

Goodpasture's only weapon was suspended from pegs above
the desk: a seven-foot bow of black chonta palm, with a clutch
of five-foot cane shafts—some tipped with carved barbs of
chonta for fishing, some with poison points that broke off in the
prey—fletched with black buzzard feathers; a leather pouch
containing the poisonous remains of his special arrow frog, his
only *Phyllobates terribilis,* a golden beauty so toxic that one
needed only rub an arrowhead on its skin. Although the Indians considered Goodpasture a prodigy with the bow, and he
had won many barter bets with his skill, he did little hunting
beyond the occasional gathering of a hard-to-trap sample. He
was not keen on killing what lived in his forest, even for science. He used the weapon mainly to propel lines over high
branches of suitable trees. He would shoot an arrow trailing a
filament line over a high branch, then use the leader to hoist a
stronger rope into position. Once anchored at the base, the stout
ropes could be climbed with *jumars.* At first, he had added these
out-of-the-way climbing ropes more or less randomly, as he
found trees bearing a burden of life that interested him. But
there had been unconscious method in it too: eventually, he
discovered that he could cross his preserve without once leaving the trees.

"Only you know the place better," he told the dead monkey,
laying it on the morgue table. He thought of getting some Polar-
oids of the poor beast, but decided to wait. He could not quite
bring himself to a working frame of mind. "Catch you later, old
son," he told the creature, and went into a small adjoining room
where he strung his hammock and kept his meager wardrobe.

Rosa lay in the hammock, snoring softly as a child, naked, the
sleeper innocently vulnerable to the hard-edged world that had
awakened around her. He was touched that she waited for him
here, this Indian girl who had so narrowly missed a harelip,
whose peanut-colored body had the young girl's peanut shape,
whose thick-stranded hair of absolute black ran down her

strong back like a sable cape. And what, he wondered, watching her, would Patricia make of you? Rosa was so much the child, and yet she might have been a hundred years old, so deeply did her touch, her odor, her soft jungle voice immerse him in the eternal spirit of his forest, out of time, out of humanity, really, down toward the very heart of this bewildering wonderful place. Somewhere at the center of this child a Guarani woman had given him, everything about the forest was understood, imprinted, shuffled in among the long strands of genetic instructions. He sometimes felt himself straining toward that knowing, timeless core—imagining her imagination was like falling from the planet into space, falling and falling.

He took off his clothes, the bleached khakis that Rosa had pressed and Patricia had wrinkled and inoculated with sharp, maritime smells, and tossed them into a basket near the bathroom. Her odor clung to him as well. He watched the sleeping child, dark-nippled, dappled with deep hollows and secret shadows, like a girl in a Gauguin. For the hundredth time, he thought that he must take better care of her, that she might be his child and ought to have a name, a future; he must not let her become just another expendable Indian female, fucked and forgotten like her sisters down the ages, eternally the victims of European men. Of course, he would do nothing, and knew it. She had perhaps more than she wanted of him now. It would be a shame, it would be insane, to spoil what they had with high sentiments. It was just another deal done between organisms in the rainforest, and when the bargain no longer worked, no one would want to sustain it. When the ants leave the tree, the tree stops making food for them. When Congreve's joke threatened the Peterson marriage, their contract with Goodpasture had been immediately broken.

He shut his eyes against all memory of women, and stalked out the back door, where he had installed a powerful shower. He stood in the chilling stream for a long time, deciding that he liked the sandy stubble on his cheeks too well to shave. He heard Rosa at the door and turned to see her watching him, the thick, dark lips turned into a child's bemused smile. "Come on," he called to her in Spanish, "the water is very good." She laughed but stayed where she was, romping in the open unthinkable. "Come on," he said, laughing too. She shook her head. "Well, then, put on some clothes before I come after you." He gave a mighty paternal growl for her, which sent her running back inside, laughing.

After a time, Goodpasture followed her in and pulled on a pair of khaki cargo shorts worn almost translucently thin and slipped his feet into faded blue thongs. She had put on a pair of shorts and a Lakers T-shirt (what did she think Lakers were?) and was collecting his breakfast of papaya, mango, cassava bread, and a pot of Indian tea, brewed black and strong as coffee. "Look," he told her, "I brought home a friend."

"A friend?" Her Spanish had a hard, tinny sound, like Congreve's. It was her jungle voice he loved.

He gestured at the dead monkey, which waited on the table like a guest, solemnly watching his host at breakfast. "He was very sick. He died right in front of me, and not in the trees—on the ground."

She jerked her head at the rows of bottled specimens. "You have many friends, Doc-tor."

"Yes, don't I," he replied in English. Reverting to Spanish, he said, "Have breakfast with me."

She nodded and sat down opposite him at the card table, eyes downcast, diffident, but also reproachful. He guessed she had smelled Patricia on his soiled poplins. "I came to your hammock last night. You were not there."

"I saw you there this morning."

"When you go away, what will happen to me?"

"Am I going away?"

"Are you not?"

"But," he laughed, puzzled that she seemed suddenly to want something from him, "where would I go?"

"The Mission."

"Sometimes you are a very foolish girl," he said sternly, then stepped swiftly away from wherever she was going with their morning conversation. "The monkey may have a plague."

"And you have brought it home to us, Doc-tor."

"But it is a monkey plague. We are not monkeys."

"They are our brothers. My father always said that."

"But you eat monkeys. Do you eat your brothers?"

She giggled, put a cupped hand over her mouth.

"Not any more, right?" He chuckled to show his anger had vanished. "Well, then." It was one of their longer and more complicated exchanges, and he was glad for her to return to her normal silent mode, a kind of thicket from which to watch him steadily. It was eternally disconcerting to have this pretty girl of the forest thus fixed upon him. He had never learned what response to give, or what response was wanted. She was all mystery after all, like her homeland. They ate in silence, and when they had finished Goodpasture stood up and stretched. *"Pues, a mi mono!"*

He pulled on a pair of clear plastic lab mittens and began to extricate the monkey, now a stiff, heavy little doll, from its plastic bag, and lay the corpse supine on the steel table. In daylight, the blue stars were only saltlike grains that seemed to ulcerate the skin around them. He got out the Amecos Polaroid for some general photographs of the capuchin, rummaging in the refrigerator for a pack of film. He found it pushed far to the back of the upper tray, behind a crazed white china plate on which a block of butter had melted into a blob, then solidified with the butterknife wedged in it like a sword in a yellow stone. Loading the film, he took front, side, and back views of the monkey, spreading the prints out on his desk while they developed their images. But when he examined them, he found only a narrow band of blurred detail in which the monkey could barely be recognized; the rest of the frame was fogged white. "Bloody tropics," he murmured, and brought a second film pack from the fridge, loaded it, and repeated the sequence. Again, the images blurred, with the same narrow shape containing some detail, and the rest of the field an exposed white. Goodpasture held the last of the images between a thumb and forefinger, studying it.

There was something very familiar, very recently seen about the freeform of detail in the pictures, and yet Goodpasture could not make the gestahlt—it was as if the monkey were being seen through a narrow horizontal aperture in the film, around which, for some unknown reason, the film was overexposed. The fogging must have happened while the film pack was in the refrigerator, he reasoned, which meant that something was getting to the film even in that protected environment. He tapped his foot, watching the useless images, letting his brain pass the problem from cell to cell, in the hope that somebody in there would figure out what had gone wrong. . . .

The shape did not have to be an opening; it could be an object blocking whatever fogged the film, a mask. Maybe what he saw was something like Roentgen's ray, its shape projected by a flow of radiation onto photosensitive paper. The metal butterknife lay between the film and source. The nearest X-ray machine was in Santa Cruz. And yet, something was producing enough ionizing radiation—X-rays or gamma particles or God knew what—to fog the film. Goodpasture's neck hairs prickled. Somehow, a radioactive source had come into his lab. He looked at the monkey. "Where could you have come upon it?" What was there in his forest that would produce the observed effects: the fogging of film through thick protective layers, and the death of a monkey? He felt himself begin to sweat. Knowing there was radiation somewhere near, one knew how the brute had died: the lesions, the hair loss and vomiting, were radiation poisoning; an autopsy would show anemia. "Jesus," he muttered, partly in prayer.

He dragged one of the lab's large white Teflon-lined sample tubs out into the sunlight and began filling it from the shower, then went back and collected the monkey, which he dropped into the tub. While the vessel slowly filled, he scrubbed the steel morgue table and began wiping down the lab, like a murderer trying to remember what had been touched. Hurrying outside, he found the tub near overflowing and sealed it with a large fitted cap, then dragged it well away from the building. When he saw Rosa watching him, he yelled, "Stay away from this tub. Stay out of the laboratory." He had expected her to flee, but she stood where she was, watching him. "Do you hear me?" he shouted. She nodded but did not move. "Oh, go to hell," he snarled in English. "Bloody-minded savage."

But there, he told himself, like a rider bringing a crazed horse under control, you mustn't stampede, my boy. It's just a bit of radiation, not any great amount of exposure, nothing to make your balls drop off or anything. You can get your film fogged in an airport security machine. It may be some high-grade uranium ore the beast got himself into, or maybe a discarded source of some kind, a lukewarm medical isotope, perhaps, or some odd concentration of the Krypton 85 tracer they had deployed in the Amecos plume studies. At least he could assess the scope of the problem without further fuss. They'd used Geiger counters to track the Krypton 85 plume. He could use one to measure how much radiation he had in his lab. But, searching with increased vexation in cabinets and chests around the room, he discovered that was the one instrument Juan Levy's people had taken home with them. They'd left every other goddamned thing, thought Goodpasture angrily, but had taken the one device he urgently needed. For a moment he felt like an animal in an experimental maze, his alternatives picked off by the observing scientists, Juan Levy among them. But, Christ, there was no way anyone could have foreseen this. Don't go crazy on me, old son.

The fact was, having radiation on the premises and no means of seeing or feeling or measuring it was unnerving. He sat down, suddenly, feeling a hundred years old, and tried to recall what he knew about radiation in the natural environment. Bloody little, almost nothing beyond the stuff from Chernobyl, and from the two American nukes that ended World War II. Well, Nagasaki and Hiroshima were still in place half a century later. Birds still sang, trees still blossomed, reproduced, and grew. Most babies had the correct number of parts. He remembered a photograph of a freshly leaved chestnut tree growing out of the rubble of Nagasaki. The Russians said Chernobyl had caused only twenty-nine deaths, plus some imponderable increase in the incidence of cancer and related diseases. Yes, and those two-headed calves. Goodpasture shook his head in wonderment. It was so scary you couldn't quite put it in perspective. You thought of hard radiation and shuddered automatically, without knowing a damned thing about it. The intrusion of radiation here felt, smelled, sounded, looked like the end of the world—and yet, one knew it could not be. Only the end of the world was the end of the world. That had been Goodpasture's motto through thick and thin. Now he cleaved to it as to a fragment of raft in mid-ocean, repeated it like a mantra. . . .

But *this* might be the end of his world after all. Once the presence of harmful radiation was revealed, the forest would fill with men in white suits and respirators, men with Geiger counters, who would crosshatch his wilderness with deep trenches in which to bury every radioactive bug and leaf, every particle . . . every *blue* particle. "Bloody hell," he growled, and ran out to the sealed tub where he had doused the monkey. The animal had sunk nearly to the bottom. Below it, scattered in its shadow, a dozen grains glowed bright blue. Goodpasture squatted down by the tub, looking at the particles. He had never seen such stuff before. It had to be new, freshly added to his forest. What was blue? Cobalt, but a deeper hue than this, not the color of starlight. The color of the Fall. Perhaps . . . and here he hesitated to proceed with the idea, so carefully had he trained himself to the use of Ockham's Razor in paring away the needlessly complex . . . then he completed the thought: this deadly thing had come into the Beni aboard those falling, white-hot rocks. The radiation had originated out there some-where, God knew how many light years away. Goodpasture peered at the sky, the bright blue bowl of troposphere behind the rising turrets of cumulus clouds, which by afternoon would have boiled into thunderstorms. Out there, where everything was radioactive. Oddly, he felt his agitation subside. The natu-ralness of it all, the idea that the source had dropped randomly from radioactive space made it less threatening. Nature had hurled another mystery to plumb, without malice, as always, without the slightest bent toward self-destruction—nature was no suicide. Knowing that, the problem came more easily to hand.

He went back to the lab for tweezers and a small, amber sample bottle, which he took down to the water's edge and packed with clay. Then, pushing a vertical pinhole in the center of the clay, he returned to the tub and plucked a single grain from the bottom, dropping it into the tiny well in the bottle. He pressed the clay into place above the blue grain and sealed the container. Back in the laboratory, he put the bottle on his desk and poured himself a stiff vodka from the bottle in the freezer. His system found it shocking, but his soul welcomed the clari-fying jolt of alcohol. Somehow, he thought, we have to get it looked at by someone who knows what the hell it is, how bad it is, where it comes from . . . all unofficially. We don't want the Bolivian army, yes, and the American drug army too, digging away at my forest.

He pulled at the vodka and wondered where he could go for advice without destroying the only world he cared about. And it came to him then that he did have a friend who knew about such things. A compatriot named Sidney Collins worked as a reactor engineer over at Brazil's Angra Dos Reis nuclear complex near Rio. Collins had been in on the radiation accident in Goiânia in 1987, when a cesium-137 source from a therapy machine had got loose and quickly contaminated a whole neighborhood. The excitement became an internationally celebrated cause and the entire place had been plowed under, more or less, by the white-coats from atomic energy agencies in São Paolo, Rio, and Vienna. Just the sort of excitement one wanted to avoid. He could write Collins, very informally of course, and send along the single grain shielded in wet clay, which he supposed would absorb any emissions. Goodpasture smiled, beginning to be satisfied that he had his calamity under control. He went to his typewriter and rolled in a sheet of bond and several carbons—he thought he must be the world's last user of carbon paper. Between them, he and Collins would have the place set to rights in no time, without a single trench being dug, without anyone knowing what that bloody meteorite had brought to earth.

Dear Sidney,

One finally achieves the age at which it seems perfectly natural and appropriate to resume contact at intervals of years, as I do now. Given our present great age, I guess we will see each other once or twice more before crossing over. One hopes it will be in sweet old Rio.

I am writing now because we have an imponderable problem here. There are signs that a radioactive source has got loose in this place, but I lack the equipment and expertise to assess the magnitude of our problem, or even to say there is one—I have seen only one dead Cebus, which is not much for casualties. What I wish to avoid at all costs, of course, is official attention. We don't want a bureaucratic reflex to bury El Beni under concrete for ten thousand years. If you cannot give very quiet help, you should break off reading now and destroy the letter and the accompanying sample. But, should you continue:

The sample is a jar full of wet clay containing a single grain of what I think may be the source, buried at about the center of the bottle. This is just my uninformed conjecture. You may come back and tell me I've sent you a bit of laundry detergent. On the other hand, for all I know it is something terrible; and, for all I know, the stuff is all over the Beni.

What I badly need from you, Sidney, if you will be so generous of your time and flexible as to your operating rules, is an expert's notion of what the stuff is, and how dangerous it is, all as soon as possible. I also wonder where the blue grain came from. Could it have come in (don't laugh) on a meteorite, for example, or run down in water from the mountains or surged up out of the ground? Of course I will meet any out-of-pocket expenses, including transportation over here.

Warm regards and thanks for any help you can give.

Joly

Goodpasture stopped typing and cocked his head to listen. From far down the river came the beat of rotors. Since last night, he found himself extremely sensitive to the sound, and paused, listening. Another army sweep, probably, the American advisors and Bolivian cops sneaking out of their enclave at Chimoré for a mid-day strike. The sound rose and fell, then faded as the machine passed behind some insulating obstacle. Down among the trees to torch another farm. He reread the letter to Collins, then wrapped the original around the sample jar, securing it with a thick rubber band, and sealed it in a padded envelope. He could get it to the Cochabamba bus for DHL that afternoon, he thought. Collins would have it on the weekend. Some reply by mid-week, perhaps. Goodpasture leaned back in his chair, beginning to feel well satisfied with himself. He had broken the code, solved the mystery (well, nearly), and acted shrewdly. His brain had not worked so well in months. He sipped the vodka, found it tepid, and returned the glass to the freezer. "My popsicle," he told it, setting the glass among the bottles, frozen beetles, and ice.

The trouble was, one wanted to do more. Writing Collins was not quite enough action. One needed further back-up, another regiment in reserve. He went back to his typewriter and cranked in a sheet with carbons. After a moment's reflection, he pecked out:

Dear Juan,

After many a summer, and all that. As you will see, an odd and troubling intrusion has occurred in our little jungle paradise, one I am not trained to understand or assess. The enclosed copy of my note to an old chum in Brazil tells you what the problem is. I trust you will respect my wish to keep the matter entirely unofficial and among the three of us. Well, I suppose I really trust you to care more about this place even than I do. The grain I sent Collins might be hot, and I would not presume to try to pass one through your postal system. They are salt-sized, a brighter blue than cobalt, I believe, and luminesce. My hunch is that the stuff came in on a meteorite that landed in the Beni several weeks ago. Most appreciative of any help. Life goes along here, although one sometimes misses the busy Amecos days. Hope you thrive.

Best regards,

Joly

P.S. Wish your boys hadn't taken all the Geigers.

He folded the note into an airmail envelope, which he stamped and filled with Juan Levy's last official address in the American government, a man with a title in an office in a division of a major line component of a sub-cabinet-level agency; that had been Levy's description of it, anyway. Would Levy ever see the note? Bureaucrats might stay in the same room for days, or centuries, sometimes they moved like bees among flowers. You never knew. Would Levy respond? Almost certainly not. And yet, the act of contacting an old comrade-in-arms who knew the territory was deeply reassuring to Goodpasture; it steadied him, filled his narrow world with intimations of large friends, and, like a voice raised in song, invited a reply.

The copter beat closer; the building began to resonate with the noise of it, and he thought by God it must be Congreve coming back to gloat about last night. Anger spread like water-color through his high good humor. He tucked the package and envelope into a cargo pocket in his shorts and grabbed his bow and arrows and the quiver off their pegs, then ran out the back door, taking cover in the high grass where the clearing shaded back into jungle. It was Congreve's *Esquilo,* creeping in for a landing, nose high, heading for the narrow space they had marked with an *H* and painted white circle for the Amecos choppers. The circle guaranteed a helicopter pilot centered on it that his rotors would not chop any wood.

Goodpasture waited upwind as though hunting a creature with no sense of smell, hiding in the pilot's blind spot ahead and under the machine. He saw that it was Arias flying it today, the same neutral, employee face looking left and right as he let the aircraft settle toward the ground. The blonde called Teejay sat in the left-hand seat, looking idly about herself, tourist fash-ion, during the descent. Conscious of the mid-day vodka mov-ing like a drug with his blood, Goodpasture waited until Arias cut power and the helicopter dropped the last inch to the ground; then he hurried through the grass, nocking an arrow as he ran. As the last energy drained out of the helicopter, Good-pasture stepped into the clear a few meters from where Arias sat, the long bow drawn nearly to the chonta barb, which Good-pasture pointed at the pilot's profile. Silence flowed in to fill the huge volume of the helicopter's sound. Arias, busy flipping switches to shut down his aircraft, did not see Goodpasture at first. Then something made him look out to his three o'clock position, into the faint transparent drool of arrow-frog poison on the barb aimed at his head. The neutrality crumbled into a terrified grimace, the pilot's hands flew protectively to his face, his eyes shut behind the mirrored sunglasses. You could see the adrenaline collide with all the chemically ruined synapses within—had Arias not been strapped down he would have flipped over on his back. Goodpasture laughed, then, and lowered the bow, letting the string slide slowly back to rest. "Arias. *Que tal?*"

"Jesus, Doc-tor," the man breathed, unable to control his voice or shaking hands. "You scared the shit outa me."

"What color is a hero's blood, eh?"

"Jesus." He touched his face, which ticked, then began to relax under its owner's touch.

"You rather scared the shit out of me last night, Arias. Why'd you do it?"

The man shrugged, recovering some of his courage. "Congreve said do it. I just fly the thing."

"Next time, think how much this will hurt." He looked past the pilot. "Hello, Miss . . . Jay?"

"Jones," she said. "Good morning." She wore a white cotton blouse and bleached khaki shorts and, as she cracked her door and got down, he saw that his ambush of the pilot had excited her. The broad face was flushed; you could see a rushing blush of pleasure as she said, "You be Tarzan?"

"At your service." He shook her slender hand.

"Remember—you invited me over."

"So I did. Come in, then." He watched her, weighed the possibility of her, then turned back to Arias. "Tell you what. Leave Miss Jones with me. I'll see she gets back to the *finca* after she's had the jungle tour. Unless," he added, "you'd like to join us."

"Hey, I've seen the jungle." Then, to Teejay, "That okay with you?" She nodded. He gave another shrug. "Well, okay then." But he hesitated.

"What's wrong?" asked Goodpasture.

"What do I tell Congreve?"

The woman reddened. "Tell him the truth."

"Can I tell him when you'll be back?"

"When we're through," said Goodpasture.

"Okay, I'll tell him." Arias rolled his eyes.

Goodpasture pulled out the packet, the long letter, and some bills. "Do me a favor?"

"What, after you took ten years off my life?"

"Nobody lives forever, Arias."

"What favor?"

"You're passing near the Cochabamba road. Be a good chap and get this to the bus for me."

"What is it?" he asked, eyeing the packet warily.

"It's a . . . frog poison sample . . . for a colleague in Brazil."

"Frog poison?" Arias drew back from the proffered packet and envelope. His expression said: Not another dose of *poison*. "Hey, I don't want that in my plane."

"Don't worry. It's sealed. Just don't open it. Will you take it over for me?"

The pilot hesitated, then grinned. "I take it, we're even, right?"

"Will you take the letter too?"

"No more surprises."

"Promise."

"Okay." Then, "Stand clear, now." He began powering up. They backed away, watching the takeoff, shielding their eyes from the dust kicked up by the rotor wash. Arias waved at them; then, both hands full of controls, he got the machine up on its tiptoes and lifted off, the rotors beating at the air like flapping wings. Again, a deep silence eddied in where the machine had screamed and clattered a moment before.

"Not a bad fellow."

"I nearly died when he saw you with that bow and arrow. Sort of incongruous, a man in a million-dollar flying machine frightened by something so primitive."

Goodpasture grinned. "He knows they aren't toys. Very bad poison here," he went on, holding the arrow tip where she could see the stain of frog venom, "and it's a godawful powerful weapon. You read Percy Fawcett's account of Indians along the rivers down here lobbing arrows at boats. Not just your fluttering little shafts. They'd go through inches of wooden hull and nail a man to the wheelhouse wall. Here, look at this." He looked around for a suitable target. "There," he said, pointing to a sad-looking papaya tree some fifty meters away that clutched a few green fruit where it branched. He raised and extended the bow, aimed quickly, and let fly. The long missile struck one of the papayas with a great *plop!* and enough force to

explode it, then thunked into a tree trunk some ten meters farther on, where it buried the entire barb.

"*Ah!*" she breathed, like someone watching fireworks.

"There's no hiding from these things," said Goodpasture.
"That's why it made the pilot nervous. Like having a cocked
forty-five at his head."

"And you're good with it."

"Oh, yes. The British Prodigy is what the Indians call me
around here. The Bloody British Prodigy."

"Thanks for taking me in today."

"My pleasure." And it was, indeed. He felt as though in the
last twenty-four hours he had handled adversity in all its
beastliest forms, and had prevailed. Congreve. Patricia. A
plague of radiation. And here he was now with this pretty California girl who had come from nowhere to visit him. By Jove.
"How much of a tour do you want, Miss Jones?"

"Teejay."

"Ah, well, then, you must call me Joly. Do you want the full
turista version, trails, canopy platforms and all, or just a quick
look at our grounds?"

She laughed, then, a sound as suggestive as warm fingers on
one's spine. "Actually, I was hoping you'd show me your dead
monkey."

At first he missed her meaning and almost said, It's just over
here in the white tub. But, seeing her blush, her broad smile, the
gold-flecked light in her eyes, he understood. "I keep him . . .
up in the canopy," he said, almost unable to breathe beneath
the sudden possibilities. "Up there," and he gestured toward
the high branches of his giant rosewood which seemed to rise
upon columns of sunlight. "Bit of a climb, but well worth it."
She said nothing, but fell into step close beside him. He noticed
she'd brought an overnight bag with LAN Chile printed on it.
"I'll just get a few things." Thank you, God. Thank you, cone-
gravy. Thank you Patricia, wherever you are.

Part II

STARLIGHT

1

The sky above Gravelly Point was the color of iron, black faded to dark grey, touched with a rusty amber where Washington's crime lights reflected from the low clouds scudding toward the southeast. Across the water, the city trembled into and out of visibility through the snow, like a wildfire seen through pale smoke, ridges of yellow lights that glowed like coals upon the winter night. The Potomac moved like a stream of white lava, choked with competing trapezoids of river ice, all drifting toward the sea, seemingly without a sound. Just the hiss of the descending snow, the faint burr of a northwest wind herding the clouds seaward. A TWA MD-80 dropped into view a thousand feet above the river, appearing magically, dragon-like, its long neck snaking around toward runway eighteen at National Airport; it wheeled past the Point and for a moment the world was entirely engine noise, then the aircraft dropped into the blurred illuminations of the runway lights and vanished. For an instant its sound was lost; then rose suddenly on the thrust reversers. Then silence, the hiss of snow descending, the plop of windshield wipers. The field would soon be closed, Juan Levy thought, watching the lights through the crescent eyes of the windscreen, and then there would be that blessed silence of a snowy night along a river.

He waited in his black Saab SPG, which murmured at the idle, its wipers slapping intermittently at the crystals that touched the warm glass and turned to drops. The car was the largest purchase Levy had ever made for his own use, and one of the least probable. A man with the natural impulse toward invisibility of his Mayan mother (but, he added wryly to himself, with the genes of an extrovert Jew father also working overtime) was an odd buyer for a car that made people look twice, although, he had decided, nobody really saw the driver of an interesting car—in fact, people were careful *not* to look into your face. Knowing better than to have affection for objects, he loved the machine, from the snug fit of its dark grey leather to the leaps its turbocharger allowed at speed; it had been made for him. He had once briefly possessed a burro that suited him almost as well. Sometimes he worried that if he had to replace the Saab he would have to think of a dog, a horse, a woman. But at the moment, the car was exactly what, and all, he wanted.

The green dash lights cast his face in sickly reflection upon the side window—a big, dangerous face, right out of the Bible, one in which a harsh beak, heavy, winged brows, and black, intolerant eyes had the hard edges of a drawing, a harsh mask beneath the friendly tangle of curly black hair salted with grey. His thick mustache just failed to camouflage the sneering line of his lips. It was the face, he thought now, of his father, all the bitterness of the assimilated State Department Jew frozen finally by a Guatemalan undertaker's cosmetic art, so that you remembered only that vivid, dead visage, not the stern, but less ferocious, living one. That, he told himself, is who you are. Levy grinned at the reflection. He could also discern the softer lines of his mother, a touch of her gentle brownness, erasing some of the hook from the severe nose, adding a modicum of warmth to the stony eyes. But mostly, he thought, noting the quietness, the languor, of his waiting, she had given him an Indian's vast repose, the ability to poise eternally, to listen, to hover at the very rim of visibility. Put Levy in a platoon of Mujaheddin, an idle crowd of Bulgarian farmers, a Guarani household, and he disappeared. That was his mother's gift to him, an ambuscade from which this man floating in the Saab's window looked upon the world with a terrible emotional neutrality; the Juan Levy that people sometimes feared, *he* was Papa's.

Levy shivered in his black pea coat, which he had bundled

up around his torso as though the Saab were not heated, as though the driver's seat were not electrically warmed, producing the sensation of sitting in a tiny pool of fresh blood. It couldn't be the cold, he thought—just somebody walking on one of his graves. He looked at the dashboard clock: ten o'clock, and nothing. Donner was supposed to have arrived at seven, but Levy had stayed on at the Point, watching the storm sweep over the capital. He would wait until the airport closed. Levy thought that such meeting places as Gravelly Point were conspicuously secret, so obvious as to attract flashing blue lights, police, questions. People like Evan Donner didn't meet former colleagues in snowstorms late at night except to exchange illicit information, substances, or sex. Donner was too solid for the police to book—he was the deputy chief of mission at embassy La Paz, a solid career man who would wind up as a minor ambassador, to Chad, to Ethiopia, to Bolivia, perhaps. And Levy was pretty solid too, grazing through civilian science agencies, looking for a project a tenth as compelling as Amecos had been. His high-priced drifting, as personnel people had begun to label it, had kept him a day or two ahead of Goodpasture's letter, until it caught up with him in Silver Spring in the forenoon. Moments later, with the synchronicity of a Greek play, Donner had called from Miami International, spooked and wanting a secret meeting.

"Ah, Joly," Levy told the snowy night, "you should have heard the man." He shook his head. Instead of waiting here for Donner he might still be up in the canopy with old Joly Goodpasture, having a cigar and a flagon of vodka, what the Englishman called, quoting Wells, the Palaeolithic in a bottle, the air warm as a wet hand upon one's skin, the night life of the forest clicking and buzzing around them. ". . . *den fliegenden Holländer nennt man mich!*" Levy sang in a soft baritone. The reflected eyes shone soft and gleaming in the glass. The libretto moved in and out of focus, like the lights of the city across the floe. He remembered only snatches, like the first lines of catchy commercials. "*Wie oft in Meeres tiefsten Schlund . . .*" He'd been away too long. He thought of Goodpasture's letter, the troubled note in the calm British voice. He might have to help Joly with his "odd and troubling intrusion." Maybe that's what spooked old Donner. These days they could have met at the Jockey Club, if they'd wanted, or at the F Street McDonald's. Nobody cared what they said to each other, two old government boys out for a beer or a Big Mac together. But here they were, sneaking a meeting like Czechs before the end of their world over there.

A United 757 rattled overhead, filled the world with flashing light and earth-shaking sound. Then silence, the snow, the wipers.

Donner was overreacting to something, as those assholes at State always did—it was in their nature. Levy thought it must have been Goodpasture's contacting an old friend at Angra-1. Maybe one could reassure Donner and that would be the end of it. One didn't want him stampeding; on the telephone he'd sounded only a quarter-turn away from hysteria. We've got a problem, he'd moaned, a massive problem, *massive*. Massive, in Donner's vocabulary, fell above awesome but below apocalyptic; half the time listening to Donner was like listening to a child. *Preemo* concept, this fifty-five-year-old diplomat was capable of saying. It was as if his cultural plug constantly short-circuited, forcing him into a pidgin vernacular of adolescence. We need to *rendezvous*, man, he'd said.

Okay, Levy had responded, how about the Old Ebbitt?

No, Juan, I mean, like *meet*. Italics *mine*.

And Levy had thought, All right, my friend, we'll make it ultrasecret. Gravelly Point, he'd told Donner. Donner quickly agreed to seven-thirty and had run to catch his airplane. By then, although Donner could not have known, it had been snowing for a day in Washington. Levy surveyed the grey expanse around him. Just the place, he thought, for a Donner party. "*Haw*," he gave the night.

As if in reply, a pair of headlamps stabbed across the snow, the cones of light lively with falling powder. Levy instinctively ducked. On the far side of the parking area, a muddy white Ford Festiva had turned off the parkway and crept toward the river. It had to be Donner, renting the bottom of the line. The little Ford slithered past and Levy peered at the encrusted window. The pale oval of Donner's almost hairless head looked back at him, a startled, scared face, he thought, the face of an old man who has accidentally locked himself in his car. He waved and the scared face bobbed. Then the Festiva went forward another fifty yards and stopped. Donner put out the lights but left the engine idling, as Levy had instructed him to do—he had not wanted the man tracking muck into the Saab. Levy backed his car away from the Festiva, then switched off the engine and got out, turned up the big collar of the pea coat, and trotted lightly toward Donner's car, the powdery crystals pelting his broad back, salting the tangle of black hair; Levy might have been a great cat hunting in the storm, imperturbable, single-minded. When he knocked on the passenger window, Donner cracked the door for him. *"Juan,"* the man exclaimed in an eager, political voice, and stuck out a gloved hand.

Levy gave the glove a rough shake and folded his large body into the small space provided. "Nice wheels, Evan."

"I thought it would be inconspicuous."

"You could have rented a Lada."

"Very funny." There was a note in Donner's voice that reminded Levy of a woman about to scream.

"How's the family?"

"Good, just great."

"Happy in La Paz?"

"I think they are, yes."

"And you?"

"Yes, me too."

Levy gestured at the empty point of land. "Private enough for you?"

"I just got here," Donner said irrelevantly, looking at his watch. "I mean, the airplane was circling for hours."

"Bad day to travel."

"I needed to talk to you."

"Well, and here I am. What's on your mind?"

"You're a funny guy, Juan. . . ."

"That's my reputation."

"I mean, like I'm worried, *real* worried, and that doesn't seem to bother you at all."

Levy grinned. "I always thought only wives talked like that."

"Thanks."

"No offense." In the driver's window Levy saw himself reflected, large-faced, dark-maned, Donner in the foreground, almost a negative image of oneself, pale, translucent, frail. As different as Cain and Abel, thought Levy. "It does worry me that you look like a mare about to bolt."

"I'm concerned about the Bolivian operation."

"Ah. The Bolivian operation." Levy felt his blood move, a seed of anger germinating deep within. "I guess your using that term *does* worry me, Evan. We had Amecos down there. We have the odd contact still on the old muchachos network through the Academy of Sciences. But no operation. Maybe I'm not understanding you."

"Maybe you're not trying."

"Funny you should call today," Levy said, pulling out two airmail flimsies. "The mail brought these from Joly Goodpasture. You remember Joly, Amecos and all that? Joly's the one who should be worried, Evan. He says that meteorite in the Beni brought in a whole shitload of radioactive material. He's asked a friend of his over at the Brazilian reactor to provide some unofficial expert help. I thought you might be worried about Joly."

"I'm . . . concerned about his expert help."

"*Por que?*"

"*Por que* I think somebody on the other side wants to use the meteorite thing."

"Gosh, Evan, don't you guys get a newspaper down there? There *is* no other side anymore."

"Fortunately, our station chief doesn't share that view."

"Who's that?" although Levy knew they'd sent Domingo to La Paz, mainly to get him into something that would take up some of the ideological slack now the eastern walls had come down.

"Domingo. You know."

"Yeah, I know."

"Domingo's bored out of his gourd. The drug warriors won't have him, they think the CIA's the enemy. So he talks to me." Levy waited for more. "He watches the Sovs, among others. He watches Goodpasture because you asked us to. Bolivia, he says, is where we're going to fight when we get out of the Gulf. He wants to know what the Sovs're up to down there."

"The Sovs, Jesus Christ. Let me arrange a newspaper sub-scription. *Times* okay?"

"Most funny, Mr. Bond. Ho and ho. Seeing Goodpasture's letter to the compatriot in Brazil, Domingo closed the loop with his opposite in Rio, who *also* has not lost all interest in the goddamned enemy. He, it turns out, happens to have been fol-lowing one of them when Goodpasture's letter arrived at An-gra. Next thing he knows, the guy he's tracking sits down with this British engineer. A *Russian*, Juan, is right there on the scene, *hours* after Goodpasture's letter comes in!"

"A Russian who does what for a living?"

"He's a Safeguards inspector."

"Sounds pretty suspicious, these two atomic men having a drink in reactor city."

"Goddamn it, Juan, it *is* suspicious."

"What's the Russian's name? We'll check him out."

"Viktor Viktorivich Krylov."

Levy's neck hairs bristled; he felt his Mayan reflex close his face, felt himself become internally very still, the hunter at the water hole. And yet, his heart hammered with the superstition of a goddamned savage, too: Krylov . . . he knew the name. Krylov. "Anyone we know?"

"Good bona fides as a Soviet nuclear engineer attached to the IAEA in Vienna. He's in Brazil supposedly because they've de-cided not to build a bomb and are opening up new facilities to inspection."

Krylov, thought Levy. Krylov was the Russian who'd talked to the pilot, what's-his-name, *Mason*, about the Fall. Krylov had been the Russian who'd heard Mason say it looked like some-thing thrown. "Good for him, Evan. Good for him."

Donner hesitated a moment, his narrow mouth gulping in some of the hot air in the crowded Festiva. "I find it pretty goddamned worrying, Juan. I think they *know*."

"There's nothing *to* know."

"Juan, I've been briefed, I know what's going on down there."

Levy closed his eyes for a weary moment. His masters, those quiet, hard, middle-aged men in thousand-dollar suits who strode the wide, tiled hallways of the Old State Department

Building, had huge appetites for other men's field work; but they were cautious about blame—cautious, to use a polite term. They had insisted on involving State, as they put it to Levy, "in some superficial way." So he had let Donner have this famous briefing. "I know you've been briefed, Evan."

"You resented my being included. From the beginning. You think, just treat those assholes at State like mushrooms, man, keep them in the dark and feed them a lot of shit, right?"

"It always worked before."

"Son of a bitch, you *never* wanted me in, but now you've got me, and I know the *Russians* know, they've put in people to fuck us up. You know what this will do?" Levy shook his head. "Bring down the goddamned government, *that's* what it'll do."

"You know, Evan," Levy began slowly, letting the silence flow in around them, letting his companion get some sense of what a lonely place they had come to, how far away the world was from this little snowbound car, and on what a night. "You're absolutely right. I didn't want State brought in. I figured that sooner or later, anybody from State who was in this would look at the enemy sails filling the harbor and experience what historians generously call a failure of nerve. Now we have it."

"A failure of nerve wouldn't be here tonight." A tremor passed across his unseasoned face and he turned away for a moment, pulling himself together.

"What do you plan to do, Evan?"

"I want to know if the President knows."

"Call him up."

"Does he?"

"If deputy heads of mission are briefed, we generally let the President in too."

"I don't think he knows."

"As I recall, you weren't given some big fucking military secret, but a slice of odd natural history. The Air Force had detected high radiation levels on an incoming meteorite. . . . Actually, one of a multitude of small asteroids that zip through Earth's orbit all the time. Most of them miss us. But not this one. Some Star Wars stuff sniffed it, found its emissions radioactive, and told the people on the ground about it. Minutes later, the thing fragments over South America and the stuff rains down on the Beni."

"Turning the rainforest into a wasteland."

"Nobody knows what it turns the rainforest into. But there it is, the Beni Fall. The hot stuff has entered the ecosystem. Because of Amecos we know it will percolate up through the canopy trees and blow out over the eastern slope of the Andes. Over the coca-growing plots in the Chaparé, for instance. America . . . me, the President, the Drug Czar, *everybody* thinks: not such a bad thing, coca getting a blast of ionizing radiation. Track the stuff using Girl Scouts with Geiger counters. Have some of the *traficantes'* balls drop off. I mean, the coca gets irradiated with us or without us, Evan. It's an act of God. It's Nature's way of telling them to stop producing coke. We *happen* to have the environmental models from Amecos that let us predict where the stuff will go. We've always wanted some kind of break, and here one comes from outer space. It lets the drug warriors follow the cascade from the bush in Bolivia to the processors farther north. Maybe we can watch it from satellites, with gamma ray counters, just like we monitor the meanders in the Gulf Stream with infrared."

"But we're knowingly withholding information that affects people's *lives.*"

"*You've* seen the lives, Evan. What's more important, a few more people lost to misery in Bolivia, or a bunch of kids machine-gunning one another over in southeast Washington, L.A., —or Peoria? This is a hell of an opportunity for the drug warriors. They can track the stuff. When word hits the street that coke, *all* coke, is radioactive, the appetite—the flywheel of all this action—dries up. Americans are so afraid of radiation they'll forego electricity to avoid the atom. Maybe they'll give up cocaine."

"We're *using* this thing. . . ."

"All we're doing is letting Nature take its course. This is some meteorite that's been out there a zillion years. Blind, dumb, creeping along at fifty thousand mph or so, randomly landing in the Beni—where, by God, it accidentally does humanity some good. Maybe not as much as landing in New York City . . . but some good. I think we should be grateful." Then, giving Donner a dangerous look, he said, "I think it would be crazy to fuck it up."

"I'm going to the White House, Juan."

"What, so that he'll go to the U.N. and persuade the world to mount the biggest burial operation since the paving of Los Angeles? Shall we inter hundreds of thousands of square miles under three meters of concrete? Shit, I think I'd rather see us pay the national debt."

"We could have *warned* them."

"Every year or so, a monster hurricane . . . they call them cyclones . . . spins up the Bay of Bengal. The government of Bangladesh sees the storms coming and warns the people. But nothing happens. Thousands drown. Bolivia's not much different. Instead of a cyclone, they got dosed. A few will die of it, whether we mobilize a rescue or not."

"And if the White House doesn't listen, I'll . . ."

Levy shook his head sadly. Please don't say it, old sport. Don't say it.

"I'll go public with it."

"But why?" Levy felt fatigue crush him into the seat; a terrible lethargy passed through him, a sad awareness of the world that would have done credit to a thousand-year-old man. "Why make such a mess?"

"We have to tell them."

"The world, you mean?" Donner nodded. "What, just to make the *indios* feel worse than they already do? You're a hard man, Evan."

"We have to clean it up."

"We don't have to do anything. It came from outer god-damned space!"

"But we *knew* about it."

"Minutes before it came in."

"It doesn't matter." Like a pouting boy, Donner crossed his arms on the chest of his khaki Burberry and stared fiercely into the black streaks of the windscreen. "If *I* don't, Juan, the Russians *will*."

"There is nothing to tell. There is nothing to know."

"Goodpasture knows what happened, and now there's a Russian."

"Goodpasture would die—he would kill, too—before he'd let the forest get bulldozed. That's why he asked for *unofficial* help. I don't pretend to know why there's a Russian in it, but it isn't because they 'know' a goddamned thing."

"Nobody else is going to think that, Juan."

"Ah." Levy smiled sadly. After a moment's silence, a moment that seemed to chill the stuffy interior of the Ford, he said, "Have you ever tried any of the stuff this war's all about, Evan?"

"What do you mean?" Girls always asked that, Levy thought, when you asked them to take off their clothes; women, never.

"Used to be considered pretty safe, everybody snuffled up a line or two. Most of the money still comes from middle-class users, trying to clear their selfish little heads. Give us another growing season, and all the stuff coming into the country will be that little bit hot, Evan, that little bit radioactive. People won't want to stuff hot coke up their noses. But . . . until then . . ." He gave Donner a large grin and fished around beneath his pea coat. Then, like a magician with a rabbit, he produced a fist, and, opening it palm upward, a Baggie of white powder. "This is what they call pre-Fall, my friend. That's how the people who like this stuff are going to write its history, pre-Fall and post-Fall. Post-Fall makes your nose rot off. Also your hair and testicles. Addicts with AIDS will not be much moved by what post-Fall does to you. But those ecologically minded movie stars, that bourgeoisie . . . well, they'll just have to go back to martinis or something." As he spoke he brought out a new bill, folded it longitudinally, and sprinkled a bold line of white powder in the crease. *"Por tu,"* he said, holding the bill near Donner's face . . . his stricken face, Levy noted, a pale visage gone paler as the blood drained away. "Go on, Evan, enjoy."

"I don't do this, Juan." That haughty girl's voice; post-scream.

"But you do."

The man's mouth had begun to work, trying to find a few pronounceable words down in the sudden nausea of fear. "I don't do this."

"There's a first time for everything, Evan."

"Don't make me." The incipient scream was back.

"Then . . . just say yes."

Slowly, wary as a wild creature, his eyes large and gleaming white, like a spooked horse's, Donner stuck his nose into the creased bill.

"Snort," said Levy.

Donner inhaled, gasped, and leaned back in his seat.

"You know, I think this isn't your first time."

Donner grinned. "That was . . . nice." Levy could see Superman begin to move around inside Donner, the old confidence returning. "You gonna . . . ?"

Levy sprinkled more of the cocaine onto the bill, steadied it, leaned toward it, only to have the bill drop from his gloved fingers, casting the powder into his lap. "Shit." He brushed angrily at himself. Donner giggled. Levy flung open the door, letting chilled air surge in around them, and brushed at his pea coat. "Here," he said, and passed the Baggie and the folded bill back to Donner. "Help yourself."

Donner made himself another line, then hesitated, studying the bill. "It's Bolivianos," he said. "Goddamn . . . ?" On the rim of laughter, Superman looked up at his companion. "What's that?"

"A loose cannon." Levy had stopped brushing his coat. He held a black Walther automatic in his right hand; his eyes were flat, his face quite empty. "God hates publicity, Evan," he said almost in a whisper. Then he shot at the diplomat eight times, missing with five, letting them shatter the window, rip through the door of the little Ford, all in pantomime, all soundless within the greater sound of a descending jet. Then silence, the hiss of snow; the Baggie, the bill, and Donner, Superman no more.

The snow had almost obliterated the spot where he had waited for Donner, and as he walked back to the Saab Levy kicked away the tracks. When they found Donner in the morning the Ford would be out of gas, the battery dead, the body frozen; there would be nothing for miles around to show who had been there, or why. It would be an interesting story on the evening news, one of those ethnically puzzling events: a white male killed in a city whose black population lost a person a day to murder. Yes, Levy thought, the white male angle, the diplomat, Bolivia—it would play well for a day. Then Donner, poor Donner, would vanish into the city's dreadful ennui about death and drugs as his own tracks vanished under the night's fall of white powder.

An American Airlines MD-80 plunged like a pterosaur from the low clouds and groped toward the dim illuminations of the runway. Levy watched it down, listened to its reversers, then to the silence. The field should be quiet now, he thought, that was probably the last one in tonight. He walked to his Saab and climbed in, careful to knock the snow off his loafers when he did. When the motor was murmuring once more, the wipers moving away the thin panes of snow, he leaned back with a ton of fatigue upon him.

Then he drove off into the storm, the Saab's big wheels kicking through the snow to the Parkway. As Levy crossed the Fourteenth Street Bridge, almost deserted except for partly buried abandoned cars and blue-lighted snowplows, he lofted the gun up and over his roof, past the right-hand railing. The ice would carry it some distance downstream, where the melting floes would release the pistol into the sea. "Guess what?" he said to the Saab. "I'm going to see old Joly!" It was time to talk to Goodpasture about the uses of an act of God.

2

Collins fiddled with his rum and soda and tried not to look at the Russian, who was carefully reading Joly Goodpasture's letter. Behind the massive figure of this unlikely companion, the bay began to deepen from the day's turquoise to the indigo of night, the first lights flickered on Ilha Grande, the first stars trembled in the dark quadrants of the humid sky. It was a comfort to have another man read the Radiation Letter, as Collins had come to think of his old friend's call for help. He had carried it around with him for days, folded into the yellowed plastic sleeve that protected his shirt pocket from an engineer's forest of ballpoints and pencils. Several times a day he had removed the sheet, smoothed it on any nearby surface, and read again of the horror that had somehow got loose in Joly's world. Then, almost ill with futility, Collins would nod sadly and put the letter neatly away. Nothing one could do for Joly, really, no way one could just pick up and head for Bolivia. The instruments alone made it unthinkable—at Angra-1 they were as dear as diamonds. Oh, he had thought about it, all right, getting together a portable multichannel analyzer and a high-range radiation monitor that wouldn't saturate as soon as you placed it in an intense field, the way the daintier little Geigers did. He'd take one of the CP-MUs they used to measure radiation levels around spent fuel rods submerged in the storage pool, what the Yanks, only God knew why, had named the Cutie Pie back in the stone age of nuclear reactors. Collins smiled. He had weighed which airline to take to which Bolivian airport, and what clothing to carry, and how much annual leave it would require, and how he would explain his sudden departure to his supervisor, to his wife. . . . Here, invariably, his daydream of action evaporated beneath the glare of reality. "Sorry, Joly," he'd told the letter numerous times, always in a whisper, so as not to seem odd to his colleagues. They thought him odd enough already.

He had the aura, he knew, of someone who might begin to turn loose of the ladder, so to speak, a man inclined to let go. His nondescriptness had haunted him from childhood, the non-entity with its red face, greying copper-colored hair, and the washed-out eyes of a middle-aged man who should never take a drink—this cipher peered at him from every mirror, like a trapped man looking anxiously through sealed windows. Collins had run into his British counterparts wherever there was technology in the third world. They worked in the Andes' elevated copper pits, in every oil field, at every reactor, in every oasis of industrial activity. Most of them had taken savage women, and were on their way to rearing a dusky, tow-headed, blue-eyed race. He believed they all dressed somewhat alike, as well, the shirt open wide over a stubbly pink chest, khaki trousers, pale feet stuffed sockless into the grey sneakers of an earlier epoch; a global regiment wore just what he wore tonight. He supposed they must constitute a kind of separate British species. Yes, but one that was not much help one member to another. A cry for aid produced only: Sorry, Joly, whispered to a piece of wrinkled paper.

"Incredible," Krylov murmured, handing back the letter. "He sounds very calm, considering. And he sent over some material?"

"Yes." Collins could feel the Russian's sharp interest, strong as a hound's, as though he, Collins, possessed something Krylov had wanted badly enough to follow its trail all the way from Moscow. The implication of pursuit, of robbery, sent a chill through his thorax and made his hands shake ever so slightly. Willing them to be still, he took out his other talisman of Goodpasture's trouble, a rectangle of folded lead foil, which he spread on the black marble tabletop between them. At first he could see nothing, which was normal. Then the single grain at the center of the opened foil square came to a kind of glowing life, as though the growing darkness had imbued it with an internal luminosity of its own. "The radioactive isotope is cesium 137," he said, watching his companion closely. "But in a queer form."

"It's blue," Krylov whispered, unable to take his eyes off the grain.

"Cesium was named for blue, but not because of this—you identify its spectrum by the blue lines in it. Really just a dumpy silverish metal. This glowing in the dark—I don't know, it's probably something to do with the isotope's emissions and atmospheric water vapor. Makes a pretty illusion, though."

"Very."

Collins understood the man's hushed tones, and thought he knew what Krylov must be feeling: to have even a single grain of such stuff only a few inches away, out in the open, unshielded, was enough to make your knees go weak; you imagined all sorts of things shooting straight into your body. Of course, that was the insidious thing about radiation—you felt hardly anything at all. "Shall I put it away?"

"Not yet."

"Under the microscope," Collins said, referring to the electron microscope the health physics people had at Angra, "you don't see the expected metallic structure, and it doesn't behave as a cesium-137 compound should. Ordinarily cesium fizzes as soon as it feels oxygen in the air—explosive reaction. But this stuff is fairly stable. Maybe that queer structure works like the micro-coatings on cold pills, letting the isotope into the world a bit at a time. It looks more organic than not. If I were a plant, I'd probably think it was something good to eat." To his consternation, he emitted a shrill whinny of laughter. "Sorry," he murmured, then shrugged awkwardly. "Well, this is me guessing. I really don't have a clue, except that it's a queer form."

"It sounds like something you'd make in a laboratory."

"Doesn't it? But Joly was pretty sure this lot came in on a meteorite."

"The Fall." Krylov's eyes glittered and he turned toward the ocean for a moment. "A few weeks ago, in Santiago, I spent the evening talking to the only person known to have seen it."

"That American pilot, you mean?"

"He wanted to tell somebody about it."

"And now here it is calling to you again."

"Yes, exactly." The big Russian seemed to shudder, although it was difficult to tell in the poor light. Someone on his grave, probably.

Collins looked at the darkening sky, the rich wash of stars just beginning to emerge. "Well," he said, nodding toward the heavens, "there's your laboratory." And, he thought, you could get anything from such a place as that. Anything. Even a radioactive cesium compound in this queer form. "Cesium 137 is a fission product, as you know. Out there, it's mostly fusion going on, but here and there, you get some fission too. Supernovae need fission to make heavy elements. Planets full of heavy material may fly apart and send fragments out across the galaxy, this radioactive stuff cooking away." He experienced something like vertigo, imagining the vast fetches of emptiness his words evoked. "I wish *I* were going over, it's a fascinating accident. I'd love to go, I'd go in a flash, even though there's bound to be government trouble sooner or later, when people start throwing up blood. But there's the refueling . . . my family . . ." The engine of his confidence sputtered out. Collins realized that he'd told Krylov one of his little personal secrets: he had not left Angra dos Reis in a dozen years, except for the odd run to Rio, just up the coast.

Krylov signalled the waiter, who hovered almost invisibly in the descending light, for another round of drinks, but stayed quiet for a time, watching the night take hold. His silence caused a faint nervousness in Collins, who began to fear that, having found help for Joly in this unlikely form, the man would now suddenly decline. Well, he had not been keen on asking Krylov in the first place. Keen! Christ, he'd never have asked a Russian for anything; it wasn't something Englishmen did. When he had first considered talking to one of the pair of Safeguards inspectors in town for the refueling, Collins had inclined toward Oldenburg, the Dane. He had watched Oldenburg putter around the reactor hall, which had gone noisy and danger-

ous as a shipyard now the rods were in and the nuclear beast
slept in its steel vessel, and they let the work crews in. Collins
had liked the Dane instinctively. Fortyish, long-limbed, agile,
always the ready smile. Mind-boggling confidence, not a care in
the world, vast experience—unofficialdom himself, just the man
for Goodpasture's job. But when he'd made his diffident approach to Oldenburg, mumbling something about wanting unofficial expert help on a radioactive source dropped by a meteorite into the Bolivian rainforest . . . well, the Dane had given
him a puzzled look, at first; then, his face had cleared as he
understood, it was clear to Collins, that he stood in the presence
of lunacy. "Really," Collins had added, for emphasis.

"Jesus," Oldenburg had fairly shouted into the ambient
clamor, loud enough that Collins felt an impulse to run and
hide, "if you've a radiation problem you'd better treat it as one,
get the government into it, pay somebody to do it, buy the
instruments to do it with. . . . Christ. I don't go into the jungle
to do informal assays. Nobody does." Then, to Collins' added
horror, Oldenburg had grinned savagely and turned to his Russian colleague, who had just come up to them. "Viktor, Collins
here needs some 'unofficial' help in Bolivia. A radioactive meteorite, he says. Pays nothing. Profits no one. Sounds a perfect
Soviet project. You know, one third worlder helping another?"

"*Job tvoju matj*, Oldenburg." For a moment, the two men
stared at one another, and the Dane made as though to reply.
But Collins, and Oldenburg too, saw something really frightening in the Russian's face that kept them both silent.

"*Your* mother," Oldenburg replied at last, almost too faintly
to be heard, certainly too softly for those big hands to grab and
shake him, and tried very hard to saunter away. He recovered
quickly, though; by the time he'd crossed the metal floor of the
hall he'd begun to strut again.

"Sorry," Collins said.

"What kind of problem?"

"Oh, I don't think . . ." He thought he must have blushed,
and looked at the floor.

"Look, I understand the British don't ask favors of Russians.
We try not to ask them of you. But at least I won't get bitchy,
like the Dane, if you confide in me." Beneath this light touch,

Collins felt the man's interest strain toward him, toward Good-pasture's letter and the cesium grain. But he also sensed that here, for the first time, was the possibility of finding help for his friend. "Tell you what, Collins. We'll have a drink after work and you can tell me all about it."

It had not been in Collins' power to say no, and now, with the rum percolating within, with Joly's problem on the road to a solution, he was glad he'd let Krylov pick him up outside the containment. Collins hadn't many friends, in-laws mostly, so that he had enjoyed their companionable stroll through Angra dos Reis toward the bay and the veranda of the Hotel Frade, where, thought Collins now, we stayed happily ever after. He took a long pull at his new drink, feeling delectably blurred. "You know, Viktor," he said, conscious of using the man's given name for the first time, "it wouldn't take a lot of gear. A Cutie Pie, perhaps, and a portable multichannel analyzer." He shook his head admiringly. "Such larks it would be, working with old Joly . . . out there." Behind half-shut eyes Collins watched his own phantom self stalk through a vine-draped forest of Kodachrome green, the instruments buzzing away, naked natives falling back before him. . . .

"I will do what I can," Krylov said at last.

For a terrible moment, Collins felt himself about to cry; the evening shimmered with suppressed tears, of joy, of grand excitement. "That's marvelous, Viktor. That's bloody marvelous."

Afterward, he was not quite sure how it had all come about. He half believed he might have approached Krylov after all, and guided him so deftly into the situation as to preclude a refusal. Then again, he would think, perhaps old Viktor had sweetly inserted himself in this business without my quite knowing, smooth as a mosquito bite. Maybe he had. You could never tell, with Russians.

3

Instead of meeting at the embassy, Krylov had decided to see Malenov, the Rio station chief, like a spy, in the Praia do Flamengo, where a light wind off the bay mitigated the December heat of the city. Sails and yachting flags fluttered as though nervously along the quay, and the place ran with children and their keepers. Rio seemed very distant, its honking and hollering and the wail of its songs subdued by the bayside expanse of trees and cultivated lawn and the soft beat of the sea. The two men looked like all the other businessmen on their way to lunch, one thick and countrified, waving a sweat-soaked handkerchief and Panama hat, the other a much younger colleague (in fact, there were only five years between them), the jacket of his tan worsted suit slung over a wide shoulder as he leaned down to listen.

"Viktor," Malenov was saying "you'd be crazy to go over there, those people hate us." He was a portly fellow now, bald and fat, his wrinkled neck like pink leather spilling over a grey collar. Krylov could remember when Boris Ivanovich Malenov was as fit as he, as quick, still able to part his blonde hair. Now he was the middle-aged neocolonial, a kind of amnesiac; a man who had lost his history. It was as if, Krylov thought, those dancing bright blue eyes, the eyes of a wily child, had seen nothing but the macaw colors of Brazil. He could remember when they had looked upon the world like two blue stones, cold as Siberia, in Angola, Afghanistan.

"Christ, I can't talk over the damned noise." Malenov waited for a white twin-engined plane to rise from Santo Dumont, and to swing off over the bay, heading off to the southwest along the coast. "I was saying that those people think the *Germans* won the war."

Krylov laughed. "Well, and so they did."

"You sound like a British."

"Even they came out better than we did."

"We just had some bad philosophy."

"A little, yes."

"Anyway, you should be thinking about going home. The Moscow snow under your boots, Viktor, that's what you need, the air freezing your nose hairs, that good Russian winter."

"You think of a Moscow winter, Boris." Here, today, such a season was unthinkable. A worm of perspiration crawled down Krylov's spine, reminding him where he was.

"I do, all the time. I tell you, Viktor, I live in constant agitation that they might send me home. My blood is simply too thin for it now. I would be ashamed. I'd behave like a girl. Worse, like an old Bolshevik with thin blood."

"But I hear they have great things planned for you."

"Oh, yes. The Santiago embassy is open again, they want me to go there. Do you know Santiago?"

Krylov shook his head. "Only a little." His only acquaintance there had been Mason, and he had died.

"Terrible air, worse than Rumania. Horrible earthquakes. And they hate us worse than the Bolivians."

"Who do *they* think won the war?"

"You can't tell. The British trained their navy, Germans trained their army, and the air force is sort of Franco-American. It's hard to get an attitude out of that." He became serious for a moment. "Since Allende, they know we are not much help in a pinch."

"I suppose everybody understands that now."

Quickly tired of seriousness, Malenov emitted a booming laugh of derision. "Except Communists, Viktor. Except *us*, my friend."

Krylov began to wish he had not come.

"Even the hardest core of all, those New Deal Americans, no longer believe. Total atheism."

"Confusing times," said Krylov. Too confusing, he had decided. For the first time in his life, a return to Moscow, to Russia, had no appeal for him. The gravitation of the vast union had weakened; often he felt like a satellite, a tiny moon, about to go flying off into the void, although he had never been even slightly tempted by defection. He had last seen Moscow just as the republics began their noisy chorus of autonomy; it had horrified him in the same way, he believed, it must have an American of the 1850s, seeing his nation about to shatter into impotent fragments. Krylov had not done all that he had done, all the hard, cruel, Committee work, for fragments. He had done it for the Soviet *Union*, for the full, maternal expanse their enemies still called Russia. "I feel like what they call in America a featherbedder. An unnecessary extra worker."

"That sounds like one of our inventions." Malenov roared, like a laughing bear. "Those Americans, always stealing from us."

"We used to work very damned hard, Boris." Krylov could not help a reproachful tone.

"Don't be stuffy. We used to do a lot of things. Now we just do what it says on our business cards. I promote trade between Brazil and the Soviet Union. You inspect nuclear facilities for the International Atomic Energy Agency in Vienna. On the other, less obvious side . . . well, you have to think of us as being temporarily neutral. But you wait, when we get our bearings, we'll be as good, or bad perhaps, as ever. It's just a matter of time."

"I always imagined we'd end up like Sweden or Austria, a big safety net under a good market economy. Now it looks more like poverty on top of chaos. Entropy."

"Chaos, perhaps, but not entropy. We still have a lot of quarreling to do, a lot of hot, bad blood to cool. There's a whole career for the younger men, watching our muddied waters come clear." Malenov forced himself to be sombre for a moment. "Of course, what I am describing is a very bad time at home." Then, shifting gears, "I remember how you used to sicken and die if you spent Christmas away from your children."

"They're pretty big for that now." Krylov tried to imagine them. André, tall, straight, blonde, a boy who had suddenly transmuted into a man, full of attitudes and views that rankled —some were downright embarrassing to hear. But the sudden appearance of a man in the boy's face had shaken Krylov more than his son's ardent politics. André seemed no longer to have any secrets, you could read everything there was to know about him in his face. The awful vulnerability of this made the father despair and turn away. His daughter Valentina still lived like a beautiful, apolitical fairy near his heart, but she was lost to him too, married at nineteen to a fortyish aerospace engineer whose visage eluded Krylov as soon as the man left the room. He thought of Valentina as a kind of hostage to this faceless man, the hostage of Star City. And the mother . . . well, he hardly thought of her now she had remarried. Sadly, he realized that he could visualize his children only as youngsters clustered on his lap, the way they appeared in the one photograph of them he carried: a young version of himself smiling, seated outside in the country, his two beautiful children under his wings. The impulse to look at the photograph was almost more than he could resist. "I don't know where I am going to spend Christmas," he said. "I've asked for three weeks' leave after the Angra-1 refueling finishes next week. But maybe Christmas in Bolivia would not be too bad."

Malenov studied Krylov for a time. Once friends, the two men had gone very far apart, that was clear. Malenov was the quintessential Soviet, like Khrushchev, overweight, with the lumpy face and bad, crooked teeth and manners of a peasant. Every language he spoke—seven, at last count—was camouflaged in a joke Russian accent. Krylov, only a few years younger, had taken the alternate path, of the chameleon. No one thought he was anything but what he said he was, for he was careful not to defy all possibility: he could not quite be an American, but made a very good Canadian in both French and English; Germans thought him a Swede. Now he sensed the tough man beneath Malenov's cultivatedly disheveled exterior, and raised his guard. At last, they would get down to business.

"But why come here to tell me about your trip, Viktor?" Malenov's gentle eyes had hardened. Krylov began to recognize his old comrade in arms.

"I was lonesome for a Russian voice."

"Horse shit, you want something from me. Not approval . . . God knows, you don't need my approval to go on holiday. So why come to me?"

"Well, what have you to offer?"

"Some good advice. Listen, you came to me because you know damned well they'd have me bring you in as soon as you went for a Bolivian visa. *Bolivia*, Viktor. Not Buenos Aires or Mexico City or any of thousands of perfectly innocent places to visit . . . no, Bolivia."

"I'm at loose ends right now."

"Why?"

"The biologist found some radioactive stuff in the jungle. Without proper equipment he can't tell a thing about it. It could be a dozen grains. The jungle could be full of it. Nobody knows."

"But why so quiet? Why didn't he just ask the Agency for help, or have Bolivia do it?"

"He doesn't want an official response to come in and bury his forest."

"They will, sooner or later."

"Later is better, he thinks."

"But don't you wonder, Viktor, don't you wonder what those damned British are really up to? What do your instincts tell you?"

"They tell me there's nothing to fear. Nothing political, I mean." When Malenov opened his mouth to say something, Krylov held up a hand to keep him quiet. "You have to keep in mind, Boris, that I really am what it says on my business card. The Englishman at Angra and I are atomic men. We like nuclear, we understand it, and we are not at all afraid of it. When we learn that highly radioactive material has got loose in the world, we feel responsible. We are the experts. We have to act." There, he had given Malenov a hundred times what he'd intended. He pushed the serious tone away. "Besides, the women of Santa Cruz are supposed to be great beauties."

The eyes softened. "So are Bulgarian women—and you've *been* there. Bolivians are like little trolls."

"Not the ones in Santa Cruz."

"I take it the Angra dos Reis girls were inadequate?"

"They did what they could."

"And now, I suppose, it's my turn."

"I don't need quite that much from you. Just a favor."

"Have a VDV brigade standing by?"

"Nothing so grand. I wondered if you'd help get my instruments to La Paz. I don't want to try taking a bunch of expensive Agency stuff past customs."

"That's it?"

Krylov nodded.

"You know, it worries me to have you involved in good works, Viktor. Where is my ferocious old comrade?" Malenov shrugged unhappily. "I still don't like it. Bolivia is running with drug warriors. And the story stinks of a British set-up. You must smell the rotten bait in it."

"I don't. That's just the point."

"The reason they'll be concerned at home, of course, is that you may rattle the Americans. After all, you've been fighting them a good many years now. Why would you not?"

Krylov stood up. "Of course your ferocious old comrade would understand all this. Will you help?"

"With the instruments, of course. Bring them to me and we'll pouch them to the embassy in La Paz straight away. Ask for Yellin when you get there. A good chap—he'll help you." Malenov's eyes twinkled. "One of us, you see." He held up an admonitory index finger and aimed its broken yellow nail at Krylov. "But, listen to me, Viktor—if you accidentally come upon George Bush himself snorting cocaine in the jungle—with a naked man—simply tip your hat and leave."

"I rarely wear a hat."

"Something else."

"Yes?"

"We'll be watching, but not to save you if it turns out to be wired and blows up in your face. There is no VDV brigade, honestly." Malenov paused, and seemed to want some physical contact with Krylov, a handshake, a squeeze of a shoulder, but then put away the troubling friendly impulse. "No, we'll be watching to see if you have some private agenda, a private war with America, or something entrepreneurial in the drug line. That is what They want to know about at home, you see. You need to be a little bit afraid of that."

Krylov grinned. "If there is a villain in this, it's old Nature herself."

4

Feeling cramped and angry, Krylov wriggled massively, trying to keep from crowding too much against the old mestizo woman in the adjoining seat; as it was, her arm pressed against his in the numb way of strangers. Cruzeiro do Sul Flight 880 always flew full on Thursdays, they'd told him, but the idiots at Angra had not got the damned reactor fueled on time for him to leave on Tuesday, as planned. So he had left Rio two days and an hour late. They were two hours behind by the time the stocky Boeing 737 was wheels up out of São Paolo, en route for Santa Cruz and La Paz. Thirty-two thousand feet below him, the forest spread endlessly across the world, the mountains rising out of valleys filled with steam, like great green crawling things lurching westward from the sea. Here and there the black verdure was marked with color, where trees bloomed or died, and the sea-colored freeforms where ranches had been cut out of the jungle for a few years' meager grazing. Bold strokes of cloud smeared the sky, low clouds sucking moisture from the breathing trees, clouds the sun would pump into cumuli before noon, and into giant rainstorms a few hours later. A rare road ran straight as an arrow to a vanishing point in the haze and Krylov could just make out the thin accretion of dwellings along the bare, orange line of it. Wherever the roads went, people set up their shacks along them and burned off enough ground for subsistence farming; put through a road one day, the shacks were there the next. The people were like army ants on the move, he thought, going nowhere with great determination. Like ants, they were simply experiencing the specialty of the house: a high-speed, no-frills journey from cradle to grave. It would become a Russian specialty as well, one day soon, retarded only by that dreadful winter Boris was so proud of.

Ah, Boris. The old fellow had been generous, issuing a kind of friendly warning at the end. Had their world changed so radically that they'd hunt down one of their own to keep from disturbing American equanimity? Perhaps. Of course, knowing that, you didn't tell the Malenovs of the world everything. You didn't tell him about Mason, or the way you sometimes felt the poor dead pilot had somehow anointed you to explore the Beni Fall, which, as Collins had said, kept calling to you. The main thing was to stop by and give an old comrade in arms a few friendly strokes, open up enough so that nobody will bother checking the Cruzeiro do Sul manifest for a Krylov, V. K. It freed you to travel on the passport of choice.

Krylov had driven back to Angra dos Reis and caught up to Collins as the shift let out, offered him a ride home, and, when he was safely in the rented Escort, explained that he wouldn't be able to do the Bolivia thing after all, that something had come up. Collins' face had crumpled and for a moment Krylov worried that the man would begin to howl before he had a chance to finish. Not to worry, he nearly shouted at Collins then, not to worry. I've got somebody else, not to worry. An astronomer chap from Victoria, yes, beautiful old Victoria by the sea, was interested—*more* than interested, *dying* to do it. He was on the way to the telescopes at La Silla, had a week's slack, extreme fascination with the meteorite idea, his field, actually, just the man for the job. And discretion Herself. Dr. Goodpasture could meet him at Cochabamba on Friday morning, he'd fly in from La Paz. Of course, Collins hadn't minded in the least. He was obviously delighted to have a Canadian—people were always glad when a Russian dropped out of play.

So off he went on his Calvin Hobbs Canadian passport, crossing the continent once more on behalf of the Dominion Astrophysical Observatory, a secret, invisible Russian, getting acclimated to life in the third world. "Fuck your mother, Oldenburg," he whispered to the scratched rectangle of his window, recalling the insult. It had caught him on a place his time in Brazil had rubbed more than raw. Everywhere he turned, he saw some appalling parallel between the ruin of this land and that of his poor, broken home, still a powerful nation but only in a brutish way, super no longer. Russians dressed no better than Brazilian Indians, and had less on their shelves, lived in worse housing, in a horrible climate. Their future still looked better only because they'd been telling themselves that since 1917: By the time you are grown, Viktor . . .

He wrenched himself around in the narrow seat. The old woman peered at him, and beyond him, Indian blind, and smiled with teeth as bad as any he had ever seen. Which, he thought, was saying a lot, considering where he came from. Christ, it was fitting that he had wound up on this little airplane with a hundred such people, all faces that might be from one of the Republics at home, everyone on the road from now to then, from bad, no doubt, to worse. "The world still trembles when we speak," a drunken colleague had declared a year ago in Moscow, "but with laughter." Perhaps he traveled as a Canadian because he was ashamed of being Russian, ashamed of what poor old Mother Russia had done to herself. And what was that? She had fallen of her own great weight, no great sin in itself. Of course, the ever-generous Americans claimed a win.

But . . . that had not put him here today. Part of it was what he'd told Malenov, being at loose ends, having a nuclear man's reflex to help with a radiation problem—a small part, Krylov decided. Mainly, he felt himself suspended between his past and all the future, which stretched out like the brown rivers meandering below, with no idea what lay ahead. He missed his former certitude, the assurance he'd had of being on the right side of things. Of course, he knew what his life would be—a job with the new government, or the Academy, or some multinational company now that "joint venture" had become a Russian noun. He could make a real career at the Agency. It was good to have a future, but all these choices seemed to weaken his hold upon the here and now. At the moment, he felt himself flying out of orbit. So, naturally, he sought that part of the world where he had been most at home. Collins had given it to him: Bolivia, the cradle of America's next secret war.

Krylov smiled, feeling somewhat better. He watched the twisting rivers, choosing yet another new course, as they had, flooded year by flooded year. Two months earlier, none of the ground should have been seen for the smoke. Now, as the rains returned, the forest emerged, a deep, nocturnal green that looked permanent and impregnable, like the tundra at home, wet with pools and lagoons, wild, untameable. A shiver of excitement ran through him.

Soon he would be back in that world he had begun to miss, where he was not quite what he seemed, surrounded by a familiar enemy. Were they flying combat sorties yet? Had they begun exterminating Indians? Had they mined the coca-growing regions with irresistible explosive toys? The odor Malenov had detected was present, but not a British scent; something American. Everything in Bolivia would be tainted with that same stinking bait; adventuresome superpowers left pungent trails. Krylov liked the prospect of walking through it, that ambiance of clandestine warfare still impending. He longed to be secretly among his old enemy again, noting their good teeth, their battledress of T-shirts and blue jeans, their unmarked Blackhawks and Cobras, their farmer accents. Apparently he was not finished with them, for he had not yet given up being present at their political creations.

Over here, he thought, everything is just beginning. Back home, they had about come to an end. Like him, the situation was poised between this moment and the next epoch of change. Their revolution was over, reduced to a kind of ideological football to be shunted among boy soldiers in places like Angola, a flameless torch for mad revolutionaries like the *Sendero Luminoso*, people who had no talent—really, no wish—to rule. And yet, he supposed they were the only revolutionaries left, crazily roaming the rubble of their ruined lands, adding fear and death to lives already doomed to wretchedness and poverty everlasting.

He was not mad, however, and had no desire to destroy. He was simply a man who could not bear to go home just yet, who could not quite face the future. Let the others rhapsodize about going to a market economy, that new synonym for democracy, let the gap between equity and reality grow as broad and deep as it ever was in Czarist times, let there be a Russian aristocracy again, this time based on wealth . . . yes, and let there be farmers with no land to till and workers without jobs and families without a roof between them and the snows of Boris' famous winter. Let the Evil Empire be trivialized into a mere economic failure. He, Viktor Krylov, had worked bloody hard for the revolution. Now, before he wound up working with the idiot son of *perestroika,* a moron playing with a nation's shattered expectations, he would make this final sortie.

The cabin attendant was speaking on the public address system, possibly in Portuguese—the sound quality was so bad the words could have been Norwegian. She switched to Spanish, but he could still not make her out. Then the seat belt lamps came on and he felt the Boeing begin a shallow descent. Off to his left, past his fellow passengers, the sky had gone black with rain in which lightning flared. He had watched rainy-season weather bloom and vanish on satellite images made into film loops. Every afternoon the atmosphere would boil up in great anvils of cloud that covered the whole interior of Brazil, thrust westward on the prevailing rivers of wind; then, as suddenly as the storms appeared, they shriveled to nothingness on the screen, leaving only the smeared sky in which the day's flight had begun.

The pilot had taken them well north of their destination and now turned southward, toward Santa Cruz, the airplane throttled back and its flaps partially deployed, killing time until the storm moved off the Viru Viru runway. Off to the west, Krylov saw the forest unfold into swamps and grasslands, detail appearing as if magically in the dark greens, the pale grasses, the brown rivers. Trees bloomed in islands that rose from the oceans of grass, crowned with white and red and yellow flowers. He could make out great tears in the forest canopy, where a tree had gone down in a storm and taken its companions with it; he could almost feel the drum of unaccustomed sunlight on the suddenly exposed forest floor. What stirrings that must bring, he thought, thrilled to be here, as thrilled by this as he had been by Siberia in winter, by the moonscape of Afghanistan. Beyond the freeforms of marsh and trees, the jungle seemed to grow blacker, more foreboding, the trees like great reptiles bound in green chains. The rivers transformed swiftly from brown to rushing white, as the upward march began. It was like a madly jumbled stairway of canyons and cliffs, all muffled in deep forest, moist as the bottom of the sea, and above it all, the pale, smoky line of snow along the cordillera.

Somewhere down there, Krylov thought, the forest has been sown with cesium 137. Its stream of radiation flowed into the unsuspecting world, which subtly changed beneath its electrifying touch. As they had at the table with Collins, the possibilities chilled Krylov to his bones. His shiver caused his companion to stir, and for a moment he looked into a frightened female face that said every landing was for her a crash. Then the Indian curtain descended and she became still, capable of enduring anything, even the long, bucking final approach. Yes, he thought, even ionizing radiation.

The airplane yawed nervously toward the long single runway at Viru Viru, which Krylov could now just make out as a pale green cleared area. The forest lay behind them now, the land all marsh and ranchland, cattle turned like windvanes toward the south. Here and there a patch of drinking oil birds pecked earnestly at the ground, feeding small cities of cylindrical storage tanks rusting away in the hard climate of the Beni. Farther south, what he supposed was the city of Santa Cruz appeared as a smear of red-tiled roofs and white walls, stands of poplars, water towers, steeples, office buildings, all vanishing and reappearing through the shafts of rain and occasional flick of faraway lightning. The storm still raged only a few kilometers ahead of them when they touched down on one wheel in a stiff crosswind, caromed, and made a final landing. The attendant explained in scrambled Portuguese and Spanish that they had reached Santa Cruz, that they would continue to La Paz in about half an hour; Cruzeiro had no apologies for the delay. . . .

Krylov peered through the scratched Plexiglass of his porthole. A few single- and twin-engined airplanes were tied down, on the puddled tarmac, looking rather miserable in the gloom behind the storm. Coca planes, he decided, for the Colombia leg of the trade. A LAB DC-9 was stirring at the terminal as they approached, and passed them on its way to the runway. A Lufthansa 747 waited to be filled with people who thought Germany had won the war. But Krylov saw no military aircraft, none of the American A-37s he had expected, or the flock of Hueys and Cobra gunships, or the occasional C-130 disgorging more supplies. Then, as he watched, an unmarked black Huey crept in almost at a hover across the field, turned into the wind, and settled to earth. Its crew quickly climbed aboard an orange Volkswagen minivan that had been waiting for them. But, at this distance at least, they looked no more military than the radtechs at Angra-1: what air force wore white flight suits?

5

"I think of it as a human avalanche," Yellin said from the window. His back was to Krylov for the moment, and to the large, richly appointed room he used as his embassy office. He sounded like a man who saw La Paz spill toward him from the high horizon of the Altiplano, beyond which a sky as blue as Pluto's rose infinitely, without a trace of cloud. In fact, he could see nothing beyond the narrow, paved interval of embassy grounds and the pink brick wall that enclosed the compound, planted with dark firs. The room might have been in Leningrad or Munich. One could just make out through a crack between the pines the multicolored shelters of a playground across the Avenida Arequipa, and, in the middle distance, the muddy spread of what remained of the River Choqueyapu.

"You have the poor cascading down the flanks of Mount Illimani," he continued, "and then, where the avalanche slows, the city centre, with some middling skyscrapers and the government buildings they occasionally like to burn to the ground. Down here in Calacoto, the avalanche has nearly ceased to move. We have our lagoons of diplomacy and wealth. Below us," he added, turning back to the room, "there is probably nothing." He frowned, looking for Krylov in the relative gloom of the place, and for a moment had the aspect of a blind man; his face, like the studiedly uninflected rhythms of his voice, held a quantity of sadness. Years before, the face had held nothing, the voice had been as empty of humanity as the tolling of a bell, and you did not want it tolling for you. Still terribly severe, still dressed in the tweed and khaki of an American dry-goods catalogue, Yellin was thin in the way someone made of a hard wood might have been. And yet, Krylov thought, one sensed life stirring within. The man's pale grey eyes had lost their frightening opacity, as Malenov's had, as had his own. Ah, Malenov . . . Boris must have known that the Yellin in La Paz was *the* Yellin. The name had meant nothing to Krylov at the time; he would never have matched it with this out-of-the-way embassy. But seeing the man had been as great a shock as bumping into Mikhail Sergeyevich himself in La Paz. Surprise, and something that mixed pity and curiosity, had kept Krylov there long after he had received his two anodized aluminum trunks of Agency instruments, which now sat anachronistically amid the antique splendor of Yellin's office.

It was not that he and Yellin had ever been close. The other was a good ten years older, possibly more, and they had never served shoulder to shoulder, as Boris might have put it. Instead, there had been the pervasive reputation of the man, a brushing encounter at a going-home party in Kabul, a long interrogation near Kandahar that was still full of nightmares. Everyone had said then that Arkady Andreovich would wind up directing the Committee. Instead, here he was, his stony eyes turned to bright, open windows to his soul, or what passed in him for one, and, beyond, an appetite or two where none had been visible before. Ah, well, it was not in Krylov's power to ignore this man; one had to listen, for he talked as though he had not spoken aloud in centuries. . . .

"An odd place to site a town, when you think of it," Yellin continued, drifting heron-like across the far reaches of the room, where he nearly vanished behind the shaft of low after-noon light streaming through the high window. "Apparently the Spaniards, who could endure anything, could not endure the Altiplano, all that howling wind, that terrible moonscape up there. And there was gold in the Choqueyapu. Gold always moved them. They put down a city straddling the river, so that all the streets run uphill from the gorge. The river still runs beneath what is now the Prado, but its gold is gone. Of course, the imperialists always pay for their intrusions. At this altitude,

European women could not carry a baby its full term. The invaders could not reproduce." Yellin smiled around long, uniform grey teeth, apparently enjoying the Spaniards' having to suffer the consequences of their actions. "Intermarry or die, that was the cosmic edict. So they intermarried and hey, presto! a race of dwarfs." Yellin came back to his desk, a monolithic piece of nearly black mahogany with nothing whatever on its vast polished surface, not a pencil, not a sheet of paper, not a calendar or water-ring; it was all reflection, like a jungle pool. "How is your breathing, Viktor Viktorivich?"

"When I first stepped off the plane, my lungs told me I was on the wrong planet." Krylov spoke slowly, conserving what still felt to him like an empty tank of oxygen. "A swarm of black spots, some floating lights." He grinned for Yellin, but it had embarrassed him, to step out of the Cruzeiro Boeing into the terrible heavenly light of the Altiplano and to be suddenly, uncontrollably woozy, as if drugged. Crossing the few tens of meters to the terminal like a man crossing Siberia in winter, he had told himself angrily: Remember *who* you are, remember *what* you are, a fighter, a powerful man, a Russian. "Everything is fine now."

"They changed the airport's name to John F. Kennedy International years ago, but people still call it El Alto. A point of civic pride, to operate an airport at nearly four thousand meters. Sometimes they have to administer oxygen on the spot."

"Anyway, I no longer feel like a fish that jumped out of his bowl."

"Then I shan't offer you a *mate de coca*, which is our remedy for altitude sickness—*soroche*, as they call it." Yellin crossed to a small white refrigerator that seemed as out of place here as Krylov's metal suitcases. "But a vodka wouldn't hurt. Will you?"

"Only a coward would say no."

Yellin took out two tapered glasses of intricately cut crystal, so bright as to be undefined, and filled them from a quart-sized thermos. When he passed Krylov's to him it was as if he handed over a cone of light. Krylov gave a nod of thanks, and, when Yellin had poured his own, held up a silent toast. Yellin clicked his heels softly and drank the vodka down. Krylov did the same, and immediately regretted it: for a moment, he thought the stuff had absorbed every molecule of oxygen in his body. The drink reverberated through him. Dimly, he was aware that Yellin had refilled his glass.

"To Mikhail Sergeyevich Gorbachev," Yellin toasted in a flat, sarcastic voice. "To *perestroika,* to *glasnost,* to the new Russia, which we shall color blue." Krylov followed suit, not wanting to be so craven he could not toast his president and motherland. On a far wall, Gorbachev's color photograph watched with a frown of disapproval. It was like one of those portraits of the Christ, whose eyes followed you everywhere, especially if you were a child. Looking at the photograph, Krylov noted silently, You have created a very bitter man here. Why did you send him so far away? Why would you waste a man like Yellin on La Paz? It made no sense.

"I think," said Yellin, his face faintly colored by the drink, "we knew one another Over There, Viktor Viktorivich."

"Our paths crossed once or twice."

"Once or twice," Yellin echoed. "Once or twice." For the first time, Krylov noticed a tremor in the pale, birchlike fingers holding the glowing crystal of alcohol. "And yet," the man went on, his words slightly slurred already, "I feel we have known one another since the Great Patriotic War. Ah, well." He shook his head and presented what he apparently intended as a rueful smile; Yellin seemed to have had to invent ways to display his feelings, and some of them were wrong. "It is just good to have a colleague in town." Yellin waved his arm in an arc that encompassed the cavernous office, the land beyond the window, the Andean sky beyond. "You must have noticed how little goes on in this magnificent room. No visitors. No interruptions. The telephone never rings." His voice grew taut with bitterness; he seemed to bite down upon something left unsaid. Krylov was embarrassed to have the man strain so for warmth.

Yellin refilled their glasses, and leaned against the dark pond of his desk, watching himself reflected as a pale blur in the wood. "This is the room to which you would send someone you could not bring yourself to kill. You'd send your man in the mask not to some provincial chateau, but here, to embassy La Paz. You'd make him a trade representative and give him the

office of a Spanish viceroy, filled with the rich woods and tapes-
tries of the old imperialist days." He spoke softly, evenly, and
Krylov could no longer hear the slightest note of rancor; instead, the tone was one of acceptance, of having seen justice
done. "I am very much like those British you see everywhere,
Viktor Viktorivich, what they call remittance men. Of course, in
a socialist society, the government, not the family, sends you
your remittance. Otherwise, it is the same. This is my exile, you
see. This is my masters' idea of death." He gave a bemused,
appreciative laugh that clanged in the silence flowing in behind
his speech. "Well, Katerina Ivanova likes it, and the children
find it 'weird' enough."

"If I may ask . . . what happened?" Krylov could not resist
the breach of etiquette.

Yellin shook his head. "Here, drink up." He poured down
another glass, shuddering as it percolated into his blood. Yellin's hands trembled intermittently; a nervousness had come to
roost in his once cold, collected body, and one saw the shine of
longings in his eyes: to talk, to drink—and what else? No doubt
he longed to be useful again, as Krylov himself did, as all of the
old guard would like to be. "I think, Viktor . . . may I call you
Viktor? . . . it was a matter of my using up too many good
men in the line of duty." For a moment, he paused, and Krylov
sensed he was naming the dead. "If my masters had not sent
me out here, I should have sent myself somewhere. God knows,
I might not have been quite this creative." He forced another
laugh. "No, not by half." His pale eyes gleamed and showed
fine veinous nets of blood surfacing behind in the whites. A
man like Yellin should never drink, thought Krylov, it is death
for him to drink. Perhaps sensing that Krylov had seen too
much of him, he veered suddenly to neutral ground. "Where
are you staying?"

"The Sucre."

"Adequate, adequate. Of course, you must go to the Sheraton
for a view."

"The whole place is quite a view."

"Very true." The chuckle this time had something genuinely
goodhearted in it, as if Yellin had scraped down to the very core
of his humanity. Perhaps they had sent him to La Paz to reclaim

him for the human race. In any event, Krylov began to like him, this talkative man who was steadfastly drinking himself to death, exiled from all that had been real in his life. One discovered traces of oneself in him. "The View," Yellin was saying. "No matter where you look, there it is. On a clear day you can see forever, Viktor. But most days, you can't find your ass for the smoke." Yellin's eyebrows arched, startled by his slip into vernacular familiarity. He pulled back instinctively, remembering to be careful. Krylov recognized the reflex: you never knew who'd be coming out to look at you. "Viktor . . . may I ask you a personal question . . . strictly off the record?"

"God, I hope we have been off the record," and he laughed.

"What brings you to Bolivia?"

"Not you, Arkady Andreovich."

"You mean it is none of my business." A hurt tone, quickly suppressed.

"I mean it has nothing to do with you, or with the Committee, or with the Soviet Union. I am doing a small technical favor for two men I don't know very well."

Yellin glanced at the metal cases. "You have a good deal of equipment for a small technical favor."

"It looks like more than it is. Some overkill, perhaps. But, honestly, I am not doing anything worth noting. To tell the truth, I am as much at loose ends as you are."

"If that's the case, why are you traveling as a Canadian?" His smile became almost timid.

Krylov laughed. It had been madness to use the passport after all. Had he known which Yellin was in La Paz, he would not have attempted the deception. Of course the resident would have checked everything—Christ, the man had a pile of reflexes and no other way to employ them except in minor mischief like this. "It's a name of convenience, not some *nom de guerre*. Can we keep it between us?"

"Where else could I possibly keep it? People are not asking much of me lately. I think I was only showing off. Not much goes on here, but I do what I can. I keep my ear to the ground, I notice things." He tossed down another vodka, the glass throwing a shower of fragmented light across the room as his arm moved through the sunbeam. "I ask questions, usually of my-self. For example, I ask why the Americans stopped flying drug sorties at the end of October? Was it the rainy season or some grand tactical decision? Then I hear that the government's anti-narcotics enclave at Chimoré went down to a skeleton force about the same time. *Then* I read in the newspapers about a spectacular meteor shower over the Beni. And now, six weeks later here comes a compatriot . . . no, more than that, a col-league . . . entering on a false passport with a bunch of Inter-national Atomic Energy Agency equipment in tow . . . to help some English. The work I have been doing for nearly forty years compels me to ask the irresistible question: how can these anomalies *not* be connected?"

"Linking me with the meteors, that is a pretty long bridge. But adding the Americans and the drug police, that is too long altogether."

"A bridge only Stalin's child would want to build."

"Also that."

"Maybe that's what I am, at bottom. One of Stalin's chil-dren." He noticed Krylov's anxious glance at the dark paneled walls, and added, "Don't worry, nobody is listening. Over here the Soviet embassy is about as interesting as Chad's." He shrugged and looked at Gorbachev. "I am certainly not one of *his* children, or he one of mine. I shall never bring myself to love America. I am still at war. . . . I have been at war since I was a boy."

"I know how you feel, Arkady Andreovich."

"I believe you do, Viktor." Yellin smiled, then, and it seemed to Krylov that some terrible tension had released within; the man's ordinarily expressionless face glowed with relief. "You know, it means the world to me to say, to a man who knows how we have lived all these years, that I am not finished, that I hate what has happened at home, that I am eternally a thorn in the foot of America—even here, where nothing happens." His eyes glistened. "It means the world to me."

"Malenov wanted me not to embarrass them. He said we were shoulder to shoulder in the middle east just now. He said if I saw President Bush using cocaine I should ignore it."

Krylov laughed. "Shit, I would pull out a video camera, Arkady. Put him on Nightly News."

"And I would help you, Viktor. We would put him in *Pravda!*"

"*Time's* man of the Epoch."

"A Nobel prize."

"For *chemistry!*"

The two men laughed like boys, relieved to be so palpably in safe company, to be free of the new chains of official freedom and openness they found more constraining than the comfortable old Communism of a few years before. They laughed until Krylov saw black specks and found he could not breathe, and still they laughed. Finally, controlling himself, panting hungrily for oxygen, Krylov held up a hand for restraint, and slowly they grew quiet, wiped their eyes. For a time they each lapsed into reverie, Krylov's mind brushing his life at home, faces . . .

"Seriously, Viktor," Yellin said then, "what are you going to do in the Beni?" Clearly, it had been the question he'd wanted to ask from the first.

Krylov shrugged. "Really, very little. An English biologist thinks the meteorite may have brought in some radioactive material. He wanted someone to help him see what it is. As I am free, I said I would do it. Now, Arkady Andreovich, you know all my black secrets."

"But not the largest one of all—the convergence that draws you to the Beni. That puts you here, with me. Something is drawing everything together, Viktor, I can feel it, numb as I am."

"It sounds mystical to me." Although, he had felt it keenly too, since word of Mason's death, since he had heard again from Collins of the Fall.

"Not mystical . . . revolutionary. Already we forget how it used to be seeing the world as one might see an ocean flowing with tides, all interlinked, rising here, descending there, vast waves moving across the world."

"Those days are gone."

"No, the *senderistas* still have that view of the world. They are worse than Marx that way, worse than Mao. But that is exactly why I find more to love in them than in us at the moment. They have the political reflexes, the sense of converging tides, of the young revolutionary. They would see the Americans' lack of sorties, the meteor, your arrival as all connected."

"Only because they're crazy."

"Highly motivated."

"*I* am highly motivated. *You* are highly motivated. It's not the same thing." Although, Krylov thought, you may have gone crazy after all.

"Have you ever so much as spoken with one?"

Krylov shook his head. "The Shining Path is not too active in Vienna."

Yellin looked at his watch, then toward the mountains, shrouded in orange light now, the sky's sapphire blue beyond the stony rim darkening behind the light. "You may meet one yet."

"They would only be disappointed. I'm not a Komsonol youngster, Arkady Andreovich—and I truly did not come to Bolivia to build improbable bridges."

"My friend, I begin to see that you yourself don't know what brought you over here." Then, "Another vodka?"

"For the road." Krylov thought he must accept, so clearly did Yellin seem to want him there a while longer. We must help one another as we are able, he told himself. One day I will be pressing a former colleague to stay. Still, the vodka had cut off much of his oxygen supply; he felt unsteady, unsafe, unreliable, and hoped there was no trouble waiting for him in the descending night.

When he had filled the two dazzling crystals, Yellin passed one to Krylov, then held his own up into the late afternoon light, where it glowed like a flame. "To Stalin's children, the Shining Path, who keep the fires we have banked at home."

Krylov could not bring himself to echo the ominous words, which chilled him with their celebration of the insane. "To poor Mother Russia," he said, raising his own glass, "and all that she has been and still shall be to all who love and serve her." Patriotism released as much warmth as the vodka had, or so he thought. He drank his down quickly.

"A fine afternoon, Arkady Andreovich," he said then, "but now I should be going."

"The temptation is to try to hang onto you, Viktor. It has been a long time since I was treated as anything besides Moscow's man in the mask. But I shall let you go. However . . ." and he waved an arm at his silent, empty office, "we have all the tools of the trade, even if we don't use them. When you find out why you are in Bolivia . . . you may want the help of a friendly resident."

But this, Krylov saw, took them too far, embarrassing Yellin as he heard the lonely longing in his voice. So children spoke to one another, candidly offering or asking to be friends. "Well," Krylov went on nervously, no longer looking at his visitor, "I shan't keep you. . . ."

The sudden trill of the telephone caused both men to jump, and to look sheepishly at one another, and laugh their relief. Yellin picked up the receiver and listened for a moment. "Good," he said, "good. We'll be right there." Then, "We'll need a taxi for my visitor, and someone to fetch his cases for him." He put the instrument back on its cradle and said to Krylov, excitement riding his voice where anyone could detect it, "Amazing, the way things come together. I will make a believer of you yet, Viktor. Come, there's somebody you must meet."

He took Krylov's arm and steered him out of the office into the dim light that drifted down into the dark-tiled reception hall. A pair of Soviet guards in brown winter uniforms were silhouetted in a bulletproof cubicle near the entrance door; a third sat with his jacket off at a mahogany reception desk just inside. Next to him stood a short, slender man of indeterminate age, dressed in the black suit and white shirt of every anarchist who had ever lived, a dark, brimmed hat clutched against his crotch as though to conceal some nakedness. But there was nothing timid in his unfinished, Indian face when he looked up. He regarded the approaching Russians with an oceanic calm, his great deer eyes as steady as those of a confident, precocious child. Krylov knew this face well enough; he had seen it in Angola, Afghanistan, Vietnam—the mask through which all revolutionaries, all purveyors of terror in the name of some idea, viewed an oppressive world. "I would like you to meet a new associate of mine," said Yellin. Neither man extended a hand for shaking, but held back, as wary, thought Krylov, as Lenin himself. "Mr. Hobbs . . . Mr. Palma."

6

Krylov had not been surprised when, the following morning, he gazed around the crowded waiting room at Cochabamba's Jorge Wilsterman airport and discovered Palma watching him. He forced himself past the illusory warmth in the deer eyes, the tentative smile of recognition. Palma was the last person he wanted to see, for it seemed to Krylov that the man had been with him all night, in dreams half forgotten, half too vividly remembered. Awakening in the pale light before the sun cleared the rim of the high plain, Krylov had been soaked in a febrile sweat, crawling into wakefulness from a terrible dream of drowning. . . . But, no, he had remembered then, it was suffocation of another kind: He had gone down in a sea of the impoverished and afflicted, all dressed in the woolens of the Andes, all Indians, he believed, until, looking into their faces, he saw the familiar ones from home, good Russian faces in Indian costumes. He had laughed at the odd joke they played on him . . . and then, in one of those temporal shudders that alters dreamscapes, he looked again and they were all Palma. Driven awake, Krylov had stared wildly around his hotel room, fully expecting to find the man seated by his bed, watching imperturbably. But of course the room was empty. At breakfast, and later, on the taxi ride up the *autopista* to El Alto, Krylov had expected to meet Palma, for dreams were often heralds of encounters; but he had not seen the man, and he was almost certain Palma had not been aboard the nine-thirty LAB flight that had brought him to Cochabamba. And yet, here he was.

Of course, the dream really had nothing to do with Palma, except as he was the Latin Everyman. It had been about being Russian, and seeing where one's great land was going; soon the streets of Moscow would teem with beggars like the alleys of La Paz. Soon the old and toothless would sit around in their homespuns, like the Indians, and lacking coca leaves and the maize liquor called *chicha*, keep themselves alive with vodka. He turned back to where Palma had been a moment earlier, this time prepared to greet him, and found him gone. One might have imagined him after all. Well, thought Krylov, nobody is afraid of you, little man, or of your great destinies: don't mistake my hangover for anything like fear.

He smiled, almost comforted by the faint but well-defined pain that ran like a minor head wound vertically across his forehead, the wages of altitude and alcohol. After dinner at the hotel, Krylov, restless and alone in a land more foreign than Mongolia, had gone out into La Paz, followed by beggars of all ages, men and women, girls and boys, enveloping him like a cloud of colorful gnats. They had waited for him when he entered bars farther and farther up the slopes from the fashionable canyon of the Prado. Soon he was the only European, in places without flooring where people drank as though their glasses were oceans in which to fish for Death herself. . . . Krylov had consumed a quantity of *chicha*, far too much at four thousand meters' altitude. It was a nerve drug, like vodka, like the apricot brandy Bulgarians called the Next Hour of Life. He had ended the evening, he vaguely recalled, wondering what to do with a bare, brown leg thrust by a sleeping *cholita* across his lap. But no one had abused or robbed him. Perhaps it was his daunting size, or perhaps they were goodhearted *indios* who enjoyed having a big half-tame bear in their midst, like Incas with a large cat. But they had treated him well and poked fun at his Spanish; at the end, he had rejoined his convoy of waiting beggars, who escorted him back to the Hotel Sucre, where he had showered them with whatever he still had in his pockets. Chilly beneath a sky pulsing with great pregnant stars, it had been a kind of Siberian evening for him. Even with the throbbing and stink of his *chicha* hangover, the outing had been reviving in just the way a night out along the Lama River would have been. He was still just the slightest bit drunk, but whether from the evocation or the *chicha* he could not have said.

"Mr. Hobbs, good morning," someone said behind him. Krylov suppressed an impulse to whirl toward the sound, and instead peered slowly around to find Palma barely a meter away, compact, humble as a priest in his rumpled black suit and brimmed hat. In the sharper light of the terminal, his face had almost no detail, as though its etcher had given up before adding the fine work needed around the eyes and mouth; as in the face of a child, there were no edges anywhere. Krylov, wearing khaki trousers, tennis shoes and a light shirt of white Egyptian cotton, felt quite the imperialist. "Mr. Palma," he replied pleasantly. "A small world."

"Well, a small country, perhaps. It would be difficult in Bolivia *not* to meet people you know."

"Considering I have met only two, it is still worth noting."

"Perhaps." A diffident glance, a lowering of the fathomless eyes. "Forgive me for intruding, but I thought you might be waiting for transport."

"I am."

"May I ask to where?"

Krylov wondered whether to answer, then decided that Yellin must have told Palma at least his destination and perhaps more. "The Beni Research Station. Dr. Goodpasture is picking me up."

"Ah, Dr. Goodpasture. Do you know him?" Krylov shook his head. "I met him several weeks ago. An interesting man." Then, melancholy clouding the soft eyes, "I doubt that he will get here today. The station is beyond El Crucero, and with the rains, the roads are terrible, even for a Land Rover."

"I can only wait." Krylov executed a shrug of Armenian proportions. "But I appreciate your letting me know."

"In fact, I came over to offer you a . . . *lift*." The vernacular tickled him, almost bringing forth a grin of pleasure. "Would you like a . . . lift?"

"But what about Dr. Goodpasture? It would be too bad if he drove here to get me and found me already gone."

"If he comes along the road from El Crucero, we shall see him. There is only one way."

"Well," Krylov began, feeling as if a trap had closed upon him, "that is most kind. I accept." He said it with a fatality he wanted Palma to hear.

"Let me help you with your cases." Palma scooped up the smaller one. "Metal cases must mean delicate equipment inside," he said, hefting the small case. "Is it very fragile?"

"The cases protect them pretty well." Krylov stood and picked up his clothes bag and the larger case, and started across the waiting room with Palma, who led them toward the tarmac, not the street.

"What will you measure over there?"

"Whatever Dr. Goodpasture wishes."

"He told me there was a kind of plague; perhaps you will measure that."

"Whatever he wishes."

"But are the instruments not highly specialized?"

"You can use a clock to measure time . . . and speed and distance. These are like that."

"Interesting. I shall remember that: a clock measures more than time." Then, "Does it have a name, this one?"

"A multichannel analyzer."

"Ah. It measures every . . . channel?"

"Exactly."

"And the big case?"

"A Cutie Pie," said Krylov. "A counter."

"That counts . . . everything?"

"That counts what Dr. Goodpasture wishes. That's why we call it a Cutie Pie, Mr. Palma."

"Ah." Ignoring a uniformed Bolivian policeman at the exit, Palma pushed through a door and led them onto the tarmac, onto the broad asphalt apron, where the moving LAB jet was beginning to fidget, ready to fly on to Santa Cruz. "Any moment," he said over the rising whine of the engines. He set down the metal case and regarded Krylov as though for the first time until the plane had taxied far enough away from them to speak. Then, "You know, it surprised me to meet a Canadian at the Soviet embassy."

"I was surprised to meet you there as well. Perhaps your

company, like mine, is sending you to the Soviet Union. You know, make a killing off *perestroika?*"

Palma laughed. "Nothing like that, Mr. . . . Hobbs." There, thought Krylov, he has expressed his doubts with that small ellipsis before the name. "My 'company' is simply the poor of the Andes, and I am a mere healer of them. So you may see me everywhere, in the alleys, the embassies, anywhere I think there may be help for their pain. We need a good deal of help, as there is a good deal of pain in Bolivia."

And if you have your way, thought Krylov, there will be a good deal more. For of course Palma was here to mobilize the poor bastards crowding in along the roads and rivers of the rainforest, working them because the people of the Altiplano had lost their ability to rebel centuries ago. Palma wanted to provide a dedicated army of Bolivian *senderistas* for the *narco-traficantes;* an army of believers was always better than one of thugs. "A worthy-sounding cause, Mr. Palma," he said, wondering why Yellin had got in it. Perhaps diverting money and guns to the terror was a substitute for nothing, a way to show he was still a revolutionary. They will be watching, Malenov had told him in Rio. Well, perhaps these soft brown eyes were Yellin's. "What takes you to the jungle?"

"There is perhaps more pain there."

"Do you stay in El Crucero?"

"In fact, I was most fortunate. A leading agroindustrialist of the area has taken up our cause. He will help us, perhaps. In the meantime, I have his hospitality. And so do you . . . he is providing our transport today."

"Do I know him?"

"Who has not heard of Congreve?"

Krylov kept his eyes on Palma. Of course, he had heard of Congreve. At one time the Committee had thought of providing some small kind of help to the tycoon, making it easier for him to feed the great American appetite. But that had been when they were still at war. "Congreve?"

"A Chilean. He has the surname of the great English playwright."

"Oh yes," Krylov replied, the playwright's name not registering. "Yes, of course."

"I hear our ride."

Krylov only heard the beat of approaching rotors, a sound that invariably made his blood move. A red-and-white helicopter was creeping toward them across the field, nose high, its blades reverberating in ground effect. He recognized the Helobras CH-55 *Esquilo,* the squirrel, a Brazilian variant of the French design. *Agroindustriales Congreves, S.A.* had been painted in streamlined red letters on its white flank. When it was a few tens of meters away from them, the craft floated in a hover, then settled to the apron.

Leaving the rotor idling, the pilot stepped back and cracked the cargo door for them, and Palma and Krylov hurried over with the bags, the Russian stooping beneath the slow sweep of the big blades overhead. Once inside, amid the noise and odors of hydraulic fluid, kerosene, and human perspiration that filled all cockpits, Palma indicated that Krylov should take the left-hand seat next to the pilot. Krylov thanked him, genuinely pleased to belt himself into the front of a helicopter—helicopters had once been his world, and he wondered how the twin-turbine Helobras compared to the MI-24. ". . . Arias, Mr. . . . Hobbs . . ." Palma was saying above the noise, and Krylov turned toward the pilot and shook hands quickly. Arias gestured toward earphones, and soon they were linked through an intercom, the roar of the machine muffled behind the padded cups. "Mr. . . . Hobbs is a Canadian," Palma told the pilot in Spanish. "He awaits Dr. Goodpasture. . . ."

Arias shook his head and replied in English, "No way anybody drives up from El Crucero today. A big slide. We will see it on the way down."

"I hope you don't mind dropping me off," said Krylov. Then, his eyes catching a horsey glint in Arias', he turned quickly to Palma. He had seen with horrifying clarity the guerrilla ready to shoot him in the nape of his neck, and let the pilot kick him into the jungle below—but it was fantasy. Palma wasn't even looking at him; melancholy and alone, the little man peered out across the high, arid Cochabamba Valley. "Perhaps that is not quite what I meant," said Krylov. "Perhaps you could just let me off at the station."

"Hey, that's good," said Arias, laughing crazily. "That's good! Can I *drop* you someplace? *Haw haw.*"

But Krylov was watching Palma. The *senderista* didn't like this talk of dropping people out of helicopters because the machines were the instruments of government. Guerrillas got pushed out of helicopters, not government troops. Helicopters were the horses, designed to torment the militant opposition, which was always, by definition, the infantry. We throw people like you out of helicopters to make them talk, my friend, thought Krylov. And you cut off our heads and hands to scare us into silence. We are both good at frightening one another— but keep in mind that I am the man who pushes, and you are the man who falls. When their eyes met, Krylov saw that Palma had been thinking along those same lines. It made the guerrilla uncomfortable to be in this flagship of the status quo—even Congreve was closer to the real, ordered world than he. But then, realizing suddenly why he understood the man so well, Krylov gave Palma a broad smile. It took one to know one. Perhaps one's instincts had not been completely scrubbed away after all.

Arias was talking to the tower on the radio. Cleared across the field, he looked around at his passengers, checking their belts, and then eased the *Esquilo* gently into the air. Behind them, Palma's expression was entirely fatal—he might have been standing against a wall, waiting for the hail of bullets. You revolt against the things you fear, Krylov silently admonished him. Arias put the ship's nose down and powered them slowly across the field, barely ten meters off the ground. A lot of planes, Krylov noted, tied down along the flight line, most of them small private planes, antique C-46s and DC-3s, the odd LAB 727 or Fairchild, one of the dark C-130s operated by TAM, the Bolivian army's cargo service, which also carried paying passengers to locations too remote to be served by the airline. At the end of the thin string of hangars and quonsets and low sheds used for cargo maintenance, a gaggle of green military Hueys stood idle outside a large, cream-colored hangar. An illusion of strength. Yellin had said they'd cut their sorties out of Chimoré, but why? The weather was not yet bad, despite what Palma had said about the roads. Why stand down? It was as if the drug war had been suspended. Perhaps, thought Krylov, it has suddenly ended, like the cold war. One day you've got knives at one another's throats, the next, the wall is down and you're shoulder to shoulder against Iraq. The Americans might have legalized cocaine, leaving R. J. Reynolds and Philip Morris to deal with the Congreves of the world.

"Mr. . . . Hobbs . . ." Palma was saying, careful to keep the suggestive pause in Krylov's name, "wants us to follow the El Crucero road."

"Why not?"

They took off to the southeast, then turned eastward, following the tower's instructions to skirt San Sebastian hill, a loaf of ground that towered over the airport where the corrugated roofs of barrio shacks scattered over the southwestern flank of the town. The Helobras strained upward in the thin air, and Krylov watched the altimeter. It seemed to him that the ground rose faster than they did. Below them, a narrow two-laned blacktop road threaded along a stream through a narrowing valley, which ended in a cluster of rough structures; the road curled into the mountains, climbing toward what looked like the cracked rim of the planet, where peaks and high ridges some five thousand meters high lay across their line of flight, as implacable as the torsos of ossified giants. Arias did not inspire confidence, although he flew with a light touch. Krylov relaxed in the way one pilot must when another is flying, and tried not to bite his lip. He thought Arias was taking the *Esquilo* down the valley a bit fast, and a bit low, considering he was operating near its service ceiling and well above an altitude where it could hover. The higher the ground forced them to go, the more like a conventional airplane the machine became. But what disconcerted Krylov most was what he saw in the pilot's face. Entering the tapered valley east of Cochabamba, it had been clear that Arias lost his orientation for a moment: you could see a tendency to go inverted as his spatial sense vanished. Then, a moment later, the frightening impulse was gone, or rather, Krylov thought, suppressed. The man had a loose wire that he had to keep reconnecting.

Below them, the narrow road ran almost straight toward the east, crossing high ridges cupping narrow glacial lakes, their mirrored surfaces like windows into a gleaming blue abyss: holes in the earth. Another cluster of buildings approached them on the road. "Corani," Arias said, nodding to the mud-brick structures that raced by under his windscreen. But now, ahead of them, the land dropped away, spilling into a tangle of deep gorges wreathed in dense forest. Arias let the machine descend, still following the road, but now through a bizarre terrain of sheer cliffs and vertical peaks as surreal to Krylov as the sudden, sheer mountains of China. The road below them was barely two lanes wide, without a shoulder on either side. The clear air of the highlands became the cold mists of the mountain forests; water gushed from cracks in the cliffs, cascading down and down the glistening rocks to streams that hurried toward a black-green sea of grasses marked by islands of trees, stretching out endlessly ahead of them.

Krylov saw only an occasional truck on the road, and nothing that looked like a Land Rover. At one point, the narrow way was blocked by a mudslide, the thin lanes vanishing into a bus-sized mound of mud and rock that had ripped out of the saturated overhang. Buses and trucks painted primary colors had stopped on either side, like stilled toys. Passengers were studying the fall, but no one had begun the digging. As in Russia, Krylov thought, hard work requires a lot of verbal foreplay. "See," said Arias, "no way to Cochabamba today. We is *it*, man." He gave Krylov that big, mad grin again, and forced himself to fly the *Esquilo* farther into the narrow V of the gorge. Krylov sensed the man's orientation flickering and wondered why he didn't pull up, fly over the land instead of through it. But Arias persevered.

In half an hour, with his lip still not quite bitten through, Krylov saw the end of the rough ground give way suddenly to a throw of shacks and low buildings he took to be El Crucero, and beyond, a broad expanse of marshy forest; they popped out of the mountains barely fifty meters above trees that rose like giant flowered broccoli stalks in the tangled understories of jungle. One could see the burden of water in the air. The pilot followed one of the rivers that streamed out of the mountains. "Hey," Arias called to Palma, "there's the Mission." He slowed the Helobras and swung it around as they came upon a small cluster of structures covered with blue tin roofs. As Krylov watched, a squad of buzzards, startled by the flying machine, ran across the blue metal and hopped into the air. Arias kept the machine almost at the hover, easing down toward the barren clearing between the buildings, touching his skids almost imperceptibly to the raw, puddled clay. At first, Krylov saw no signs of life beyond the odd chickens pecking their way between freeforms of rainwater, and a thin dog that crept miserably from one patch of high ground to another. Then a door in the central, cross-shaped building opened and a man and woman emerged into the clearing. They were dressed like Bulgarian peasants, their drab attire electrified with a splash of color, he in khaki cutoffs and a vest badged with bright appliqué, she in a sleeveless sack covered with tiny blue flowers, except for a panel of primary colors like bright weeds in a garden. Krylov could see she was too thin and rather plain, her mouse-colored hair skimpily plaited in a stingy braid, her face merely gashed with eyes and mouth, like a scarecrow, seemingly without lids or lips, and a nose as sharp as Kosima Wagner's. The man with her stared unblinkingly at the helicopter with blue eyes. He was ascetically thin, mustached, his blonde hair thinning to pink patches of scalp, his complexion a pale sea for small, maroon islands. At first glance, they had the sickly, outcast aspect of lepers, but, looking more carefully, Krylov saw in them the odd complacency he had seen in the ruins after an earthquake—the complacency of survivors. And something else: they seemed to share a joke; he could see a species of inner mirth at work in their faces, as though at any moment they might fall down laughing. Their hands groped together and intertwined conspiratorially. "Who are they?" he asked on the intercom, conscious that he was inclined to whisper.

"The Petersons," said Arias as he powered down. "Missionaries. I like to drop in, see if they need anything." Then, as if that had been a lie, he added, "Congreve asked me to stop, said Peterson had something nice for him."

"What?"

Arias shrugged. "Got me. I don't ask." He unstrapped himself and opened his door. "Don't touch anything, okay?" He stepped down into the muck of the clearing, ducking as he

picked his way along the harder ground beneath the idling rotor. The pair greeted him, and the man, after a short exchange,
went back into the house for a moment, emerging a moment
later with what looked like a shoebox, which he handed to the
pilot. Like actors closing a tableau, the three exchanged a few
more words, then Arias started back toward the *Esquilo.*
"What's the matter with them?" Krylov asked Palma.

"Who knows. We were their guests on the American Thanksgiving. Now they have lost their hospitality."

"They look as if they'd lost more than that."

"They are North Americans," said Palma.

"That doesn't explain much."

"I find it usually explains everything, Mr. . . . Hobbs."

Arias climbed back into the Helobras and placed the shoebox
on Krylov's side of the cabin, then put on his headset. He
waved one last time to the couple, who responded with a slight
gesture of good-bye. Then Arias brought the power up and
pulled the helicopter out of the clearing. Neither man nor
woman moved to escape the blast of hot air and muddy spray,
but seemed hypnotized by the rising machine. "What's in the
box?" asked Krylov.

"Something nice was all Congreve told me."

"A piece of a falling star," said Palma.

"Maybe," Arias replied. "It's heavy, whatever he put in
there."

Krylov reached down and hefted the box, then handed it
back to Palma. He didn't want a piece of a falling star sitting
there between his legs. Palma said, "Peterson promised Congreve a piece of the meteorite. Perhaps he found one."

"Or maybe it's a fruit cake, for Christmas," said Arias, chuck-
ling. He put the nose down and steered them out across the
river, climbing very slowly. "Fruit cake'd be just the thing,
cause those people are crazy." Then, with a pilot's reflex toward
tidying up thoughts with dark humor, he added, "Maybe they
caught something off that dead monkey."

"What dead monkey?" Krylov wanted to know.

"Ask Dr. Goodpasture," said Palma, and Krylov heard a cau-
tioning note in it for Arias. "It is his story, not ours."

"Goodpasture was screwing the wife," Arias put in, ignoring Palma's signal, or perhaps missing it.

Ah, thought Krylov: the earthquake; *that* was what they had survived.

"We saw them that night. Old Congreve put on the landing lights, man, you should of seen it." He laughed excitedly, like a boy. "He says, 'Hey, Doc-tor, you showin her your dead monkey?'" The *Esquilo* yawed as its commander shook with laughter. Then, sobering, he added, "Course, Goodpasture just went on to that blonde cunt."

"Arias," Palma said, his voice dangerous with exaggerated patience, "leave it."

Krylov thought it had to do with the blonde.

"Okay, okay." He climbed the helicopter above the trees and cut across the loops of the meandering stream. "Rio Chipirirri," he told Krylov, nodding down at the brown curls of water. "Piss in the river here and they smell you next year in Belem." Then, "Here's the station."

He slowed the Helobras and got its nose up, then beat his way toward an overgrown clearing between the muddy river, where Krylov saw a Zodiac tied up at a grey ruin of a pier and a scatter of derelict frame buildings. "I don't think anybody's here," said Arias as he set up the landing with great care, almost with his tongue seized between his teeth in concentration. Krylov could not look at him, so hard was the pilot fighting the impulse to flip over on his back. Instead, he watched the approaching station, thinking that this was a lost world after all. On one of the metal roofs he made out a faded insignia with the white letters AMECOS bleached out of a rondel made of spiralling blue and green arrows. Ancient history, thought Krylov. He remembered Amecos; they had got some of the technical papers having to do with radioactive tracer experiments. But the project had been a joke—not even environmentalists had believed it accomplished anything. Perhaps it had been intended only to devour a small surplus of money discovered somewhere in the American government's budget. But all it had left behind was this sad, transient ruin in the rainforest. Christ, he thought, it's like landing in Panama after the French gave up.

The skids of the *Esquilo* touched down and the machine rocked to a halt. Arias left the rotor at idle while Palma opened one of the side doors. Krylov got down, feeling the wet clay beneath the grass suck at him. He reached back to shake hands with the pilot, and picked up his cases. "Thanks for the lift," he yelled at Palma over the sound of the turbines. Palma nodded humbly and Arias gave a thumbs up. Krylov waved and backed away with his cases until he stood on the other side of the helipad's painted circle, and watched while the craft leapt back into the sky. He watched it flutter down the river, watched it out of sight, and when he could only hear the beat of its rotors he still did not move immediately.

Krylov had never felt more alone. A wave of bird and monkey chatter flew from the trees, and the insects, quiet while the flying machine was there, renewed their song. In the distance, a distressed howler monkey marked his location with a series of explosive barks, evoking all that was mindless in the world. Not even in Afghanistan had Krylov felt more isolated from his kind; he experienced a sudden irrational loneliness, as though he were the last of his species. He waited for someone to come out of the dilapidated buildings, but the place remained deserted and still. Perhaps, he thought, Goodpasture had already analyzed their problem. Perhaps they had evacuated the site. Perhaps Goodpasture had been killed by gamma rays. Krylov squeezed his eyes shut. For all he knew, he had just spent twenty minutes within two meters of a powerful source of ionizing radiation—or a fruit cake. He had come to a place of mad incongruities. Now, for all he knew, he stood in a radiation field strong enough to kill him. Resolutely unafraid of the atom, Krylov nevertheless went cold to his center. The moment held unexpected terror in the way that sleep holds the potential for terrifying dreams. He did not want to move, or breathe, or look about him at the desolation of the station. The tissues of his body dumbly soaked up gamma; it was as though he had stepped in his sweat-soaked clothing into a shattered reactor hall, where neutrons zipped through his very cells, and each breath coated his lungs with poison. Watching himself from some more distant perspective—forcing himself to do so—he saw a large, sweaty animal, paralyzed by unaccustomed fear, by superstition, really, for he had no knowledge there was radiation here. For all you know, he told himself carefully, this place is as clean as the beach at Angra dos Reis. How can you be afraid of radiation you have not yet detected? This is not the wrecked hall at Chernobyl. Here you are simply at the zero point, you know nothing. You are afraid . . . of *nothing*. Like a chastened serpent, his fear slithered away from him, his head cleared. And, as if courage had been a condition for life in this empty place to resume, a door opened in the main bungalow and an Indian girl stepped into the grasses, watching Krylov like a wary animal. "Dr. Goodpasture? Is he here?" he asked in Spanish.

The girl shook her head.

"Then, where is he?"

"There," she called back to him in a shy child's voice. "There." She pointed toward the dark wall of trees that rose around the rim of the clearing.

"May I put my bags in the house?"

"Yes, why not?"

"And then you will take me to him?"

"Yes, why not?"

7

Goodpasture started from his fitful nap, listening to the forest. For a moment he thought he'd heard a human voice, but now there was nothing but the platform creaking like a wooden ship in the light wind, his branch rubbing its fellows, the sigh of lianas as they stretched and slackened between the canopy trees. "Teejay?" he asked the bright glare of sunlight that darted through the rounded leaves of the rosewood. The sound of her name caused his heart to rise, to thump happily, as his body remembered the great compliment of her love-making. "I'll always do everything I can for anyone I'm with," she had murmured to him once, evoking a hated legion of Others who had shared extraordinary favors. "But, well, Doc, you . . . *you* . . ." and she left it unsaid, left him happy as a sandboy with his environmental girl. He had not once dreamed of Patricia in the days while Teejay was with him, and afterward when he had at last experienced those dreams there had been no anxiety in them, or much of anything else. He thought he had begun to fear for Patricia in his sleep because of what the Fall had brought into his forest. Fear for her, for everything. "Teejay?" he asked.

But, no, she had gone back over to Congreve's *finca,* he remembered now. "You're not the only one with work to do, Doc," she'd told him, then talked far too much about the evil defoliant called Spike. He had wanted to say, we've got bags of ionizing radiation here, and you're worried over Spike. Except

. . . he had decided not to tell her about the blue grains that Collins wrote were cesium 137, "in a queer form." He had not wished to stampede her, or have her cause Congreve to take some crazily destructive action when he realized what the radiation must be doing to his product. Instead, Goodpasture had quietly turned the event into a research project. As his continued foraging had turned up further signs of the Fall—a few heat-fused shards of what looked to him like the fired chondritic rock of meteorites, more of the luminous grains—he had installed fine nets to catch dead leaves and seeds, marked and numbered trees where cesium was found, wrapped their ripening fruit and blooming flowers in gauze to catch their seeds and pollen, searched like a hungry ant for infected animals: a howler monkey, the blue stuff glimmering in the red fur, hair loss, vomiting, hemmorhage, death; a sloth seared by the blue grains trapped in its fungified fur, but too deeply immersed in equanimity to die of radiation poisoning. The birds gave no sign, but bravely preened away Death itself, expressionless behind their beaked masks; he admired their courage most unscientifically. The reptiles and amphibians seemed not to know anything was wrong, although he had seen a tree boa with blue grains festering in its leaf-colored skin. He had dispatched the dead cebus and buried the tub of water he was using for storage more deeply in the ground, so that it sat at the bottom of six feet of water, with the blue grains sprinkled on its white base. He put the newly found cesium in there, gradually amassing a handful of the stuff. Although the station was not visible from the platform, at night he could just discern the ghostly Cherenkov glow, dreamily formless, dangerous, as beautiful as stars. "It must be," he murmured abstractedly to himself now, "a kind of life."

"*Goodpasture!*"

There it was again, the voice that had awakened him. A man's voice, rising from the gloomy, littered world of shadows beneath the canopy. Goodpasture pushed himself up on his pallet, one arm waving aside the cloying shroud of mosquito netting. Finally in motion, he felt a powerful inertia tug at him, one that seemed more massive every day. He was not convinced it was the radiation beginning to slow him down. It could be too much sex, or too much vodka. But it simply couldn't be the bloody radiation. His brain worked too well, his project had taken too sharp a form, for there to be anything like *that* wrong with him.

"Goodpasture!"

"Yes," he cried out angrily. *"Yes, yes, YES."* He stood up and went onto the platform, leaned out over the rail, careful not to disturb a leafcutter highway that had sprung up overnight, with empty ants scurrying out, the others, like fiery boats with tattered green sails, tacking toward home. Rosa appeared in the shadows, wearing her Washington Redskins T-shirt, her face raised to him. As always, the sight of her produced a flicker of guilt—he really must spend more time with the girl. Next to her was the stranger who kept calling his name, a big bloke in khakis and a white shirt with the sleeves rolled up above the elbows, the way Russians always did in summer. He was all sweat, his large round face uplifted like Rosa's toward the platform. Goodpasture supposed this was the Canadian Collins had written about, the astronomer named Hobbs. "What is it?" he yelled at the watching figure.

"I am Hobbs," the man replied. He had a fine, strong voice, Goodpasture thought, wondering if he could sing. "Collins sent me."

"I thought so," Goodpasture said in a voice no one could hear. The man with the bad news; hell, no hurry for *that*. "Come aboard."

The visitor shook his head, "You come down."

"You're not afraid of heights, I hope."

"We have a lot to do. You'd better come down." By God, he had taken a *tone* with him, hadn't he?

"Look, be a good chap and come up." As he spoke he lowered the tangle of ropes, sling seat, and *jumars* over the side. "We can talk better up here," he said. "The problem becomes more *visible* up here, you see." The man called Hobbs merely watched him. *"Really."*

For a time, the man said nothing. Then, in a low, furious voice, "I'll come up." To Goodpasture's surprise, he didn't take the *jumars* and seat; instead, he looped one of the ropes over one foot and under another, and began to climb, pulling himself up on the strength of his arms, then holding himself in place by tightening his foothold on the rope. A powerful bastard, even to presume to climb thirty meters up a swaying rope. Or a foolish one. Goodpasture leaned on the rail, ignoring the small stampede of leafcutters swirling about his elbows, and watched the visitor rise toward the light, waiting for this exhibitionist to fall. But when it was clear the man would succeed, Goodpasture went back into the enclosure where he slept and had his platform supplies, and opened the ice chest. To his delighted surprise, he found a chilled liter of Russian vodka still there. He'd thought that had gone the day before, or the day before that. He shut his eyes against the confusion of days, that and the prospect of having to interact with another human; most of the time Rosa was more than he could handle.

The platform shook beneath his feet and he heard the underlying branch protest the added weight: the stranger had arrived. Goodpasture opened his eyes. The man stood almost within reach, breathing hard but evenly. His shirt was transparently pink with soaking perspiration, and his trousers bore a bloom of dark moisture on the knees. He was as tall as Goodpasture, but powerfully made, early forties, one would guess, a dark mane of hair sprinkled with single grey fibers, and the arched eyebrows of an Oriental, or, perhaps, a red Indian. His mouth was full, broad, and held now in a narrow, mean line; his small black eyes glared at Goodpasture. It was a face, the Englishman thought, that would always be smooth, that would not crack with age. The man's two big hands rubbed one another as though independently, massaging the rope burn. Well, now we see if you hurl me into the understorey, thought Goodpasture, beginning to grin. "Welcome aboard, Mr. Hobbs. Joly Goodpasture, at your service." He extended a hand, which the visitor declined to take.

"Let's get on with it," the man said.

"Here now, don't let a bad temper spoil this. Shake hands like a good fellow and *then* we'll get on with it." When Hobbs merely glowered, Goodpasture added, "I mean, it wasn't my doing that you felt compelled to pull yourself up here like bloody Tarzan, was it?"

"It got me here."

"Yes, and just listen to you. Next time use the *jumars*, arrive in a sweeter mood. I wasn't being whimsical, having you come up here. Look around yourself, look at the light streaming down upon us, feel the cooler air, the absence of all those biters you get down at ground level. Down there you may get to see the fleeting view of a monkey's rump, or a sloth as a brown blob fifty meters overhead and hidden by leaves. You miss the life of the place altogether, except for the ants. Looking at the forest from down below is like studying the ocean whilst standing arse deep in whale dung, watching the crabs and worms eat detritus. The canopy, this sweet-scented natural cathedral you're in right now, this sacred place to which you've brought that great load of anger, is what my forest . . . sorry, I meant *the* forest . . . is all about. This is where it lives and breathes, where its flowers bloom, where it touches the rest of the world. Up here, in this clear light, in the hard-edged shadows all around it, is where you wish to be if you're a creature of the forest. Plant, animal . . . everybody ascends as far as weight and diet permit, everybody but the shit-eaters and undertakers down in the litter. Just look around yourself, man. You're more than ten storeys up in a tropical rainforest, and you've come a thousand miles to help save it. If you *are* here to help, then put away your anger and shake my goddamned hand so that we shall have begun properly."

Hobbs gave Goodpasture's hand a hard jerk, and returned it. "You do a great imitation of whimsey herself," he said. "So glad it wasn't real."

"Well, and so am I, Hobbs. Thanks for coming to the rescue."

"The sooner we begin . . ."

Goodpasture held up a restraining palm. "In a bit. In a bit. Now, tell me. How was your trip?" He sat down on a plank along one side of the platform, and gestured for Hobbs to do the same.

"Fine," said the visitor, sitting down. "They gave us ham sandwiches for lunch. The airplane was a Boeing. I spent the evening in La Paz. Have I omitted anything?"

Sod you, thought Goodpasture, choosing to ignore the sarcasm. "But how'd you come here? I was going to pick you up. . . ."

"Yes, I know . . . the rains. I got a ride with Palma."

Palma. "What, from La Paz?" Nobody would let a man like Palma walk around loose in the regular parts of Bolivia, "Terrorist" just about tattooed across his forehead.

"From Cochabamba."

"Well, the roads are all muck now."

"He gave me a seat on his helicopter."

"His? You mean Congreve's."

"Yes. It made a quick trip."

"Record time," said Goodpasture. For a moment he thought perhaps he had heard the aircraft landing, although it was hard to say: he'd been napping. Maybe he had dreamed it. Hell, maybe he was dreaming right now.

Hobbs peered out across the high branchings of the trees, the pillars of mid-day light beating down into the gloom below. "We stopped at the Mission," he said.

Goodpasture's heart gave a ripple of excitement that shamed him, and for a moment he went giddy with memory, longing to hear some word of Patricia, the woman who persisted as a jagged hole where something had been ripped out of his life. "And . . . how were they keeping?" He had driven the Rover by on a dry day a week ago. They had emerged from the Vicarage at the sound of his engine. Elmer had peered miserably in his direction before she turned him away, she in a full white skirt that, to Goodpasture, had made her light and beautiful. Their hands groped together, demonstrating solidarity. Had such a show been necessary? Perhaps, for Elmer, he'd decided. Still, his heart had kept heavy as a tungsten plug in his chest. He had begun to miss her. The prospect of enduring Christmas without Patricia was almost more than he could bear, and he had thought of packing into the forest for the holiday, or, alternatively, visiting the considerable fleshpots of Santa Cruz. "The Petersons, I mean."

"They came out to meet us. He gave the pilot something for Congreve."

"Ah."

"Palma thought it might be a piece of the meteorite."

"Congreve said he wanted one."

"That's what Palma said. The pilot, Arias, thought it was probably a fruit cake."

"Congreve had better hope so."

"The radiation?"

Goodpasture nodded.

"I find that part very puzzling. Why is this meteorite so hot? You'd expect them to come to Earth with some radioactive material . . . but I don't see what made this particular one so hot."

Goodpasture shook his head. "I have a flea's memory of an undergraduate astronomy course taken back when the most exciting thing they could have us do was celestial navigation training—and bloody awful it was too. Almost everything they now know had not even been thought of. I was taught a universe closer to Newton's than to Hubble's." He shrugged. "If I thought of it at all, I suppose I assumed everything out there," and he glanced skyward, "is 'hot,' as you say."

"Less of it than one would think. But I need to do some reading. My astronomy is not much better than yours. . . ."

"Really, and you an astronomer?"

"I mean, my knowledge of where fission is going on out there. I do globular clusters very well."

"I'm sure you do, Hobbs."

"And this little chat," the man went on, "is the reason I had to make that bitch of a climb?"

"On behalf of your bad temper, more like," murmured Goodpasture. He hadn't liked that astronomy business; it left a hole in the air between them, a kind of vacuum that plucked at you. Christ, why would anyone come here under a false flag? There's nothing here to deceive. For a moment, he studied the stranger, trying to make the man less the intruder, and gave it up. He yielded no more than the goddamned animals of the forest. Less, really. "The fact is, Hobbs, I've more than a little ambivalence about your being here at all. We've found what Collins writes is cesium 137, in what he calls a queer form, whatever *that* means. We've found a little more of it, and a few more victims, so we know it's serious. But, taking the other side, I would also say that there's hardly an animal disease that doesn't take more victims than we've seen here. Epidemics kill with abandon, not this silent, occasional death. That makes me think we have something less than the end of the world. At the very least, it gives us some breathing space. That's why I had you come up here to what I call Arachne's Palace. I wanted you to have some feel for the place and the creatures in it before you give us what may be supremely bad news a day or two from now. So, before you get out your gear and tell us we're as badly off as Hiroshima in September 1945 or, God willing, the victims of a mere dental X-ray's worth of radiation, take a few hours to look around at all of this." He gave an actor's flourish, a sweeping gesture that encompassed his whole world.

"Dental X-rays don't kill monkeys."

"Of course they don't. Most monkeys can't afford a dentist." Goodpasture chuckled and watched his stubbornly sullen visitor, willing him to laugh. Finally, shaking his head, he did. "Good," said the Englishman. "Hard to say what kills, of course. Three Mile Island, which caused great excitement, excreted just a tiny whiff of radioactive stuff. No one was hurt, no lives were shortened. . . ."

"Unless you count the nuclear industry's."

"Yes, unless you count them. Chernobyl killed only about thirty people right off the bat . . . neglecting many-headed calves and lost fetuses, and a presumed increase in cancer incidence, it isn't much death and destruction for a failure of that magnitude. Chernobyl gives me hope."

"Then you can get hope from anywhere."

"Not really. Not from Goiânia."

"No, that's the one that scares."

"It was 1988?"

"No, it was September 1987. A radiotherapy machine's cesium-137 source got loose in the community. You know how much cesium was involved, Goodpasture?"

"Not much."

"About three and a quarter ounces, packed into two cubic inches of space." Hobbs stared out across the middle storey of treetops, black and dark green in the splotches of sunlight raining through the canopy. "It killed four straight out," he said.

"Then the government stepped in, Brazil, the Agency in Vienna, and began to obliterate the contaminated sites."

"I've found more than that much already," Goodpasture ventured in a low voice.

"Where do you keep it?"

He had to hand it to Hobbs, the man was a cool customer. Christ, he might be sitting on a little pile of cesium right now, and yet he refused to give the slightest sign of his discomfort. "I've improvised a storage pond over by the station. A Teflon basin dug into the earth, submerged in several feet of water. The Amecos chaps . . . do you know about Amecos?" Hobbs nodded. "Well, that puts you in a select company indeed. Anyway, that lot took their Geigers home with them, so we haven't a clue to what the radiation is really like. But I think it's contained where I have it. You can bring Polaroid film right up to it without it's getting fogged."

"At Oak Ridge, they used to store stuff in a pond. Twenty years or so later they discovered it drained into the Mississippi and Gulf of Mexico."

"You're saying I could be fouling the entire nest with this amateur bungling. But that's why you came."

"A friend explained to me recently that I really don't know why I came, Goodpasture." He stood up, calm now, ready to work. "My tour will keep. Let's get to work while we have some light. Exposure times are very important."

"Ah, I know that, I do know that. But the thing is, Hobbs, the bad news you're going to get from those instruments of yours could be so bad, so bloody, *bloody* bad, that all of this will have to be destroyed." He waved sadly around the dome of branches and bright leaves. "The trees will have to come down, the ground plowed under, the really bad stuff encased in concrete . . . the sort of thing they do to one block of houses in a village, but Christ, extended to cover a hundred, a thousand, hectares of forest. They may have to dam the streams to keep the stuff out of the Amazon, out of the Atlantic." He hesitated, biting his lip. Then, in a slow, deliberate voice kept tightly reined, "Every living thing for miles around here may have to be destroyed in order to contain your bad news. So . . . perhaps the bad news can wait one more day. Just a day. Then we get out your Geigers and whatchamacallits and get down to business."

"The way radiation works, Goodpasture . . . nothing happens, and then people begin to die."

"I know that. I know. But I also know that delaying a day is not going to kill you, or shorten your life. I've been here, Rosa's been here, for more than six weeks since the Fall and we've got no symptoms of radiation poisoning."

"Is that the girl I met?" Goodpasture nodded. "She didn't seem quite well to me. Have you examined her?"

"I'm sorry to say I have not. I haven't done much of anything for the people here. I've been busy trying to make this into an experiment."

"It seems to me that Nature has already done that."

"You think Rosa is ill?"

"I think you need to find out."

God, it made you want to wring your hands. "You're right, of course."

"Does she have a family?"

"I don't know. She was a gift." He could not bring himself to tell a stranger that the girl was likely his daughter, his only child, whom he kept here, in the midst of lethal radiation.

"We'll start first thing in the morning?"

Goodpasture nodded.

"Then I can wait."

"When we know where we are, Hobbs, I want us to figure a way to contain it. The thing is, I know with every cell of my body that radiation is not going to wreck the ecosystem. A marvelously strong creation, is the tropical rainforest. Oh, things will change, there will be tapirs born with two heads, Siamese twins, legged snakes, and other sports. The plants will change their strategies a little, adapting to a slightly altered environment. But this stuff from the meteorite is not the end of my little world. I know that as surely as I know we're sitting here," he added. "*Fire* is the end of my world, Hobbs, fire and the fucking chainsaw, not radiation from some distant fissioning out there." He jerked his head at the offending heavens.

"I used to think the same about my world, Goodpasture."

"What, Canada?" How very puzzling.

"You know . . . the secession of Quebec . . ." Hobbs shrugged unhappily.

"You've nothing whatever to worry about, old boy. They'll never secede. Come on, now. I'll give you the tour." Like a performer on the high wire, Goodpasture stepped off the platform into thin air some thirty meters above the forest floor; his trained foot found the single, lower strand of cable, his hands gripped the two higher ones for balance, and he set out, one foot following the other. It was the most frightening thing he had ever done, but he had come to love it, much, he believed, as a bird begins to love the terrible fall that ends in flight. Twisting around, he watched Hobbs follow him into the air, another flying man.

"It's in the hips, you see," he called back to Hobbs. "A step out," the line sagging under him, "the opposite hand out on one side, then another step," again, the line sagging, "an opposite hand advances, all rather like the tango."

"Too bad you don't have music." The voice was preoccupied with making headway along the cable, but Goodpasture heard no fear of falling in it. Perhaps astronomers became immune to such things, crawling around those huge domes and telescopes in utter darkness.

"First time?"

"First time what? Bolivia, yes. And the forest, yes."

"Lovely, isn't it?" He stepped, sagged, stepped, sagged, his torso moving rhythmically toward one steadying hand or the other. "Takes time to see anything in the forest, even up here where the lives truly unfold for you. They're pretty much accustomed to me now, you know, old What'shisname, Heisenberg to the contrary notwithstanding, my being here does not seem to change the observations. I'm just part of the aquarium, so to speak. Never quite on speaking terms, but always out there trying. But at first you see almost nothing, because it occurs mostly at a scale much finer than what the eye has trained itself to resolve. We go around looking at a world as though it were an oil painting, and a Seurat at that, trying to make the dots into something recognizable. But the fact is, you have to look down and down, between the dots. That's where it all unfolds."

"What are the nets?" Hobbs asked, his voice rising and falling with his ginger steps along the cable.

"My experiment. If we have a source of ionizing radiation out here, we won't see cute animals falling to earth . . . whatever happens, happens down in their cells, down in their blueprints for future generations. Instead we'll see its effects . . . its truly important ones . . . in things like seed mutations. A body of work, it shall be." He laughed to minimize his investment in such stuff, although to see such things—to do real biology again—meant the world to him. Half-turning, Goodpasture watched his visitor make his way along the cable behind him, already moving like something arboreal, so that he seemed less the intruder, more the large creature of the canopy, like Goodpasture himself. Bobbling up and sinking down with each step, they flew slowly through the treetops, the platform out of sight behind them now, the only sounds, the subdued mid-day clucks and buzzings of the forest. The men became more ordinary with each jouncing step into the high branches of the canopy. Behind him, Hobbs had paused. The man had seen something and here it came now, the oddly sweet face of a sloth hanging from a cercropia, garlanded in the large round leaves. "Sweet, is she not?"

Hobbs grinned like a boy. "Very."

In fact, they were rather like boys, Goodpasture thought, boys bouncing on bedsprings, or spiders, exploring the ramshackle skeleton of an old wire umbrella. "Ready to start back?"

"Not yet."

"Let me know when you are."

"I will." But Hobbs was entirely preoccupied with the new world unfolding about him. You could hear in his voice a kind of warmth, a kind of affection, for the place—he would be no more able to destroy all this than Goodpasture was.

He decided to be silent for a time, and let the rainforest speak to Hobbs alone. As if on cue, a ferocious blast of sound flew at them from a nearby tree, followed by a booming bark that shook the air. "You know what he's saying, Hobbs?"

"Nope."

"I'm right here in this tree, he says, and I'm so wicked that it'll be the end of you should you be so unfortunate as to cross my path, so listen carefully and give me a wide berth."

Hobbs laughed. "The coward's threat."

"Indeed."

"But look at them!" A troop of howlers, led by a boxer-sized male with long rust-colored hair and an expression of indescribable belligerence, shook a fist at them and bared his teeth. In the background, the others massed like a group of small, hairy, stooped-shouldered humans, all pulling faces and flashing fangs, with the odd male letting loose his disconcerting boom of warning.

"At night they sound like kingdom come," called Goodpasture. "But they're pretty innocent. Just mobile composts, really . . . takes them forever to metabolize the leaves they live off. Of course . . . they're not all sweetness, either."

"Nothing is."

"Exactly. You know, people in my line of work go to extraordinary lengths *not* to ascribe the slightest rational intelligence to the non-human world. It is considered vital, scientifically, that they be dumb beasts, behaving in more or less predictable ways, just a few electrons drifting through rudimentary neuronal circuits. No thought process, you see. But then you'll see a troop of howlers invaded by a new male who takes over. His first act as emperor is to kill the infants fathered by his predecessor. But sometimes a pregnant female will come along, mate with him, and go to great pains to convince him that the baby she's carrying is really his. Meanwhile, we naturalists feel we must portray them as unthinking brutes."

"Not all happiness, then."

"I would say hardly any happiness at all."

"Then what do we care if it burns down tonight?"

"We care because . . . we come to love it." When Hobbs said nothing, Goodpasture turned to look at him, worried that he might have lost his footing. But the man stood transfixed, peering out across the upper storeys of the forest, the grand atrium built from pillars of hard light and opaque shadow, the flag-like flick of bright color when a parrot, or poison frog, or flower was suddenly revealed; and behind it all, the overarching tower of the rising storms of a rainy season afternoon. When Hobbs faced him, Goodpasture saw that the man had been deeply touched. "I say," he asked timidly, "can you sing?"

8

Rosa listened to the men in the trees, distant, excited, their voices raised in just the way Indian boys did when they played in the swollen, rainy-season river, exhilarated and frightened by drifting branches that might be caimans, or dead men, or anacondas; leaping away from turbulence that one could imagine being a cloud of piranhas, or a *puraque,* ready to electrify them. You never heard that note of high excitement from the women —you never found women high up in the trees like that, daring the forest or its other creatures. Squinting upward, she could just discern the thin line of cables that looped almost invisibly through a camouflage of bright light and black shadows. Off to the east, like something summoned by the men's play, thunder thumped and growled and lightning flickered in the darkening sky. The day's rains would soon begin, she thought, half hoping they would catch the men out on the thin lines, balanced high above the ground. Of course, she hastily amended, she wished them no harm, but only a moment's terror as a giant hand of wind shook the cables out from under them. . . . She smiled at the image, the two *caraybas* tumbling through the air, their faces no longer smiling, the excited laughter stilled. . . .

Perhaps she merely envied their easy access to the treetops. Soon after she had arrived at the station, what passed in her history for antiquity, the doctor had offered to take her up, but she had refused—it was another world, and it would know that and shake her into space, and she would fall and fall. Perhaps that had been a mistake; it was why he seemed to like her so little now, perhaps. The girl lowered her eyes, dizzy from gazing upward into the dappled glare of sunlight. She had never gone up there because she was not one of the small tree people who lived like monkeys among the lianas and high branches of the forest. And even they did not ascend into the canopy, any more than jaguars or tapirs did. Nobody wished to fall from that great altitude, to be impaled upon the thorny roots of a paxiuba tree, or worse.

A sudden gust of wind puffed down upon her through the trees, then, like a spirit, fanned out across the ground, invisible except where it bent the grasses, raked the brown surface of the river. She shivered beneath its touch, and coughed, surprised by the thick phlegm that rose in her throat. It must be part of the sickness. In the mornings she vomited, at noon she coughed, her body produced runny, ill-smelling stools. Clearly, clearly, she had somehow become pregnant, although she knew that, barring magic, she was still a maiden, if an old one at fifteen. She had kept herself for the one man who was important to her, for Doctor Goodpasture, who now seemed no longer to care for her, or even to like her. The child moaned softly, raising her eyes once more to the canopy. She would reward his neglect by becoming the Mother of God, unless, of course, she suffered an affliction that God had put upon her, the price, perhaps, of watching the doctor, of thinking about him as though he were a man.

She could just make out the flicker of movement on the platform, tiny figures, the branches sagging beneath their weight. They had returned just in time, for now winds arrived like great invisible birds, to whip the upper storeys of the forest, and behind them came a spray of rain. The gloom where she stood turned black as night as the sun was devoured by the advancing wall of cloud and wind and water, crackling with great sparks and the muttering of thunder. For a time she watched the two men where they clung like parrots to their tossing branch, knowing that the storm would excite them, turn them into boys again; they would drink together, and smoke cigars, and sing songs in tongues, and then climb down late at night, as gingerly as hanged men descending from their nooses, and the doctor would crawl into his empty hammock, still warm from her body. And it would be as if there was no Rosa, as though Rosa were only a person who lived in her mind.

The storm gained fury, and she backed away from it, turned toward the station, leaning forward beneath the torrent that pummeled the forest around her. On the outside she shivered with the cold, but she remained warm at the core, warm with a kind of worm of sexual desire that coiled and uncoiled, that moved about behind the rise below her navel, intimations of pleasure and need, which, as near as she could remember, God had not aroused when He impregnated her. She wished to be lying with the doctor, to have him enter his hammock and find her there, to have their bodies touch, his hands showing that he did like her after all. And more. She stopped and closed her eyes, letting the rain flow over her. Perhaps this was how God had done it, perhaps this rain was His touch upon her. Feeling hollow and voluptuous, she tore away her Redskins T-shirt and raised her volcano-shaped adolescent breasts to the storm, and kicked away her shorts, so that her young body, naked but for her scapulars, shone in the streaming rain. She was a woman, a woman with needs and desires, a man's touch, a name, a future —a woman who was about to have a child, perhaps. She had never experienced her femaleness so keenly, not even when she had lain in her doctor's hammock, half hoping he would come to her as a man. God had found her there instead. She thought her pressing palm could feel a hardness below the waist; her nipples stung when she touched them, scarlet and hard as thorns. The Mother of God.

Then, in the half-light of the storm, she saw the pool where the doctor stored what he called the plague stuff. The water suffused with light of the purest blue, almost a smoke of luminous color that suspended in the pond like a blue sun. She had seen the glowing pool at night, and been afraid of it, seeing in the light the work of spirits, *duendes;* but coming upon it in her present mood, it seemed only miraculous—perhaps the blue crystals were not the stuff of plague at all, but *had* come from the stars, as man himself had, and woman. Perhaps they were a sign. Perhaps, on the very night of the falling star, God had slipped into her somehow without her knowing and got her

with His child. Rosa squatted down beside the pool, partly sheltered from the rain drumming around her by an overhanging
branch dense with clutching lianas and bromeliads, which
waved like wild hair in the dark winds of the gale. She could
not take her eyes off the steady blue fire. Finding the blue
grains herself in the forest, she had rolled them into her scapulars, where they blazed secretly between her breasts. But tonight she could imagine herself diving into the glowing water,
diving down and down, and emerging with the blue sand
gleaming upon her body. She would rise, and the blue sand
would be as a face upon her, her nipples its eyes, her navel its
nose, the mouth below. . . . Rosa smiled. She would be so
beautiful that the caymans would gaze at her with stupefied
delight and the courageous *surucucu* would slither into hiding,
unable to look upon her glory. And when the doctor came,
when he saw her, he would know that she was the woman at
the center of his life, she, and not the scrawny *inglesa* at the
Mission, not the blonde *inglesa* who lay with him in the treetops. No, he belonged to Rosa, and for him she would become
Our Lady of Starlight, a queen of the Chipirirri, wearing the
powder that shone with the light of stars, where everything
began—that shone with the truth about her: she carries the little
son of God.

Even as this came to her, fully drawn, fully seen as a kind of
mental illustration, the rain slackened and late afternoon sunlight poured in for a moment between the storm clouds and the
sierra; another sign. Then the sun was gone, swiftly eaten by the
mountains, and Rosa found herself once more in the vast
shadow of the eastern cordillera. She sprang up and fetched a
hoe leaning against the laboratory building, and returned to the
doctor's storage pond. At the bottom, like sand, a generous
handful of the precious grains was scattered like a cluster of
stars on a white sky, staining the water with the blue that was
purer than God's. She reached down with the hoe and began to
scoop them up, raising the hoe carefully to keep the water from
washing the grains away. And when she had most of them on
the ground beside her, she mixed them with a thin gruel of
water and red clay and began to decorate her body.

9

The vodka ran out near midnight, long after the last faint light was shut off by the sierra, but the two men stayed on the platform, which still dripped with the afternoon's rain, the air filled once more with the buzz of insects, the click of hunting bats. Goodpasture looked at the northwestern sky, which had begun to clear, revealing a throw of brilliant stars. "It was just there," the Englishman said, "just there," and he gestured like an actor at the northwestern sky. "Just a few points of moving light, then nothing. Then, as though each of those had multiplied, dozens of them, descending silently toward me. I tell you, it was as if it came flying out of . . . I don't know, Victoria. Yes, your stomping grounds, Calvin, the old Dominion Astrophysical herself. You didn't send that thing flying at us, did you?"

"Not us." Krylov shut his eyes and thought of the moving lights. They stirred some visual memory that eluded him. "Try God."

"Well, and so, I fear, I do." Goodpasture laughed and Krylov felt compelled to join in, although the afternoon had left him somewhat drained and melancholy. He had been profoundly moved by his introduction to Goodpasture's aerial world, and by the likelihood that the Englishman might be losing it, as Krylov had lost his. He liked Goodpasture . . . well, he thought, the man is irresistible . . . and felt some kinship with him too. No matter the false Canadian passport, no matter all the old-chap Britishness, no matter their raising their voices in a few lines from *Eugene Onegin*—they were serious men. "I think we should go in, Calvin," said Goodpasture. "Rosa will have breakfast for us soon. I don't like to keep her waiting. I mean, she might vanish into the bush, perfectly capable of it. Although, God knows, she takes pretty fair care of the old boy."

Krylov stared at him across the darkness of the platform. He had seen her turn her face upward toward Goodpasture, toward the sunlight like a Catholic greeting Christ, and knew she would never leave his side. She loves you, he thought, and you are very damned careful not to notice it.

"But come, we have to be goddamned ginger going down the ropes in darkness. Come over here and I'll help you on with the sling."

"I'll go down the way I came up," said Krylov, unable even to think about wrapping himself in a harness of chains and rope.

"But the rope's soaking."

"I'll be fine. Go ahead, I'll follow." Give me a few moments alone up here . . . like a good chap. He waved through the lightening darkness at his host when Goodpasture disappeared over the side, harnessed like a paratrooper. Then Krylov leaned back against the wooden railing, his eyes lightly closed, letting the remains of the jungle night soak into him. With hearing that seemed to him supernaturally keen, he heard the movement and hunting signals of everything, just everything. Looking up suddenly, alerted to some subtle flicker of sound, of heat or vibrating air, he found himself staring into the eyes of a tree boa, the eyes flat and bored, incapable of expressing the snake's surprise at finding a man in the treetops; then, like a ray of extinguished grey light, it became darkness. A few inches from his eyes, Krylov could still just discern the steady stream of leafcutter ants, hacking away and sailing home beneath their ponderous sails, like men carrying houses, like Russian women carrying a bushel of coals on their backs. He shook his head, tired of being haunted by Russia, and stood up to stretch.

Goodpasture had opened his world to him on their long, careful flight through the canopy on the cable web. "Look," the Englishman would say, and they would pause, Krylov trying madly to see what was there. Then, like a scene resolved by a focused telescope, the subject would emerge from the background: an arrow poison frog the color of leaves and blood backing into a bromeliad pond to drop off an egg for her tadpoles; long leaves transformed suddenly into a family of military macaws, chatting to one another in their cheerful masks, like gentle people at a fancy dress ball; ants pouring out along a limb to protect their tree. "The tree gives them a place to live, you see, and a little treat beside," Goodpasture had explained. "Here, by the leaf stems, you see these little bumps. They are little hydrants of nectar for the ants. Shelter and dessert, then. The ants, for their part, keep the branches clear of epiphytic plants, and leaf eaters. A wonderful bargain, for all concerned. But the thing is, one has to wonder how the tree, the ants, these things we regard as utterly without intelligence, negotiated this elaborate bargain in the first place. Ah, you may say, they didn't, it was all in the genes. Of course, how absurdly simple. But then you notice that some of the same kind of trees are not in the ant trade, and *they* don't have the little nectar bumps. How do they know? How do mother frogs know which pools, of the thousands of pools, have *their* tadpoles, of the thousands of tadpoles? In short, how does the word get around so well up here?" He had given the cable an angry shake.

Within a few moments, Krylov had lost all awareness of the halo of little bugs Goodpasture referred to as *bichus*, of the ponderous heat and humidity, of the foreignness of the place. At first, he had seen only the smooth grey bark, the leaves, the flowers. Then he had found himself only a few centimeters away from a frowning organ grinder's monkey, a serious pink face in a furry coat, studying him quietly before withdrawing into its hiding place of leaves, light, and shadow. He saw hanging bird nests overrun by ants. "Looks dreadful," Goodpasture had explained, "but it's another bargain. Shelter for protection. The birds build where they are likely to get ants, which keep the botflies from laying their eggs. Their larvae will destroy a baby bird. The flies are easy to swat . . . *there*, by God!" and he cracked his palm against his cheek, coming away with a small mess of broken black fly and blood. "So they may get others to do their egg-laying for them. They'll manage somehow to put an egg on the leg of a mosquito, for example, since they're so much less detectable. If you get a mosquito bite that swells horribly, it's probably a larva." He had laughed.

Their march through the air had taken them on and on, into the forest. Here and there Krylov saw mist nets for capturing bats, nets for collecting seed and pollen from the trees.

"The horrible thing is," Goodpasture had said near the end, "we don't understand the place very well. We like to say that diversity is where life is supposed to go. The more genes you have about, the more possible combinations. The tropical rainforest is genetically diverse beyond telling, which means that every little dent in the place wipes away a species. But, you see, we have no idea where we are in Nature's experiment. If diversity is where she is intended to go, why isn't the entire planet some variant of the rainforest, with zillions of species everywhere? Or maybe our system is wrong, differentiating species along trivial lines, like differentiating men by the growth-rate or color of their beards. So we have the problem of not knowing what is right. You find great thinkers who see nothing at all wrong with a universe intended to be populated by a single species. Peterson, over at the Mission, will tell you that species is *homo sapiens*. Others will tell you the virus is a stronger candidate: not alive until made so by the cells of others, you see. It can endure anything. But, again, maybe the Fall is part of Nature's experiment. Maybe she wanted to see how her pet viruses take radiation. Of course, nobody knows that Nature is doing anything, or going anywhere. She may be running under a full set of sails, but without a visible crew—a journey with no maps and no destination—the good ship *Flying Dutchman*."

Krylov had found himself extremely, intensely happy, in a way he had not been for what seemed years. Think of the Moscow winter, Malenov had urged. Christ, and here he had begun to wonder whether he would be able to leave this remarkable place. But it was not the forest; it was the plangent clarity of Goodpasture explaining. Krylov wanted to spend a year listening to Goodpasture; he wanted to have the place taken apart for him, piece by piece, so that he would have in his brain what the Englishman had in his. . . . He laughed. Coveting thy neighbor's wisdom. There must be a law against that. Then, melancholy drifting in like a patch of fog: that had been the Soviet game, coveting others' wisdom.

He peered over the side of the platform at the ropes, which dropped into blackness. "You may have to call the fire brigade to get me down, Joly," he called. A rich chuckle floated up from the understorey. Then, with an almost fatal hilarity rising to his lips, Krylov threw a leg over the wooden rail and looped the rope around his feet, as he had for the climb, and used foot pressure on the rope to ease himself down into the dark hole of night below the platform, a world with that palpably velvet opacity he had found in Afghanistan, when there was no moon and clouds covered the stars . . .

"ARRRH!"

The roar froze Krylov where he suspended, still ten meters off the ground.

"ARRRH! ARRH!"

A jaguar, he thought, or a howler, although he knew this must be something else. The terrible sound was not ferocious, and held no threat: it was an announcement of despair.

"AH, GOD, AH GOD!"

Sweet Jesus, it was Goodpasture! Krylov dropped the last three meters to the soft litter of the forest floor, the detritus soaked from the rain, the wet clay slick and sucking at his tennis shoes. He could just make out a ghostly light and ran along such track as he could discern, but carefully, not wanting to go down on a viper or poisonous thorn. Soon he saw the darked-out buildings of the station, their white sides glowing faintly in the fading night, and realized where he was. The light he had seen was moving toward him. "Joly, is that you?"

"Hobbs, my God, look, just look."

Goodpasture cradled Rosa in his arms. She was naked, the girlish peanut shape of her torso childish with small, conical breasts, her black hair streaming downward. On her chest she had drawn a face, using clay and the grains of radioactive cesium from the pond, a face that flickered insubstantially over her body, its Cherenkov radiation like St. Elmo's fire along an electrified wing or mast. "She came out of the darkness like this," Goodpasture groaned. "A frightening apparition, she was, I had no idea what she'd done. Christ, look at her."

The Russian touched the girl's face, which was hot and clammy. Her carotid artery beat gently but erratically beneath his fingertips. She panted softly, and the whites of her half-opened eyes shone. "She's alive," Krylov whispered, but he knew what she had done. Feeling the bony hand of death upon her, she had dropped in her tracks, like a wildebeest feeling the fierce paw of a lion on its flank; she had accepted death like a jungle creature, stoically as a bird, and would wait for it now. It took Krylov a moment to remember where he'd seen this same drooping toward advancing death, and then it came to him: she had lain down as one lay down to sleep in the Siberian snow. "She's alive," he repeated softly, knowing she would not be for very long.

Part III

FINGERPRINTS

1

The mud stopped their survey some ten kilometers beyond Puerto Patiño, where the gravel ran out and the rubble and idled equipment of the highway builders stood like the relics of a lost civilization in the drumming rain. On one side, the foothills steamed and heaved toward the cordillera and on the other, the jungle, great strips of great inverted broccolis, marched somberly out through the wet, grey afternoon. Krylov welcomed the end of their labors. The hard ride in the Land Rover was destroying the calibration of the instrument, hardy as the Cutie Pie was, and he thought that the pounding rain might even mess up the ion-chamber probe, mounted on an improvised rack on the rear of the Rover. This was a more demanding kind of work than being dangled gently into a pool filled with spent fuel rods and he worried that it might ruin the device altogether. Besides, they had got nowhere—you didn't survey anything from the road in a country without them. He switched off the electronics and pulled a tarpaulin over the extended probe, which protruded into the free air above the vehicle's roof, a large black pencil of metal connected to the readout unit by twenty meters of black coaxial cable, which Krylov had coiled in the back seat. "Bwana," he told his companion, "I go no farther." For the first time since Afghanistan days, Krylov thought he might like a cigarette, but of course there were none.

Goodpasture snarled at the Rover, then leaned his head upon the white-knuckled fists gripping the wheel, his eyes squeezed shut against despair. They would have a rotten time getting out of the muck that oozed like peanut butter around the uselessly spinning wheels, and curtains of rain obscured the roadway. We are like blind men on ice, Krylov thought in Russian. His mind had turned to the past, to the fine, harsh taste of a Gauloise, to the mother tongue. Soon, he thought, he would be a good Communist again as well.

"We're fucked," said Goodpasture, killing the engine.

Krylov thought of the Briton's steadfastly pushing the Rover beyond its limits, and rancor flared briefly within, like a match in a wind. "Maybe a new driver . . ." The anger blew out. Bad nerves, exposed nerves, between us, thought Krylov. He may become like those Siberians, so nervous they cut their companion's throat. Part of it was the radiation. Each day, according to his preliminary measurements around the station, they were getting more than five units of radiation, five rads, more than people who worked with atomic material were permitted in a year. An entire career's exposure every thirty days. In a quarter, enough radiation that laboratory rats began to die like . . . laboratory rats. He smiled, watching the rain. In half a year, enough to kill you, unless you're very tough. The very tough last a year. And some, mysteriously, don't die at all.

"Something wrong with my driving?"

"Sorry."

"No, really, is there? You can tell me." Goodpasture's face was flushed and ugly, the face of an angry child.

"Let me try to get us out."

"After the rain stops."

"Yes, after the rain." Krylov imagined the blue smoke of a cigarette curling up into the roof of their compartment, the smell of tobacco against the thick humidity of the storm, the chilled jungle air seeping through the metal sides.

"Trouble with you, you think the radiation will kill us before we figure it out."

"It could."

"You should go home."

"Well, that's just it, I don't think I can." He smiled for the Englishman. "That's just the problem."

"Dangerous game." Goodpasture's voice softened; his face

became the more familiar one, ruddy, narrow, and full of long, sad lines.

Talk of radiation was rare for them, and when they broached the subject it was usually with calculated dispassion, as though the Beni were a cardboard maze with animals hunting a way through it. They were careful not to identify themselves as the specimens, or to speak of the deadly flurry of emissions their bodies soaked up day by day. Krylov, who felt the danger more keenly than the Englishman, tried not to think about it; when he wondered why he had come to Bolivia he would shake his head and, as though answering Yellin's clever question, murmur, "To die." Sometimes he would shut his eyes and see in a kind of biological schematic the fight beginning in his bone marrow, his blood and nerve cells, his jittery gonads, and quickly veer away from such images. A man could scare himself silly.

More than their own degree of risk, talk of radiation evoked the night Goodpasture had come upon Rosa with that deadly stuff swinging between her breasts in the scapular, painted on her body. It had taken her a week to die. Without knowing how long she had worn the scapular containing half a thimbleful of cesium grains, Krylov could not even guess at the dosage she'd received. Enough, he thought. One only knew it was enough. It had destroyed the white-blood-cell production of her active bone marrow, so that even a cold virus became a foe. It had exterminated the friendly bacteria within that made digestion possible; every drop of fluid, every morsel of food, shot through the ruined, sterilized body of the girl. She seemed to bleed everywhere and vomited until there was nothing left to expel, and the copperish freeform the scapular had burnt into her chest began to hurt her terribly. She remained aware of her disintegration, of the loss of the long black hair she had never cut, which lay about her like dead vines. Reviving for a moment, surveying the vast damage to herself, the girl would ask, "*Surucucu? Surucucu?*"

"It means bushmaster," Goodpasture had explained. "All the bleeding, she thinks a bushmaster got her but can't remember when it was. The venom isn't just toxic—it helps vipers to digest their prey. You bleed everywhere, your *fingertips* bleed." For a moment he was silent, watching the stricken girl. "At first she thought the vomiting was morning sickness and she was carrying a little Jesus in there. Now she thinks a snake got her. Imagine old Cosmo making radiation sickness somewhat along the lines of *surucucu* poisoning. The red death. Christ, *that* makes it scary."

Krylov thought it was scary enough already, and knew the end had come long before Goodpasture. He had perceived her approaching death as he might have heard the pale horse clattering toward them from a distance. Rosa's nervous system poised amid the rubble of her crippled organs, then tumbled suddenly toward dysfunction, sparing her further confusion about a forgotten encounter with a *surucucu*. In a way, the men hated one another for the girl's death. Goodpasture mourned his neglect, which had let her put on the fatal scapular out of sight, beyond his help. Krylov cursed the hand, heavenly or otherwise, that had set such stuff loose in the world. I felt nothing, she had told them, nothing. . . . Even at Chernobyl, exposed men with twenty-four hours to live had felt nothing but a tingling in their fingers, and then their biology collapsed.

"We may have to winch her out," said Goodpasture, his voice flat and tired. It took Krylov a moment to realize he was talking about the Rover, not the girl.

"I can get her out."

"We'll see. We may need the winch."

"Whatever."

Only the day before they had wrapped the girl in large plastic sheets left over from Amecos and carried her to a pitifully shallow grave scraped out of the mean, rust-colored soil at the forest edge, shallow because, Goodpasture said, the rainy-season water table would fill any hole they dug. They had anchored her there with large stones and chunks of a fallen ironwood, and they had put the cesium scapular with her as well. She would be like a star underground, said Goodpasture, his eyes gleaming. A star underground. When they had finished her mound and marked it with a rough wooden cross and her worn rosary beads, the Englishman had put on rubber gloves and squeezed an arrow-poison frog to make a fairy ring of venom around the grave, then propped the clown-colored amphibian's remains like an unstrung puppet against the cross, as a warning. Animals big enough to dig would be smart enough to avoid it, he said. Now, grief sat upon the Englishman like a great, dark-feathered bird that would not fly away, and Krylov's own spirits bumped against despair, as though the girl had been somehow his as well. On the drive today he had seen her in every brown face, in every child who came begging. The girl, her naked body painted with radioactive glitter, danced eternally in his mind. All across the forest, there would be others, tantalized by the glowing grains, and quietly killed by them. When he'd mentioned this to Goodpasture, the Briton had replied; the jungle is filled with old bones.

Today, they had risen early, leaden with the experience of her dying, rigged the Cutie Pie and its probe on the Land Rover, and set out on their first broad-area radiation survey. Goodpasture had whipped the Rover down the faint track of bent grass and mudholes to Todos Santos, then south along the Rio Ichillo to Highway 7, the grand, hardtopped two-lane *autopista* between Cochabamba and Santa Cruz. He had driven at the snail's pace ordered by his expert, who hunched over the readout equipment in the back seat, and this had made their oddly equipped car more conspicuous yet as it crawled westward from town to town. The crowded buses blared at them, then swerved past, forcing oncoming traffic to drift off the hardtop out of their way, and now and then bands of children overtook them, a pair or trio of Bolivian dogs who even down here in the forest, Krylov noted, looked as if they had a good life. Once, creeping along Highway 7 toward Puerto Patiño with a gang of kids racing the Rover, they had stopped for traffic and the children had gathered about them. But then, as they saw the ion-chamber housing, black and lethal as a gun barrel, their faces changed, the open smiles became the closed faces of Indians confronting another unfamiliar object from Outside, and they had dispersed. After that Krylov had concealed the probe, so that when they stopped, and children materialized from the rough shanties along the road, to beg, to sell a comb or bar of soap or candy bar, to ogle the two big foreigners and their shiny, mysteriously technical gear, there was nothing to frighten them. "We measure the amount of dirt in the air," Goodpasture told them. Then he drew a great breath and announced, *"Muy limpio, todavia."* Very clean, so far. Noting the grey cirrus of diesel exhaust, they giggled at the *ingles.*

Krylov had bought four Double Colas, four empanadas, a box of cookies, and had handed over some metal bolivianos to a ring of children. He could barely look into their faces, so conscious had he become of the invisible poison in the air they breathed, so strongly did they evoke the children of Afghanistan, living sadly in their terrible minefield. . . .

"You should see your expression," Goodpasture said. "Who were you ripping apart? Not me, I hope."

"If I'm ready to kill anybody, it's me—for not figuring this out."

"We've only just begun."

"I hope we're not still saying that a week from now." Krylov cocked his head, listening to the drumming on the cabin. "I think it's letting up."

"You want to drive?"

"I want to get out of here without marching through ass-deep mud, yes."

"Why would you be any better?"

"Canada is a very muddy country." Not to mention Mother Russia.

"Well, come on, then." Goodpasture eased his long frame out of the driver's seat and plopped down on the right-hand side. "Want me to do the winch?"

"Not yet." Krylov started the engine and let it idle for a moment. The rain was abating, as he'd thought, and he could see the ruin of the unfinished roadbed, brown and gleaming where the water streamed off the clay. Goodpasture had pushed into this by taking the corner too fast, but perhaps they had sat long enough to have evolved a little traction. Gingerly, Krylov pulled the Rover into low four-wheel reverse and, using almost no power, nudged it back toward Puerto Patiño. Back, back, he willed the old Rover, which slithered a few centimeters, then a meter in reverse, then another. Goodpasture was silent; one could smell his fear of saying just the wrong thing that would cause them to founder. Krylov concentrated on easing the Rover back and back, as though moving it with will. At last the rear wheels scratched upon a gravel base. Krylov gunned the engine, and the Rover clambered out of the mud like a drowned man dragging himself from the surf.

"Nicely done," said Goodpasture, a pained note in his voice.

"The difference between science and engineering," Krylov explained, grinning at the Englishman. Through the thinning curtains of rain he could see women and children watching from mudbrick huts a hundred meters away on the edge of a burned-off clearing. "They must think we're mad," he said.

"I would have to agree."

Krylov nodded and backed the Rover around to point it toward the east. As he did, the rain ceased altogether, creating a deep silence around the two men, and shafts of early afternoon sunlight pushed through breaks in the low clouds. For the first time since discovering Rosa, since watching her step toward an ugly death, Krylov felt himself more or less at ease with the world, and sensed that perhaps the great bird sitting on Goodpasture's spirit had begun to stir as well. It had been just a day since they'd buried the girl, which was not long to mourn her; but a week's hard dying consumed one's stores of grief, and now, Krylov believed, they had used up much of the residue. He looked at Goodpasture, wondering what the man was thinking, whether he also felt some relief now they had pushed out of adversity together. Then, without saying anything, Krylov headed east, the tarpaulin crackling like wings behind them.

They passed through the wretched town of Puerto Patiño, a depressing clutch of mudbrick shanties with tin roofs, seas of mud in the ruined streets, closed faces and masked eyes in every doorway, watching the gringos pass. Beyond the road, visible through breaks in the forest, the brown rivers twisted out into the lowlands, searching snakelike for a decent grade so that gravity could take them down to the sea. The gravel clattered upon the Rover's underside as Krylov pushed the car along, through Rio Eteramazana's clustered shacks and squads of idle immigrants from the Altiplano, sombre and somehow defeated by the rain. At Villa Tunari, they picked up the paved road from Cochabamba where it left the mountains and turned east for Santa Cruz. Buses pushed by clouds of diesel exhaust darted at them, as before, honking aggressively before hoisting themselves out into the paths of oncoming traffic. The road carried a good deal of it, mostly buses and trucks but also a number of the small, worn-out Ladas and Fiats many people drove here, cars that made Krylov feel more at home. And there were the American four-wheelers with black windows and cowboy names painted in streamlined lettering on their hoods, following the money into Santa Cruz.

When they reached the turnoff to Todos Santos, Krylov pulled over to the side in a place where there were not too many watchers. "Back to work," he said, and lifted himself into the back seat, where he began reviving the electronics. Goodpasture slid behind the wheel and quickly got back into the traffic. Overtaking vehicles went by the Rover like attacking fighters, careening past as if beyond their drivers' control. Krylov switched on the sensors, resuming the survey where they had turned west that morning. The readout needle stiffened and Krylov felt the cold hand of an ionizing plague fasten once more upon his spirit. The clatter continued, enough roentgens per second to produce a daily dose of about five rads —the conditions of the noncombatant world after a nuclear war, perhaps. Without feeling a thing, the thin population in scattered shacks and *tiendas* along the road were being rigged for some future, imponderable failure: an increased incidence of certain cancers, trouble in the genes. But in this place, few would live to see the effects. For people whose lives were as hard as these, statistical distributions were banal indeed.

The needle held for another twenty kilometers, which took the man an hour to traverse. Then, as the Rover crept into the village of Chimoré, the needle dropped. They passed through the tiny settlement of mudbrick and tin, watched suspiciously by police and the idle men along the streets. The women, Krylov thought, must be out working in the fields, the children in their school. It was like home, where the men often had little to do.

"Rather lost its snarl," said Krylov. "Go a few kilometers farther, though. It may pick up again farther along." But by the time they reached the new steel and concrete bridge across the Chimoré, Krylov was ready to quit. "That's it, Joly. It's down to background."

"Meaning?"

"The world is full of natural radiation. Down here, where you have a lot of radioactive rock, background is relatively high, enough to give you maybe five-hundred microrads a day. At the station this morning we had ten thousand times that. A thousand times that on the road west of Chimoré." He switched off the equipment to conserve its batteries and leaned over the back of the passenger seat. "Let's stop here."

"Bad place for that." Goodpasture gestured at the river, still wreathed in steam from the day's rains. "Famous thoroughfare in the Drug War. The police'll pick us up if we stop."

"I don't see anybody waiting to pick us up."

"Very well. I hope England will fight for us when the time comes." He swung the Rover into a U-turn and brought it to a stop just off the bridge, facing back toward the river. "The notorious Chimoré," he announced, cutting the engine. In the silence that flowed in around them, Krylov heard the roar of the rain-swollen stream tug at the pilings. He got down from the Rover and walked out upon the span, conscious of its slight buffeting vibration in the flood. Off toward the sierra, the river narrowed and straightened, its currents quickening as it rose toward the Andean source. "Lots of coca grown up there," said Goodpasture, joining him. "Up there and all along the foothills, far beyond where we got stopped by the mud. It's the Chaparé coca here, grown mainly for export. Farther along, much higher up, you get the Yungas stuff, mainly for domestic consumption. Life in Bolivia requires a certain amount of coca leaf to be worthwhile. And it's perfectly legal. Just the processing that's against the law."

"But they process it."

"Oh, sure. The Congreves . . . you know about Congreve?"

"I know Palma gets to use his helicopter."

"Well, the Congreves used to run their business like family enterprises. Now they're more like their Colombian and Peruvian counterparts. Terrible thing, because Bolivians have a marvelous streak of non-violence that's rather hard to overcome. They're insulated from some of that ideologically propelled cruelty you get in Peru, for example. Hard to ignite them. Ask Che."

"Che Guevara?" The name produced a concealed shiver, the way "Behind the Iron Curtain" once had.

"He died just over there," Goodpasture said, pointing toward the low mountains to the southwest. "They caught the poor bugger half dead from illness and starvation near La Higuera, then flew him into Vallegrande and shot him. October 1967. I was teaching freshman ecology at Stanford and trying to get to the Costa Rican forest. Where were you, Calvin?"

Krylov had to bite his lip to keep from answering: Hanoi. "Oh," he managed to say, "I hadn't got out of Vancouver yet."

"My students got rather agitated by it all. Communism hadn't yet been discredited then. But I'd visited Bolivia and I know a gentle people when I see one. They've had some bitches of wars over the years, rather like Bulgaria, always on the wrong end of the martial baton. But only a fool would try to mobilize their sense of being wronged. You need a grievance to get a good revolution going, and these people think this is how life was intended to be. Besides, you need the ideology. They don't have their own Shining Path over here to give a revolution sense, none of that here."

"But you think they're importing it?"

"I think the Congreves of the world are the Congreves of the world, and there is nowhere for them to go but to the fortified estate, private armies, car bombs, and assassins on motorbikes. Even if they start out as good-hearted Bolivians, that is where they ultimately have to go to make their way. Maybe that isn't importing so much as imitating . . . following one's destiny." Goodpasture shook his head. "You know, I haven't been this far east in five years. I mean, you catch the scent of all that money and rising violence as you approach Santa Cruz. You can see they're preparing for war." He gestured across the brown water of the Chimoré. "Not that we aren't. Look."

At first glance, Krylov thought he was seeing an American firebase in Vietnam, and it surprised him not to have noticed the resemblance immediately. It wasn't the runway paved with a five-hundred-meter overrun at the far end, that angled toward the river—air strips were everywhere in the jungle. But in a crescent of clear forest, he could make out an oval of empty hardstands just off the runway, and buildings unmistakeably

fashioned by a military hand: seven low Quonset-like structures, guard shacks, a mess hall, a motor pool. Around the perimeter a wall of concertina wire had been laid down. But the
look of a firebase was only skin deep. There were no real fortifi-
cations, no artillery dug in. "Whose is it?"

"The American DEA, *day-ay-ah* as they call them here, Bolivia
drug police, some American military advisors, some Bolivian
army units. A dog's breakfast of drug warriors. They use Amer-
ican-owned Huey copters flown by Bolivian pilots to make their
inter-*dictions*," he went on, laying heavy sarcasm on the last
word, "and think they're doing good works."

"Nobody around today."

"Probably out persecuting some poor sods who've started
processing coca into paste . . . or into cocaine, for that matter.
It's *verboten*, but the *campesinos* still do it. Easier to haul a pound
of paste than a bushel of leaves. Mainly, the *federales* intercept it
when its ready for pickup, when the plane flies into one of these
jungles strips, or to a wide spot in a road. They're better about
leaving the growers alone. They used to go in with the helicopters and burn the fields."

"Palma would like them to keep setting fires, I suppose."

"No doubt. That boy really stinks of revolutionary intent,
doesn't he? A man like that, a miracle they let him roam about
Bolivia loose." Goodpasture sniffed. "Ignores the lesson of old
Che, does our man Palma."

Krylov watched the roiled water for a moment in silence,
then walked back to the Rover and brought out his store of food
purchased from waifs along the road. The empanadas felt like
dead flesh and sagged in the humidity, and the Double Colas
were tepid. "Lunch," he announced, and gave Goodpasture
half the ration. They sat down with their food on the edge of the
bridge and ate and drank in silence, like one of those married
couples, Krylov thought, who eat without exchanging a single
word. "I think," he said at last, "the bad radiation is behind us.
Behind us and out there." He gestured toward the river winding out across the lowlands. "I think it's mostly out there."

"We need to find out."

"We won't on the ground. The instruments can't take it. And
we've finished with the roads, which gives us data along the

highway and a couple of stalks off to the side. It's like looking at a piece of paper end-on. What I think we have is a contaminated area hundreds of kilometers on a side, almost all of it where there are no roads to take us into it." He rubbed his eyes, suddenly exhausted by the futility of their work. "I hate this job."

"Then quit."

"Stop telling me to quit, Goodpasture."

"You might take me up on it?"

"I might do anything." Hearing the tread of fatigued anger within, Krylov got up and walked to the railing to watch the water, and the deserted enclave beyond. "Too bad they're gone," he said. "We might get them to donate some helicopter time to an aerial survey."

Goodpasture shook his head. "That brings the government in, full of crazed good intentions. It'd be the end of the forest."

"It could be the end anyway. For all we know, the contamination out there is ten, a hundred times what we've seen thus far. We can't drive over the area, we can't walk in with the instruments. We have to fly it . . . or forget about it."

As he spoke, he heard the faint beating of rotors, far down the river. The sound grew and soon he saw a flash of reflected sunlight from the blades. "They're coming back," he told Goodpasture.

"It's not the Hueys. They always travel in pairs."

"It's Congreve's," Krylov said. The *Esquilo* fluttered near the water, keeping just outside the perimeter of concertina wire, and climbed as it approached their bridge. "Palma's aboard," he said as the craft roared overhead. He had seen—and, he was sure, he had been recognized by—the pale olive face in the left seat. He watched the helicopter circle and dive back toward the enclave, following the runway centerline this time, slowing almost to a hover as it crept along the paved strip. Nothing stirred among the buildings. No figures appeared. Little man, he thought, you must be awfully disappointed. The place was an ideal target. You could make a Che-like statement by attacking a police barracks, and this one seemed poorly defended—a mortar on the ridge behind them could lay down a lot of destruction. Machine guns on this high ground would look down the defenders' throats. Go in, shoot it up, damage or destroy the helicopters, and pull back into the forest. Krylov grinned. Palma would be furious to find it deserted. The man was ready to start a war and nobody was around to fight it.

"You know, Calvin," Goodpasture was saying, "old Congreve's a bit of a Robin Hood figure around here. Wouldn't you think he'd lend us Arias and the helicopter for a day or two, if it were for the general good?"

"That's lying down with the devil."

"The devil owes the world a living." He watched the *Esquilo* lower its nose and head down-river. "Tomorrow, we go to the *finca.*"

2

Teejay watched the grey, shrouded woman take away her baby, plucked from her arms outside the Newport Beach commune—one knew it was Newport from the blue line of ocean, the gulls, the baby blanket she had woven there, a pink woolen rectangle enclosing a large white peace circle. At first, the baby had gone quietly enough; but then, as something nameless and horrible appeared on its short, new horizon, its little face crumpled into a scream that filled the world, a single high note held, it seemed, eternally, of terror. Something—Teejay believed it must have been the screaming—caused the shrouded woman to hesitate, to look back toward her. The grease-green cowl fell back, exposing an ivory skull, as expected, which peered from its empty eyes at Teejay, then grinned with gumless teeth, and held up the baby for the mother to see, another skinned face of glistening bone. . . .

She awoke in a sweat, trembling from the reverberations of her baby's cries which, she realized now, had been only the shrill scree of the cicadas, which had begun their daily single-noted song outside, punctuated by the boom of a troop of howler monkeys, loud cowards letting the world know where they were. Teejay lay back, aching and nervous, and watched the flat tropical morning light flow across the high-ceilinged room, causing its white walls to glow and a woven Colombian rug to spring to life like a garden on the warm terra cotta of the floor. A rich room, full of woods whose grain seemed to descend to an inner vanishing point, as if transparent; thick curtains of forest-green cotton framed the lightening sky, as boldly flowered as the forest outside their clearing, where islands of trees stood in a sea of ploughed fields and rough meadow. From somewhere, cattle replied complacently to the howlers.

Teejay closed her eyes, thinking of the baby. She had dreamed of the child again and again, the woman from the agency always Death, the cry of terror always at maximum amplitude, as was, she believed, the undescribed horror that provoked it. She remembered the quilt, she had woven it for her best friend, Leslie, at Newport Beach. There had never been a baby for Teejay to give away—and yet, the dream had the unmistakeable texture of memory. She knew why. It was just as they told you; the protagonist of one's dreams is always oneself, no matter what mask it's wearing. The baby was Teejay, betrayed by her mother. And the terror? Everything, she thought. Everything. Waking up with your mother no longer with you, waking up knowing in some infantile way that you were not loved, not worth keeping. She wondered if that had really happened to her as a baby, if she actually remembered being carried off by a strange woman, or whether it was just a cautionary puzzle for her to solve. Cautionary, because the baby's terror appeared always as a warning of some closer danger, just behind some real, immediate door.

Well, she *had* come to a spooky old place, and to a spooky old time in her life, so of course she would drift toward the heebie-jeebies in her sleep. Somewhere deep within, her life had begun to scare her, although it wasn't any fear of Congreve or his boys or the cocaine or of being so far from her shallow root system of a room shared with Roger, who ran the Greengo anti-Spike project in Cuzco. Teejay feared no one but herself, and what that self might want. Maybe, she thought, looking around the room, thinking of how the *finca*'s main house unfolded, one white, beautiful room after another, I'm afraid of having money . . . but, no, it wasn't money, but the need of it. She was afraid of needing to have money. A money-needing person would find it difficult to say *hasta luego* to the nightly lines of cocaine, the dangerous sex, the shopping excursions to Santa Cruz in the helicopter, from which she returned wearing rings with real gemstones, bracelets of soft solid gold, suits fashioned from grey leather as thin and sweet as skin, silk underwear. . . . She moved her hands down her naked body, the small-breasted, always tanned thorax of a fit baby-boomer, as she thought of it, big rib cage for those diver's lungs, strong legs with peasant calves, a bottom that bloomed like the proverbial rose. . . . She smiled, touching herself gently where she opened. Amazing device, she thought. But her touch awakened pain within, as well. That goddamned Congreve wanted only her rear end. In fact there was a lot of anal lust among men, treating women as the old Greeks treated boys. She had begun the night wearing a short nightdress of silk lace, which was now a rumpled pile across the room, where Congreve had thrown it.

He had wanted to fuck wearing that horrible thing he'd got from the missionary, a charred fragment of some light, strong metal shaped in a rough crescent, the kind of object a child might cut from the lid of a mayo jar, except it was nearly two centimeters thick. She thought it looked like a piece from one of those thick, wooden children's puzzles of trees, animals, and moons. Peterson had drilled a small hole in one end and threaded a leather thong through it, which he had tied in a loop so that Congreve could wear it like a scapular. He already had worn it too much, for it had rubbed a chafed oval in his chest hair, an area that looked more and more like an unhealing sore. Teejay hated the dead, grey look of the metal in the light; in darkness, she hated it more, for it flickered with a faint bluish light. "It's part of a star," Congreve had whispered admiringly, urging her to touch it, in the black room. "A sign, the missionary said it was. An omen. And, you know, already I feel like a new man." The damned thing was unnaturally warm to her touch.

"What next? A condom that glows in the dark?"

Pouting, she'd forced him to take off the talisman and had thrown it across the room at her nightie. Angry and excited, the bastard had jumped her from behind, had poked her before she had a chance to think of some past sweetness that might soften her up back there. While he had her, she lay prone, her arms spread, her fists clutching the bedclothes, watching the freeform of blue light in the darkness across the room.

"Christ," she whispered, the tough nut suddenly feeling a crack in its hard exterior, the mush within . . . it felt like despair. There seemed nowhere to go, except more deeply into being this person whose needs gave her evil dreams. Her life here had become the odd rape, the residues of semen coiled in her backside, the electric memory of cocaine flickering in the nasal tunnel to her brain, all because she had finally become a money-needing person. She supposed she'd got tired of having two khaki skirts and a white cotton blouse and a cheap watch and stereo without a CD player, without that pure sound when she loved music so. Once she had sung like a sweet bird when she was happy. She uttered a small laugh of pleasure. She'd sung in the treetops with that Englishman, floating in his arms on tree branches that creaked with their effort, threatening to cast them into the darkness—not for him, really, but for being way up there, floating in black space. That aside, he had given her nothing, told her nothing about this "plague," or what he thought about Palma and Congreve and what was happening in the Beni. Instead, between sessions, when she had lain back against him in the night, he had teased her about Greengo. "Easiest thing in the world to love something as remarkable as a whale, my dear," he scolded. "The real challenge is figuring out why two such predators as whales and humans were put in the same ocean. Well, it has to be one of Nature's busted experiments, doesn't it? There are all these mighty contradictions around and here you Greengo people are lying down in front of cropdusters and driving rubber boats into harm's way. Not the same thing as comprehension, what?" Quickly now, she steered away from the memory of him, patronizing, deriding bastard that he was. Thanks much but no thanks.

Music still rose in her. She had hummed softly when Congreve had walked her around his beautiful house, and graciously, for him anyway, sort of handed it over to her, and she sang on her way to the fancy boutiques of Santa Cruz, her voice lost in the engine noise. Used to be, a long time ago, she had sung in the old stone streets of Cuzco too, but no longer, and not for her faithless boy. Roger had urged her to go with Palma to Bolivia, telling her how horrible it would be if Bolivia acquiesced in a defoliation project. But what he had wanted, really, was to get his girlfriend out of town so he could jump a new girl named Michelle, from Corpus Christi, thin, the color of milk, grand tits. . . . Teejay touched her own smaller ones. Too bad, fellas. Of course, she added, a grin spreading across her lips, she had to admit she hadn't been quite candid with Roger, and didn't care then or now whom or what he jumped. She had finished singing for *him* months ago, months that Cuzco had made as long as years. Across the room, a blonde girl in the flowered mirror smiled conspiratorially back at her.

Go with Palma to Bolivia, Roger had commanded earnestly, disingenuously. She had looked into his soft, brown-bearded forty-year-old face and willed her eyes to flash: *liar.* Then she had left everything—oh, God, yes, *everything* being a hundred dollars worth of clothing, a couple of books, and the rotten stereo—except a suitcase of khakis and her Nikon and boarded the Juliaca train with the small man in black and they had come over the Altiplano to La Paz. Palma had not been an unknown quantity or anything. They had known him about three months by then, after he'd come to the Greengo office to offer his help. As a healer, he had told them, as an Indian himself, he could help them verify the government's use of Spike on coca farms in the high valleys of the Ene, the Tambo, the Urubamba. She had found him comically charming, a little man in a cheap black outfit and white shirt buttoned at the neck, Mennonite plain, deferentially clutching a broad-brimmed black hat in hands that had somehow not been ruined by hard work. There had been something appealingly soft about him, something that feared pain in the deep, brown eyes, the vulnerable mouth, that made it difficult to tell him no. Driven by that quality in him, they had traveled together in the forested chasms northeast of Cuzco, and lived, to a degree that sent thrills of pleasure through her, the cold, wet, hard life of the mountain people— well, of healthy American visitors anyway. Wrapped in soft *ruanas*, their needs deadened with a coca tea, they faced their newly discovered world like comrades, together, she and Roger and their strange guide. Roger had begun to wake up with an erection again, but it was too late; Teejay had been seduced by something else.

Sometimes Palma would bring them to a coca farm that had

been blasted by time and neglect, or a fire, and he would point to the ruin and tell them it had been chemicals. The North Americans—he could not use the term without a shiver of hatred that moved dangerously behind his gentle façade; it was, she had decided later, his one emotional excess—were using Spike up here where no one ever came. She and Roger were comfortable with his claims; somehow it felt right to see what he wanted them to. But everywhere he took them, Teejay perceived the presence of the *Sendero Luminoso*, the Shining Path. She heard its proximity in the voices of villagers, read it in their frightened eyes; she smelled the fear that white settlers must have experienced on the land of a ferocious tribe. It had taken her some time to realize that this palpable fear was inspired not by something in the air, but by Palma—that he was himself a *Sendero* leader, once of the Ashaninkas, now a figure of great power in his rugged corner of the Andes. Few had ever put the legend and the man together. Hardly anyone knew that this guerrilla chief was the small man traveling with the Gringo man and woman, but she did. Looking into his neutral face, then, she had seen a cosmic indifference that chilled her to the marrow. He possessed the interior warmth of outer space. His eye had caught hers at that moment of recognition, and he had smiled, letting her know that he, not her own discerning eye, had parted the curtains.

Palma had arranged to have Roger, who never knew his guide's real identity, recalled to Cuzco, where, Teejay thought, he could put that erection to work. Then Palma had taken Teejay into the very structure of the vast *Sendero* web that stretched out through the forests and gorges of the high country, leading her as though she were a pet animal, something as harmless as a llama, but less tame: a honeybear or marmoset. She had gone with him into their sombre assemblies, where coarse ideology like smoke from smouldering coals lay upon the watchful silent soldiers, always, it seemed to her, poised in tense repose. She could smell their readiness to destroy in those gatherings, their fatal commitment. For Teejay, that odor had been powerfully attracting. When she reached out to it she felt through her spirit the addict's tremor. As though graduating her, Palma had drawn her further into his life, to villages where his men hectored, tortured, and killed merely, it seemed to her, to have their way with the people—to have people *agree* with them. And yet, she found herself able to find a kind of probity in it, although it was written in a language she still barely understood. She had seen a man of eighteen crucified alive, castrated, disemboweled, left to die wearing a sign that said it was death for anyone to touch him. A piece of resistance, Palma had called him. More like a loser in a medieval war, thought Teejay. She had seen Palma, without seeming to exert himself, without his expression changing, use a Spanish garrote improvised from a red bandana and a short length of bamboo to strangle a man before his stricken, silent family. . . .

Suddenly touched by a stifling claustrophobia of the spirit, Teejay veered away from such memories. One tried not to think about that side of what Palma called The Struggle. But, even wanting to with some deep part of herself, she never found the way to full belief; only the deadly gravitation that drew her. Back in Cuzco, she had for a time suppressed that sharp need of Palma, the need to share all that this small once-comical man did for a living. It was not love, she'd told herself, wondering secretly how it could be anything else; it's ideology, one committed person drawn to another, a kind of fit between two people. She carefully avoided asking what it all meant to him, beyond having the safe conduct of a lively North American girl— a *senderista* did not travel with blonde girls from California. If he had other feelings, he kept them in the spirit-chilling nihilism behind the opaque backdrop of his earnest, deer-like eyes. Now Teejay gave her reflection a rueful smile. Go with him, Roger had told her, and of course she finally had gone. By then she had been Palma's anyway, as bound to him as he was to The Struggle. *Adios, mi amor.* Good-bye forever.

So they had come to Congreve's *finca*, which the part of her that feared her needs wanted to leave, but which she could not bring herself to decline; no more could she move apart from Palma. "It is rich," she sang now in a clear, melancholy voice, "and I . . . I—*I* am poor." Once she had been a girl who meant every word she'd ever uttered, who slept only with people she could love, who committed to men, women, causes she found just without the slightest holding back. Then she had become another, lying girl, a duplicitous blonde discovered living in the shadows of that other, truthful, self. And now . . . she had become a money-needing person, a person committed to what she found in her lover's eyes: to nothing. She might never find the strength to leave this place, or Palma. The baby in the dream had been herself: money-needers gave themselves away to others.

An engine revved in the near distance, someone beating his way through the mud to the *finca* in a four-wheeler, no doubt. A carload of Congreve's gunners, boys in football jerseys, carrying Uzis. Or maybe some of Palma's gang, quiet men and women drifting in unarmed from their crossing points in the Altiplano, a long way to come for a fight. Except, there would probably be no fighting here for a time. "You have to understand that we are in no hurry," he'd told her in the mountains beyond Cuzco, speaking English, as they habitually did. "Our movement has no temporal dimension. And," and here he had smiled, "it has no center, it is hollow at the core. We are not a political party seeking office. We are a political force engaged in a struggle for minds, for the levers of human behavior. Our ideology offers nothing for those who would govern. It cannot manage an economy, it cannot even feed itself. But it is very adept at a struggle, at disruption, at foreclosing upon the success of others. And *that* is enough."

Teejay shook her head, thinking how odd it was that such a man as Palma, who needed nothing, had introduced her to great wealth. She gave a mighty stretch, her torso rising naked from the flowered sheets. She watched herself in the mirror across the room, the reflection like a separate person, remote, and . . . beautiful. It surprised Teejay, finding her rough self so pretty in the light, noting that her breasts were probably about the right size and shape and color after all, and that her hair shone like gold. "Hi, beautiful," she told the mirror.

"Hi, beautiful." It was Palma, and the unexpected sound of his voice made Teejay start with frightened superstition: it was as if her powerful reverie had summoned him, for he seemed to have materialized out of thin air. In fact, she saw now, it was more ominous. He had waited in the mottled light and shadows behind her bed, his black-and-white coloration as effective as a bushmaster's brown whorls against dead leaves, watching her undetected, reading her movements, listening to her thoughts. "Good morning," he said, stepping fully into the light.

"Just beam down?" Her voice trembled faintly, her hangover making it difficult to shake the fear that lives within surprise. Inside her, she felt the kernel of that other need begin to crack.

"*Cómo?*" A ripple of irritation.

"You know, from a star ship?" In a cartoon, Teejay thought, she'd be giving a huge shit-eating grin now. "You could knock."

"I could."

"Then I could slip into something." She looked at her exposed breasts. Christ, they were reaching out to him. "More comfortable."

"What could be more comfortable than nothing?" He sat down on the bed next to her, his leg a troubling plane of heat where it touched her flank. "My beautiful *gringa*." Hatred flickered like fever in his eyes, but she knew it was only for all North Americans. Still, unconvinced, her mind murmured, Don't hate me, don't hate me, a mantra of forgiveness for having come from California. Palma moved his left hand under the sheet and lay it on her belly, a spade of heat. As she had on that night when Roger had returned to Cuzco, lying naked with Palma in a frail shelter beneath the thundering mountain rain, she felt desire fan through her like blood in the sea, debilitating, febrile, the awful sickness of her need. It had been for that hand, that touch of heat upon her body, that exfluorescent wanting of this man, that she had left Cuzco and Roger and the rest of the world to be at the side of this little fellow, so serious and focused, so committed, and cold and cruel as the stars. "There is something wrong with Congreve," he said, his fingers stroking down toward her tassle of blonde hair. Her throat went dry with wanting more.

"Maybe he broke something off in me." She tried to produce a bitter tone, but could not; her definition, her outline, had begun to flow like melting rock beneath his hand.

"He hurt you?" She nodded, turning a little to watch him. "Where, back here?" The hand slipped behind her, cupped a buttock, then slid softly, yes, she thought, her spirit beginning to blur, and *deftly*, along the cleavage there. "Here?" She nodded, shutting her eyes. He stroked the hurt parts, murmuring, "I am sorry he does this to you. He is a pig about sex. But he is the man who will put us to work. Afterward, we will put a lovely naked statue of Teejay in the plaza." He smiled for her; his hand crept further toward her warm center. "Aside from him, you begin to like the *finca* life, don't you?"

"I like being rich," she said. "You're teaching me capitalism."

He laughed. "This is not capitalism; this is revolution." His hand returned to her stomach, stroking softly downward. "But I regret your lessons bring you pain."

"It's not so bad."

"Our host will not bother you for a while." The hand poised, she could feel its fingertips like warm dimes on her skin. "There's blood on the sheets."

"Maybe the snake's casting his skin."

"I think he has the plague."

"What plague?"

"The one the Englishman is working on," he said. She wanted his touching now, not his talk. Her body moved urgently toward him, forced itself along the stroking hand. "Do something for me?"

She nodded, high-strung, impatient. Anything, she thought. Sing. Screw. Spy. Anything. "Anything," she whispered, wondering, in a dazed, half-conscious way, how she had come to be this person. . . .

"What a fine girl," he said, leaning closer to her so that his breath touched her throat. She tried to rouse herself, to get her bearings: the auto engine had gone quiet, there was just the buzz of the cicadas out there now, a razor of sound slicing the still, hot air. "The Englishman just arrived," said Palma. "He wants to see Congreve about that plague. There is a man with him . . . he claims to be Canadian. When I saw him in La Paz he had been drinking all afternoon with the KGB resident. A suspicious person." His hand moved down, touched the outer petals of her rose, which awoke, engorged with hot blood; behind its unfolding, Teejay felt a vast sea of desire, hot and moving. "When they leave today," Palma continued, "I want you to go with them. Spend some time there, help them, make them happy, fuck them, if it comes to that." His thumb moved like an inquiring serpent, pressing, testing. "Will you do that?" She nodded, finding it difficult to breathe. "I want to know about this man, and about the plague. I want to know what they are measuring. I want to know why there are no helicopters at Chimoré. I want to know everything." His thumb slipped into her, his fingers explored more distant parts that were unable not to signal pain. "I want to know everything," he murmured, his voice filling with his frightening cruelty, the clanging hardness of his *Sendero* heart. "Everything," repeated in a rhythm that matched the slow rotations of his thumb, which seemed to gather her very being as a hand would a puppet's strings. Her heart filled suddenly with her dream baby's fears of needs she could do nothing about. *"Everything,"* said Palma.

"Everything," she echoed, panting, feeling herself begin to crack beneath the burden of her need of him, her urgent need to have him touching her, *in* her, causing a great wave to build and run against some imaginary shore carrying her swiftly along, and more swiftly, until she felt the swell begin to break, her body to yield up its ocean of desire, which then began swiftly to ebb . . . but no, he was starting her again, again, again, oh God, she moaned, writhing beneath his explorations, oh God, anything, anything, anything. . . .

3

Congreve was dying. But it was odd, thought Goodpasture—
he seemed to be the only one who was. His boys looked well
enough, their eyes the flat, reptilian ones of the healthy thug.
But something was killing their boss. Propped up on pillows,
Congreve wore the scalded look one saw in cancer wards, his
face unnaturally white with deep red trapezoids where the
skull pushed against the thin cheeks. When he leaned forward
to hack into a white bandana, his loose shirt fell open, revealing
an ugly burn mark on his chest, a sore that, Goodpasture
thought, would have a life of its own, like the bite of a spider—
like Rosa's.

The tableau had a distinctly medieval feel to it, the king dying of a mysterious ailment that would soon cause him to summon his magicians and priests from the hospital in Santa Cruz,
induce days of entrail reading and penance, all to no effect. The
long, narrow room with its high ceilings and towering windows
at either end evoked the nave of a tenth-century cathedral, full
of light. Congreve's broad rosewood desk shone in the morning
light, so deeply grained that it seemed to have no exterior. The
walls were covered with mahogany shelves lined with books no
one would ever read, and rich rugs from the East flamed here
and there on the tile floor, polished to a flat, rusty luster. The
place was wealth itself, thought Goodpasture, everything
wrought by some exquisite hired taste—well, almost everything. Here and there you saw something that must have been

Congreve's personal selection—a dreadful painting, garishly framed in metal, a pair of table lamps whose stems were kneeling porcelain nudes, the odd, clangingly bad touch. Well, it didn't matter about his taste. Congreve was dying.

Goodpasture glanced at his companion, the big bogus Canadian with those dark, Russian eyes. He'd be getting goosebumps about the amount of radiation required to bring Congreve so low so quickly. It meant that, somewhere in the house, perhaps in this very room, a powerful, lethal source was pumping out the gamma at them, drying up their blood and semen, rigging them for cancer, arranging a two-headed grandchild somewhere down the line. Russian eyes indeed, thought Goodpasture, watching the formidably relaxed figure. Krylov. The name took some getting used to, but he thought it must be the right one—he'd got it from a chance (well, not entirely chance) encounter with the man's official passport, the one issued by the International Atomic Energy Agency. Krylov. Goodpasture shook his head. Why the false flag? His first impulse had been to be guarded with this disguised Soviet, to probe, to find out more. But the man had been working so hard, and taking such risks, that Goodpasture could find nothing ulterior there, beyond the anomaly of the false identity.

"You don't get out to the *finca* much, Doc-tor," Congreve said in his sneering voice. Even feeling himself begin the slide toward death, he remained unrepentant. One had to give him something for that.

"We have an emergency," said Goodpasture. "That plague we talked about on Thanksgiving . . . it is much worse than I first thought. Mr. Hobbs," and he inclined gently toward Krylov, "is an expert on plagues like this. We need to do a survey of it, but we cannot do it on the ground. We need your help."

Congreve laughed harshly, and coughed into a handkerchief that had gone pink with ejected blood. "You need my helicopter, you mean."

"We think the plague covers a wide area."

"What is it, this plague?" Congreve watched him like an ailing viper.

For a moment Goodpasture made no reply. He had told

Krylov on the way over that he would be open and honest with Congreve on every point but that one: he would not call it radiation. "Once the ugly word is let loose," he'd said, "our control of the situation goes up in smoke. In atomic particles. The very word would put Congreve on the horn to La Paz and the government would come in, with help from outside, and dig up the whole bloody Beni. So . . . let's keep it just a plague. Plagues are frightening enough, don't you think?" Now he told Congreve, "That's why we need to make a larger survey. We don't know what to call it."

"What does it do?" He asked the question of Krylov, the expert.

"It kills, sometimes quickly, sometimes over a long period of time," Krylov replied. "You see victims with some hair loss, some burns that refuse to heal, some damage to the blood and bone marrow, and no immune system to speak of." Goodpasture shut his eyes, thinking of his lost Rosa. "Sometimes the nervous system dies first," Krylov went on, no doubt thinking of the girl too, "and the end comes more quickly."

"Shit," said Congreve, his eyes sliding off in reverie that, at last, Goodpasture thought, held a gleam of fear. "It sounds like that AIDS, man," he whispered.

"It does."

"But you don't get it from bending over in the shower, huh?"

"You get it from breathing the air," said Krylov.

"You think I got it?"

"I think you might."

"You think it's killing me?" Congreve's voice was almost inaudibly soft, and yet it seemed to Goodpasture that it filled the hall.

Krylov shrugged. Goodpasture liked it that he was smart around dangerous people. An interesting man, this secret Russian.

"Maybe I change the subject." Congreve coughed into his handkerchief, and asked, "What about agro-industries? What does the plague do to agro-industries?"

"I don't know what it does to plants."

"And coca?"

"It's a plant."

"No shit." The sick king gave a shiver of impatience and seemed about to say more, but a door carved with iguanas, broad leaves, and bundled spears opened behind Congreve's desk. Without turning he said, *"Palma,"* with such obvious pleasure that Goodpasture felt the others in the room vanish in the glare of the small Indian who entered, followed by the blonde girl, Teejay. Goodpasture was struck by the clarity of the man's hold upon her. At the Petersons' she had seemed to be merely a guest of Congreve's, and, given the reputation of the *finca*, perhaps a bit more than that. But now he saw her leash belonged in Palma's small brown hand. A moment later, he felt his spirits sag beneath a further realization: she had come to him at the station because Palma had asked her to. For a moment, his eyes met her green-flecked ones, and he thought she must have sensed what he was thinking, for she gave him what he took to be a bittersweet smile. It doesn't matter, it said. Goodpasture thought it did. He watched as she distanced herself from her man, exuding independence and courage and purpose. Too late, my girl. She was Palma's, through and through.

"Dr. Goodpasture," Palma said in greeting, without moving to shake hands. "And Mr. . . . Hobbs." Goodpasture heard the ellipsis of sarcasm and thought, Why, the little bugger knows he's Russian too.

"Hello, Palma," he said. "Nice to see you. Calvin," he went on, giddy with deceit, "this is Mr. Palma, a healer from Peru, I believe, and um, his friend, Teejay. Miss Jones."

The girl came over and extended her hand. "Hi, people call me Teejay."

"Calvin Hobbs," he replied, taking the proffered hand.

"From the funnies?"

Krylov threw a baffled looked at Goodpasture, who shrugged. "No, from Victoria. Canada."

"Ah." She looked at Goodpasture as if he had suddenly materialized there, and the bittersweet It-doesn't-matter smile returned. "Morning, Joly."

The Englishman grinned for her. "How goes the green, Teejay?"

"It goes good." He marveled at her poise. Without making

the slightest overt effort, she had assimilated herself into the pair of them, had made a trio.

"They came about this plague," Congreve said to Palma; it was as if the others in the room had disappeared.

"The monkey plague?" Palma asked, giving Goodpasture a look of impenetrable innocence.

"Yes," laughed Congreve, "the dead monkey plague." He brought up a mouthful of blood and spat into his handkerchief. "Don't make me laugh, man. Please."

"We need to run an aerial survey, Palma," Goodpasture said.

"And you can measure the plague with those instruments Mr. . . . Hobbs . . . brought from La Paz?"

"Precisely."

"But how do they measure germs, or sickness?"

Krylov stepped in. "I told you. They measure it indirectly. It is like taking a temperature."

"Ah, the temperature. So this plague changes the temperature." He looked toward the sky, already slick with the day's budding storms. "I had not noticed."

"Hey, don't make me laugh, man," croaked Congreve.

"They want the helicopter?"

Congreve nodded.

"But for how long?"

"Two or three days, once we get the instruments set up," Krylov replied.

"I think you should get the helicopter . . . and some help as well," said Palma.

"Arias . . ." Goodpasture began.

"I was thinking of Teejay."

"Gee, I'd like to help," she put in, smiling earnestly. "I've taken a lot of data at sea. I know how to read instruments. I can reduce data."

"I think we can handle it, just the two of us," said Goodpasture. "But thanks."

"I think you need Teejay," said Palma, looking at Congreve, to whom he added, in Spanish, "I *really* think they need her."

"Done," said Congreve. "Arias and Teejay will fly over to you in the morning."

Goodpasture itched to protest, but decided to let it rest. Without the helicopter they were helpless, and if having it meant having the girl with them as Palma's spy, well, then, they would just have to be a bit restrained. "What about fuel?" he asked.

"No problem—it's all over the place," said Congreve. "Arias can work it out after you talk tomorrow."

"It would be good to talk to him today," Krylov said.

"Then we will find him for you, Mr. Expert." He held up a restraining hand. "But, no more," he said, his voice barely a murmur. "It's done. You get the helicopter and the girl to help. And afterward, you tell us what this plague is all about. You have to do that." He coughed, then seemed to rally. "But, you know, I can beat the plague." Congreve turned to Krylov. "I don't see it killing me, man. The *selba* is full of secret medicines, and I got an ace in the hole." From beneath the pillow supporting him, he lifted a leather thong attached to a heavy-looking metal crescent a few inches long. "That missionary, Peterson, gave me it. A piece of a star, he says. A piece of something from *God*, man." He smiled with the complacency, Goodpasture thought, of the fatally ill. "So I don't worry much, not with this thing from the Fall."

Goodpasture watched the amulet dance on its leather strings, and glanced at Krylov, who had gone quite pale. The crescent swung in the air, silent, merely warm to the touch no doubt, no jagged rays of light or anything; and there it was, pouring its emissions into your blood and bone marrow. Christ, what an evil thing this radiation was. Just think how hot it would have to be to finish Congreve this fast. "I guess that's that," said Krylov, his voice tight and diminished. "Thanks for your help."

You cool, clever sod, thought Goodpasture, you're acting as though we're not having our balls singed off by that thing. "Good-bye, Congreve. Many thanks. You've been very kind." The man waved his arm in a Think-nothing-of-it gesture and Goodpasture turned to go. "*Hasta luego*, Palma. Teejay." A moment later he was trailing Krylov toward the Land Rover, finding it difficult to keep up with the man. But once they were struggling back along the muddy track toward the station, he said, "You got a bit peculiar there at the end, Calvin."

"Sorry," was all the devil said.

"Actually, I remarked on it in the hope you could tell me why."

Krylov shook his head. "It's nothing, leave it."

"I don't believe you."

Krylov looked at him with those extremely Russian eyes. "Did you get a good look at the amulet?"

"Well, you saw . . . I guess we were both a few meters away from it." Goodpasture grinned. "A good thing, too, don't you think?"

"Oh, it is definitely hot. But the material looked odd to me."

"The color, you mean?"

"The curve of it, the texture. I thought . . ." He shook his head. "It doesn't bear repeating."

"Repeat it anyway."

"I thought the metal looked machined."

Goodpasture wanted to speculate, but they had reached the first of several truly challenging oceans of muck they had to cross. "Hang on," was all he said. But as he wrestled the car he asked, "Not a piece of our star, then?"

"How could it be?" Krylov was quiet for a moment. "I wonder," he said at last, "why Peterson thought it was."

4

"I'd be a durn sight more comfortable with those blinds pulled, Juan. Wouldn't surprise me *none* if the Sovs'd started scanning our panes again."

"Where does it hurt, Ricardo?" Levy watched the autumnal dusk sweep down across the scattered buildings that seemed to have been carved from the ochre soil and rock of the mountainside, an avalanche of houses bearing Coca Cola and Argus advertisements on their exposed walls. The narrow canyon of the avenida Mercado resounded with small cars, Ladas and Fiats and gloriously ruined Fords and Chevrolets gasping for air, moving at what, by Latin standards, was a snail's pace. He could just make out the road's progress uphill, beyond the limp stars and stripes outside Domingo's embassy window, following the seeming fall of buildings back to their source on the Altiplano, the rim of which he could just discern through a coppery gap of sky between distant buildings. Going down, following the cleft of the old city, the street ran off toward the valleys below.

"Hurt?" The worst thing about Domingo's voice was that he had chosen it. It had driven Levy from an occasional meeting, so grating was its sound, its derivation, to him. Domingo had fashioned a calculatedly stupid speech in which an eager, servile note always floated, along with a steady signal of mendacity; and then he'd added a sleazy Speedy Gonzalez diction that hit Levy on the same nerve that portrayals of Fagan always had.

"Hurt?" Levy shut his eyes against the apparition he knew was seated behind him, cowboy-booted feet on the old maple desk, denim pants and jacket, a border-sheriff belly hanging over a big tooled belt, and space-age sunglasses, like two amber-blue holes in the face. Somewhere in those holes were two small black eyes with no light in them, peering out of a middle-aged face on which life had drawn no dignifying lines, or raised a beard, beyond a squad of straggling hairs that peered from the soft chin. Levy understood why they kept Domingo on: he possessed a kind of goodhearted cruelty, that rare ability to produce good-old-boy bullshit even in those concrete rooms where you took people to break them. And his Spanish was okay. "Oh, hey, I get it. But I meant *window* panes, man."

"Oh." Everywhere, he saw those sweet little *cholitas* in their bowlers and bright, many-layered polleras, distant within a brusque, simian manner; the sight of a *chola* woman invariably made him smile, with a pleasure that touched the Indian he carried within—the Jew's bodyguard, down here. For a moment, he felt a powerful impulse to join them, to abandon English for Aymara, to tear away his tweed jacket, paisley tie, and khaki trousers and run into the streets of La Paz—to struggle heroically to accomplish little, like those stoic men you saw riding old fat-tired bicycles along Altiplano roads that seemed to come from, and to go, nowhere. Levy smiled at the image; as it was, his lungs were sucking the thin air for oxygen like a pair of beached fish.

From what seemed a great distance, Domingo said, "That was terrible about Donner."

"I couldn't believe it," Levy replied. A pair of Bolivian dogs swaggered along the sidewalk; they always looked as if they'd just come in from a splendid time, like nineteenth-century Parisian gentlemen. He smiled. "I guess I still don't."

"You didn't get a chance to talk to him, did you?"

"Didn't know he was in town . . . until I picked up the paper."

"Jesus, that must of been some shock."

"It was." A faint headache had begun to tap behind Levy's eyes. He wanted this ordeal by Domingo to be over.

"Only reason he went north was to see you."

"Why?"

"We had something. I think they snuffed him because of it."

"They?" Let me guess.

"The Sovs, Juan. Evan just knew too blamed much. They got him out in the snow there, I know exactly the place where it happened, the boys and me used to wind-surf at Gravelly Point. . . . They got him out there and spread some of that white powder around to make it look like a drug killing and then wasted him. KGB must find drug killings pretty easy to imitate."

"The cold war's supposed to be over."

"It ain't over till the guy with bad teeth dies."

"Why'd Evan want to see me?" He thought he might have a touch of *soroche* after all. He'd get some coca tea at the hotel. They always kept some in the embassy mess, but he didn't want to ask. Domingo was easily excited by the discomfort of others.

"We got us a Russian down here, Juan."

"Tell me about your Russian."

"Few weeks ago, Joly Goodpasture asked for some help from a British friend of his over in Brazil. . . ." Levy listened somnolently, his mind returning for a moment to the night with Evan Donner at Gravelly Point, hearing the dead man's voice telling him the same things. "Okay," Domingo said, punctuating his tale and rousing Levy somewhat. "Maybe a week ago, this big dude arrives here in La Paz. Not the kind of person I'd normally care about, no drug profile or nothing. But the first place this guy goes after checking into the El Sucre is the Soviet embassy, down in Calacoto. We still keep some watchers on the place. I mean, we're going to have to fight down here sometime, and they're the enemy. . . ."

"Please, Ricardo."

"Yeah, right, just the news. He's there for, like hours. *Hours.* And when he comes out, he's got all this Atomic Energy Agency stuff with him. Know who he is?"

"Somebody's expert help?"

"You bet. It's Krylov, the Russian we ran into over in Brazil. But when I check the El Sucre, he's a Canadian, see?" Domingo gave a great beaming smile of disbelief. "Well," he went on, "it beats the hell out of me why this guy's traveling on a fake passport. I mean, he's got good IAEA bona fides. I can't figure it. So . . . I poke a little harder."

"A spy."

"More. A colonel in the fucking KGB, Juan."

Levy leaned his forehead against the cool glass and shut his eyes. Why would *they* be in it? What did they care? "Maybe," he said at last, "he's just another agent trying to make a living in quiet times. Things have changed, Ricardo. People are what they seem."

"Sure, like you and me and this Krylov dude. There's more." He paused for effect and Levy imagined a big, canine grin spreading behind him. The *soroche* was worse; the tension created by Domingo's campaign of subversion was tightening the screw behind Levy's eyes. He would ask for oxygen at the hotel. "About an hour after our Mister Krylov comes out of the Soviet embassy, here comes this little Peruvian guy named Palma. We can tell by looking: *Sendero Luminoso*, Juan. They're beginning to trickle in across the Altiplano, trying to get the local *indios* fired up. So we ask ourselves, how come Palma's in there with the Sovs anyway? And how come, next day, he runs into Krylov down in Cochabamba and gives him a ride in a chopper . . . from *Agroindustriales Congreves?* How *come?*"

Very wild cards, thought Levy. It was goddamned unfair, in these peaceable times, for the Russians to put in their own man at just this crucial point in the operation, unfair of them to come along and fuck everything up, as they were so adept at doing. And now, a *senderista*, ready to blow up the world in the name of nothing, teaming up with Congreve, the Robin Hood of the Beni. When they'd begun, back in the planning stages of Amecos, Bolivia had been everybody's first choice: the lines there were not so clearly drawn as they were up in Peru, there wasn't that ideological *violencia* to deal with—hell, as somebody reminded them, Bolivia was where the army had run down and killed Che Guevara, not to mention Butch Cassidy and the Sundance Kid. Now he felt a heavy malaise: they might be lagging events after all, even in this backward, timeless land. Behind him, Domingo seemed to whir like an electric clock, waiting to announce further evidence of cosmic interference. "I sense you have more," said Levy with some bitterness.

Domingo chortled happily. "You betchum. The Soviet resident in La Paz. Know who he is?"

Levy shook his head.

"Arkady Andreovich Yellin, that's who." He let the name sink in, then, "Ring any bells?"

"Russian impressionist painter?"

"Aw, shit, Juan, *you* know Yellin. Everybody in the business knows *Yellin.*"

"I may have heard of him." So goddamned *unfair.*

"Yeah, right, I guess you may've heard of him."

If I turn around, thought Levy, there will be this big old boy with his hands on his denim hips in ardent cowboy disbelief. "Is that what Evan wanted to tell me?"

"Evan was goddamned worried. Me too. Why'd the Sovs put a man of Yellin's experience and reputation into La Paz?"

"They do a lot of dumb things. We try to take them in stride."

"I don't think this is just some 'dumb thing.' "

"Okay, maybe they want to know why the biggest American embassy south of Mexico is in La Paz."

"They goddmaned well *know* why. We got a war going on down here."

"So Yellin's down here watching our war. Where's the surprise?"

"That . . . ain't . . . it."

"What do you think *it* is, Ricardo?"

"I think they *know.*"

"There is nothing to know."

"Evan didn't agree."

"Did he tell you what it was?"

"Nope . . . but he sure's hell thought there was *something.*"

Levy turned to look at the man, anger moving about within now like an intruder in the darkness, knocking things over, making noise, breaking lamps. . . . "Evan was full of shit."

"Nice way to talk about the deceased, Juan."

"You say it." He gave Domingo a dangerous look, calculated to frighten: it spoke about careers.

"I don't like to just say stuff like that, Juan."

"Say it."

"Evan . . . was . . . full of shit."

"Now you can stop worrying. Tell me about Joly Goodpasture. What's he up to?"

Domingo shrugged, looking small, disheartened by the rough treatment. "They been taking measurements from his four-wheeler, him and this Krylov. I don't think they got too much so far." Then he seemed to revive a little, for the grin that signified further complication spread across the soft dough of his face. "Looks like they're going airborne."

"With what?" Levy could not conceal his surprise.

"They've been putting their instrument on that *Agroindustriales* chopper."

Levy turned back to the glass, the enshadowed city. He looked out upon this poor land of fellow *indios* and thought that there was something terribly ominous waiting for him in Bolivia. The Indians had won here, as they had, to a degree, in Guatemala—it too was a nation of Indians. But La Paz was also a city in which Klaus Barbie could live comfortably for forty years, fluttering with those other fine-boned little old men in black suits and magenta-tinted glasses to drink expresso and lima juice at the Cafe la Paz only two blocks from where Levy now stood. Maybe, in such a city, the Jew could not be protected by the Indian. Suddenly, almost sweating, he saw that too many vectors had been made to converge right there, virtually beneath his feet. They had begun to tangle: soon events would slide beyond his control. "I need to get over there," he murmured. "I'll need one of the Hueys."

"Easier said than done, Juan. Hueys can't get up to La Paz. Couldn't take off if they did. Even going up to Coach from the jungle, they cross the sierra a couple thousand feet above their service ceiling."

"You saying I can't get a chopper?"

Domingo held up a small, placating palm. "Not to worry, Juan, course we'll get you down there. By sundown tomorrow we'll be injected right into the area. Count on it."

"Just me, Ricardo."

"Whatever." But he heard Domingo's spirits rise. "We'll put

you on the military attaché's King-Air down to Coach, and then we'll find your chopper."

"You have a dozen Hueys down here."

"Yeah, but *we're* only flying one. Bolivian Air Force has the others, the ones that aren't in that depot maintenance Washington ordered back in November. They're doing a project southeast of Santa Cruz." The ability to obstruct, to complicate, began to heal Domingo's spiritual wounds. "And that one Huey we got, Juan, it's on that radiation survey you requested, after that meteorite."

"How far along is that?"

"Far enough to know it brought in a shitload of radioactive stuff. Far enough to know somebody out there's getting a hell of a dose. I think they've flown a couple lines from the Beni River on down toward Santa Cruz." He shrugged dramatically. "Counters don't like the climate none, so it's been kind of slow." He chuckled at the well-known vagaries of science. "I mean, our boys aren't exactly nuclear physicists, Juan. And they're not real keen on wearing protective gear in that heat."

"Protective gear?"

"Sure. They're military, they got procedures. You fly on that chopper, they'll put you in a white suit too." He chortled happily.

"What does Goodpasture wear?"

"Shorts and sneakers, looks like." Then, into the silence that spread from Levy, he added happily, "Hey, I hadn't thought about that. One of those things where, you wait, the problem goes away?"

But Levy had stopped listening. He was thinking of old Joly and the Russian, in shorts and sneakers, sailing the gamma seas. Joly, he thought, old friend—you go too far.

5

It had taken Krylov three days to get the helicopter survey going, even with Arias over every morning to help them, along with the American blonde who used only her initials. At first, something in the *Esquilo*'s ignition system had messed up the calibration of the Cutie Pie's electronics, so that the instrument kept sensing things that were not there. Krylov had finally got the sensor settled down, although the readings, he understood, would be relative. The background radiation changed its character daily; every time a storm blew through, which meant every afternoon, the radiation altered, the highs were worn down slightly, the lows slightly elevated, as the cesium percolated out into the environment. They'd be able to detect the stuff forever —on dense pasture grasses your lower limit for detection was six millionths of a gram of cesium 137 per square kilometer, and here they were sitting on a great keg of the stuff. He and Goodpasture had worked out a rough kind of strategy, a two-man assault on a brigade-sized problem, as Krylov thought of it, that required the highs to stay in place: the highs were the only clue to where they would find relatively dense concentrations of cesium. After the survey, they planned to do some burning, some burying, some diversion of river water, to move what cesium they could out of the ecosystem. Then, when the rains had washed it all into the forest, the average radiation level would be lower. Krylov thought of their clean-up efforts with a kind of pity, puzzled to be doing something so bad for his health. And yet, he had not once considered saying no.

207

On the third day, Arias and Teejay had spent the night at the station—Krylov believed she may have lain with Goodpasture, although they were all too tired for sex. But he had thought of her, lying a few steps away in the darkness. He had liked her immediately, ignoring the cautionary glances from Goodpasture. It would be marvelous to possess her, out in this wild, radioactive country, a final, desperate lunge of the life force. Except, he, all of them, had been too fatigued to leap. At least he hoped it was just fatigue, and not the damned emissions eating away at his manhood.

In the morning the four of them had marched out to the *Esquilo* before dawn, and clattered into the air just as the forest began hooting and howling below them. Krylov paid out the twenty-meter instrument cable, attached to a weighted line to keep the ion chamber below the tail rotor. He had laid out a long rectangle for their survey area, about 250 miles long by 60 miles wide, angling from northwest to southeast along the Andean foothills and covering the forest halfway to Trinidad. The first mission had taken them along the perimeter of the rectangle, searching for a drop-off in radiation that would indicate where the boundary really ought to be. The helicopter had no Loran and very little navigation gear of any kind. Goodpasture had the left-hand seat in front, and Teejay, also wearing headphones and a boom mike, knelt nearby, loosely strapped into the back seat on the right. Krylov sat in the open door wearing a parachute harness tethered to the cabin by a long canvas strap. He spread an American tactical pilotage chart on a small drawing board bearing the ubiquitous Amecos label. He would give Arias a compass heading to fly, then mark the count and the time where their course crossed some recognizable feature—a road, a track, a twisting brown river, that he could find on the chart. As they flew farther out over the jungle, the chart matched reality less and less, so that Krylov had been forced to alter his data-taking procedure. Out toward Trinidad, he began calling out times and counts, which the girl wrote down on a tablet. He could go back later and, using the specific speed over the ground, calculate where the counts had been read along the line of flight. They had flown thirty meters above the trees with a hundred kilometers—about sixty miles an hour—forward speed, slow enough for a good count. It made the perimeter more than ten hours' flying time, plus two hours on the ground for refueling, a piss, and an empanada. They had fluttered back into the station at dusk, utterly exhausted by the wracking vibrations and noise of the machine.

From that first, day-long run, Krylov had been able to narrow the heavily irradiated area somewhat, moving the eastern side of the box ten miles closer to the mountains. But the radiation levels had not dropped to background until they had crossed the Beni River, at the northern end of his rectangle, so the long dimension had not changed. He was rather proud of his improvised assay. Everyone said Russians were no good on their feet, but here he was, forcing poorly calibrated instruments to march as he wanted them to, taking the risks of a lifetime in a cause best described as strange. The original idea of catching the Americans at some dangerous kind of play in Bolivia had evaporated, so intensely had he and Goodpasture set about making this survey, and so fully had they replaced apprehension with fatality. Krylov thought sometimes that he had never had a friendship of quite this quality, except as a soldier in combat. A kind of love, he supposed it was.

And he liked working with the girl, Teejay, who smelled like soap and was constructed along the lines of a pretty Russian, if a bit small in the chest. As they worked together, leaning close together, jostling into one another in the narrow cabin, touching, as he heard her clear, California voice on the intercom, he had thought there might be a kind of love for her as well. If, he told himself, she was just what she seemed, she was wonderful indeed. If not, if this wonderful warm exterior were merely a disguise for a committed revolutionary, then she should be ruling a country somewhere. Her remarkable clarity, the way she held herself out to the world as open and transparent, seemed to him to exclude only the Congreves and Palmas of the world; and yet, she was theirs. Always, remembering her entering Congreve's office with Palma, the unambiguous revelation of whom she belonged to, Krylov could struggle back to a clear view of her. She was Palma's, he had told himself, which meant she had something screwed up in her head.

Sometimes he wondered what had happened with Teejay

and Goodpasture. They'd made love, of course, you could see that, and they had parted friends of sorts, but there was none of the residue of affection you always saw between former lovers. Goodpasture, impassive and quiet in the front seat, spent the flights observing his domain from a vantage point he had never had before, a moving platform toward which the trees loomed upward, exploding into leaves and, here and there, bright yellow, white, and crimson flowerings. Always something blooming, he had told Krylov. To stay alive down there, it must always be springtime for somebody.

But Krylov wasn't watching the great trees wheel below. He was preoccupied with his probe while sitting in a pounding downwash, held in the door by what he considered a mere thread. When he leaned back, needing to get out of the blast for a moment, he found his back resting against Teejay's tanned shins, and felt her warmth through the damp cloth of his shirt. The temptation to turn and nuzzle his way into her lap was powerful, although he resisted. For one thing, he decided, Goodpasture would wet his pants laughing.

In three days, they had flown five parallel southeast-northwest lines, one along the fifteen-hundred-foot contour of the foothills, where radiation levels dropped toward background, and the others spaced about ten miles apart. Back at the station, Krylov had replaced the Amecos operational wall chart with a mosaic of aeronautical charts—great white rectangles where no terrain data appeared were bounded by the bright greens of the low-lying jungle, the tans and deeper rust colors of the Andes, blue rivers like tangled veins. He had grease-pencilled the survey counts on an acetate overlay and watched them like an astronomer trying to see the faint displacements of something moving across a dense field of stars. If you looked at something, anything, long enough, single-mindedly enough, you would find it . . . whatever *it* turned out to be. And yet, he could not find order in his construction. The numbers rose and fell haphazardly across the survey area, suggesting a terrain of high and lows, of hills and valleys, that Krylov still could not quite discern. "If we could put it on a computer," he complained to Joly, "we could get isopleths . . . contours."

"Good God, *I* know what isopleths are. As it happens, we've

a very capable program for plotting such things, one left over
from Amecos. We used it for drawing pressure maps of the
atmosphere. I think it will serve."

After Goodpasture had taken him through the isobar program, Krylov loaded their survey data into the Amecos work
station computer, which, after some internal agitation, began to
draw contours. They emerged as four elongated freeforms, as
patternless as pools of spilled paints. "We need more survey
lines," he told Arias, who hovered nearby. "Five more."

"Christ," the pilot muttered. "More than a thousand miles,
man."

"One very long day."

"*Very.*"

They began the last day's flying an hour before first light,
only the three of them. Goodpasture had decided to explore one
of the areas with relatively high radiation levels, on the ground.
"It's so close to the Mission," he'd told Krylov. "One can't help
worrying." Krylov had watched the Englishman diminish in
the darkness as the *Esquilo* rose into the morning sky, the insect
chatter silenced by their commotion. He leaned against Teejay's
knees and craned his head around for a look at her. "Do you
mind?" he asked. She shook her head. A moment later, she
softly touched his hair with a hand of exquisite warmth.

"Do you mind?" she asked.

He laughed and took up his post in the open hatch. As they
clattered out across the black trees, he fiddled with the Cutie
Pie, getting it ready for a last day's work—he didn't see the
power packs taking them much beyond today. "At Todos Santos," he told Arias on the intercom, "turn to three-two-zero,"
and lowered the ion chamber toward the trees.

"Roger."

"Hundred kilometers, thirty meters above the trees."

"Roger." The bored, uncommitted voice of the driver.

Krylov leaned against the metal rim of the door, letting himself drift more or less pleasantly. For the moment, at least, his
mind was not on the instruments, or radiation, or the work
ahead, or the warm girl behind him. He felt extraordinarily
clear, and sucked in a great, reviving breath of jungle air.

Christ, maybe radiation was *good* for you, in the right dosage. He chuckled.

"What's funny?" asked Teejay.

He started to reply, but quickly stopped. He had seen something for an instant against the lightening sky to the east, something flicking invisibly in the low, transpirated haze above the forest canopy. There it was again, more distinct this time: the slender silhouette of an American Huey, standing like a barracuda at the very rim of detectability. It flew without lights on a course that paralleled their own. If they were closer, Krylov thought, he would see the crew's white costumes—not flight suits, as he had thought at Santa Cruz, but protective clothing. No doubt they had their own Cutie Pies going. "They know," he whispered, too softly for the intercom to carry. Immediately he thought of Goodpasture, of the bulldozers and chainsaws and oozing pits of buried trees this news would conjure for the Englishman.

But that was not quite right.

They know about the radiation, thought Krylov then—but they don't care.

6

Goodpasture watched the *Esquilo's* lights out of sight, then stood by the limed landing circle, its white circumference barely discernible in the gathering first light, and waited for the beat of the rotors to die as well. He felt a great nervousness, and thought it might be the dosage—he had sensed lately that his body was not moving as well as it had, but could not tell if he were merely succumbing to worry. On this morning, he suspected his jitters had nothing to do with cesium—they arose from the drumming heart of the fossil adolescent within. The prospect of seeing Patricia had made him anxious as a boy.

He had worried about the people at the Mission—well, he had worried about *her*, he didn't give a damn about Elmer—from the first day's flying, when he had seen his secret Russian mark high millirads where their line of flight passed over the compound. When they had flown that line, Goodpasture had looked down, almost like a thief, he thought, flying over the scene of old crime, and found it empty, the bare dirt clearing beginning to turn green with the absence of footsteps. Apparently, nobody came there anymore, no school, no congregation. The Petersons would be alone, hiding from the world with some dirty secret that Elmer had come upon in the forest, and shared with Congreve in the form of that metal crescent. Then the *Esquilo* had flashed past the Mission and he had forced his mind back to the work at hand, still full of latent worry.

Of course, the dose rates seen at places like the Mission, as

Krylov had explained to him, would smooth down to some kind of average. "Cesium is the most reactive metal known," Krylov had explained to him. "Soon it will vanish into the chemistry of the forest, and the whole place will have some average amount of radioactivity. Right now, we can switch part of it off by removing the cesium we can find. But before much longer, the only cure will be the one you've tried to avoid." Goodpasture squeezed his eyes shut against that prospect, seeing his forest all in flames.

Starting out in the old Land Rover, with the world not quite lighted, calmed him, and his inner nineteen-year-old regained an uncertain leap of the heart as he remembered former intimacies with Pat, the clandestine touch, the lying with her in an area he had swept clear of snakes and ants. Now all of those bowers, as he thought of them, would be more or less radioactive, along with the water soaked up by the trees and pumped into the atmosphere, destined to fall again as hot rain on this side of the mountains. It was as if, Goodpasture decided as he wrestled the Rover across a deep smear of mud on the narrow track to Todos Santos, nature had created a kind of regional radiation pump, using the tools readily at hand: the way rainforest trees cycled water upward, the easterly winds that swept it against the foothills, a meteorite chock-full of cesium 137. It was the most puzzling act he had ever observed, or heard of, in nature, more bewildering than the wildest bargain struck by ant and bird, bird and tree. . . . What did the old girl have in mind?

Here and there, as he drove slowly through the sodden brush, he saw a mud hut or one of those tin-roofed frame shacks put up by squatters, and behind them the chaos of downed, half-burned trees, the tangled barricade in which they raised their little crops, and the odd patch of coca. Knowing about the radiation, one expected to see bodies everywhere, to find it a regular Jonestown. But nothing seemed to be amiss. Children crept cheerfully about their mean homes, not yet somber with poverty, the mothers labored as they always did, the men continued off somewhere, cutting, digging, scratching away at the earth for a living, or learning to serve white men. The dogs seemed as pleased with themselves as ever. Chickens strutted everywhere. It was as if the silent, imperceptible presence of the gamma were something he had dreamed.

Birds, he thought, avoiding a parade of chickens that pecked their way across the Rover's path ahead of him, must be almost immune with their hollow bones, and reptiles and amphibians must feel it hardly at all, and trees could take it or leave it. He shook his head in admiration. The bloody trees, why *they'd* find a way to put radiation to work! So perhaps all it meant was that you'd have a few sports, mutations, born here and there: some two-headed calves, some six-legged pigs, maybe an iguana capable of counting to twenty, a human generation rich in harelips and unseparated twins, perhaps. And down the line, bags of cancer. "The point, for Christ's sake," he growled at himself, driving mightily at the bog between him and the grass runway at Todos Santos. "What's your point, man?"

Well, the point must be that it was not the end of anything, really, not of life, not even of his small corner of the world. Everything would proceed more or less normally, except that, gradually, word of abnormally high radiation levels in stuff from the Beni would begin to percolate around and the place would become isolated from the commercial world, except for the uranium prospectors, of course—they'd be very excited for a short time. No more macadamia nuts or cashews or rubber from around here until the place cooled off. Still not the end of the world, for people can eat everything but rubber. Even their coca crop, their main source of ready cash, would be contaminated. Christ, thought Goodpasture, what consternation *that* will create out at the *finca*. He uttered a happy cry. Maybe it was nature's way of drying up drugs. Maybe it *was* Elmer's sign. Goodpasture shuddered.

Watching the growing numbers of shacks along the track on the mountain side of Todos Santos, he thought that these people, these women and children and the men out trying to clear a bit more forest to feed themselves, would be killed by poverty and insect vectors long before radiation got them. Miserable lives would be rendered marginally more miserable, as Gorky might say. They would live, endure, like the people for many miles around Chernobyl. God knows, there were worse things. Well, Joly, he told himself sadly, your heart has hardened at last. Nevertheless, he looked into the eyes of the children he passed on the road to El Crucero, their faces raised, open and innocent, wanting something. I shall do something about the worst spots, children, he silently promised. You'll have this one white man with you to the end. He grinned and thought of his secret Russian. "Make that two."

Seen from the helicopter, the Mission had looked empty indeed, but the rotor noise had imbued it with a kind of vitality. Now, as Goodpasture cut the Rover's engine, he found himself in a silence that evoked a time before sound existed, an emptiness suggesting not only that no one lived there now, but that no one ever had. It was as though all the years, all the holiday dinners and sweaty interludes with Patricia, had happened in a dream. "Christ," he said, putting a voice into the empty air, and got down from the vehicle. Of course, the horrible silence was an illusion—his single word elicited a defensive howl from the forest, the steady song of the cicadas arose once more upon the hushed sigh of the river. It had been he, not the place, that had gone silent. Soon, he thought, the dogs would appear, and chickens, and kids, and the Petersons themselves.

But nothing did. The animals had gone away, or crawled off somewhere to die. He hoisted the multi-channel case out of the passenger seat, pulled out the sensor head, which he thought looked like a singer's microphone, and turned the instrument on. Immediately, the gauge flicked toward the high end of its range. Goodpasture's neck hairs prickled. He would find them both dead.

"Pat?" he called uncertainly. "Pat, are you there?"

Something replied from the treetops. Macaws.

He crossed to the Vicarage, the pretentious name drained of all irony by his rising apprehension. He knocked and listened for a voice, and thought he heard the faint sound of someone moving, but no one appeared. He pulled the door open.

"*No!*" someone cried out and ran against the door, scrabbled at the knob. It was Patricia, he saw, wraith-like, disheveled, and sick. Several years before she had come down with a dreadful flu during a long *surusu*, the interval of cold winds from the south. She had looked then as she did now, her small eyes red and puffy, her skin sallow, her hair lank and thin. "No," she said, gasping for air from her exertions. "We don't want you here."

"Pat, take it easy." He spoke as to a nervous pony. "There, it's only me."

"*We* know who it is," she ranted, "we don't want you here." She released the door and fled into the gloom of the house, and Goodpasture entered, letting the door bang shut behind him. The place smelled of illness. "Go away, Joly," she said in a voice that moved him with its deep fatigue.

"Where's Elmer?"

"I'm here, Goodpasture," came a faint voice from a dim corner of the room. "Don't worry, I'm still very much on the scene . . . *old boy.*" He emitted a squeaking laugh. Goodpasture saw the figure wrapped in a *ruana* raise a frail arm as a signal. "Never mind, Pat," Peterson said, "it doesn't matter. He isn't a part of this."

"Of what?"

The figure shook its head. The blonde hair that caught the light had thinned greatly, and Goodpasture imagined loose teeth, hemorrhage, vomiting. "You're very sick, Elmer. I came to get the two of you out of here."

"Tested. Being tested." He emitted the squeaking laugh again. "Not sick."

"Pat," Goodpasture said, turning to the other figure in the room, "it's very dangerous here. Look . . ." and he switched on the multi-channel box. The room filled with the angry chatter of the counter, which rose as he aimed the sensing head at Peterson. "That meteorite was radioactive, Pat, it brought in bags of cesium isotope. It's all over the forest. But there's a great lot of it right here."

"You're lying," she said. "You're just trying to hurt Elmer." She did not have to say "again."

"It's killing you, Pat." And, from the look of things, it has already killed Elmer. "Let me get the two of you out until it's cleared up."

"This is our home, Goodpasture," Peterson said. "This is the place God has brought me . . . us . . . to, to do some of His greatest work. Leave us." The figure leaned forward, adjusting himself in what they had always called His Chair, and Peterson's face was illuminated for a moment. He was nearly bald now, and looked twenty years older than he had a few weeks earlier. It was the transparent visage of the terminally ill, incapable of concealing anything. Yes, thought Goodpasture, and it is the face of a man who thinks God is blowing in his ear, utterly complacent. God had made Elmer a courageous man. He wore a khaki shirt unbuttoned at the neck, and, in that instant of illumination, Goodpasture made out a leather thong around the wasted neck. Peterson had kept a metal crescent for himself.

"Your amulet is killing Congreve." Goodpasture caught Patricia's eye, which had gone wild-looking, like a terrified animal's. "It's killing you too, Elmer."

The figure retreated from the light, and waved a hand. "I'm not Congreve. I'm the Reverend Peterson. Don't you see the difference?"

"What, you think God will protect you?"

Peterson made no reply, but merely exhaled, the sigh of a disappointed parent. Then he said, "It's *supposed* to kill Congreve."

"Patricia, for God's sake, you can't stay here."

"I must." She must stay, she was telling him, because he had led her into a betrayal of her husband from whose resolute insanity she now refused to escape. Elmer was making her pay with every coin in her possession. "Anyway, it isn't up to you . . . Joly." Speaking his Christian name, her voice held a trace of its former warmth toward him, and for a moment he hoped that he might get her out of there after all. He strained to see her better where she stood across the room, enshadowed, vague as a ghost. Something gleamed there, and Goodpasture's heart sank. She held a shotgun at waist level, aimed not at his belly, but at his feet. "Please go, Joly. I don't want to hurt you. But . . . if I have to . . ." Her rheumy eyes shone, and Goodpasture said nothing, frozen in place less by fear than by an aching heart. He thought he must be seeing something pretty in this old girl again.

7

Peterson stared at the Englishman, trying to see detail on the tall, spare man silhouetted in his doorway. He wanted to see the eyes, the face, of a man who had seduced his faithful wife and drawn her so far into a sin that, but for the presently unfolding miracle, would have destroyed their marriage—their indestructible, once-perfect marriage. A play of light in the room showed him Goodpasture's face, a bit drawn with profound fatigue. "You don't look too good yourself, Goodpasture." He could not bring himself to use this love thief's given name. "Maybe it's killing *you*."

"Maybe it is. Look, Elmer, you can sit here in your blood and feces, dying from that thing around your neck—but let her go."

"Nobody's making her stay with me. It's *her* choice. Isn't that right, Pat?" He saw her nod, but she said nothing. A tremor of irritation passed through him. He wanted more enthusiasm, not a silent acquiescence that looked, smelled, like a failure of nerve. She *owed* him this. "Isn't that right, Pat?"

"Yes, that's right."

Her voice held the same collapsing note, however. This man was trying to take her away, and ruin everything. He still had some seductive hold upon her. "You see?" he said to Goodpasture.

"I'm not convinced."

"You will be when she shoots you."

"She won't shoot me."

"Oh, but she will. Won't you, Pat?" He tried to beam his

thoughts into her head. "Won't you, Pat?" He thought he saw her nod.

"I'm going outside, Pat," said Goodpasture. "I'll clean up what I can. If you can get that thing off Elmer's neck, do so . . . it's very dangerous. When you get it off, bury it deep in the ground and cover it with earth and stones. I'll come back for you. I won't let you die here."

"Oh, Goodpasture," Peterson laughed, "come off it, nobody's going to die."

But the Englishman was gone, the door vibrating where it banged closed behind him. Nobody's going to die, thought Peterson, not here, at least. Congreve would die, but he, Peterson, would not. That was God's will, that was the understanding between us. But he would be sorely tested, he saw that now. You couldn't make an arrangement with Him, you couldn't manage one of His miracles, without being sorely tried, perhaps destroyed. No more could you stand in the whirlwind, no more could you endure against the sea, no more could you survive deep space where, incredibly, His hand had fashioned the object Peterson now wore about his neck. He had come upon it in the forest, the semicircle of burnished, silvery metal around which tiny, glowing particles seemed to dance in the air, like tiny stars brought to earth. He had known immediately that this had come in on Goodpasture's meteorite, and at first had thought the object a fragment of meteoritic rock. But then, looking at it more closely, he saw that it was in fact a kind of brushed metal. He had picked it up, and found it light and warm to his touch, as though it had an inner life. The starlike grains fell earthward, like blue sparks, as he held the crescent up to study it.

It was then that he made out the runes. Not much more than a sixteenth of an inch high, they had been etched along the very rim of the grey metal crescent. Peterson's legs had almost buckled, and, in fact, he *had* let himself sink to his knees in the reddish mud of the forest. A vast stillness had seemed to reign for that moment of discovery, a stillness that resounded in his mind like a chorus of angels. His fingertips had felt the sharp etchings in the metal, and he had closed his eyes, clutching the object as he would have a sliver of the True Cross. This was no mere fragment of meteoritic rock, he realized then, but something *fashioned*, Out There. It was a sign, a message from God . . . to him. Yes, it had been made by Someone, and inscribed with the literal word of its Maker. Tears had blinded the missionary then, and he had stayed for what seemed a long time, kneeling in the soft clay, clutching the artifact in his two clasped hands, like the cross of a Rosary.

Finally, he had stood up, and returned slowly, as in a kind of one-man procession, to the Mission. Pat had said little when he entered. She had become silent in these last few days, as though she no longer cared about her sin with Goodpasture, as though she were prepared to flee her life with Peterson; oh, she gave no definite sign, of course, but his dreams filled with her leaving; awakening each morning he had been surprised and as pleased as a child to find her at his side. He took the object to his desk and brought out the magnifying glass he had found useful on some of the Lord's finer print. He read the etched characters:

Oh, Lord, tell me what it is, what does Your word say, how may I pronounce it? His hand trembled.

Words, *sounds*, rushed through his mind: espala, masara, sendri. . . . How, he wondered, in the flood of thoughts did one identify that which was God's? *Hordra.* The word came to mind as though illuminated, mysterious, without meaning. *Hordra.*

"*Hordra*," Peterson whispered now, causing his wife to glance warily at him. "Do you know what that is, Pat?" She had shaken her head. "It is the *literal* word of God."

He had drilled a hole at either end of the crescent, and run a leather thong through them so he could wear the object next to his skin. But he soon found its warmth to be troubling, and saw that it had raised a patch of scorched red skin, although the metal was not nearly hot enough to produce such an effect. He had realized then that it was not intended just for him to wear, to worship, but also as a tool with which to carry out God's hitherto concealed intentions. The metal crescent held a potent poison of some kind, a poison from the center of the universe perhaps, intended as a weapon against evil. Of course, he had known from the beginning that his discovery of the crescent with God's word on it could not have been an accident—such things never were. But he saw that he was meant to use it in some way. As with the sound of the strange glyphs, he had known his first impulse must be an inspired one. It had come to Peterson then: God had intended that he give part of the crescent to Congreve, to destroy an evil man. Once he had seen God's intention thus clearly, Peterson had cut the crescent in half, and sent half—well, he conceded, perhaps a bit less than half—to Congreve. But the piece with God's inscrutable message he had kept for himself. *Hordra.*

"Elmer?" When she spoke, Peterson experienced a leap of fright, so far from her had his mind taken him.

"Yes, Pat?"

"What if Joly's right?"

"About what?" His voice, operating beyond his control, filled with venom.

"That this is all radioactivity from the meteorite."

"Oh, you mean not a Sign from God?"

"What if he's right?"

"Come over here, Pat," he commanded in the same involuntarily nasty tone. His wasted fingers scrabbled inside his shirt for the amulet. "Come look at this."

But she would not. "I've seen it."

"I want you to see it again. I want you to *touch* it."

She shook her head and backed farther into the shadows: the shotgun held as a talisman, now, like a cross.

"That Goodpasture really shook you up, didn't he?" Yes, he *did* sound like somebody braying. God, give me more control as I do Your Will. She was silent. "A visit from the seducer and your faith crumbles. You forget what you have done. *How* can it be nothing but radioactivity? *I* am not dying, *Congreve* is, and yet he and I wear almost identical amulets." He shut his eyes for a moment, frightened briefly by the possibility that he had misunderstood God's terms. Perhaps he would have to die after all. That was always the way, though. You asked for a Sign, and got one. And then you asked for another to confirm the first, and on and on, driven by doubt. He would not fall into that trap. "The Lord's intentions are crystal clear, Pat. They go far beyond what your Englishman . . ."

"He's not *my* Englishman."

"He doesn't even believe in God, for Pete's sake. But . . . say he's right, that the power in the meteorite is radioactivity. What could be more powerful? I mean, this is what the *stars* run on, Pat, this is the power of the Universe, right here, in this little piece of metal."

"The radiation may kill us," she whispered.

"Only if God wills it."

"We should go with Joly."

"Oh, Pat, this is so *disappointing*." He felt his eyes glisten with tears; he had the ups and downs of a stroke victim. Then, "You won't leave me?"

"I said I wouldn't leave you, Elmer. I won't." There, her tone had softened. He felt she was back with him.

"This thing, this holy object," he said, sounding calm once more, "came from somewhere out in space. You can tell by looking at it that somebody made it. It isn't just a piece of rock. Maybe it *is* radioactive, but that's just its power in this world, God's shorthand for something . . . something . . ." He shook his head. "I wish I knew more," he murmured. "I feel so . . . inadequate," and he shrugged hopelessly, conscious of dissembling.

She watched him, her thin body stooped and weary, her face set by her illness in an odd blend of extreme youth and age. Perhaps God was going to take her to Him after all. Peterson would be left alone, down here, to complete His work. A well of sadness opened under the minister's spirits, thinking of himself, struggling for God, with his poor wife buried out on the edge of the clearing, which would *serve the seducer right.* . . . He shook himself, trying to order his thoughts. Somebody engaged in

God's work, in a bargain with Him, had no business being jealous of some carnal aberration.

"Elmer," she said, "what if the meteor was just a satellite coming back to earth?"

"But that's just what it *can't* be, Pat. You know, the *Runes*."

"Couldn't they be Russian, or Chinese?"

"Gosh, no. They're nothing from *this* world." He smiled complacently. Cocking his head, he listened to this world, whose sounds in the last few days had seemed to come to him with extraordinary clarity. He heard someone scraping around outside, and the occasional whir of that instrument the seducer had brought in with him. "He's still out there," he murmured. "With his 'radioactivity.'" In the distance he could hear the faint roar of the river, and, far beyond that, the beat of helicopter rotors. They had been coming over the Mission frequently the last few days, first Congreve's little red-and-white one, he could tell from the sound of it, and then an American Huey, with its great thudding noise. Peterson grinned. He knew what they were looking for: he wore it around his neck. "See, it isn't just that this holy thing came to us, to *me*, from space. It came with *writing* on it. Tongues. I believe, I feel I have been *inspired by God* to believe, that this is His word, his literal, very *word*." He thought of the glyph, so strange, so terrible, so devoid of meaning, so much the kind of word you would expect from the All-powerful:

"*Hordra*. I don't know what it means, not yet, although I know in my heart that, when the time is right, He will enlighten me. But . . . just for the sake of argument . . . let's say it isn't from Him directly. Then, you know what this is? It's a message from another civilization. Extraterrestrials. God has chosen *me* to be the first human to receive their message. So, either way, you see, we're dealing with something far beyond a radioactive rock. *Hordra*, Pat, *Hordra*."

8

Krylov's final line was flown in total darkness, the trees like a black sea under the *Esquilo*, and, out across this ocean of jungle, the faint glow of the Huey's turbine, where the others watched them. He had asked Arias to come back into the station on a curved course that took them somewhat to the southeast and back again, hoping for that extra increment of data. By the time Arias thumped the helicopter into the limed circle on the ground, a landing that said he might never fly again, the power packs were so low that the probe sensed nothing at the station. One way or another, the survey was over.

"Jesus Christ," Arias complained in the front, stretching and rubbing his neck. "That was some long day, man. I may never be the same after that one."

"When were you ever the same?" said Krylov, providing a laugh for the pilot.

"And that's it?" asked Arias.

"That's it." Krylov untied the sensor cable and began to coil it from hand to elbow. Then he picked up the Cutie Pie case and started for the laboratory building. Teejay followed with the day's measurements and the readout unit, and Arias stumbled along behind them, almost too tired to leave the *Esquilo*. Krylov turned to him. "Take a good shower tonight. You don't want to get . . . whatever it is. When you get to the *finca*, give the machine a good scrub, too."

While Arias took first shower, Krylov began reducing the

day's data, marking numbers along lines drawn on his wall map's acetate overlay. Then, half-shutting his eyes, he sat back to look at the odd conglomeration of quantities. He could almost make it out, now, the invisible terrain of radiation covering the long rectangular course he had laid out. Here were peaks of various elevations, reckoned in dose rates of millirads per hour. And there were valleys of relatively low values—high valleys, still thousands of times background radiation levels. He began to copy off the latitude and longitude of each point, so that the data could be put on the computer.

"Where's Joly?" Teejay wanted to know. She had fixed coffee and put yesterday's empanadas on a plate.

"Out." Krylov paused, wondering himself why Goodpasture had not returned.

"Search for lost love?"

"Maybe."

She came up behind him, standing close enough that he felt a kind of aura from her. "May I ask you a personal question?"

"You can ask." He laughed, preoccupied with the map.

"What have we been measuring?"

"What do you mean?"

She sat down next to him with her coffee. "I will speak in parable. Long, long ago, I was watching this airplane movie. The plane was in trouble, and the camera kept showing a gauge fluctuating madly. I guess it was oil pressure or something, but all the dial showed was the manufacturer's name, Smith. So I began to get very tickled and finally I yelled, 'My God, we're down to three Smiths.' " She laughed, "We all just cracked up. Only three Smiths. The end of everything."

Krylov looked at her, puzzled. "What's a Smith?"

"That's the point. That's what I mean. What've we been measuring. Bicrons?"

"Bicrons?"

"Bicron is the only name on the instruments. So I watch the needle point and here we're up to so-many Bicrons."

Understanding at last, Krylov chuckled. "Just look at the map. A lot of Bicrons."

"Meaning you won't tell me?" She put on a hurt look, added a measure of pain to her voice.

"We'll talk when Goodpasture comes back. It's his forest, not mine."

"His Bicrons, too, probably."

"Probably."

Arias came in, wearing his flightsuit, which he had put back on dripping wet. "Coffee and last year's empanadas," Teejay called cheerfully.

"Shit," he said. "I don't think I can do that. Maybe I'll have some of Goodpasture's vodka."

"Bloody good idea," said Teejay, mocking their host. "Blooooooody goooood. Me too."

"Me too," said Krylov.

The pilot poured out three glasses of the stuff. "Enough left so he can have one when he comes in."

"Fair enough."

Teejay held up her glass. "To the Bicron epidemic."

"What?" asked Arias, mystified.

"We've been measuring Bicrons, my boy," she replied. "Bicrons by the milli."

"What's a Bicron?"

"One Bicron equals twelve to the minus fifth ilks," said Teejay. "Don't pilots need to know stuff like that?"

Arias shook his head. "We just fly the plane."

"What's an ilk, then?" asked Krylov.

Teejay giggled. "Three times ten to the minus one Rotarians."

"*Salud*," said Arias.

They touched glasses and sipped their vodka, Krylov careful not to throw it down Russian style.

"Well, folks," said Arias, getting up, "I'll sleep in the plane. Don't want some fucking *indio* dinging it."

"Night."

For a time, Krylov and Teejay sat in silence as though embarrassed to be alone. Then he said, "Your turn in the shower."

"We could share."

One last lunge, he thought. What a wonderful death. He looked into her eyes, the green-flecked grey irises open, warm, intelligent. Ah, tell me you're not just Palma's *Cyka*, Teejay. Tell me you're just what you seem. Open her face certainly was, to a point; but Krylov could see a kind of curtain in there, too. It didn't much matter, the idea of joining her, shining and naked in the jet of tepid water, outside, in the night, was more compelling than caution. A cautious man would not have been there in the first place. "We could at that," he said. Christ, he thought, what a wonderful way to die.

But the death by shower, holding this sleek, blonde California girl in his arms, making love beneath the powerful stream of water and the cry and flutter and click of the jungle night, was only a figurative one. Afterward, he carried her back into the laboratory soaking wet, and they made love again, slippery as two eels, and then he gently toweled her dry, and found himself unable to leave her alone, and she unwilling to let him rest. Finally, with the forest entering its transitional silence before the dawn, they lay quietly, her head resting on his chest, one of his arms gathering her in. Krylov had rarely been so content. Perhaps, he decided later, he had felt a kind of love for her, enough to want her safely out of the forest; perhaps he felt he owed her something for the use of her body. Perhaps he had simply grown too rusty, too human, too radioactive himself, to think secrets mattered. At any rate, when she whispered, "What's a Bicron, really?" he told her. He must have dozed, then, for he did not awaken until the clatter of the *Esquilo* and the cold, empty place along his flank told him she was gone.

9

Teejay leaned her cheek sadly against the cool, damp surface of the *Esquilo's* perspex window, watching the jungle rise, unfold, and bloom barely a hundred feet below them. Arias flew impassively, sensing perhaps that she did not much want to talk. His only comment to her had been when she arrived at the helicopter at dawn, to find him awake and readying the machine for flight. "Never seen it so dirty," he'd told her, like someone explaining that his maid had not appeared that day. "Needs a good wash." And once aloft he had commented, "Something's moving in. We've *had* our flying weather." Beyond that, he had given her the silence she so badly needed.

She concentrated on her immediate, outermost layers of feelings, thinking how the night with the big Canadian had left her feeling spent and exploited, but not very much by him. No, not by him. He had made her feel as if someone's heart thumped for her, a sensation she had nearly forgotten; certainly she had not experienced it in Cuzco, perhaps not since nameless boys had fixed themselves upon her in old Orange County, when she had come home from a night's necking at Huntington Beach, lips raw from a companion's dental braces. But this Hobbs person had also seemed not to smell the dank odors of the money-needer on her, or the sharper scent of her partnership with Palma. Or, maybe—better—he had detected and then ignored them. What a guy.

Exhausting as it was to think it, she believed that something yet to be seen clearly had set her free from all that. She felt an unaccustomed tremor of intent, a nervousness imparted by a man; ordinarily, she could walk away without anything, almost without memory, but last night she had crossed some unexpected line that, although she'd got the information Palma wanted, made her less likely to stay with him. She smiled. He liked abstraction, he would understand. After she told him, he would accommodate her leaving with that dark, impenetrable self of his, fix it with Congreve to have her flown to the airport at Santa Cruz, ticketed to . . . where? Not Cuzco. California, maybe. Maybe it was time to see her folks again, and her nieces and nevvies and all those vanished best friends she had more or less walked out on years ago. California. God, was that really where she had to go? Home, she thought bitterly, where people give their babies away?

Her eyes filled with tears and she bit her lip, leaning against the window. All of this was as nothing, and she knew it. All her thoughts were just a thin skin of atmosphere blanketing a planet of fear. It throbbed beneath everything she thought or remembered. Fear was the line she had crossed. For she had asked her big Canadian what they were measuring, and, finally, late at night, he had turned to her, watched her closely for a time, and replied, "Radiation."

"What do you mean?"

"Ionizing radiation. Gamma rays, with some alpha and beta thrown in."

"Somewhere out there?" She had gestured in a way that suggested Distant Jungle.

"No, everywhere."

She had almost lost her ability to form words with her lips and tongue. "We're dying."

He had chuckled in the darkness. "From the moment we are born."

Her brain had begun to roam, to cast wildly about for exits. "But it's not so bad—I mean, listen to you, the philosopher." She had tried to laugh at him.

But he said, "Worse than around Chernobyl. Not as bad as Nagasaki or Hiroshima—well, we've had no explosion."

"This is just *jungle*, there's nothing here." She meant nothing so menacing.

"It's from space. A meteorite brought in a lot of cesium isotope. Improbable, but there it is, all over the jungle. That's what we've been measuring."

"Bicrons are rads?"

"Well, millirads per hour. But add them all up, and, yes, you get rads. Lots of them."

"But you don't wear anything, no masks, no . . . *robes*."

He had grinned at her. "We take huge risks. I think we're doing it because Joly wants to protect his forest from everybody else's good intentions."

"But you have to get the *government*, the U.S. . . ."

"What, would you have all this burned down and bulldozed under? What kind of Greengo is that?"

"A scared one," she whispered against the *Esquilo's* window. A scared utterly shitless one. Her body might not be what you'd call a temple. She abused it, she let it be abused, but, on the whole, she took good, very good, care of it. It was like a high-performance car, driven hard now and then, but meticulously maintained. She might do the odd line of cocaine, but she watched fat intake, cholesterol levels, sugar, preservatives, additives; she exercised, she kept her weight where it was supposed to be, she fasted occasionally, all to keep the pretty machine healthy and alive. But here, from the beginning, she had been like a healthy fish in an aquarium full of radioactive water. For weeks, her lungs had been taking in radioactive particles, her intestines processed radioactive food, she had left a trail of radioactive wastes. The white powder she inhaled carried radiation up into her nasal passages, into her blood and brain. When Congreve or somebody poked her full of semen, well, that was radioactive too. "Christ," she murmured hopelessly. *That* was the line she had crossed, of course, nothing to do with Hobbs, everything to do with running scared, fleeing into a clean part of the world, if there were such a thing, rinsing for the rest of her life in its clean waters, a part of her consciousness always waiting for the lump in the breast, the incurable headache, the potty full of blood. She would stop smoking, even. She was nothing except afraid. She kept hearing the Canadian's calm reply: *Radiation.*

That, she realized suddenly, was the sickness killing Congreve. That gizmo he wore around his neck was radioactive enough to kill a man. Jesus. Radiation had killed Goodpasture's famous funny monkey, oh, yes, *hilarious.* And the girl who had been at the research station, the girl who was there no longer— perhaps it had killed her too. She wished she could stop breathing, but brought out a Camel filter and lighted it with shaking hands. One more for the road. After a few puffs, she flicked it out the cargo door into the slipstream . . . the stream of radioactive air, she amended, the radioactive air through which they flew in a radioactive helicopter. Jesus. God. *Somebody!*

"You okay?" Arias wanted to know. She wore no headset, so he had to yell his concern at her.

She nodded, nervous as a junkie, Yes, *yes,* fine, *fine.* "I'm okay," she said, her words lost in the roar of engine and wind.

The *finca* materialized in the haze several miles ahead of them, the big house gleaming white beneath its red tiled roof, surrounded by outbuildings that, in this early light, also seemed somehow glorious. Cattle swarmed like ants across one distant field, the planted acreage fanned out across the low, flat, ground, marked at intervals by small islands of dense forest. Here and there, she saw his squad of Arabian horses, gathered, as horses always seemed to be, in a meeting near the fence. A double fence formed three sides of a large trapezoid roughly centered on the main buildings, with the fourth side being a high stone wall topped with razor wire and broken glass. You heard that there were minefields there, and fields of fire for hidden machine guns, but Teejay rather doubted it. Congreve didn't worry much about attack. When the Bolivian Air Force helicopters and the Drug Police came for him, as they sometimes had, he was gone; if they came every day and every night, she supposed, he would move away to Brazil or Spain, but not until then. Of all his properties, he had told her once as she lay face down, exhausted and hurting, beneath him one long night, he liked this *finca* best. He had put his first automobile, a brown-and-white 1957 Buick Century hardtop, on a concrete pedestal just outside the main gate, and had bougainvillaea planted all along the wall; the vines had grown into springy trees of lavender, red, and coral-colored flowers.

Roses had once bloomed in profusion near the house, but they had turned out to be too succulent for their own good; everything down here, Congreve had complained, every fucking thing, eats *roses.* Knowing now what Congreve was dying of, she felt a species of affection for him. Well, they had been intimate, hadn't they? And he was dying, horribly, wasn't he? Teejay gave her head a melancholy shake, to order the babble of voices she thought might rise there. She thought of the *finca,* of leaving it.

Until today, she had loved his favorite property too. Her heart had leapt whenever she saw the big house from a distance, white as a grand ship on a green sea. Sure, it was the leap of the money-needer, she understood that, but it also had to do with beauty and serenity and being with the right man. Now, the sight depressed her. A radioactive *finca,* with her radioactive man . . . yes, and there he was, black-clad as a crow out by the landing circle toward which Arias now persuaded the *Esquilo,* flying with both hands and feet, keeping the machine steady in a rising buffet of wind.

The sight of Palma chilled her further. The closer they got to him, the clearer and more recognizable his face became, the less Teejay believed that he would let her go. Her heart drummed like a bird's. If she told about the radiation, he would smell fulfillment and want her to stay with him. They would die together, because dying was what his struggle was really all about. Her jaw worked, she could not firm up her mouth. She wanted to tell Arias to rise into the air, to restore her to the research station . . . no, that was too radioactive, everything in the goddamned world down here was radioactive . . . to Santa Cruz. Please. *Please.* And even as she, paralyzed with this interior prayer, felt the skids settle to the earth, heard the rotor begin to wind down, she murmured, "Please, please," hoping someone would hear.

But Palma did not have to. One look at her, she saw, and he knew that she had been turned to fear. One look. "You worry me," was all he said, reaching in to give her a hand out of the helicopter. It looked gentlemanly, but she knew what he was doing: he was taking her hand in his, not to steady her as she got down, but to show her that his hand was vast, and that she was a small, terrified bird enfolded in it.

"I'm fine," she lied. "Tired." She gave a febrile grin. "We worked hard over there."

"On the plague." His lip curled on the term.

"Yes."

"You must tell me."

"I need a shower. I'm really worn out."

"You must tell me, and Congreve too. I think his sickness has begun to scare him, even with that thing, that talisman." Palma laughed coldly. "It's probably killing him. The missionary is a Borgia."

She did not reply, not trusting her tongue to form the words now. Congreve's talisman was no doubt *the* most radioactive thing in town. And she had had it touch her. . . . Teejay shuddered involuntarily.

"Are you all right?" Palma frowned.

"Got a chill."

"Maybe it's the plague."

"I hope not," she whispered fervently.

"Is the plague *so* bad?" He stopped and turned her to face him. "Is it so bad as that?"

She shook her head. "I'm tired, that's all." Then, looking into his face, she said, "I can't do this anymore. I have to go. Away."

"Where on earth would you go?" Palma asked pleasantly, his eyes warm and interested, something friendly and easy in his face.

"Not Cuzco, I wouldn't go back there," she replied, finding herself beginning to hurry. She might be able to leave this morning—by dusk she'd be on the far side of the mountains and safe. She studied him more closely. He *was* taking it well. He was accepting her needs as real and important. "Maybe I'll go home."

He chuckled. "How will you get *me* into America?"

"I didn't mean . . ."

"I know what you meant, Teejay. I was just kidding you. You need to go away, but alone. A fresh start. New place. New friends. New job. New everything."

She nodded frantically. "That's *right*. I knew you'd understand."

"Oh, well, I have always understood you." He resumed walking toward the residence, drawing her with him with a gentle hand on her arm, that made her wilt beneath his touch. And yet, as great as her fear of him was, it was nothing to her fear of radiation; she might survive Palma. "But you haven't said what the plague is. What were they measuring?"

Was it too late to be truthful? She felt suddenly confused. "Something called . . . Bicrons. I don't know. They never said. I *asked*," she added quickly, "but they never said."

"Ah." He stopped once more. "Arias," he called to the pilot, who was just coming up to them from the *Esquilo*. "What were they measuring over there?"

"Radiation."

Palma turned to Teejay. "Never send one spy when you can send two. Why wouldn't you tell me?"

"They wouldn't tell *me*. I couldn't tell what it was, I don't know instruments."

"Arias, how do you know?"

Arias shrugged. "Nothing else *to* measure with that thing."

"She says she didn't know."

"Maybe she didn't."

"Why would she lie?"

"Christ, don't ask *me*," the pilot grumbled, wanting out.

Palma stepped to one side, pulling her with him, to let Arias go past them. "Don't tell Congreve just yet," he said. Arias shrugged.

"Why would you lie?" Palma whispered to her then, his hand tightening on her arm. She was faint with fear now and could not stop trembling.

"I was going to."

"I thought you didn't know."

"I didn't. . . . I mean, I was afraid. . . ."

"So you were going to say nothing? You come back today and tell me you want to leave. Fine. But you also come back clearly terrified of something, and it turns out to be that astounding North American fear of radiation, that irrational terror that sends you people out with your placards and protests. You are as bad as the rest of your race."

"It's everywhere, you can't feel anything, or see it, but it's everywhere. It's killing us." She stood huddled, as though in a driving rain, her eyes shut, her head inclined to the ground. "I was so afraid . . . I couldn't think straight."

"But straight enough to abandon your comrades. You wanted to run away and say nothing."

"I wouldn't have gone through with it. . . ."

"I think you would."

"Please, I was just so scared. . . ."

"I understand." His voice denied ever having touched her, ever having had her in its power, or ever having contained a single note of warmth for her. It was as cold and empty as the Altiplano, this voice that she had heard him use with enemies, in those minutes, hours, or days it took for them to die. "But, Teejay . . . there are worse things than radiation." Death would have just that voice, she thought.

"I'm sorry." Had he heard her? Had she spoken? She no longer knew. Her very blood seemed made of fear.

10

Goodpasture had still not returned when Krylov decided to give up his pleasant sexual reverie and begin his day. The American blonde had returned to her bad companions, which was all she could have done, in the absence of some better offer. For a moment, he imagined having made such an offer, imagined having her on his arm in Moscow in winter, and laughed aloud. Those big swimmer's calves would fit right in, of course, and her face, why it was *glasnost* herself, with all the interior curtains that the word had started to connote. A survivor of anything, no doubt. He felt some mild regret that he had told her about the radiation, a moderate spiritual hangover from it; it was not something a former Dzerzhinsky School gold medalist should have done. But perhaps it was the new world order after all, where one kept no important secrets. And maybe she would use the information only to help herself. The worst that could happen was she would alert Congreve to his condition, and send him flapping off to bone-marrow specialists for help. Even that would unfold so slowly, so clumsily, that Goodpasture's forest would not be much compromised at all. More likely, Congreve would die long before he could keep an appointment in Rio or Buenos Aires.

Beyond his faint nervousness over breaking Goodpasture's silence, Krylov felt extraordinarily fit and clear, his mind like a great, cold, windswept steppe overarched by infinite blue sky. It was as though, cleansed by his encounter with the girl, he now had access to every corner of his mind, to parades of memory, mountains of detail, all bathed in a bright interior light. Perhaps, he thought, this is the beatitude that came before the radiation killed you, like the clarity one was supposed to experience upon being burned at the stake. He chuckled. Whatever its source, he welcomed the mood. Perhaps it would see patterns a tired mind had not.

He stood up without his clothing and stretched mightily, feeling like a young man, a man not quite in love, but considering it. . . . But, there, remember that she pumped you, and went home. She's not in the kitchen fixing breakfast; she's fucking Congreve, or that little *senderista*, Palma. Insulated from further daydreaming, he gathered up his soiled clothing and started it through the washer. It was part of their strategy to shower at every opportunity and to keep washing their clothes, not so much to escape as to thin the radiation risk. After showering and dressing in clean, unironed khakis, a white cotton shirt, and leather thongs, he made himself a pot of coffee and broke the last, stale empanada in two, so that Goodpasture could have some when he returned.

Where was the Englishman?

Krylov thought he would wait for Goodpasture until noon, then strike out to search for the Land Rover. It might have let Goodpasture down in a bog. There might have been an accident, Goodpasture's body may have failed; he might have been shot by a jealous husband. Krylov thought of that one for a moment, and finally emitted a great *Haw!* Then, with the confidence of a master moving to a piano, he went to the computer work station, to begin punching in yesterday's harvest of data.

For a time he studied the wall chart, where he had plotted the day's measurements. The last five lines had added real density to the survey, the dose rates gathered closely enough together, he thought, that they would produce some meaningful contours. He methodically typed in the geographic coordinates of the new data and set the machine working on its new set of contours. The courser spun as though randomly about the screen, like a mad artist dealing in widely separated points rather than lines, linking approximately equal millirad values. Distinct oval forms began to take shape, and Krylov asked the computer to interpolate between the contours at ten-millirad intervals. Although this created a false contour—a value for an area where he actually had none—it had the effect of showing which way the slopes ran, and how the ovals might be linked.

Krylov leaned toward the screen. The contours did not show the half dozen hillocks of radiation he had expected, but a set of whorls arrayed with a kind of symmetry. They lay along the rectangular survey area in four sets of three, each of these forming a rough chevron pointing southeast, twelve blurred fingerprints of some alien, thumbless hand. Twelve, he thought. Why twelve? Why symmetry?

But, then: If the meteor Fall was truly random, why not?

Each print, he saw, was really quite different from its fellows, deformed, or smudged, by the movement of air currents where the stuff had entered the forest. They had been smeared further as the cesium began to react with the environment, disappearing into chemical compounds that now would contain at least one radioactive atom.

Why twelve?

Why the symmetry?

Why . . . cesium?

Cesium 137 was common enough. Every living thing on Earth had carried a trace of the stuff since the first atomic explosions, and, later, from bomb tests and accidents like Chernobyl. But it did not occur in nature, that anyone knew of. It was a child of nuclear fission, created when you split an atom of uranium in a bomb or a reactor core, about six atoms of it for every hundred atoms of split uranium. But why would nature split an atom? She ran off just the opposite process; instead of splitting heavy atoms to release energy, she fused light elements to power stars. Where, out there, is fission?

He shut his eyes, the better to see what lay on the larger vistas of his exposed memory. What had Collins, the Brit at Angra-1 said, all those centuries ago by the bay, the dot of cesium compound between them, the Atlantic sky going dark?

Cesium 137, but in a queer form.

What did that mean, exactly?

If I were a plant, I'd probably think it was something good to eat.

Perhaps, then, it seemed like some organic substance, a form that doesn't occur on Earth or in reactors, a form fashioned by vastly more powerful forces Out There.

Where would nature go for a queer form of cesium 137?

Supernovae need fission to make heavy elements. Planets full of heavy material may fly apart and send fragments out across the galaxy, this radioactive stuff cooking away.

Supernovae were the explosions of massive dying stars that collapsed with enough force to forge heavy elements like cobalt and barium . . . and cesium, no doubt . . . before blowing apart, sowing space with heavy metals. But the only supernovae in this galaxy happened centuries ago, the last maybe three hundred years ago. Krylov smiled at this remembered scrap of college astronomy. The Milky Way galaxy, he recalled from the same source, was about a hundred thousand light-years in diameter. Let's be generous and say a supernova detonated a mere ten thousand light-years away—close enough to be felt here, but never mind. It would take the light ten thousand years to reach us. And the pieces . . . the cesium, the meteors, or whatever . . . moving at an unbelievable ten percent of light speed, would take a hundred thousand years to make the same journey. Therefore, a meteor created by any known supernova would still be tens of thousands of years away. But an old, *old* supernova, exploding before there were humans to see it, might have made a meteor that, after crossing space for hundreds of thousands of years, *had* arrived over the Beni last All Saints Eve.

But what was the radioactive cesium doing all that time?

Decaying into another element, and another, trying to become stable, nonradioactive barium. Cesium 137 had a half-life of about thirty years. That meant half the atoms in the famous meteor would have decayed in the first thirty years, half of the remainder in the next, and so on. Krylov picked up a hand calculator and punched in some numbers. A hundred-thousand-year journey had more than three thousand thirty-year intervals in it. With each one, the cesium 137 would decay by half. In three centuries, only about a thousandth of the original isotope would remain; in six centuries a couple of millionths. And the long journey would barely have begun.

Therefore . . . the meteor must have come from a nearby star.

Maybe. Proxima centauri was only about four light-years away. Maybe an unknown planet detonated in the solar system and spewed large chunks out into space, one of them toward the Beni. But a chunk, a meteor, would only travel at a few hundred-thousandths of light speed, stretching a trip that took only four years into a journey lasting hundreds of centuries. Again, the original cesium 137 would decay to a relative thimbleful en route. Krylov leaned back. "Calvin, if you were any kind of astronomer you would have figured all this out at the beginning."

To explain the amount of cesium 137 they had detected, you needed to bend the rules of the universe, and invent wildly improbable scenarios: a moon-sized meteor from a nearby star system, moving at a large fraction of light speed, fragile enough to disintegrate on impact with the atmosphere without destroying the Earth—and only into a dozen pieces, rather evenly dispersed.

Like something thrown, the pilot, Mason, had told him that night in Chile, weeks ago. *Like something thrown.*

In fact, he decided, returning to the screen, the odd symmetry of the ovals was very familiar, the one thing, apparently, he was unable to remember on this clearheaded day. He had seen those twelve fingerprints clutching something, somewhere, before. He stared at them for a long time, but nothing came. Annoyed, he shook his head and commanded the computer to print a copy of the iso-map. Then, reflecting, he typed in new commands that averaged the values, smoothing the smeared deformities of the whorls.

While the machine worked, he poured himself more coffee, and pondered where the morning's deep thinking had got him. The rule of thumb was that you never tried to explain anything by the most elaborate means: things were usually what they seemed. Of course, that was just the trouble here. The cesium had to have come in on the meteorite that both Mason and Goodpasture had witnessed. That was a given; the stuff had to have come from space. But the meteorite . . . there was no explaining how a meteorite whose impact had not destroyed half of South America could have carried so much cesium, a metal that, even in its natural form, was rare.

He returned to the computer. The fingerprints had been tidied into fat, teardrop-shaped bodies with the highest dose-rates gathered at the broad end. Krylov studied them. "I know you." Exasperated, he told the computer to print out a second map. For a moment, while the printing head scurried over the page, drawing its isopleths, Krylov thought he had grasped the elusive memory. If he had, he lost it, the memory driven out by another more distracting: he heard the unmistakable beat of a Huey marching slowly toward the station.

For the first time since his arrival in the Beni, Krylov wished he had come armed. He glanced around for a weapon, even looking for Goodpasture's bow and arrow, but these were off with the Englishman in the Rover. And then it came to Krylov: this was not an assault—the helicopter must be bringing word of Goodpasture. Relieved, he went outside, watching the dark green insect float in a ground-effect hover, reluctant to touch down. The crew wore white suits, and the man in the doorway had a respirator over his face. But Krylov was more interested in the big man who hopped lightly from the machine to the soft turf of the landing circle.

Even at fifty meters' distance, Krylov could sense that the stranger had been there before, that he felt very much at home at the research station. He wore a blue work shirt, denims, and, incongruously, white cloth booties over his shoes. *They know about it, but they don't care.* The visitor waved at the pilot, who nodded, put the Huey's nose down and slowly drummed away from the circle, heading, Krylov thought, for the vacant Drug War enclave at Chimoré. Then, as the rotor's thumping sound diminished in the distance, Krylov found himself staring into a remarkable face, a pale oblong framed in a mass of tangled black hair that had become flecked with white, keen and deep-set black eyes, a black mustache; and yet, while as definite as a figure with an outline, he seemed almost to flicker, not quite Indian, not quite American, his identity shifting among shaded differences. He might be Afghan or Russian, or, Krylov thought, Canadian. He might be from the Altiplano.

Now the stranger cocked his head, as though noticing Krylov for the first time. "Hi, my name's Levy. Joly around?"

"He's out."

"Juan Levy," the man said, coming over close enough to extend a hand.

"Calvin Hobbs."

"The astronomer?" Levy's lip had curled.

Krylov nodded.

"Here for the baths?"

Krylov forced a friendly laugh, wondering as he did whether he could take the American, for American, he saw now, the man surely was. No doubt Levy was solving the same equation. "I have some coffee on."

"Not just yet. Want to look around. I ran Amecos, you know, a year or two back. Marvelous experiment. Kind of miss the old gang, all the action. God, we had boats, planes, balloons . . ." He shook his head, signifying admiration.

"We've been using your equipment."

"It was cheaper to leave it than ferry it back to the States."

"Looks like you left everything, Goodpasture says, but the Geigers."

"Not much call for them down here."

Krylov looked at the stranger's protective footwear. "Nice shoes."

"Yeah, well, no point wrecking perfectly good loafers."

"Your aircrew also looked pretty stylish."

"The glass of fashion."

"What brings you back to the Beni?"

"Business. I needed to talk to Joly."

"You could warn him about the radiation."

"Radiation?"

"I thought you knew—hence the booties."

"If there's radiation, booties aren't a bad idea."

Levy shuffled awkwardly, hands in trouser pockets, head down. "I think we got off to a bad start," he said at last. "Let's pretend I've just arrived and come over to you and stuck out my hand." He extended his right hand to Krylov, who, disarmed to a degree, went slightly off balance as he leaned toward Levy with his own hand. Levy gripped it in a sincere, friendly vise, pulling Krylov slightly forward; and as he did, he drew a Glock 19 automatic from his trouser pocket and aimed it at a point near Krylov's navel. "And then I say: Colonel Krylov, I presume?" He laughed. "Isn't that more like it?"

Krylov said nothing, furious with himself for letting Levy get so far. When you smelled trouble this keenly, you took the matter out of your opponent's hands, *before* the gun came out.

"Strange bedfellows. Here you are," he went on, his free hand holding up a finger for each name, "and Joly, the American girl, the *senderista,* the drug lord . . . What are you doing, making a movie? *The Bridge of San Luis Rey?*"

"I am not here as a Soviet." Krylov had become very still inside. If you came all this way to live and work here without protective clothing, he told himself, a pistol is the least of your worries. Pick your moment, get to know him, and take the gun away. After all, he is the one with the white booties—and you've been shot before.

"May I ask why?"

"Soviets are conspicuous down here."

"They're pretty conspicuous anywhere."

"To you, maybe."

"Does Goodpasture know your dark secret?"

Krylov shook his head. "I thought of telling him . . . but . . ." and he shrugged.

"Why spoil a lie?"

"Or a friendship."

"Why'd you come here?"

"To help."

Levy sneered. "All this way, just to help?" Krylov nodded. "That was very generous of you, given what's in the air."

"I thought so."

"Now that I'm back on site . . . we won't be needing your help."

"I hadn't planned to leave just yet."

"But you will. I'll have my chopper take you to Cochabamba today, then off you go to La Paz and Minsk, Pinsk, whatever."

"Let's wait for Goodpasture."

"Tell me about your survey."

"You've watched us at work, you know what we've been doing."

"Results?"

"We're still . . . reducing the data." He decided he did not want Levy to see the twelve ovals on his computer map. "We've got a few maxima . . ." He shrugged again, like a Bulgarian farmer.

"What does your gut tell you?"

"You know how we are, Levy. Socialist automatons. No hunches."

"But sarcastic."

"Yes, I think so."

"We alone?"

"Except for the girl."

"Rosa?" Levy grinned. "Rosa still here?"

"She's around somewhere." She haunts the place.

"Have you told anybody about your survey?"

Krylov shook his head. "There's nobody to tell. And Goodpasture didn't want any official action. He thought the rainforest could assimilate the stuff. Maybe it can."

Levy looked at his watch, at the sky, around the compound, until his eye settled on the covered pit near the laboratory building. "I don't remember *that*."

"It's a storage pit."

"For what?"

"Cesium grains."

"Ah. Must be pretty at night."

Krylov remembered the week Rosa had taken to die. "Very," he said.

"Going to miss the jungle?"

Krylov looked out across the islands of grass and lianas and trees. He thought of his first night there, drinking vodka and singing with Goodpasture high above the forest floor in Arachne's Palace. "Yes, I shall miss it." Looking into Levy's eyes, he thought, He means to kill me now. He wondered why he was so calm—it must be Teejay, or Rosa's ghost, or the gamma. He smiled. "How did you know about the meteorite?"

"Purely by accident. One of our Star Wars satellites passed through a region of very hot particles, radioactive stuff, that nobody could explain. Everybody thought at first it was World War III . . . wondered where you boys'd got the money." He regarded Krylov thoughtfully, like a soldier sizing up a prisoner of war. "It turned out to be the wake of a big meteor. Going nowhere, dropping into the Bolivian jungle. Like the proverbial tree falling in the forest, you see, except we saw it fall. Somebody . . . gosh, it might have been me . . . said, Hey, remember how those rainforest trees processed our Krypton 85 tracers in Amecos? They'll take this other radioactive stuff and keep pumping it into the foothills . . . where the grapes of wrath are stored. Not my exact words, but you get the picture."

"Not really."

"Bolivia's got two coca crops. Up in the Yungas country, up north, it's mostly for domestic consumption. Mostly okay from our standpoint."

"Our?"

"The United States', the Drug War's . . ."

"Goodpasture said you were a meteorologist."

"So I am. Like you're a nuclear engineer."

"I understand."

"From about the Rio Beni down to about here, coca's mostly grown for illegal export. Not much luck with crop substitution, or massive armed interdiction either. So, seeing the meteorite come in with all that gamma source in it, we thought: The next export coca crop will be *hot*. It'll be visible as it goes into the pipeline in Colombia, and in the pipeline to the States. At each stage, it'll leave a trail anybody with a Geiger counter can follow. The stuff they process in Bolivia will blaze a trail to middlemen in Argentina and Brazil, to Spain, to the base appetites of Europe. Quite a windfall for the Drug Warriors. Safe, too. At each stage, the stuff becomes a shade less radioactive. By the time it's in New York City, the radioactivity problem is about as bad as radon gas in Queens—I mean, at some level of society you stop worrying about dainty risks because people are killed every night with automatic rifles."

"How do you keep it quiet?"

Levy shook his head sadly. "We can't forever, of course. We can for long enough to let that first hot Bolivian crop percolate through the entire system. It's a kind of research and development program. We'll study the first round. By the second crop, we should know what the parameters are. They get four coca crops a year down here, Colonel—numerous opportunities to do well."

"But eventually . . ."

"Eventually, word gets out, sure. They, meaning those fellow-Americans whose greedy appetites keep the dope wheels turning, are as jittery as goldfish where personal risk is concerned. They smoke, they dope, they fornicate, drink-and-drive. They collect handguns and Kalashnikovs for hunting . . . ever hunted with a Kalashnikov?"

Krylov shook his head. "Not game."

"More sporting to poison the salt lick. Anyway, these same people want their kids' clothing to be fireproof, they want warning labels on champagne corks, airbags. Baby seats on airliners. An end to Freon. They worry about the ozone layer, polluted seas, dead seals, and saving the whales. A shrink might say their concern is a facet of their greed. And they're scared utterly shitless by radiation. They'd read by the light of whale oil, rather than go nuclear up there. Call it Wonderland."

"A patriot speaks."

"You can be a patriot and still see things clearly. Isn't that what you've been doing all your life? But the point is this: although they stuff cocaine up their nostrils *knowing* it will rot it off in time, they won't go into a city that has the equivalent of a dental X-ray in the air. Not even the most deathbound Hollywood starlet's going to snort radioactive coke. Finally, we see a real honest-to-God drop in demand."

"All this from a single act of God." Krylov held out his arms in mock wonder.

"Krylov, this is God at His *best*."

"It may be at that." He felt time, his time alive, running down and down, and began to steel himself to attack Levy. But the visitor, watching him closely, had drifted a few meters farther away, as though to study the storage pit. When he looked up at Krylov, he brought the pistol up to eye level as well, and held it aimed steadily at his captive's chest. "I know how it is, Colonel.

You're getting the feeling that time has run out on you. Time to make your play. I'm going to save you the trouble."

But Krylov had begun to move, lunging swiftly off to his right, lowering his head for speed, each great step seeming to take minutes to complete, one, two, three, some distance, but, *shit*, his feet sliding sideways on the wet grass, and down, trying to roll to his feet and behind him a first shot, a slap of grass and muck thrown up near his face as he rolled, another shot, a slab of flesh ripped off his shoulder, unable quite to get his feet positioned under him. . . . His momentum drained away. He had lost. Krylov raised himself on the elbow of his uninjured side and watched with a calm he had rarely experienced. Levy aimed the pistol at his chest.

"Job troju matj, Colonel."

"No more, Juan." Goodpasture's voice seemed to come from everywhere.

Levy looked wildly around. Krylov could not see Goodpasture, but he was close by, in the grass, behind the nearby wall of trees. "Joly," Levy said, "gosh, am *I* glad to see *you.*"

"Come on, Juan, you can't see anything. But I can see you. Throw down the gun."

"With you in a minute, Joly." Levy shook his head and took aim at Krylov, who half turned away from the muzzle, tired of being brave.

"My arrow's right behind your next bullet, Juan. I'm using my best frog: *Phyllobates terribilis.*"

For a moment, Levy hesitated, scanning the grasses, the dark trees, for any sign of Goodpasture. "He's a Russian."

"Not the only one present who is not what he seems."

"A Russian *spy*, Joly." Levy strained for the reply, trying to locate the voice.

"As you are an American one?" Krylov thought that Goodpasture must be moving silently closer, over ground he knew as intimately as an Indian would have.

"He's going to fuck everything up, Joly."

"Everything's already fucked up."

Levy slowly raised the pistol toward Krylov again.

"Don't do it, Juan. *Don't . . . do . . . it.*"

"My chopper's coming back for me."

"When you tell them to."

"They'll bring reinforcements."

"Only if you ask them."

Yes, thought Krylov, the voice was moving, and Levy was beginning to track it. They both caught a wave of movement in the grass, and Levy quickly fired at it.

"Oh, Christ, Juan, just put down the fucking gun." Something hissed out of the tall grass not twenty feet behind Levy, a five-foot bamboo shaft fletched with black buzzard feathers, hurtling like a javelin, on a trajectory that surprised Krylov with its flatness. It whistled between Levy's spread legs, an inch or two below the scrotum, and buried itself in the ground ahead of him. He leapt, more with anger than with fear, and whirled toward the source, firing from the hip into the swaying grasses.

"Checkmate," said Goodpasture, stepping into the clearing with a second arrow nocked and a third held with the hand that gripped the bow. He drew the big bow as he came forward, the long arrow aimed at Levy's back. "You can't kill either of us now, Juan. You lose."

Levy stood for a moment, the pistol hand drooping at his side. Then, listlessly, he dropped the gun behind him, and turned to look at Goodpasture. "This won't change anything."

"I don't intend to change anything," said Goodpasture. He squatted down, still holding the nocked arrow like a spear to keep Levy back, and picked up the automatic, then stepped back to put some distance between himself and Levy. "Have a seat on the ground, Juan. Put your legs out straight, put your hands in your trouser pockets." Goodpasture ejected the magazine and squinted at it. "Didn't leave much. Better than nothing, though." He reloaded the pistol and cocked it, and lay the bow and arrows on the grass.

"What you don't understand, Juan . . . I don't care if you boys put this Fall business to work in a good cause, far from it. But I don't want the place destroyed by it. Let's make a deal . . . isn't that what you people like to say?"

Levy did not reply. A model prisoner, thought Krylov.

"The deal, of course, is that we keep all this quiet . . . that we've come this far in silence, we can go the rest of the way the same."

Levy remained silent, his face impassive, but hatred shining from his black eyes.

"A damned shame," said Goodpasture, turning to Krylov. "We used to be the best of friends, Juan and I. I may have been the only friend he's ever had, as a matter of fact. And now he's ready to make me into a lampshade."

Krylov pushed himself back to his feet and stood up, his shoulder hurting. "Thanks."

"*De nada,* Viktor . . . I can call you Viktor, mayn't I? I mean, I'm bloody well not going to call you Colonel."

"You heard that?"

"I heard it all." He leaned against the building, watching Levy, who remained as motionless as an Altiplano Indian. He might have been seated there for centuries, he might have been made of stone. "I spent the night in the Rover, over by the Mission. Trying to get Pat out of there, you see, but nothing doing. Elmer's very sick with radiation. She's stricken as well, but not so severely. He's got an amulet like the one he gave Congreve around his neck, but he says it won't kill him. Well, perhaps not. But if something else is going to, it had best hurry up." He gave a shrug of anger and impatience, dismissing the missionary. "On the way in I heard the American helicopter, so I crept up on your little panto. Glad I didn't sweep my old chum up in my arms."

"You were there when he shot me," Krylov said, his eyes wide.

"Viktor, my friend . . . we are risk-takers."

"He nearly killed me."

"He may, too, if you don't get out of here. Bolivia's a bad place to be a Russian, which I suppose is why you invented that odd Canadian."

"You weren't fooled, apparently."

"Oh, of course I was, until I stole a look at your official passport. But the Colonel part surprised me." He frowned at Krylov. "Are you a spy?"

"Not at the moment." No, that was not quite true, thought Krylov. Not until I met Juan Levy. From that moment, yes, you would have to regard me as a spy. "Of course, I only met your friend a few minutes ago."

"I imagine he could bring out the spy in one," said Goodpasture. He looked sadly at Levy. "I can entertain my old chum here for a few days. The weather's turning nasty, nobody will be flying in to get him." As if his words had conjured an approaching storm, the trees around their clearing bucked suddenly in a chill gust of wind. "Yes, I believe we're in for it. Or Juan and I are. For you, Viktor, it is time to go home. Take the Rover, drive to La Paz. It's six hundred kilometers or so, some of it rather awful, but the Rover knows the way. Take your Cutie Pies, I've got more data than I'll ever need."

"I'm not ready to quit."

"But I am ready for you to. Don't be a problem." He peered inquisitively into Krylov's face. "Don't, that is, unless you came here for something else." Krylov shook his head. "Well, then, let's pack it in. You only have a few days' head start. I doubt Juan can be kept much longer than that . . . people in white booties generally don't stay here very long."

"I'll come back."

"Oh, I don't think so. No need." Goodpasture gripped his hand and seemed about to speak, but didn't. Finally he said, "Well, words fail us."

Krylov only nodded, as reluctant as the Englishman to say more. He went into the laboratory and stripped off his ruined shirt to look at his creased left shoulder in the mirror. The wound was a dirty indentation perhaps three centimeters wide where skin had parted to reveal the dark meat beneath it. For a moment, he felt a keen impulse to throttle Levy, but put it away, along with the throbbing pain in his shoulder, which he reduced in his mind to a pulsating crimson light that could be forced toward a distant mental horizon. Krylov cleaned the wound, swabbed it with antibiotic salve on a sterile pad, and bound it. Then he put on a clean shirt and gathered his belongings into his bag, put away the Cutie Pie and sealed its aluminum case. Yellin could send them back to Rio, where he could restore them to the Agency himself.

On his last trip out to load the Land Rover, Krylov noticed the computer screen. It still displayed the twelve fingerprint-like whorls, and had completed the map he'd asked it to draw. He looked at the paper for a moment, then folded it and put it in a trouser pocket. On his way out, he aborted the screen display as well. Levy would recognize those fat, teardrop-shaped ovals, as he had finally done himself. He had seen the same shapes years before, on an American map—of Leningrad.

Part IV

BUSHMASTER

1

For as long as anyone at Lake Union could remember, Yuri Igorivich Petrakov had appeared at seven sharp on Saturday mornings, to fly what most people considered the love of his life: a 1960 Cessna 180, recently repainted white with a thin red lightning bolt down the sides. Weather never seemed to make much difference in his schedule. If he had a few hundred feet between the water and the cloud base, and visibility of half a mile, he headed out. No one knew, or much cared, where he went in the Cessna, although the plane was seen from time to time over Puget Sound or up in the San Juans between Bellingham and Victoria. Rumor said he had a cabin on one of the islands, although it couldn't have been much: a chief petty officer second class would have a place that was like his plane, old and small, but beautifully maintained. Mostly, the people at Lake Union left Ray Morris, as Yuri was known there, pretty much to himself. The Navy was full of men who preferred to live alone, and, God knew, flying every Saturday morning, rain or shine, was pretty innocent—some lonely chiefs molested little boys and girls.

This Saturday morning had dawned behind the passage of a winter storm heading for Montana, leaving in its wake thick curds of ice, some slick hills in downtown Seattle, and a pelting rain of nearly frozen raindrops the size of marbles. The sky and water were fused pewter atmospheres of similar consistency, and only the base of the Space Needle could be seen. From the dock at Kurtzer's one could just discern the ochre and white and maroon buildings across the lake, but nothing was flying—even the gulls floated dismally beneath the overhanging structures of the lakefront. But Petrakov appeared right on schedule, wheeling his ten-year-old Subaru wagon, its beige flanks dinged by a long life on and off the highway, its back seat shredded by the claws of Jemima, Ray's excitable Doberman bitch, into the Kurtzer parking lot. He was a stocky man with greying blonde hair that had gone thin in back, blue eyes empty of all malice, and mean-looking little hands on the thick wrists of a dangerous fighter. He favored Black Watch Pendletons with paisley ascots tied in the collar, and faded jeans, and jump boots, but today he wore a waterproofed anorak as well, in deference to the genuine nastiness of the weather. For a time after he cut the Subaru's lights and motor, he sat in the car, finishing a Camel, watching the weather through the smeared windscreen. He could see very little from the car. In the Cessna, without wipers, he'd be blind forward, able to see perhaps a quarter of a mile to his front right and left. The rain was so close to freezing that it might turn the Cessna into an iceball and drop it into the Sound. Ray Morris would not go out in such weather. But Yuri had no choice. Yellin had called in his marker.

Petrakov shook his head and grinned miserably. Yellin had probably been the death of him, too. They had been quiet lately, things at home being what they were, so that his regular Wednesday call at the Bremerton Thriftifill drop had produced nothing, as usual. But on Thursday night, after his shift at the dispensary at Submarine Base, Bangor, where they called him Doc Morris, he had caught the ferry back to Seattle, taken a few beers and a cheeseburger at Louise's, up in his Westlake neighborhood, and gone home to his one-bedroom flat two blocks farther up the hill, where he could hear Interstate 5 roar eternally, like the sea—just the place for an artificial man to keep his artificial things. He liked the flat because he could see the lake and the Cessna, its white wings part of the multicolored tangle of docked seaplanes tied up across the lake. The ringing telephone had made him jump, which he later took to be an omen, although he knew it must be a solicitor of some kind—

those were about the only calls he ever had. But it was Yellin, a familiar voice from that previous, actual life floating out of the buzz and hiss of ether. "Ray-mond," Yellin had said, his voice making fun of the name. "Is that you, Ray-mond?"

"Yes . . . who is this?" Perhaps Yellin had gone over. Perhaps he was shining a bright light on Petrakov that the FBI could follow to his door.

"Father Christmas," Yellin had replied, laughing. "Happy New Year."

"A bit early."

"I may not be able to call you on the day. How are you doing?"

"Well." Petrakov longed to reply in Russian, the fluent mother tongue like a flood within, but dared not. "And you?"

"I need something."

"This is not the way to get it."

"Don't worry. We've taken precautions."

Petrakov had laughed. "What, tied a bell around my neck?"

"No one is listening."

"If you say so. If you're wrong . . ." Petrakov shrugged, as though Yellin were in the room with him.

"Trust me. I need a favor." A pause, space songs. "It's personal."

Ah, there it was, an evocation of all that was owed him: his life as an American, as against prison for an incident with a Czech girl in 1968, his mother's annuity and quarters in Kiev, the guarantee that they would pull him out if blown, twenty-five years' friendship . . . for the latter, one did anything, of course. One died for one's friends. "Personal?"

"I mean . . . unofficial."

"Well, you know . . . anything." He shut his eyes, feeling his false life contract around him. They could not do this undetected in the modern world.

"When you fly this Saturday . . ."

Petrakov stubbed out his cigarette and got out of the Subaru, ducking his head against the big drops of freezing rain, and locked the car behind him. There was a light in Kurtzer's operations shack and an anonymous figure, who waved. Petrakov waved back, frightened by the silhouette—he wanted no friendly strangers today. He heard imaginary wolves behind him as it was, and pounded down the T-shaped floating dock like a man pursued until he reached the shelter of his Cessna's overhanging wing. There he stopped, expecting to see a wave of armed men move up, door to door, house to house, like soldiers freeing a town, converging upon this suddenly illuminated false sailor, this enemy of the people. . . .

The anorak made him perspire and he unzipped it, then opened the pilot's side and threw it on the passenger seat. The cabin smelled of fish, machine oil, and perspiration. But the cold wind felt good. And . . . he thought he must be alone. He got out the bilge pump and began emptying his floats of the water that seeped through the rusting rivet holes. Get an old plane, they had told him, something a chief petty officer might afford. Perhaps they would let him move up to a newer model one day. Perhaps they would bring him home. Walking around the fuselage, he tugged at elevators and ailerons within reach of the dock, drained the fuel-tank sumps of condensed water— there was never much, as he kept the tanks topped up—and added the two quarts of oil the ageing Cessna always needed before a flight. Then, after another long look to confirm that the wolves, the attacking infantry, were not real, he cast off the lines and leapt onto the near pontoon, then pulled himself up into the cockpit. When the plane had floated a few feet clear of the dock, he cranked the engine, watched the oil pressure come up, listened to the sweet, even racket of the big six-cylinder powerplant. Always perfect.

He taxied out across the rain-spattered chop of waves, heading toward the southern, downtown-Seattle, end of the lake, with the wheel pulled back into his lap to keep the prop out of the spray while he did his run-up on the move. Then he retracted the sea rudder, fastened his seat belt, sealed his door and turned the Cessna into the wind. Adding full power, he kept the wheel back, hauling the airplane up on the step quickly so that its pontoons planed across the water, skipping from wave to wave with a shudder that diminished with each successive impact. Then he tore them off the lake and felt the airplane transformed suddenly into a creature of the sky, a sensation that would always fill his heart to overflowing.

Nearly blind in the rain, steering, he thought, like Charles Lindbergh, out the side windows, he climbed toward the line of railroad tracks and restaurants lining Pacific Avenue, then turned northwest when he had enough altitude to clear the skeleton of the Aurora Bridge. From there, he dropped to two hundred feet, following a narrowing line of silver water out past the Ballard locks and the park that had once been the Army's Fort Lawton, and broke out over Puget Sound, where he felt less shut in by weather. He could just discern the dark, low humps across the Sound, the cranes and docks of Bremerton, and thought of crossing the narrow waist of land to the submarine base, buzz the great boats that floated like icebergs, most of their enormous bulk eternally submerged. But he did not. Kitsap passed off to his left, and Kingston. Across a low hump of land, he could just make out Port Gamble, where another created American monitored the *Trident* submarines as they came and went past the swinging bridge at the mouth of the Hood Canal.

The Cessna had only a gyrocompass, a two-way radio for communications, and a radio direction-finder—Petrakov rarely flew high enough for an omnirange navigation system, which was line of sight, to do him any good. He flicked on the radio, monitoring the tower at Whidbey Island Naval Air Station, off to his north, and turned on the RDF, which he tuned to 1220, Victoria's radio station CKDA, with its antennae offshore on one of the Discovery Islands. CKDA was his standard beacon; everything in his aerial world lay on a bearing from that point. Yellin had told him to fly northeast of CKDA where a bearing of sixty degrees touched the tiny islands freckling the sea north of Shaw Island. Islands multiplied off to the east now, their curved spines rising from the grey water like the backs of immense greenbacked whales. He was to beach the Cessna at that point and wait until noon. If nothing happened, he would try again on Sunday, breaking his long-standing routine—and bathing his artificiality in light. The thought of detection brought an involuntary shudder.

He thought the rain diminished toward the north, for he could see the larger backs of San Juan and Lopez Islands dead ahead, and aimed the Cessna at the narrow strait between them.

There were airfields and seaplane harbors everywhere up here, but no one was flying today. Even Whidbey Island NAS was quiet. Petrakov cocked his head, listening to the even sound of the Cessna's engine, scanned the instruments, looked at the dark forest passing on his right, the low flanks of San Juan Island on his left. He kept to mid-channel, descending to a hundred feet above the grey water, oddly comfortable to be so low in a grey sphere with no horizon. Well, he had once flown out of Vladivostok, after all.

He realized only now how nervous Yellin's call, like somebody at the corner drugstore, had made him. But out here, he felt he had regained his element, and relaxed a little. He switched the radio to the Coast Guard air station at Port Angeles, but heard nothing on their frequency. There were worse things than being left alone by the American military on a day like this, with Yellin's call still vibrating in his ears. In his soul, more like.

"Something happened on the *Indiana* last October. I want to know what. It's very important."

Important enough, thought Petrakov, to throw me to the wolves.

Shaw Island appeared ahead of him and he banked gently toward the northwest, and began to get the Cessna ready for landing, quickly running through the cowl flaps-gump (gas, undercarriage, mixture, prop) checklist, pulling his power back to fifteen inches' manifold pressure, and adding ten degrees of flaps. The wind was howling right down the channel, driving a stiff current to the southeast. As the end of Shaw Island passed his right wing and was replaced by a throw of small islands, he put on another ten degrees of flap and eased the power back until he had a hundred-foot-per-minute descent. One really could not tell where the water was, except that it was the bottom of the grey, horizonless sphere through which he had been flying. Not until he was barely ten feet off the surface did he see the whitecaps, the froth and moiré of the rain, and then the pontoons touched. Quickly, Petrakov pulled the wheel back—Cessnas flipped over if you didn't—to slow it, but added enough power to keep the floats on the step, so that the airplane would skip across the waves rather than wallow among them.

Taxiing on the step, he saw where the RDF showed a sixty-degree outbound bearing from CKDA, and headed into a narrow cove on a sparsely wooded island. He cut power and let the airplane drift to the stony beach. The pontoons rasped upon sand and gravel. The Eagle has landed, thought Petrakov. He throttled the engine, and switched off the electricals. Then there was only the sound of moving water, the cry of wind, the creak of the aircraft against the beach. Petrakov lighted a Camel and put his anorak back on, waiting for . . . what?

Wolves, no doubt, and soldiers.

At first he thought the new sound was just a change in the voice of today's bad weather. But, listening more closely, Petrakov recognized the buzz of an outboard motor. Through the grey veil of rain, he saw an inflatable boat like a French Zodiac push into the relatively still waters of the cove, three men aboard. They watched his airplane with suspicion he could sense from fifty meters away, and beached their craft well out of good pistol range. One man stepped ashore, a small fellow with a Lenin beard, probably bald as well, and probably, beneath the fisherman's heavy weather gear and sweaters, somewhat frail; his face had the luminosity of the weak. Instead of walking to the airplane, he strolled across the beach to the dark line of the pine forest, stopping in the shadows. Behind him, the others pushed off and took the boat back toward the sea, leaving the visitor to face whatever came by himself.

Petrakov lighted another cigarette. This was not very well done, when you thought of it—telephone calls in the clear, boats of strangers pulling up on unfamiliar beaches. A Navy trap would spring in just this way—although, it *had* been Yellin on the telephone, and there stood a pale Russian of a man, his face turned toward the airplane. "Shit," Petrakov murmured. "*Shit.*" He took a chamois packet from the map pouch in the door and unwrapped a nine-millimeter Browning automatic, put a round in the chamber, and slid it into his anorak pocket. At least he would not go into this as a lamb to the slaughter. Angry at being where Yellin had placed him, he shoved open his door and stepped down on the pontoon, then jumped ashore, his feet clinking in the gravel. The man waiting in the shadows stepped forward, matching him step for step until they met halfway up the slope of sand and rock. "I am looking for Shaw Island," said Petrakov, following his instructions.

"North of Takoma," the other man replied.

"Thank you. I must go there sometime."

"Before you go . . . do you have a Camel?"

Petrakov grinned and walked up to the man. "Christ, who thinks of these dances? Petrakov is my name."

"Zubov."

They shook hands, the stranger's very cold to the touch, and so thin you could feel the small bones rattling around beneath the skin. He quickly restored his gloves. "I believe we have a mutual friend," said Zubov, his voice a clear resolute tenor.

"Yes, and see what it has got us." Petrakov laughed. Without even knowing it, he had slipped back into Russian. His language still waited for him to put it on, like a fine suit of clothes. "I haven't spoken Russian in a long time," he said almost in a whisper. "Where are you from?"

"Novosibirsk."

"No, I meant tonight. What ship?"

"The *Ekholot.*"

Petrakov thought it over. She was a 750-ton intelligence ship of the *Okean* class, about fifty meters long, older than he was. "Vancouver bound?"

Zubov nodded. "I'll be back aboard by the time she clears the islands."

"Yellin called you too?"

"Easier for him to call me. . . . We have secure communications."

"He called me on the telephone."

"Christ."

"What is he after?"

"I don't know. Something to do with a missile test. We were out in the Pacific, watching as usual when we know a *Trident* will be launched. It was spectacularly beautiful . . . but a failure. The thing popped out of the water, but began to cartwheel, like a giant firework. They blew it up before it touched the water. Fantastic show, but nothing for us. Still, Yellin wants everything I have . . . unofficially. I suppose he called you 'unofficially' too."

"He may face a three-hundred-dollar fine for this," Petrakov replied with a grin. He removed a folded manila envelope from the anorak's inner pocket. It had a U.S. Navy return address on it, along with a warning of penalties for private use. "These are interviews with *Indiana* crew members who've gone on sick call since the test, and autopsy reports on the three sailors who've died . . . apparently of natural causes." He handed the envelope to Zubov. "What happens now?"

"I'll get everything to DHL in Vancouver today. Yellin should have it on Monday."

"Where is he?"

"He asked me not to say."

"He may have destroyed me here with that call. Where is he?"

"At our embassy in La Paz."

"La Paz." Petrakov chuckled. The ends of the earth. "La Paz. I wonder what he did to deserve that?"

"He probably asked unofficial favors of old friends."

"And here we are." Petrakov looked apprehensively at the weather, the darkening water. "I'd best head back. It's suspicious to fly in such weather, even for me." The other man did not move. "Well, perhaps you can give me a hand getting her off the beach."

Between them, they managed to rock the Cessna back into the water, and get it pointed seaward. Then they shook hands and Petrakov climbed into the cockpit; the engine roared to life when he cranked it, pulling him gently into deeper water. He looked back at Zubov, who had returned to the shadows, and waved. He thought Zubov returned the gesture. As he taxied, Petrakov checked the mags and prop and mixture, looking for the longest fetch against the wind. Then he was off the water, blind in rain again. Looking down from his side window, he made out the wake of the rubber boat going back for Zubov, and felt an odd, elated relief.

In fact, he felt actually lightheaded. A difficult mission, nicely done, leaving him drowning in misspent adrenaline. It had taken him until late Friday night to obtain copies of the records, which he had not had a chance to read, which he had not even removed from a cache beneath the Subaru's floorboards, until he'd started for Lake Union this morning. There were so many things one didn't want to know. He climbed the Cessna to two hundred feet, and trimmed it for level cruise at a hundred miles per hour, then set an outbound bearing of one-three-five on the RDF; when he crossed that line he'd be close to Port Townsend. He could find his way on all fours, if necessary, to get home from there.

Petrakov did not see the helicopter until it had moved into formation with the Cessna, appearing so gradually out of the grey rain that it might have materialized there. It was a Blackhawk, painted flat black, and he thought he could see where some identifying numbers had been overpainted, like the numbers on a smuggler's plane. Jesus, Yellin, he thought frantically, is this your precautions? The Cessna's cabin was getting warm again, and beginning to smell of its pilot. He wriggled free of the anorak, watching his unwanted companion. He adjusted the RDF to see how far he had come and discovered that he must still be well out in the Straits, over the miles and miles of open water north of Puget Sound, flying not ten miles east of the Canadian boundary. The Blackhawk's helmeted pilot watched him inscrutably, then held up fingers, one, none, eight, none, five, to indicate a hailing frequency. Petrakov grinned for him and pointed at his instrument panel, then turned his thumb down. No radio. The pilot shook his head, sadly, it seemed to Petrakov, and made a movement with his hand to indicate a change in direction, and did his finger signal again: two-seven-zero. They wanted him to fly west with them. To where? He glanced at his fuel gauges, saw that he still had better than two-thirds fuel remaining, enough to go another four hours. Perhaps he could outlast them. He banked toward the suggested course, playing for time.

If they knew who he was, his American world had already crumbled. There would be an arrest, months of interrogation, and finally perhaps a trade for someone. . . . In the new world order, what did one do about spies? "Yellin you've fucking *cooked* me," he cried out in English. The sound made him feel better. Why was he so worried? The *Ekholot* was steaming toward Vancouver. The Soviet consulate would get him aboard if he could reach Canada. In a few weeks he would be back in the

Soviet Union, his past sins forgiven, his career taking some new and interesting turn. He grinned, then looked at the sombre escort. The rain had thinned, but still drummed on the Cessna. It would be freezing a few hundred feet above them, up in the clouds that blanketed them even at two hundred feet. But the Blackhawk couldn't track him through cloud. He could climb, get rid of them, yes, and take the ice, then drop down farther north and melt it off, and make for Vancouver.

But the Blackhawk was crowding him, he saw now, forcing him steadily to the north of their westward heading. They must be over Canadian waters, he thought, and then made out the trees of Vancouver Island, the high banks, a vast darkness behind the veil of rain, and *still* they crowded him northward. Sensing that he had got too far behind his situation to recover, Petrakov frantically applied power and began to climb, the helicopter staying always on his left, rising with him, always a meter closer than before, so that he had to turn farther toward the rough land that now hurried by not fifty meters beneath them, climbing the Cessna as he did, trying to get up into the cloud, which swallowed him, forget the ice, forget everything but getting away from this goddamned helicopter, the stick back, full power, the Cessna shuddering upward, ice forming along its wings, the windscreen glazed, and still Petrakov climbed, and the helicopter, still visible as a grey ghost on his left, nudged him farther north, until the Cessna was too heavy with ice to gain another meter's altitude, and leveled out, shaking, ready to stall, at only two thousand feet. Petrakov racked his memory and thought he might be far enough west to clear the hills. In fact, he was fifteen miles east of Port Renfrew, where a coastal ridge rises more than three thousand feet above sea level.

He scarcely saw the dark form of the forested ridge leap toward him. All he had time to see was the opaque, blurred shape of the earth, like an enormous bear, like God himself, dart at him, and then the scream of his fine old airplane breaking up in the black pines, the hiss of fire . . .

2

"The trouble with you, Viktor, is you think you can do it all yourself." Yellin stood before him like a ghost, the light flooding the room from the window behind him. Outside, Krylov could see the line of trees that enclosed the embassy, and beyond that the blue and yellow walls of the playground across the way, the trickling remains of the Choqueyapu River; an ochre pile of dirt and weathered rock made a rough horizon, a moonscape, between them and La Paz. "I could have saved you a few steps . . . well, now I have. Do you feel up to a fairy tale?"

Krylov nodded, smiling privately. One heard that, in the old days, Yellin had displayed a self-possession that required only an occasional word or two to steer him through the world. Now, in his La Paz exile, the man ran on and on. "I can hardly wait." He sat on a brown leather sofa in Yellin's embassy office, wearing the white government-issue pajamas the doctors had given him when he'd arrived. They had taken one look at his wounded shoulder, which had turned the color of old steak, and put him to bed, which he was glad to do while they waited for Yellin's people to verify his peculiar—and, he thought now, unreliable—gestahlt. In the jungle, the doctors said, he had lost eight kilos and his red blood count was down a third. Arias had told him, during the survey flights, that he would be going to Panama to have his blood changed, "Especially *now*," and the pilot had nodded toward the counter. Krylov had thought of

Arias as the doctors changed his blood, turning him, as Yellin put it later, into the world's largest Bolivian. They also itched to check his bone marrow for blood cell production, but he had put them off, even when they argued that he might be clipping years off the end of his life. Christ, how did one know where the end was, anyway? It might have already come and gone several times.

"That was a remarkable insight you had, Viktor." Yellin had sat down behind his broad wooden desk, now littered with paper, the tendrils of discovery. He radiated the pleasure of an idle man restored to his profession, and Krylov was glad to see it: he took Yellin to be a friend. "As you said, those shapes . . . those 'fingerprints' . . . look very much like a multiple-warhead footprint. The twelve re-entry vehicles in a *Trident II* D5 warhead would produce a very similar dispersion. The trouble was, no one appeared to have launched anything like that during a time period corresponding to the Beni Fall. We cannot watch the whole planet with our radars, of course, even the Baranovich phased-array sees very little south of . . ." and he smiled, "the border." His long fingers laced themselves together, as though they had a life of their own. "Not even in Argentina, Israel, or South Africa. We looked everywhere, you see, even at the outlaws. And no satellites dropped out of orbit on the night of the Fall. He leaned back in his large leather chair, and watched his fingers make a steeple. "The only attempt to launch a ballistic missile in that time frame was a clear failure. Have you seen Zubov's tape?"

Krylov shook his head. Yellin knew he had seen nothing; this was just theatre.

"You'll find it interesting." Yellin pointed a remote control box at the far wall, which opened to reveal a large television screen, covered with a confusion of lines. "Watch."

The tape must have been made aboard the *Ekholot*, Krylov thought, using a thousand-millimeter lens, or better. The movement of the Soviet ship had been somehow damped out, so that the surface track of the submarine could just be discerned, centered in the frame. Suddenly, like a breaching white whale, a *Trident II* missile leapt from the water in a great cloud of spray, rose without power into the air, and seemed to poise for a split-

second before its solid-rocket motor ignited. Standing on its
column of smoke and flame, the missile rose skyward, but
seemed suddenly to falter, as though its robot pilot had died—
Krylov had the eerie sense of a dead midget slumped over the
controls. The *Trident* rose barely a hundred meters into the air,
then turned back toward the sea, its exhaust trail forming a
white *O* above the water. But near the end, again, as though the
pilot had revived, the missile pointed its nose skyward and rose
perhaps fifty meters before, stalling, it toppled sideways. At
that point, someone must have pushed a button that destroyed
it; the missile detonated in a flash that cast a great pall of smoke
and falling debris across the sea. "Christ," he murmured.

"Listen to what Zubov says. 'When we saw the *Trident* go
crazy, most of us ran on deck to watch. There was no point in
watching telemetry when the missile was going to blow up in
such a spectacular fashion. It was too good to miss.' " Yellin
shook his head and stood up. "Let me show you something,
Viktor. He walked over to the television as the tape rewound,
and started it forward once more, this time one frame at a time.
Again, the dark ocean showed a white point that grew into a
kind of fountain, and the round nose of the *Trident* appeared in
the column of spray, moving upward, frame by frame, through
the loop, the seeming recovery. . . . He froze the frame. "Look
just to the right of the smoke in this frame." A patch of white
water had appeared there, like the one in the first frame of the
launch sequence.

"Debris?"

"Watch closely," Yellin murmured, himself transfixed by the
images on the screen. He advanced the tape another frame. The
white patch spread, became vertical, grew, and then, in the
fourth frame, was obscured by smoke. "You think it is falling
debris?"

"I don't know. Can I see it again?"

Yellin walked the sequence back through the half-dozen
frames. "I don't see anything dropping into the sea at this
point."

"Nor do I."

"So . . . what do you think?"

"I don't know. A second launch? Why wouldn't the *Ekholot* have seen it?"

"Zubov says the weather was poor that day, visibility down to about three kilometers. You can tell by the quality of the tape that it was the wrong day for a test shot. The submarine—the *Indiana*—was south of Hawaii, down at the very edge of our radar coverage. We got something, nevertheless. The PVO got —the *Voiska Protivos*—a ghost, something. When Zubov was queried, he said he thought it must have been the radar signal of a piece of the missile, blown sky-high by the explosion. Maybe so. But suppose it is one segment of an arc, and you take the Beni Fall as another segment of the same arc. The two line up."

"Maybe we just want them to. It is very circumstantial."

"It becomes more so. My old friend Petrakov sent me something more. After the 31 October test, the *Indiana* returned to her base in Bangor, Washington. Eight crewmen reported sick, with symptoms you would find familiar: fatigue, general malaise, anemia. Five were easily treated. Two who were involved in loading the missile tubes reported more severe symptoms, such as vomiting and diarrhea, extreme weakness. The eighth one died soon after the submarine returned to port. The autopsy report says he succumbed to a heart attack, but it also describes skin lesions, anemia, low white-cell counts. One of the surviving pair died in a collision on Interstate 5 near Everett. The last was killed when a propane tank exploded at his mobile home. He was the only officer, a lieutenant j.g., and he left something interesting in his medical record. Listen. 'I believe that during the loading and post-test cleanup on 31 October and 1 and 2 November, I was subjected to abnormally high levels of ionizing radiation, causing illness and exposing me to a high future risk of cancer among other diseases. Because the U.S. Navy will not acknowledge my exposure, I am going to a private hospital for further diagnosis and to see whether or not I have been made sterile.' "

"The *Indiana* must have had a radiation incident. It happens. Think of the *Komsomolets* off Norway."

"That was a fire, not radiation. Besides, we . . . one wants to say *even* we . . . did not kill sailors for talking about it."

"So that's what you think is happening in Seattle? The silencing of the stricken? The American Navy doesn't operate that way either."

"But some Americans do."

Krylov shrugged. He began to regret making the leap from teardrop shapes to missile footprints. After all, it was like finding animal shapes in clouds, anyone could find anything. "Of course, you can find people who'll do any dirty job."

"I think the fellow who made the affidavit was talking about radiation in the missile tube itself."

"Nuclear warheads all emit something."

"The odd neutron. But this one emitted enough gamma to sicken the men installing it."

"Why build such a thing?" It was crazy. You could build a bomb that would crack the planet in half and not release so much gamma.

"Why indeed?"

"And a warhead isn't a grain sack. You don't just fill a *Trident II* D5 with twelve cans of radioactive material."

"You're right, Viktor. A lot of science has to be done beforehand." Yellin returned to his desk and got out a thermos of cold vodka, and poured two of the brilliantly cut glasses full. "For your bone marrow, Viktor."

"Thanks." But Krylov didn't toss the vodka back against his throat, as he might have at home. Instead, he sipped it, letting the cold fire spread slowly downward through his body, which, he realized, had needed warming up. The alcohol washed through his mind and he thought, Anemia is the key to a cheap drunk.

"I am a vodka dispenser from way back," said Yellin, his voice seeming to come from far away. "During the Great Patriotic War, near the end, I was just a boy, but I joined the Army anyway. The winter of 1944, there I was, eleven years old, my feet wrapped in rags, ladling out vodka for the men." He held his glass so that the facets cast a lace of light across the room. "That was the beginning of a new world order, Viktor, the Great Patriotic War. I liked it. . . . I liked the hard edges, the sharp blacks and whites. I frankly enjoyed a world in which two superpowers were poised against one another, too power-

ful to go to war without destroying the world. It was like social-
ism itself, you know, like the rust in an old engine, it held
everything together. Clean it out and the engine falls apart." He
hesitated, reflecting, then leaned toward Krylov. "I'll tell you
another fable, Viktor." Yellin returned to the window, peering
out at the pale sky, the lunar surroundings, but, Krylov understood, really looking at the past.

"It is a fable," he began, "because we know nothing, really.
We have a name, rumors, and that's all. You remember the
neutron bomb? We propagandized the Americans out of building it years ago. Only capitalists, we told anyone who listened,
would be so cold-blooded as to develop a way to destroy life
instead of property. It was more than they could bear. They
gave it up.

"But an idea like that never quite goes away. Now and then,
we would get a slight whiff of something, always very nebu-
lous, never confirmed. It sounded like the ghostly son of the
neutron bomb, and we never put money into running down
American ghosts. We were concerned with those sharp edges I
referred to, the easily distinguished blacks and whites. But here
was this thing, this ugly rumor of a weapon, waiting in the
shadows. Or not. As I say, we never knew." Yellin turned back
to the room, and refilled his glass. Krylov declined, not wanting
his mind clouded.

"Viktor, did your British friend show you one of the big vipers over there?"

"I never saw one."

"You never do, unless someone points it out. Then, someone
will say, look there, a bushmaster, and you'll peer at the mottled shadows and see . . . nothing. Nothing, that is, until
you're nose-to-nose with a seven-foot snake. It makes your
knees go weak finally to see it." He filled his mouth with
vodka, and let it trickle into him. *Lachesis mutus.* You know
Lachesis?"

"Clotho spins, Lachesis takes the measure, Atropos cuts."

"The three fates. Lachesis measures out the thread of life.
When you see a bushmaster waiting for prey, you believe in
them." He chuckled.

"Is the snake part of your fable?"

"*That* was the name we used to hear. *Bushmaster*. A wonderful name for this . . . ugly rumor." He seemed almost to shake himself then, and returned to the window. "I can imagine some visionary going to the technicians in Los Alamos or Livermore. Gentlemen, he says, we are about to see a new world order. It will have no sharp edges, no obvious contrasts. It will have one superpower and scores of third-world countries motivated by zealotry, poverty, envy, famine—the new horsemen of the new order. Their arsenals contain only terror. Now . . . build us a weapon for the new world order.

"So . . . my mythical technicians go to work. The strategists tell one another that, in this new world order, there is no thought of seizing ground, and no reason to destroy cities. The weapon, therefore, would be used to punish terror and aggression against weaker, or favored, neighbors. If a superpower's citizen is taken hostage, the weapon can punish the captors, their families, their city, in open-ended escalation. And this weapon offers terror as well. It does not merely blow things up —it terrifies, it comes upon the people of the less-developed world as from their worst superstitions—like the *surucucu* comes to the dreams of rainforest Indians." He paused, seeming to reflect. Then, almost as if he awakened from a trance, he turned back to Krylov. "It could be a dream. As I say, we heard the name, but it always had the sound, the feel of rumor. In the end, I think our Powers decided it was the Americans trying to sell us yet another load of technological shit. When we heard that *Bushmaster* would be used to get the hostages out of Iran, to cure Iran of hostage-taking, we did not believe it. In the event, nothing like that happened." He uttered a low, self-deprecating laugh. "Nobody knows."

"You'd need a very dirty war to use it."

Yellin's eyes gleamed. "And what war is that?"

"The Drug War."

"Yes, exactly. A war with the third world. They attack your society with narcotics, you counter with an invisible poison that also tags contraband with a radioactive signature." Yellin poured himself another vodka, and held up the thermos for Krylov, who again declined. His mind was racing.

"Still," Krylov said then, "the stuff is no better than gas. Once the genie is out of the bottle, you have no control." But even as he made the argument, he realized what the Americans—what Levy—must have done. He raised his eyes to Yellin's. "Amecos," he whispered.

"Amecos?" Yellin was genuinely puzzled.

"The Amazon Ecosystem Study," Krylov said. "I should have smelled it. They come down to Bolivia and get enough data to build good predictive models of where the cesium will go. The meteorology of a rainy season over ten or a hundred thousand kilometers is not difficult to simulate in models—it is very predictable. Amecos," he added, "is the part of *Bushmaster* we can see."

"Wonderful, isn't it? Here we've more or less invented a project, a weapon, a motive, everything. But we still haven't anything to take to trial, Viktor." Again, Yellin leaned toward him. "However, I *know* we are right. I have proof of that."

"What do you mean?"

"Petrakov never returned to Seattle."

Because, thought Krylov, you illuminated your old friend with a telephone call. "You expected it."

"Only if someone were listening. And . . . someone was."

"One of your sharp edges, Yellin?"

"Remember when you first came to see me, Viktor? I said that I may be one of Stalin's children, after all. I told you: I am still at war, I have been at war since I ladled vodka in the snow." He chuckled, glancing almost shyly at Krylov. "You told me you had not come to Bolivia to build improbable bridges. And now, here we are with a regular Golden Gate of an improbable bridge. Perhaps that really was what brought you here."

But Krylov barely heard him. He was thinking of Goodpasture, and of being under Levy's pistol; he was thinking that Petrakov had never got back to Seattle. They knew. They had begun to care. "I have to tell Goodpasture." Then he thought of Congreve's amulet, the grey crescent of forged metal. There would be more where the missionary had found it. *Bushmaster* had left a trail. "We'll bring down their fucking government."

Yellin smiled and raised his dazzling glass into the light.

3

That bastard Goodpasture had poisoned him, Levy was certain of it, for he had not intended to sleep at all, and now, here he was starting suddenly awake with his head throbbing like an axe wound, full of some goddamned crushed leaf from the forest, compliments of his grand old friend. "JOLY!" he yelled, his voice tight with anger and pain. Bastard. He moved to get up and found himself paralyzed. Christ, he thought, Goodpasture's given me curare! Then he realized that he had been trussed with a slipknot of braided vine around his wrists behind him and his ankles, linked by a third loop around his neck. When he tried to stand up, the knots tightened at both ends. "JOLY GODDAMN IT!" He knew his yelling did no good, but it was all he had left at the moment. And he knew there was no one there to hear him. The place resounded with an emptiness that seemed ageless, as though he had been lying on his woven mat, hog-tied, for centuries. Levy thrashed unhappily for a moment, then lay back to let the knots ease up again. Goodpasture had kept him close and had tethered him since his arrival, but nothing like this.

A yellow Amecos Post-it note was stuck to his left knee. With some difficulty, Levy maneuvered into a position from which he could read it without strangling.

Must rush. Careful with the harness, some arrow-frog on it. Juice in fridge.

Levy shut his eyes, rage like an oil-well fire in his chest; he imagined blood vessels exploding in his brain, imagined himself actually *dying* of anger, and forced himself to calm down, to think, to think. . . . Then, lying quietly, he began to laugh, slowly at first, then more wildly. "My God," he howled. "My God!" I mean, he thought, think of how you look, Juan. God. The fact was, Goodpasture very likely was his only friend, and he one of Goodpasture's very few, whatever their . . . operational . . . differences at the moment. He made himself relax, watched the vague discolorations of the white-painted ceiling, listened to the world beyond his bonds: the weather that had threatened when he arrived had swept in on them over the weekend, and now the station floated like an island in a grey sky full of rain, the big drops roaring on the metal roof. Perhaps that had awakened him, although, after a day or two, you tuned out noise like that.

An enemy would have killed him in the night, as, he thought now, the rage flowing back in behind the mad chuckles, he should have done to Goodpasture long ago, after Amecos. He should have wiped the goddamned research station off the face of the earth, burned it, and left Joly in a shallow jungle grave where the animals could pick him apart and fight over his bones, so that *Bushmaster* could proceed without all this extraneous horseshit, without the introduction of a *Russian*, for Christ's sake—so that he, Juan Levy, armed and very dangerous, could not be outfought with a fucking bow and arrow, or left trussed in a venomous noose.

There, he told himself, there, there. Joly would want you to be angry, he wants that red haze in your brain. But he wasn't trying to kill Levy, or he would have done it on the first night, or the next. He merely wanted to delay the inevitable, which was . . . anger seethed once more, imagining the ruin that would now befall the Englishman. "I'm coming back with some firepower, Joly," Levy hissed. "I'm going to get rid of all this goddamned *static*."

If Joly were not trying to kill him, he thought, driving himself back to a more relaxed state, then the vines would not be lethally poisoned. He tried to view himself from outside, to look at the machinery of his tethers, and began exploring his real ability to move. He could not stand up, but he could get to his knees. Then, leaning back, his fingertips could just touch the vines binding his ankles, although as soon as he touched them, he felt the venom blister his skin. Still, he scrabbled at the vines, feeling them begin to shred, fingers burning, but, there, something began to yield as he let the rage fly up once more. He bent backward another painful inch, grabbed the vines in his two bound hands, and ripped them away. His legs freed, Levy spread himself out, and rested for a moment. Then he rolled back on the woven mat, brought up his knees, put his feet through the loop of his bound hands, and rolled lightly to his feet. With his hands in front of him, he could manipulate the neck noose over his head, relieved to find that Goodpasture had not put poison on that part of the truss. Then, trailing vines from his tethered wrists, he went into the kitchen and turned on the kerosene burner. He watched impassively as the blue flames curled along his wrists, blistering the skin, burning the dark hairs away, burning the vines, thinking that this was what he would do to this place when he returned. When the vines had nearly burned through, he yanked his wrists apart and held his arms in the air like a man who has cast aside his chains. He felt powerful now, and dangerous. Moving quickly, he went to the basin and ran cool water on his fingers, then soaped them, diluting the frog poison. Still, his fingers were numb after he dried them. He looked around for his shoes, but Goodpasture had taken them, leaving only the white booties.

A second Post-it note was stuck to the door jamb.

I could have fed you to the ants.

"Thanks for nothing, Joly." For a moment he contemplated the torrential rain outside, the cold blast of high-altitude air sweeping downward from the slowly moving storms, then kicked the door open. As he did, his eye caught a flicker of movement, a trip wire, and he threw himself to one side against the inner wall. One of Goodpasture's long fishing arrows flashed through the opening and lodged in the far wall.

The rain, the cold, were sweet upon his body, washing his head clear, rinsing away the poisons and the blinding rage. Levy moved cautiously, testing the ground before he put his foot down on the trail. At the edge of the forest, he saw the low mound of stones, a wooden cross that was all sadness in the rain, its garish crucified frog. They had buried the girl, Rosa, out by the trees, Goodpasture had told him on the first night. "The cesium killed her, Juan." His eyes had gleamed, speaking of it.

"You make it sound like *my* cesium, Joly."

"Ah, well, you're right," Goodpasture had said. "I know an act of God when I see one. You can generally tell by the amount of terror in it."

Levy stalked toward the darkness beneath the canopy of trees. The forest, buzzing in the heavy rain, went silent as he entered, its sounds erupting after he had passed, as though he were followed by a crowd of onlookers. As though, he thought, I'm wearing a bell. The fall of rain was broken into splashes and streams by the trees, and Levy, who had bent beneath the torrent, now straightened up, trying to sense more than he could see of his surroundings. He felt strongly that Goodpasture was nowhere about, although he saw that the Englishman had gone into the treetops. The ropes and *jumars* that had formerly dangled from the platform had been hauled up and secured where no one could reach them, and Levy supposed Goodpasture had done this across his entire arboreal network of cables and walkways. He must have extended that realm considerably since Amecos days, when there had been just a platform and a couple of short cable walks—the better, thought Levy, to drink vodka and sing the odd line of opera. For a moment, his spirits fell; back then, despite the central lie of Amecos that lay between them, they had been close, shared real laughter, real affection, they would have died for one another, perhaps . . . if it didn't affect the operation. Yes, thought Levy, there was always that. He felt suddenly as though the natural part of him, the Mayan within, had been deformed, stunted, possibly slain, by the activities of his other, operational self. *Bushmaster I*, a mere test of an idea whose time appeared to have come, had cut him off from his one friendship. What would he be like after *Bushmaster II* went into the high valleys of Peru? He shook his head. "You'll be like a radioactive firefly if you don't get out of here, Juanito."

For the first time since his arrival, he thought clearly, sharply, of what floated in the air he breathed, what lay upon his clothing, his skin . . . and experienced a vast interior calm. He had exposed himself to that same venom he had sent into the forest with the Fall, and here he was, alive, given to fits of anger, occasionally ready to blow up the world—but alive. Yes, and slightly radioactive. Gamma rays had gone into his blood and bone marrow, into the hearts of his cells, and did so now, as he stood in the rain, in the forest. It was time he got out of here, and did the necessary. If you had only one friend, after all, you could probably get by with none. It was time to be, as those hardhearted old men in the executive office building liked to put it, extracted.

Back in the laboratory, Levy helped himself to the juice Goodpasture's note had mentioned, drawn from some bitter-sweet jungle plant, slightly mouth-numbing, that only an Englishman would drink, and to half a loaf of cassava bread. Chewing, beginning to feel good now that the drugs, the rage, the sense of terrible futility were wearing off, he sat down at the radio, switched it on, and began to try his Huey's shortwave listening frequency. "This is Levy," he said into the microphone, "Levy, Levy, Levy, over." A resounding silence swallowed his voice. Goodpasture had done something to the goddamned radio. Quickly, now, he turned the unit around and searched its interior for obvious damage, but found none. And it was plugged into a wall outlet. . . .

The silence. Aside from the roar of rain, there was only silence at the research station, where, somewhere in that roar, he should have heard the sputter of the diesel generator. He ran back into the rain, to the low shelter where the Amecos generator had been installed. Goodpasture had severed its fuel lines, cut its throat. Rage flickered like lightning within, but Levy held it in check. Rage would drive him over a cliff that Goodpasture had put in his way, would stop him thinking as he moved through the Englishman's domain—for, he had to concede that it was definitely Goodpasture's, not his own. Levy knew this rainforest intimately only at the mesoscale, as he knew foreign governments: he knew its storms and chemical pathways, without knowing much about its population of trees and animals, its secret arboreal terrain. Goodpasture knew every goddamned bush, no doubt. Not a sparrow falls, he thought, wondering if there were sparrows in the tropical rainforest. Of course there were. There were sparrows everywhere.

He had to get out of here, quickly, immediately. He had to get into clean clothing, get his skin clean, get a doctor in Santa Cruz to check his blood. Abruptly, his heart rate increased, he felt it hammering away, as though the strangeness of the ground, his utter isolation, had frightened him. Christ, when had he ever been scared?

A sound beneath the roar of falling rain came to him then, and he thought, the river, and then: *the boat.* Amecos had left a Zodiac behind, he could get out in that. He sprinted toward the river. The boat was where he'd left it all that long time ago, inflated, sitting lightly on the swollen brown eddies of the Chipirirri, a sight to make the heart leap . . . except, Goodpasture had also been here before him. The outboard motor was gone, and now lay, no doubt, in the muck of the river bottom at a point only Goodpasture knew. Without a motor he couldn't go against the current, and there was nothing, absolutely nothing, for a hundred miles downstream. He saw a yellow rectangle fastened in the sheltering curve of the Zodiac's inflated sides, and climbed down to read it.

Welcome to shit creek. Sorry about paddle.

Son of a bitch. Son of a *BITCH!*

Joly, Levy thought with great care, stepping between the mines of rage, I will get out of this and come back with a squad of infantry and pulverize this place, burn your station, burn your goddamned forest, turn everything that's here to ashes. When we are finished, my friend, animals will compete for your bones. Indians will speak of it as the time the forest burned. We will burn it down even in this rain, old chum. You lose.

He would have to walk out. Four hours to Todos Santos. Four more to the highway. Another couple of hours getting a ride to Chimoré. "Tomorrow," he told the buildings, the trees, the river, the silence that flowed in around him in the rain, "You have until tomorrow." Then he put his head down and began to walk.

4

The sky outside the hut was crying as she had wanted to, Teejay thought, but could not. She watched the windblown sheets of spray, the trees jerking crazily in the gust that flew down, invisible angels of the air, to smite the earth. To smite her, perhaps, to make her writhe, somehow to increase her misery. The mud walls of the hut streamed with water, and puddles formed on the earthen floor where it was not quite level, while, overhead, the thatch crackled and thumped in the wind, and filled the tiny space with the smell of wet hay. The sun was a silver ghost behind the torrent, and Palma had taken away her watch, the ruby-rimmed Juvenia from Santa Cruz, so that every moment of her day would be like every other. She thought it must be dusk, so long had the light taken to grow, and to diminish, the passing star hacking another notch in a life gone seriously awry.

Her entire body hurt, not a lot, but everywhere, from her three days in the cold hut, a one-room structure on the fringe of the outbuildings that radiated, each one poorer than the last, from the residence. Palma had installed her there on Congreve's orders. Congreve would have done worse, had he been strong enough to beat her. His small, ruined face had blanched in its frame of wildly uneven white hair, then suffused with hatred, as he'd listened to Palma say that she had lied about the nature of the plague, that it was radiation; that she had thought to leave them to their fates. Congreve had lifted the amulet from its place beneath his pillows, then, had held it before him for a time, then flung it across the tiled floor, where it landed with the clunk of a false coin. "Peterson," Congreve murmured. "Fucking missionary. I want to *see* him." His hands had shaken. "Where's Arias?"

Palma had gestured at the day, the walls of falling rain. "Not flying."

"When it stops . . ." and Congreve had seemed to lose interest. His eyes had flickered to hers, watched her intently for a time. "Her," he'd told Palma, then, "Give *her* to the boys."

Christ. The boys.

Palma had let the boys look her over, touch her, mock her, stirring them up so that she could see what hatred lay behind the thin veil of their obedience to Congreve, and their fear of the *senderista*. Like sharks they had come close to her, brushed her with their rough skin, excited to be near this most expendable of all women, this blonde *gringa* who had been too good for them, this traitor to their boss, whom she had screwed as coldly as a whore. He had let the boys rough her up a little; her lips felt swollen to her fingertips and tongue, and she thought a tooth twice root-canaled had loosened in her gum. He had let them flash their cocks at her; the boys, she thought, lacked grace and style. Beneath the roar of rain, he had let her see how badly the boys would hurt her, she, who had done everything for every man she'd ever been with, keeping love clear and clean by taking less, always less, than she gave. But he had not given her to the boys.

Palma had returned to the hut that night and, without speaking to her, punched her in the face, then took his time defiling her, penetrating her without warmth, wherever he wished, without even taking his pants off. He might have read a newspaper while he did it. He might have raped her with a pointed stone. And, at the end, he had left Congreve's amulet hanging by its leather thong on a nail in the far wall. "If you touch it, I'll give you to the boys." That was all he'd said to her, and she understood that he intended it to frighten those nasty little fuckers, who swam by her hut like sharks in a moat. Well, she thought, it ought to work—it sure scared the shit out of me.

In a way, it didn't matter. The boys would only have hurt

her, after all, made her feel dirty, a bit ashamed to be a big, strong California girl who could be made to do anything by the greater strength of young men. But they could not touch her center. Anything they might have done to her could have been cured by rest, a long hot bath in a big tub, a night with a loving, gentle man, or, maybe, a loving, gentle woman. Every whore who'd lived had endured more every night than the boys would have inflicted upon her, and she, like a whore, would have survived, grown old, and succumbed, as everyone finally must, to misery, malfunction, or a loss of mind. And it must be said, she thought, watching the seep of rain across the *finca*, the distant lights of the fine white house from which she now was exiled, where one could take a long hot bath, where one could rest, and tell the time of day, and be served delicious food. . . . It must be said that the boys would have been reality, at least, even if the most degrading kind. Palma had known that, and kept her to himself, confident that when he touched her he penetrated to her core. Teejay gulped sadly and groped around on the pallet until she found the crumpled box of cigarettes. She lighted one, drew deeply, wanting its small, solitary warmth, a tiny red coal against the vast darkness of her universe. This was real, the faint constriction in her lungs.

But the object on the wall, that, at night when the air was wet, danced with tiny ghosts of blue light, was *not* reality. It did nothing, it merely suspended there on its leather thong. And yet, it sent an invisible beam of deadly rays right through her body, right into the nuclei of her cells, creating new combinations, erasing existing blueprints, making her body a stranger to itself, and inoculating it with the secret stuff of cancer.

She knelt on the pallet. "Oh, God, please don't let me die of that. It isn't a lot to ask, from a girl in the kind of fix I'm in."

The bad part, the really terrible part of all this, was that Palma would eventually kill her. He might do it with radiation, but he could as easily cut her throat while he defiled her, or slip the garrote around her neck and, as she strained beneath him, tighten the stick. And yet, she thought, as a kind of silent prayer of thanks, in my heart, I think it's better than being given to the boys.

She cocked her head, listening. For a moment she thought she had heard a disembodied voice, a cry, a response to her simple but eloquent prayer. But, no, it was just the pounding rain, the whispers of the zillion drops, the hiss of tiny rivers. She hugged herself, willing her body to be warm, and thought how you'd think something radioactive would heat the place up a little, as radioactive rocks had once melted the planet's surface, back in the beginning, in the old days before Cuzco. The amulet, the thick crescent of grey metal, would be warm to the touch, she knew; she could pick it up and put it between her breasts and draw some warmth from it. The thought caused her to shudder involuntarily, a sudden chill—it was, she thought, like finding yourself thigh to thigh with Death.

Teejay got to her feet and peered out the barred window with its filthy, broken screen. Nobody stirred. The guard was nowhere in sight. The boys must be giving the hut a wide berth. If she could break the lock, she could run away into the storm, out into the farmlands, to the fence, the razor wire, the legendary landmines they said had been laid everywhere. . . . The futility of flight made her very tired, killed her before her escape even began.

"Teejay." A male voice, and not a Spanish one, whispering her name.

She pressed against the moist wall by the window, afraid it was Palma or a courageous boy, wanting her enough to ignore the amulet.

"Teejay."

Her heart bounced within, she could not speak, and when the flimsy door to the hut splintered and flew open, she could not bring herself to look at the man she knew would be standing in the grey rectangle of rain. It had to be a cruel trick of Palma's, a way of breaking, obliterating, her. . . .

Something encircled her, something dark, gleaming, and wet, and she flinched furiously away, lashing out with her fists as a cry formed on her lips. But the arm pulled her in against its body, also wet and shining, slick. . . . Teejay's heart hammered madly at this apparition and she strained to see what it was . . . then smiled. She thought she smelled an Englishman.

"I heard they'd moved you," Goodpasture said, not bothering to whisper.

She stepped back to see him better. She did not remember his being quite so tall, or so thin, his body poking against his rubber poncho like a skeleton beneath a dark green skin, his long face covered with a sandy stubble, and strained with an almost palpable fatigue. The naturalist was gone, she saw then, leaving a tired warrior. A bark quiver of blowgun darts swung from his belt beneath the poncho, and a long knife in a worn snakeskin scabbard; where the poncho parted, she saw a pistol tucked into the waist. He had kept one hand behind him, as though concealing an injury. "What's wrong with your hand?"

He grinned and brought it out where she could see. Teejay gasped, not knowing at first what it was: the hand and forearm gleamed with blood and water, as though freshly skinned. But then the thing took form in the poor light. He wore the great, evil, spade-shaped head and neck of a large viper on his right arm, like a grisly hand puppet. The eyes peered from skin the color of dead leaves, looking no more, and no less, alive than they had ever done, pale and slitted, stony cold. The mouth was fixed in an enormous smile of extended fangs that dripped rainwater. "I hated to take it," he said, holding the head up where he could speak to it, "they're such wonders, you see. But it also makes a wonderful surprise for these *finca* chaps . . . well, it scares the shit out of them, actually, having my *surucucu* spring at them." He looked at her more closely. "You've had a bad time. What happened?"

"I lied about the radiation." Sad to say, I lied about nearly everything.

"Congreve knows, then."

She nodded.

"Can you travel?"

She nodded again. "I'm okay."

Goodpasture gave a snort of laughter. "So you are." He glanced around the room. "Not quite so nice as the residence."

"A room of one's own."

"And that," he asked, indicating the device on the far wall, "Congreve's lucky charm?"

"He thought I deserved it."

"No one does . . . but we'll take it along just the same." He slid the snakehead off his hand and stowed it in a string bag he

produced from beneath his poncho, like a magician material-
izing a cage. Squatting by one of the puddles, where the earthen
floor had softened, he fashioned a clay ball the size of a grape-
fruit, then picked the amulet off the wall and pressed it into the
rough sphere. After adding another layer of mud, Goodpasture
put the ball in the string bag too. "I'm becoming quite the col-
lector," he told her. "But we'd best be off . . . we have a way
to go. Old Hobbs . . . well, no, old Krylov . . . the man's a
Russian, did you know?" She shook her head, amazed. "Krylov
has the Rover in La Paz."

He stepped out of the door, surveyed the grey rainscape before them, and gestured that she should follow. Her guard was
waiting, after all. He sat against the earthen wall in the shelter
of a thatched overhang, his Uzi slung around his shoulders, the
muzzle resting on his thighs. His bare brown feet stuck out into
the rain. Four small punctures oozed on his left cheek, which he
touched with rigid fingers, as though eternally surprised. She
looked interrogatively at Goodpasture. "Looks like a snake got
him," he said, studying the corpse as though forensically. "In
fact, he was slain by a wee froggie." He leaned toward the dead
man, and lifted the rifle over his head, then patted the pockets
and found a spare magazine, which he also took. "Know him?"

Teejay shook her head. "Just one of the boys."

5

Krylov had driven through the night, pushing the Rover along the pocked blacktop ribbon of the Pan American Highway where it curved south and east from La Paz along the Altiplano, the road nearly a straight line drawn across the twelve-thousand-foot-high valley, watched by columns of tooth-like mountains that glowed with snow beneath the southern sky's dense wash of stars; animate, sombre figures that loomed on each horizon. This journey up to La Paz had passed in a fevered dreamstate—he had just managed to contain his wound, his profound fatigue. Now, for the first time, he experienced the alien, extraterrestrial quality of the place. Towns, mere handfuls of mean structures, lay as dark and silent as the rural villages of Bulgaria; the unbounded emptiness touched him as the Asian steppes had; it evoked a crossing of Afghanistan. He reached Caracollo at midnight, and turned toward a gathering of peaks that seemed to lie in wait for mortals willing to pass through them on the sinuous descent to the Cochabamba Valley.

Crossing the pale, dry patchwork of irrigated valley farmlands, he pulled off the road near Suticollo, and forced himself into a fitful sleep filled with unremembered, anxious dreams that caused him to jerk and flinch, like a dreaming dog. In Cochabamba, as the eastern sky began to brighten, he drove through the dusty streets of the city, where the only pedestrians he saw were cheerful Bolivian dogs, returning with broad smiles from another evening on the town. Here and there mud-

286

brick walls were spraypainted with political slogans and the occasional threat to *yanquis*—the wish that they would go home —sprayed as though with blood.

He found a station open and tanked up the Rover, fed it oil and water, checked its treacherously worn tires, then bought breakfast at a kiosk on the edge of the city. Before the sun cleared the eastern cordillera, Krylov was heading up the narrow valley he had first traversed in Congreve's helicopter. At Aguirre he turned sharply to the northwest, following the winding path of Highway 7 up and up, until the pavement sputtered out and the Rover chewed away at a rough dirt and gravel trail that took it nearly to fifteen thousand feet, where Krylov stopped. From this vantage point, he could see the road twist its way down through the foothills, could even discern patches of forest, where brown rivers reached the lowlands and immediately began their meandering search for gravity. But the forest was mostly obscured by a sea of cloud that washed against the foothills, with here and there the towering anvil of a thunderstorm. Beneath it, he supposed, the Beni swam in a torrent of rain—cover for returning Soviets.

The Rover drove into the rain at about the eight-thousand-foot mark, and he forced the old machine along, straining to see the narrow road, straining to sense when the odd bus or truck would fly at him from a blind curve. A slide had blocked the road a few kilometers past Corani, causing a pileup of traffic; some pulled off as near the edge as they dared; the others, mostly four-wheel-drive vehicles, slithered across the spray of rock and clay. Krylov followed in his turn, like one of a procession, trailing the others down and down, into the dense, wet air of the foothill forests. The rain began to ease as he passed El Crucero, and had diminished to a drizzle by the time he reached the Mission.

The Petersons must finally have fled, for there was no light in the gloom of day, no animals, and utter silence. Even the ambient jungle lay quite still. The rain had washed away much of Goodpasture's work, but Krylov could still discern several mounds near the far end of the clearing, where the Englishman must have buried the cesium he'd found. He pulled the Rover up by the cross-shaped main building, cut the engine and got down. The only sound was that of water, dripping, running, rumbling in the swollen brown river nearby. No one had been there in weeks, he thought; it might have been a ruin in the jungle. He waited for a time, listening, then pulled open the chapel door. The room seemed never to have felt a human presence, there was not even the scurry of mice or click of insects. He went outside again, and splashed across the clearing to what appeared to be the Petersons' living quarters. "Hello?" he called, pounding on the door. "Hello?"

Nothing.

He pushed into the building, blinded for a moment by the poor light. They sat across the room from one another, motionlessly watching him with the fixed, open faces of the insane. "My name is Krylov," he told the silent figures. "I've come to help you."

"We don't need your help." It was Peterson, his voice barely a rasping whisper. Krylov was shocked by the man's appearance, the patchy baldness, the boiled visage of the cancer ward. He smelled of frailty, excrement, and death.

Krylov looked at the other figure, the woman, her face partly obscured by a red *ruana*. Her eyes gleamed with a febrile, angry light, seeming to illuminate the fine-boned, sharp features, the thin, chapped lips, the frame of scraggly brown hair. "I'll take you to Goodpasture," he said. She shook her head almost imperceptibly, a signal as faint, as ambiguous, as a spirit's.

"We're coming to the end of something," said Peterson, gulping for breath as he spoke. "We're going to be all right."

"Congreve's dying."

"Course he is. He's *supposed* to."

"That piece of metal you sent . . . it's killing him."

"I know."

"And yours is killing you."

"No," Peterson whined, "it's *testing* me. Pat, too. But we're not going to die. That's not God's way, to kill off those who do His bidding."

"What is yours like?"

Peterson smiled coyly. "Just like Congreve's."

"Exactly the same?"

"Well . . . not exactly." The missionary snickered faintly, like a secretly bad child.

"May I see yours?" Krylov's stomach went weak, thinking of the gamma rays.

But Peterson shook his head. "Mine's different, that's all."

"It has writing on it," the woman said in a low voice.

"Don't tell about the runes," Peterson cried out, agitated but not inclined to move anything but his head.

"The word of God," she added, ignoring her husband. Krylov was surprised by the venom, the irony, in her voice. "A message from God, just for Elmer." She had come to hate him.

"Where'd you find them?"

The man, sullen now, jerked his head toward the window. "Out yonder."

"Was that all you found?"

Peterson nodded. "Just that silverish stuff."

"What does God say?"

Patricia gave a cold chuckle. *Hordra.*

"Pat," Peterson began to beg. "*Please* don't mock the Word."

"The Word." She seemed about to spit. "Show him."

Peterson shook his head. Then, "I wrote it all down . . . on the desk."

Krylov found the cluttered table, the pad where Peterson had copied:

He studied the characters for a moment, then grinned. They were obviously coded numbers: □ must be 5; ⬚, 7; ⬚, 3; △, 0 or 10—like Roman numerals, nine was one less than ten. A seven-digit number etched into a forged crescent of a light, tough metal. A part. *A part number.* You couldn't build anything without numbered parts; it keyed them to a blueprint somewhere. *Bushmaster* had left more than a trail of fragments—it had left this pointer back to its origins. He copied the symbols on another scrap of paper, and put it in his shirt pocket.

"They're numbers," he told Peterson. "7590932. They put them on the thing where it was built."

"And where was that, *Mars?*" Peterson brayed, wanting to sound triumphant, and failing.

"Sunnyvale, Los Alamos?" Krylov looked into the luminous, moribund blue eyes. "Take your pick."

"God *told* me it was His," he whispered. "God . . . *assured* me. . . ."

"A part number," Patricia said, beginning to laugh. "Oh, Christ, a *part number.*"

"*Hordra*, Pat. Remember: *Hordra.*"

But, watching the man's ruined, puzzled face, Krylov understood suddenly that Peterson himself knew the markings were not really God's. They compromised his miracle, reduced the cosmic whisper in his ear to a psychosis, and marked him for death from the poisonous object he had placed around his neck. When had he come to this knowledge? Krylov suspected he had realized men had forged the metal amulet when he'd felt the certitude of his death a few days before. "Let me get you out of here."

Peterson shook his head. "I have to stay. I have to see God's will obeyed."

"I don't," the woman said, getting slowly to her feet.

"You said you'd never leave me."

"I was wrong."

"You're going to Goodpasture, aren't you?"

She nodded.

"I'm *dying*, Pat."

"I don't care." Her face, Krylov saw, was streaked with tears. "I can't give you any more."

"I won't ask anything else, not anything, ever again." Krylov could not look at the man's face, which had filled with a terrible fear. "I'll get rid of this thing," Peterson went on, holding the amulet up in the light, then pulling the thong roughly past his ears. "See?" He cast it aside. "I'll get *well*." His frightened countenance poised, partially illuminated, and seemed to listen. Krylov listened too: there, very faintly, came the beat of the *Esquilo's* rotors. "Hear that?" asked Peterson.

"Congreve," Krylov said.

"I know." The fear had drained from Peterson's face, replaced by a fatal confidence, as though his prophecy might still run true.

Outside, the helicopter wheeled slowly on the axis of its rotor, like a dog circling to lie down, and settled on a relatively dry bit of higher ground, its downdraft causing the puddled water to shiver. Krylov could see Arias clearly, and another man he realized must be Congreve, and Palma . . . Palma, like a little blackbird bearing a fatal disease. He leapt from the machine's open door, clad in the usual black suit, black hat, the white shirt with no collar, dressed a bit, thought Krylov, like Leon Trotsky, and as anachronistic now as a man in armor. Krylov stepped through the door to meet him.

"Mr. . . . Hobbs," Palma began, suppressing all surprise.

"Actually, my name is Krylov. Viktor Krylov." He knocked his muddy heels together and gave Palma a slight bow of the head. "Yellin's man in the Beni."

Palma regarded him skeptically for a moment, then, "I have business inside."

"The Petersons have the plague."

"Whoever you are . . . Hobbs . . . Krylov . . ." He put both surnames in quotes. "I know about your 'plague.' "

"Ah."

"The American girl told us everything."

"Where is she now?"

Palma's mouth became a cruel line. "She left the *finca*. Recovering her"—and he looked in the general direction of the research station—"is our next piece of business." He stepped past Krylov into the gloom. "Good afternoon, Mr. and Mrs. Peterson," he said. "Congreve wants to talk to you. Please come with me."

"I think he only needs to speak to Mr. Peterson," said Krylov.

"I think you should mind your own business."

"Here, look," Peterson called to them, "I'm coming, see?" With great effort he raised himself to his feet, then stepped toward the bright rectangle of the door. "Give me a hand?" His face wrinkled with distaste, Palma offered Peterson an arm to cling to.

"Palma," Krylov said, "Yellin urges restraint."

"I am restraint herself," said Palma, guiding Peterson out into the clearing. Arias had not shut down the engine, so that the rotor swept past, with a *whoof, whoof,* as Palma guided Peterson along beneath it. "I will come back for the woman," he called to Krylov. "Congreve wants to give them a ride in the *Esquilo.* They've never been, he says."

"Yellin will cut you off if you don't return Peterson."

"Don't worry, Mother Russia, we'll bring him back."

"I'm coming with you."

Palma shook his head, and showed Krylov his knife, a long, sharp, curve of metal; you would use such a knife, thought Krylov, to flense an animal, or a man. "Only seats four. Sorry."

Krylov backed away, watching the missionary stumble along with the Peruvian's knife just touching him, watching the door open and swallow them both. For a moment, his eyes met those of Arias, the pilot, anxious, perhaps a bit ashamed. Krylov shook his head to admonish the man not to do it, but Arias looked away, as pilots in such work invariably did. As soon as the door closed behind Palma, he brought up the power and lifted the *Esquilo* into the air.

"Patricia," Krylov called to the woman, who stood just behind him near the door, "do you have a gun?"

"A shotgun," she said. "For birds."

"Bring it, please."

6

Superstition, ancient and despised, had flickered like aurorae in Palma's mind since he had come upon the girl's guard, dead, his face marked and swollen by the bite of a large viper, and Teejay gone, swallowed by the rain and the forest, as though spirits had carried her away from him. The rain had obliterated any outside tracks, no one had seen her, no land mines scattered near the fence had been triggered. Spirits had floated everywhere he looked. Congreve's boys were too frightened to look at him, or come with him into the hut. Even when he had seen a single footprint on the softened earthen floor, a print larger than any of the boys'—the Englishman, laying down a trail of frightening jungle magic—Palma still had to force the idea of spirits out of mind. He had kept knowledge of the footprint to himself, and later had returned to rub it out, wanting no one to know of her latest betrayal. Her treachery in the matter of the radiation had stung him incurably, but he had protected her from the fate Congreve had ordained. And for that, for sparing her, she had now betrayed him again, fleeing with the Englishman, abandoning him to whatever came—worse, abandoning the Struggle.

Of course, hers was a terrible mistake. You gave up the Struggle only when your hand had been stilled. If they hacked off your hands, you pummeled with your stumps, and when those were gone, you kicked until they took your legs, you bit, you writhed, you fought like a dying snake, with every cell, every muscle that remained alive; they must chop you to pieces. How had she thought she could simply walk away? "Oh, Teejay," Palma had muttered darkly, squatting by the footprint in the hut. He had dismissed all memory of defiling or beating her himself, of wanting her broken, of wanting her dead, and remembered only that he had given affectionate care to a *norteamericana*. Well, he had decided before dawn, he would do her one last favor. He would free her from the Struggle in the only way one could be freed; he would kill her like a snake.

But not, he thought now, looking at Peterson and Congreve in the back seat, until we have satisfied my patron. The two dying men looked like oldsters being taken for a Sunday ride, each trapped in reverie, in a worn-out self, unspeaking. He watched Congreve. Before this benefactor died, Palma needed his endorsement, an infusion of Congreve money and power. With those, one could bring the Struggle to the gentle people of the forest, to the hard lives of the Altiplano. Che had failed here because he had tried to mobilize a revolution in a land without hope. The Struggle would succeed because it required nothing, and offered only death. An impoverished country could be transformed into a ruined one. A fragile economy could be broken. A faltering government could be put out of its misery. Palma grinned, thinking that perhaps he would end by governing this place, then gave a private, internal shrug of indifference. Governing was nowhere near the top of his list.

He leaned back between the two front seats, where he sat on Arias' left, plugged in a headset for Peterson, and gestured for him to put it on. Congreve was already wearing his, the big green plastic earphones giving him the look of a sickly bug. Palma donned his own. "Can you hear me?" he asked Peterson. The missionary nodded. "Congreve wants to talk to you."

Peterson turned interrogatively to the man beside him. They might have been strangers on a bus together.

"How come you act like a friend, and then send that thing to kill me?" The intercom rendered his aggrieved tone flat and metallic.

The missionary turned and looked out the open door on his side of the helicopter, watching the heavenly blue roofs below them become steadily smaller as Arias spiralled the craft upward several hundred feet. "I know it was wrong to pretend to be your friend," he said at last. His voice, Palma thought, possessed surprising resonance. "I apologize for my . . . duplicity."

Congreve tossed his head impatiently. "I don't *know* duplicity," he complained. "But I know you killed me."

"God told me to."

"Ah, shit, don't tell me *that*."

"He wants the world rid of you, Congreve. He asked me to help." Peterson grinned inanely at his victim. "Don't you understand?"

"Oh, sure, I understand." Congreve lifted his eyes skyward, cupped a translucent hand behind one of his earphones. "Hey, is that you, God? What's that? What you saying?" He smiled then, nodded, and turned to Palma. "That was God. He just called up to tell me something. Know what he said, Peterson?" he asked, leaning toward the American. "Know what he said?"

"That wasn't God," Peterson muttered. His face had gone very white, his hands trembled in his lap.

"He said: Throw the motherfucker out."

Palma brought out his knife and flicked it at the preacher. "Take off your seat belt."

The missionary looked down into his lap, even contemplated it, sitting there by the open door, and released the belt. He looked at Palma, his pale eyes calm, suffused with belief, as he sat there by the open door, no longer tethered to the ship—a flying man.

"You heard what God said," Congreve snapped. "Toss the fucking *perro* out."

"Congreve," Peterson cried out then, "Please," the weak, sick fingers scratching at the white suit, the stained silk shirt, Congreve writhing away from the assault, "Please, *please*," except Palma heard the lie in his pleading, and turned to slice him away from his master when, in a motion that had the seamless, graceful pattern of ballet, Peterson flicked Congreve's seat belt's quick release, seized the silk lapels, and leapt backward toward the open door. Congreve screamed in the intercom until the line went taut and yanked the jack out of the panel, then tore the headphones away from him. For a moment, the two were suspended in the door, Congreve's fingers scrabbling wildly at the metal sides, and then they both were lost, flying down the center of the helicopter's spiralling climb, diminishing against the bare brown mud of the mission.

"Holy shit," whispered Arias into his mike. "Holy *shit*."

Palma could not speak, or think. His brain roared with the beating wings of spirits, inner voices taunting him with having to return to Peru. Peterson had destroyed him along with Congreve. The boys would spit on him when he came back without their boss, when they learned he had been unable to protect Congreve even from a crazy *norteamericano* missionary. "Go down," he hissed into the intercom.

"I am, I am."

On the ground below, Palma saw Krylov, the sudden Russian, another touch provided by those mischievous spirits he could not believe in, running in a crouch from the residence to the two bodies splayed in the mud. The woman walked slowly behind him. Too bad, Yellin, Palma thought. I have to kill your man in the Beni. He took an Uzi from its metal clamp beneath the panel, cocked it, and released the safety. "Make a slow pass by them on your side," he told Arias. "Then pivot this thing around so I have them in my window. Okay?"

Arias nodded. They would kill the Russian and the woman, they would bring Congreve home as though he'd died courageously in the Drug Wars. Palma would tell them that the other side lost badly. We are on the march, he thought, his heart hammering like a child's.

Arias had ceased the spiral dive, and now tracked slowly toward the clearing, toward the bodies. The Peterson woman knelt by her husband's, which seemed to have no bones and lay as loose, and jointless, as a discarded puppet. Congreve had landed badly, his body crumpled and leaking in the mud, a small man rendered smaller. Krylov knelt beside him. They would have to stretch Congreve's body out, thought Palma, as the *Esquilo*, nose high, skids floating only a foot off the ground, stalked slowly toward this sad tableau. The woman did not even look up, but the Russian did; Palma could see the whites of his eyes where he knelt, framed by the windscreen just ahead and to the right of Arias . . . *but what was he doing?*

Krylov had leapt to his feet and sprinted toward the *Esquilo's* nose, bringing up a shotgun as he moved, not a big automatic or pump one, Palma noted, but a primitive two-barreled gun, a bird gun, whose pellets would bounce like pebbles off the *Esquilo's* skin. Arias could whip it around quickly now and put Krylov and the woman in the Uzi's field of fire. "Bring it around, bring it around."

But on his right Arias frantically moved the controls, with the Russian growing larger and larger in the window, the engine power taking an eternity to spool up, and then, in a reflex, the pilot took his right hand off the controls, trying to protect his face, and the ship faltered. Krylov fired from less than two meters' distance. The blast showered the interior of the cockpit with shattered perspex and bits of Arias' face. The pilot screamed on the intercom, and Krylov, now close enough to touch the fuselage, fired his second round into the pilot's face. Palma brought up the Uzi, but Krylov dived past the nose of the helicopter, which began to wheel about.

"*Arias,*" Palma yelled, "*We're spinning.*" Some pilot's reflex interceded. The *Esquilo* steadied, limped farther into the air, yawing like an injured fish, like an animal wandering blindly toward the river to die.

"The river," Palma said.

Arias looked around at him, surprised, perhaps, that he was not alone, and yet not quite comprehending who Palma was, or why the two of them were there at all. The left side of his face was more or less intact, with a brown eye luminous with fear, whose lid fluttered autonomically, as though it were a light about to fail. The right side of his face was all blood, birdshot, and bone. The mouth, ripped apart on its right corner, tried to speak, but only bubbled into the intercom, along with an unnerving rattle of breath. Palma ripped his headset off and looked down at the turbulent brown water only a few meters beneath them. "Arias, the river," Palma told the terrible, puzzled face that still watched him.

The pilot seemed to understand. He cocked his good eye at the water, then brought the power up and took the helicopter into a shallow climb. Palma relaxed. Arias had not been so badly hurt as he looked. Just birdshot, after all, gunpowder burns. They would go back after a little while, and he would kill the Russian and the wife, he would bring Congreve's body home . . . triumphantly back to the *finca*. . . .

Arias suddenly cried out, threw back his head, and his hands, operating now entirely on their own, pulled the *Esquilo's* nose up nearly vertical. The ship climbed a few tens of meters that way, then shuddered, rotating backwards with a slowness that reminded Palma of a carnival ride, that permitted him to see Arias was dead, the light gone from his one good eye. The helicopter struck the mudbank on the far side of the river, transforming the world into pure noise and fire. Palma was thrust by an invisible hand through the crushed door on his side of the fuselage, and thrown through cutgrass and thorns, thinking that he must die, now, or lose consciousness . . . but he did not. Finally, he lay on his side near the edge of the forest, the heat of the burning machine warm on his face, on his body. He watched the flames walk up the remains of Arias, and cringed when the fire accelerated just before the wreck exploded, showering him with wet shale and hot metal. And still he lived, still he was conscious. Palma grinned painfully. It was true. They had to destroy you piece by piece, cell by cell, like a snake.

Overhead, the clouds had thinned somewhat. He saw a patch of blue, a shaft of sunlight. The sun shone on the Mission, too. The Russian was a tiny figure who, if one had just held on to the Uzi, could be killed even from here, the woman too. But, of course, the gun was gone, melted in the helicopter. Everything had turned to shit for him, after all. In some way he did not fully comprehend, he thought it had begun to turn bad just when it had seemed best, on that night in the hills beyond Cuzco, when he had first lain with Teejay beneath the pounding Andean rain. How had she managed to bring all this down on him? Was it simply that she was a *norteamericana*, and that all *norteamericanas* were doom for men like him? Palma thought that must be it. He had tried to do more than fight; he had loved, in his way, and he had governed her—and this was what he got for it. He wished he could take these hard lessons back to Peru, to spread among his comrades in arms in the high river valleys. Stay away from *norteamericanas*, he would tell them. They are poison. They fill your life with spirits you are not supposed to believe in. And stay away from helicopters. They are imperialist machines, the mechanical horses of your oppressors—to go near them is to die.

Across the river, he watched the two figures in the clearing. The Russian was digging graves near the edge of the forest, the woman sitting nearby. Palma watched them for a long time, until Krylov had carried each body across the clearing and lain it in the shallow depressions he had scraped in the ground, until the graves were mounds of rock. Then the Russian and the woman went into one of the buildings. Finally they emerged, Krylov carrying a bag, the woman walking slowly on his arm. They went out of sight, and Palma heard the sound of an automobile cranking, the engine fading as they drove away. Then it was just the steady roar of the river a few meters away, the hiss and ping of hot metal looking for its former shape, and the single clear burr of the cicadas, singing now the rain had passed.

Alone, then, he thought of all he had done for the Struggle, the terror he had wrought, the men he had sentenced, the people he had killed. He thought about the belief that had sustained him, and the way it had almost brought success within his grasp here, in Bolivia. Well, he thought, for him the Struggle had ended. "I am ready to die," he told the river, the forest, the grey, cloud-strewn sky. Vultures turned overhead now, some flying down to within a meter of him, and he tried to shake his little fist at them. Perhaps he was not ready after all. There was still Teejay, who had done all this to him. He thought how it would be to kill this girl, to extinguish that bright light in her that, he believed, had drawn him to this place in the Bolivian mud. Fortified by hatred, he tried to get up, intending to walk to the research station to kill her. But he could not. Something had ripped him open. His life drained away when he moved; his body leaked his life into the grass and mud. "Teejay," he murmured thickly, and, in his mind, he twisted a garrote about her lovely neck a quarter turn, heard her try to cry out. Then, fixed, as ever, upon the death of others, Palma died.

7

The extreme youth of soldiers always amazed Levy, even
though he understood that they were only young to him, not to
themselves. He had gone into battle with just the same sort of
unmarked face worn by the boy sitting next to the M-60
mounted in the Huey's door, the same impassive expression in
which, when the eyes looked back at you, at the responsible
person aboard, you saw innocence and sometimes fear. Everybody on the ship seemed terribly young to Levy. Perhaps, flying to destroy your only friend made you suddenly old. Perhaps it was death to do it.

He looked out to port, at the two other Hueys flying not
much more than a rotor blade away in a staggered echelon
formation, each with its handful of young men, each with that
innocence, that intimation of fear, behind their Ray Bans. Nobody wore uniforms, but low canvas boots, blue jeans, short-
sleeved knit shirts bearing alligators and horsemen. Today, they
also wore the white protective coveralls of the nuclear industry,
with rubber respirators dangling beneath their chins and radiation badges clipped to their chests. All of us, thought Levy, look
like lab technicians, incongruously armed.

"Smoke dead ahead," the pilot said on the intercom. "Chopper down." He spoke what Levy called aero-western, the flat,
calm accent of aviation. "Not ours."

"Let's take a look," said Levy.

"Roger." The pilot's face was marked only with carefully

crafted wrinkles at the corner of each grey eye, concealed now beneath the visor of his gold-painted helmet. He fingered the mike button to call the other Hueys. "Beni One," he said. "We're breaking for a look at that fire. Orbit us for cover, if you would."

"Beni Two, Roger."

"Roger, Beni Three."

Their helicopter sagged, the big rotor slapping the atmosphere, and started down toward the river and the wreck, which, Levy saw, was Congreve's *Esquilo*, its red-striped tailboom leaning like a shattered mast above the burned-out fuselage. As the Huey picked its way slowly past the smoking framework, Levy saw the small body, dressed in black, cracked like a seedpod in the muck a few meters away. Its dark hair fluttered in the rotor downblast, but it had the heavy look of death. Buzzards scattered at their approach, but strutted back toward Palma's remains as the Huey passed overhead. "Let's try the Mission," Levy said.

"Okey-dokey."

The pilot swept the Huey into a sharp turn, then beat slowly around the river toward the low block buildings. Levy saw nothing, and no one emerged to greet them. Well, nobody ever came out to wave at olive-drab Hueys, not here, not anywhere. As they crossed the clearing, he saw footprints in the soft earth, and the two fresh, rock-covered graves, and thought that the Petersons must have succumbed after all. Too bad. Bystanders were the flaw in every operation. "Okay," he said. "Let's go see Goodpasture."

His ship rejoined the formation, which wheeled toward the Beni Station, following the general trending of the Chipirirri, which twisted, brown and rain-gorged, through its canyon of trees. Levy glanced at the men behind him, saw once more their odd expression of innocence and apprehension, the spring screwed down tight within. They did not reflect on wonders and, afterward, they would not brood. All they knew was what he'd told them: the British naturalist at the research station was suspected of using the facility for cocaine production. Levy would talk to him about it. If it were true, they were to raze the place. Ah, *that* had made them gulp. It bore the sound of orders

that corrupted, it infected them, suggested consequences somewhere downstream. He'd chided them out of such heavy thinking. Without Maggie Thatcher in there, he'd said, there's no
chance of a counteroffensive. *Haw haw.*

All he really wanted was a few minutes alone with Goodpasture, to see how far his runaway secret had spread these last
several days. A hundred men and women, give or take a few,
had worked on *Bushmaster.* But only three men, all of them in
Washington, had known about the launch into the Beni: Levy;
his master in the Old Executive Office Building; and the weap-
ons man who'd seen it aboard the *Indiana,* rigged it on its *Trident* booster, and keyed in targets for the twelve re-entry vehicles. That sailor had died of radiation poisoning, leaving only
two to share the secret. Two was more than plenty; when those
other swabs had come forward, pleading burns and nausea,
when they had called attention to the warhead's leaking
gamma in the missile tube, they had been silenced, along with
Yellin's spy. And now, he would have to find a way to kill the
Russians, Krylov and Yellin, and anyone else who could come
forward with a beam of light to shine on *Bushmaster.* And
Goodpasture. He shut his eyes and rubbed their lids gently
with his thumbs. A real daisy chain, stretching as far as one
could see. But he would do it all, because *Bushmaster I* had
worked, and there was still all that coca to ruin in Peru.

As they approached the station, Levy strained to see any sign
of life. Nothing moved on the ground, and the Rover was nowhere to be seen, although he knew it had left La Paz the night
before. The Russian must still be on the road someplace. They
could pop him after they'd finished here. Levy began stripping
off his coveralls, and the white canvas booties covering his
shoes.

"Rather you didn't, sir." The pilot seemed to frown at him
behind the visor.

"I won't be on the ground very long."

"Still rather you kept your gear on."

Levy did not reply. He clipped a walkie-talkie to his belt, and
slung his M-16. "How fast can you get here from Todos Santos?"

The pilot grinned. "About as long as it takes for you to press that transmit button, sir. Five minutes, max."

"Okay. Put me down. I'll call."

The Huey floated noisily toward the landing circle, then hovered, swinging like a pendulum from its rotor a few inches off the ground. Levy gave the pilot a thumbs-up, and jumped down cradling the M-16 slung across his chest. As soon as he touched, he crouched and ran for the grass, which flattened under the downblast of the departing craft. Levy waited until the three ships had formed up again and clattered up the river to wait at Todos Santos. He listened to the forest—the shrill buzz of cicadas, the rough tongue of the macaws, the booming sounds of a distant howler voicing his fear of others. "Okay," said Levy to himself. "Let's get this over."

Nothing moved or made a sound at the station. Joly must have gone into his famous rosewood, thought Levy, walking carefully toward the edge of the clearing, where trees seemed to stand on great vertical grey bones. A part of him sensed that another man walked with him through the sharp blacks and whites between the trees, the sudden shafts of sunlight breaking through the canopy; he imagined another silent person matching him step for step, moving just out of sight through the brush, and yet he knew he was alone, that no one walked with him. It was his spirit, he decided, smiling privately, roaming outside his body; it was the Indian.

But there was life here after all. He saw the ropes and *jumars* dangling from the platform up in the jacarandá, where before they had been secured out of reach. They moved very slightly in the still air, and glistened from days of rain. "Joly?" He didn't like the way he sounded. *"Joly."* He watched the platform more than a hundred feet overhead.

"Du kennst mich nicht, du ahn'st nicht, wer ich bin . . ."

Christ, Goodpasture was up there with his vodka. Levy stepped into the leather harness and adjusted the *jumars*, then began to pull himself up, alternately sliding the devices up their separate ropes.

". . . befrag' den Seemann, der den Ozean durchstrich. . . ."

He paused in his ascent when twenty meters off the ground,

turning slowly on the ropes, listening. Joly, he thought, I'm trusting you not to pick me off. Don't violate that trust.

". . . *er kennt dies Schiff, das Schrecken aller Frommen.* . . ."

Levy pulled himself toward the platform, liking the strain on his arm muscles, the relative ease with which he defied gravity.

"den fliegenden Holländer nennt man mich!"

They call *me* the Dangling Guatemalan, thought Levy. For a time he swung just below the railing, out of sight, the M-16 cradled in his arms, the ropes dropping out of sight through the understorey below. He could hear Goodpasture shuffling around on the platform, and the unmistakeable clink of the old vodka bottle. It began to feel very safe, safe as it had in the Amecos days. Levy grinned. Nothing had to happen right away. They could talk, he could be with a friend . . . for a time. His spirits rising, he gripped the railing and hoisted himself the last meter, swung lightly over the barrier, and landed on the platform, stripping off the harness quickly, like a paratrooper on the move.

Goodpasture stood in the shadows of the tree's clustered oval leaves, staring at his visitor. The vodka bottle sweated in the shade nearby. "Juan," he murmured, his voice somewhat slurred, his eyes squinting to see. "Are you a figment?"

"The real thing, Joly."

"Help yourself."

"Thanks." Levy took a mouthful of vodka, then put the bottle back in the shade. It felt like chilled lava going down.

"I didn't expect to see you again." Goodpasture sank heavily onto a plank seat that ran along the far railing, causing their tree to shiver. He reached for the bottle and took a long pull at it, then wiped his mouth and chin with a dirty hand. "Thought I'd scared you off."

Levy laughed.

"You're loaded for bear, I see," Goodpasture observed, nodding at the M-16. "I heard helicopters too. We being invaded?"

"I wanted to talk to you."

"About what?"

"I didn't think you understood . . . about the radiation." He watched Goodpasture closely, waiting to see a flicker of comprehension, a faint sign that this friend of his had somehow learned about *Bushmaster*. Nothing came. Perhaps he could leave this harmless man in place, after all. Exchange occasional letters. Cards at Christmas, now right around the corner. "It was a stroke of luck, Joly, to have it bring in all that source. Things are happening. The first exposed coca crop is on its way into the pipeline as we speak. It's going to win a dirty war for the right side . . . for a change. We want Congreve to send everything he's got into the pipeline, every little irradiated crumb. We don't want him to get spooked by word that his crop is radioactive, though. In a year, maybe less, Bolivian coca will be finished. Everybody on earth'll be afraid of it."

"I've asked myself whether I care if America runs out of co-caine. I don't." He took a tug at the bottle, and handed it to Levy, who drank another mouthful. "Besides, Bolivia isn't where all the coca's grown. They'll just increase production in Peru. Nothing will change."

"Peru could change."

"You know what? In another few months, you boys are going to want another meteorite." Levy peered into Goodpasture's face. He wasn't at all drunk. His eyes were keen and cold, his body poised, ready for a fight. "You'd have God jumping through hoops for you." He studied Levy, then shook his head, half-sadly. "I used to miss you, Juan. I'd come up here with my bottle and my rather truncated memory of opera . . . and sing . . . and think about our good old days. You know, Amecos, all that."

"I think about those days too, Joly."

"I mean, I really thought we were doing something serious. New understanding of the ecosystem, predictive models that would do somebody some good. God, how fine it all sounded." The Englishman stood up and made a tired gesture with his hands, a gesture Merlin might have fashioned, near the end. "I know your dirty little secret, Juan."

"I know."

"Amecos . . . *amigos* . . . was just a load of crap."

"No, we needed the models."

"Right, so you'd know how to target your MIRVs on the Beni. What do you call it, a pre-emptive strike?"

"Something like that."

"You've filled the place with ionizing radiation, Juan."

"I . . . *we* made it the way the world will be in fifty years. Look at it that way. We've given you a chance to get ready for the future."

"And pretty soon you'll give the poor Peruvians the same advantage?"

"It's a dirty war, Joly."

"It's a dirty world, *Juan*." Goodpasture took a step toward him, and Levy brought up the M-16, flicked off the safety. "Oh, relax," the Englishman went on. "I just wanted to show you something. Everything is imperfect, at least everything that we do. I mean, we just aren't nature, Juan. We can't begin to simulate a good rainforest, we don't do good environments. We can't even predict the weather. And what we do secretly, we do as children: we always leave a trail. Our meteorites suck, as you might say. Take the Beni Fall." He leaned toward Levy and extended his two hands, which held a rough clay sphere. Without speaking, Goodpasture pulled out a knife, causing Levy to retreat until the small of his back touched the wooden rail. "Not to worry," said Goodpasture, and sliced through the dry clay, which crumbled around his knife. He put the implement away and offered the severed ball to Levy, opening it like a clam. Imbedded in the dirt were two dull, silverish crescents of thick metal, with a leather thong drawn through a drilled hole at one end of each. "That poor imitation meteorite had a part number on it, Juan. Can you imagine such clumsiness? Have you ever known a bushmaster to leave a trail?"

Levy could not take his eyes off the amulet. "What is it?" he murmured.

"Black magic. Turns you seventy in a week."

"It's hot."

"It's so hot only a madman would hold it. It's so hot it's sending gamma right into your bone marrow, your blood, your thyroid. Zap, zappity-zap."

"I don't need this."

"Touch it, Juan. It's actually warm . . . you can *feel* the stuff decay." He took another step toward Levy.

"Enough, already," said Levy, and brought out his radio,

switched it on with a thumb. He'd bring in the choppers. It was time to kill one's friend, to turn all this to charcoal.

But, in a graceful, looping movement, and with a smile, Goodpasture tossed the amulets in their severed clay ball at him. Levy dodged aside, but the thong caught on the radio's short, flexible antenna, and for a moment, astonishingly, he seemed almost to juggle the things, trying to get them away from him, trying to avoid their touch, their ambient sphere of gamma. . . .

Suddenly somebody else was on the platform. Levy felt the planks and supporting branch sag beneath the added weight, and looked up to see Krylov just to Goodpasture's left, and moving fast. Levy swept the amulets away into the cloud of leaves surrounding them, and brought up the rifle, firing first at where he thought Goodpasture should have been, but was no longer, then wheeled to stop the big Russian with a shot that he barely squeezed off before a powerful hand slapped the radio and sent it spinning down and down into the understorey. A hard palm smashed into his neck below his right ear, Krylov going for the artery. Some inner structure splintered with an explosive crack that only Levy heard. He twisted away from the killing hand, tried to block the Russian with the gun, went for the man's crotch with the stock, missed, and spun away, trying to bring the M-16 once more to bear. But Krylov was on him at once, the heel of his open palm jamming upward into Levy's nose, trying to drive the cartilage into the cortex, but Levy got his head down before the hand could kill him, brought up the muzzle like a bayonet, pressed against the Russian's shirt, and fired. . . .

Krylov's eyes flickered with pain, the punishing hand withdrew. The Russian dropped to his knees, holding his abdomen in both hands, huddled around his pain, and Levy leaned forward, bringing the muzzle against his head. Then Krylov came up suddenly, his hand caught Levy's crotch, and with an effort that made the Russian moan with pain, hurled Levy into space. He fell backward, flat, down through the thin upper branches, the understorey palms and lianas, and thumped into the leaf litter and vein-like roots covering the forest floor. Levy lay there, thinking that he would regain the breath that had been knocked out of him, then find the radio, call in the cavalry, and char these goddamned enemies of society. Gingerly, he drew a breath through the mess of his broken nose, then another, and smiled. His lungs worked, his brain was jangled some, but okay, nothing felt broken. . . . But when he told himself to get up, nothing happened. Feeling the inner mice of panic, he examined himself more closely, sending commands to toes, to fingers. It was like speaking into a dead mike. A terrible conviction filled his mind, along with news of pain that radiated outward, that must be visible to anyone who saw him; pain like this would make one glow in the dark. He swallowed hard. Joly. He wanted to say: *Joly.* But nothing came.

8

The young men in white radiation gear had come and taken Juan Levy away, removed the body that watched them, that had tried, Goodpasture thought, to speak. "A ghastly accident," he'd told them on the radio. "Mr. Levy's had a nasty fall."

So the Hueys had brought in the young men, awkward without a leader to comand them to destroy, embarrassed that they had once considered mayhem, anxious to get back to Chimoré. One of them, perhaps a second-in-command, had approached Goodpasture more or less suspiciously, and told him about, uh, rumors that the station had been used to process drugs. Goodpasture had laughed like the boy's favorite British uncle, and explained how Mr. Levy had found that pretty funny too, since he'd built the station in the first place for Amecos, you know, *amigos,* and knew there was nothing there to give aid or comfort to the enemy in this dirty war a few brave men were fighting down here in Bolivia. He'd sounded a bit like Churchill, Goodpasture thought afterward; certainly everybody but Levy had gone away inspired.

Now he sat in one of the lab's swivel chairs. His secret Russian was up on the stainless steel autopsy table, the one slug that had stayed in his body removed, his wounds swabbed with palm sap to stop the bleeding, a bit of sterile gauze smeared with *virola* against infection. The stomach had not been pierced, thank God, or the intestine either, so that Goodpasture had been able to administer copious vodka to get Krylov asleep before he sutured the ragged punctures shut. His only medical regret, now he had his Russian all wrapped in clean bandages and resting comfortably, was that he'd employed sterile needle and thread, and not a line of *Eciton burchelli*—he'd always hoped to suture a wound with army ants.

It was curious, he thought now, that a man who'd spent a life pretty much on his own, as he had, should suddenly find himself in the bosom of a family, even a sad little group like this one, all of them carrying some burden of radiation, and, tonight, a bit tipsy to boot. He looked at them fondly. Teejay sat cross-legged on the floor near the metal table, refreshed by a shower in the powerful stream outside. He found himself hoping she would stay, and thought she might, nothing to do with him of course, but because she wanted good works to do. "There are worse things than radiation," she'd told him, but he had always known that. What she meant, he believed, was that one of those worse things was to have lost your rudder. Palma had taken her a distance from every reference point. She might want to stay until she'd figured a way back.

Patricia, who sat curled in the other swivel chair, drowsy, was very sick. She would need new blood, new bone marrow, what Krylov had called the works. No doubt they all would, in time. He had helped her shower, rinsing away her old life, rinsing away the horror of the day. Looking at her now, in the dying light of their candles, he thought she might not be for everybody, but would do for him. We'll make you beautiful again, my girl, he told her silently. We'll put roses back in your cheeks.

Near midnight, Goodpasture stood up, rising against his fatigue as one would rise against the gravity of Jupiter, and went out into the night. The clouds had cleared away, the dark dome streamed with stars. When a meteor skipped across his field of view, he looked away. He walked to the storage pit, where he kept the cesium grains that had killed Rosa, and lifted off the concrete disk he used as a cover. The water was a cylinder of blue light, the center of a star. Goodpasture watched it for a time, moved by its mystery, its beauty, its ability to kill. Levy might be right, he thought, the future is radioactive; and what we know about the way it touches life may finally come from this great cockup of his.

He knelt near the pit and used his knife to dig into the clay, then lifted the two amulets into view, held them up in the shimmering blue light, and sliced their leather thongs so that they dropped, first one, then the other, into the water. They spun gently down and vanished in the blue freeform of Cherenkov radiation that floated like a star at the bottom of the pit. Krylov had asked him to keep them for him, that they were a kind of insurance against a new Levy, against Levy's nameless boss, against all that America might do. But Goodpasture thought he might protect Krylov from himself a little too. The spy in his secret Russian might want to use them. Spies would blow up the world.

Still kneeling, he dragged the heavy cover into place, and darkness flowed in about him once again. He felt a slight touch upon his shoulder, a touch he had known, it often seemed, forever, and turned to the familiar form, and took a hand containing all her frailty. Goodpasture leaned his head against the warm disk of her belly. "Ah, Pat," he sighed, "It's a funny old world."